THE CURSE OF BRAHMA

Jagmohan Bhanver has handled national and international roles for top multinational banks, and is rated among the top leadership coaches in the country, mentoring industry leaders across the globe. He is considered one of the most powerful speakers in Asia and addresses half-a-million people every year. He has also been the recipient of the Rajiv Gandhi Excellence Award and the Global Achievers Award, among several other felicitations in education and public service.

He has previously authored three non-fiction bestsellers. *The Curse of Brahma* is his first novel.

He can be found at www.jagmohanbhanver.com and tweets at @JMS007.

THE
CURSE
OF
BRAHMA

• KRISHNA TRILOGY • VOLUME 1 •

JAGMOHAN
BHANVER

RUPA

Published by
Rupa Publications India Pvt. Ltd 2015
7/16, Ansari Road, Daryaganj
New Delhi 110002

Sales Centres:

Allahabad Bengaluru Chennai
Hyderabad Jaipur Kathmandu
Kolkata Mumbai

ISBN: 978-81-291-3533-9

First impression 2015

10 9 8 7 6 5 4 3 2 1

The moral right of the author has been asserted.

This edition is for sale in the Indian subcontinent only.

Typeset by Saanvi Graphics, Noida

Printed by Gopsons Papers Ltd, Noida

Dedicated to Komal, the woman who saved me from myself...and from my own version of Tamastamah Prabha

Dear Susan,
Happy reading!

Jagmohan
23/04/15

Contents

Prologue

It was an extraordinarily large room, dimly lit with terracotta oil lamps dangling from the walls at various corners. It could accommodate more than a hundred people without appearing to be cluttered. A dozen couches of varying sizes and shapes were scattered tastefully across the cavernous room. Everything was aesthetically done up yet at the same time, gave the appearance of being ominous and murky. More than a thousand brightly coloured flowers of different species adorned the room, looking incongruous in the shadowy space, and heightened the sinister element of the place. It was as if the flora had been deliberately put there as a façade, to try and mitigate the otherwise malevolent persona of the place.

The three creatures stood in the centre of the room awaiting their Master's presence. The one on the left was a pisaca, a creature with a snake's body and octopus tentacles for a head. A spike lay hidden under the tentacles for close encounters with enemies. The monster in the middle was a kalakanja, whose body resembled dried leaves, with scarcely any flesh or blood. He stood three gavutas high (one gavuta being equivalent to six feet). His eyeballs jutted out from his head like crabs, and his mouth, situated on top of his head, was as small as a needle's eye. The third monster, standing on the extreme right, was a bonara. He was slight in size, barely taller than a midget, but looked the most treacherous. He had only one eye in the centre of his forehead and his entire body was covered in scales. In place of his feet were two long talons sharp enough to slice through an elephant.

Three deadly and vile-looking fiends; but right now, all three were shivering with fear.

They had been ordered there by the Dark Lord, the embodiment of evil in all the three worlds. There could only be two reasons for the summons. Either they were to be rewarded for pleasing their Master, or they would encounter a ruthless death for having offended him in some way. All of them knew they hadn't done anything to please their Lord in the recent past. That signified only the other alternative. It meant Death, and it had them terrified. Not that any of them was afraid of death. They were not even alive, in the real sense of the word. They were creatures from the lowest levels of Pataal Lok, who had already died several times and then been resurrected by their Master to do his evil bidding. But death at the hands of their Master meant they would never be given life again, and would be doomed to remain buried in the lowest pit of hell for eternity. It terrified them.

A door opened and a shrouded figure glided into the room. All the flowers in the room instantly shrivelled and turned to dust. The shrouded figure exuded death, and the smell of pestilence pervaded his being. He stopped a few feet away from his three followers. A hoarse voice from somewhere inside the cloaked figure snapped an order to an unseen guard at the door, who quickly closed the door and fled. A pair of blazing eyes from under the shroud glared piercingly at the three monsters. 'You have failed me,' the Dark Lord said softly. The tone was deceptive, and the three monsters knew that their Master was seething inwardly with some unknown fury. They waited for him to speak further. None of them wanted to invite his wrath if they could help it.

'The mortal woman, Devki still lives,' the Dark Lord hissed, looking at one of the creatures. 'L - - Lord,' the Kalakanja stuttered, his tall and skeletal frame shivering in terror.

'Silence!' The shrouded figure glared menacingly at the

Kalakanja. 'I should ideally send all three of you to your eternal graves in Tamastamah Prabha.' Tamastamah Prabha was the seventh and the lowest level of existence within Pataal Lok, where serpents fed on the dead and those who had been sentenced to eternal death.

He paused to look at the shaken trio of monsters and continued. 'But you have served me well in the past, and for that I will make an exception this time.'

The look of relief on their faces was palpable, as their Master continued. 'Go and kill Devki before this month is over, and you will have earned your place forever, in my mind.' He paused to look penetratingly at them. 'But fail again and there will be no corner in the three worlds where you will be safe from my wrath.'

Cowering in fear, the three monsters bowed.

'Go now!' commanded the Dark Lord in a raucous voice. The command was like a whiplash and his followers made a hasty retreat, each of them vowing to himself that he would be the one to kill Devki. Her death would be her salvation, and theirs too.

◆

The Dark Lord took off his hood when he was certain that his followers had gone. He rubbed one side of what should have been his face. There were only the tattered shreds of burnt skin that had still not healed in the past two hundred years of agony. *Brahma, you shall pay for this, and so shall every deva in Swarglok,* he vowed to himself. *I will have my revenge when your treasured Mrityulok is mine. And when that is done, I shall transform every mortal there one by one into the Demon that you made me. I will raise an army of Demons from Mrityulok, and together with my trusted soldiers in Pataal Lok, the Demons will take over your precious Swarglok.*

His laughter echoed through the cavernous room. But there was more anguish in it than there was joy.

Battle over a Princess

King Devak lay prostrate on the ground. He had collapsed immediately on hearing of his wife's death while trying to give birth to their second child. The royal vaid had intended to personally convey the news of the queen's demise to the hapless king, but before he could do that in his patent sensitive manner, the news had travelled through the royal corridors in the form of Devak's first born—the three-year-old Princess Devki. One look at the stricken face of his daughter had told him what a million words from the Royal Vaid might not have communicated. He knew the queen was dead. She was gone forever.

Devak was not a warrior king with a heart of stone. His nature was more poetic and he was loved by his people not because of his conquests on the battlefield, but because of his impeccable administration and the care he showed for all his subjects. His three treasures were his wife, his daughter and his poetry; the first being the greatest. With his wife gone, he knew he would not be able to bring himself to do justice to the other two. This was the first thing that struck his desolate soul as he regained consciousness and found himself lying on his bed.

I have to meet Ugrasena, was all he could think of as the hours passed.

◆

The messenger raced to Ugrasena's court carrying the urgent message from his younger brother. After two days of relentless riding, and going without food and water to conserve time, the messenger reached Madhuvan and was ushered into Ugrasena's private chambers.

King Ugrasena took one look at the messenger and mouthed a command to one of his attendants, 'Get the man some water, in the name of Vishnu!'

As the attendant moved to do his regent's bidding, Ugrasena nodded kindly to the man standing in front of him, half dead with exhaustion. 'Messenger, take a seat and catch your breath. Then tell me what news my brother sends for me.'

The messenger bowed his head in respect, but kept standing. 'Your Majesty, King Devak sends you his greetings and requests that you read this letter in my presence and give me an answer that I can return with.'

If Ugrasena was taken aback by the messenger's request, he hid it well. He extended his right hand to take the scroll and broke open the royal seal himself. His face grew grim as he read the two words scrawled in his brother's hand: *Come immediately.*

He looked at the messenger. 'I shall be leaving for Haripur at once,' he said softly.

Then as an afterthought, he added, 'You should spend the night here and get some rest. Leave tomorrow.' The messenger shook his head apologetically. 'Forgive me Your Majesty, but my king awaits my return with your answer. I can have no rest till I have completed what he has commanded me to.'

Ugrasena looked at the messenger with admiration. He knew there was a high possibility that the messenger might not survive the trip back in his current state. He had clearly not slept in the past two days and would not get any rest during the two days' ride back to Devak's kingdom. If he had some food and water, there might just be some chance of his making it back alive.

'Messenger, you shall eat and have some water before you leave. That is a command!'

The man bowed yet again in respect. 'Your Majesty, I cannot eat, nor drink, nor rest till I have carried back your answer to my Master. With your permission, I would like to leave now.'

Ugrasena looked long and hard at the messenger. The King of Madhuvan was accustomed to having his commands followed. But in this case, the messenger's loyalty towards his brother warmed his heart. 'What's your name messenger?' he asked gently.

'Airawat, Your Majesty,' the messenger replied respectfully, with just the mildest signs of impatience at the delay.

Ugrasena took the messenger by his right shoulder and looking into his eyes said, 'Go then Airawat, and do your master's bidding. Devak is indeed fortunate to have men like you in his kingdom.'

As the messenger left, Ugrasena asked for his first born and favourite son, Kansa, to be summoned to his chambers. He didn't know what had happened at Devak's court that had made his brother call him like this. Protocol had prevented him from asking the messenger. If Devak had wanted him to know the reason, he would have commanded the messenger to let him know. But he hadn't. Whatever the reason for his brother's urgent request, Ugrasena knew he would feel more comfortable if his valiant son, Kansa accompanied him on the journey.

◆

'My brother!' Ugrasena embraced Devak as he entered his bed chamber. He was shocked to see his younger brother's condition. If he had met Devak anywhere else, he may not have even recognized him. The king of Haripur had aged twenty years in less than five days. The once-large frame was now gaunt, and the eyes that used to twinkle with laughter had nothing but the shine of fresh tears in them. Ugrasena's son Kansa had accompanied his father to his uncle's palace and he stood respectfully in a corner while Devak poured his heart out to Ugrasena. Ugrasena listened as Devak told him that he no longer had any desire to live. That he would retreat to the forest where he would go into meditation and give up his mortal body, so he could be united with his wife in the afterworld.

Ugrasena was shocked at Devak's plans. 'It is too premature for you to take Samadhi, Devak,' he said in a shaken voice. 'You have much to complete before you depart from this world,' he continued. Devak shook his head. Now at the brink of death, he was more determined than he had ever been during his lifetime. 'Think of Devki,' Ugrasena pleaded, his tone ridden with agony over his brother's decision.

'I am doing this for Devki,' snapped Devak in pain and frustration. 'I can no longer be a father to her. I am already a dead man! Can't you see it? How can a dead man give love to anyone? If she stays with me, she will neither have the love of a father, nor any other family close to her. With you, she will have your love and a large family of brothers and sisters. She will be happy.'

Devak's breathing was laboured. He looked at his brother and a tacit agreement was reached between them. Ugrasena nodded as Devak clasped his hands in relief. 'I knew you would not fail me Ugrasena.'

◆

Ugrasena and Kansa stood waiting for Devki in Devak's inner chambers. Devak sat on a diwan. He had asked his late wife's chief personal attendant to fetch the child and pack whatever clothes and play things she may want to take with her to her Uncle Ugrasena's palace. Her best friend, Mandki, daughter of one of the former attendants of Devki's mother, would also accompany her as her companion and playmate. Mandki no longer had a family, and it would be easy for her to move with the princess. Devak turned to look around as he heard the familiar soft tread of his daughter's footsteps, accompanied by two other, slightly heavier ones. Devki entered the room, followed closely by Mandki and an attendant. Devak extended his arm towards his daughter and beckoned to her. She approached him timidly and held his middle finger with her small hands, as if willing him to let her stay with him. Devak bent down to kiss his daughter and for the fraction of an instant, his resolve seemed to weaken as he stared into her doleful eyes. But then the thought of trying to wake up each day without his beloved wife by his side came unbidden to him, and strengthened his purpose yet again. He held his daughter's gaze and said softly, 'Go with Uncle Ugrasena; he is your father now. His sons will be your brothers henceforth, and his daughters, your sisters.'

Devki looked at Devak and Ugrasena, from one to the other, knowing she had to go, but not wanting to. She was still clinging to the hope that this was all a prank and Devak would stoop down any moment to take her in his arms like he used to, before her mother died. But Devak did not bend down to lift her. Nor did he offer any further expression of love. His face was set in stone. It was as if he had already entered a state of samadhi and couldn't wait to relinquish his eternal soul from his temporal body.

Devki stood rooted at the same spot, unable to move or feel anything. Tears rolled down her eyes, and she unsuccessfully tried to blink them away. In the next instant, she was lifted gently off her feet and for one joyous moment she thought her father had had a change of heart. She looked into the eyes of the person holding her and instead of her father's lined face, saw the youthful and loving smile of her cousin, Kansa. 'Don't worry little one,' Kansa murmured gently into her ear. 'You are my sister now, and no one,' shall harm you while I live.' Devki looked into the eyes of her cousin and felt a strange sense of security in his arms. She leaned her head against Kansa's mighty chest and closed her eyes.

Ugrasena looked fondly at his eldest son and knew he had done the right thing in getting Kansa with him. The boy was just fifteen but he was older beyond his years and he would take care of Devki as he had told her he would.

Devak took one last look at his daughter and waved goodbye to all of them. He would now give up his royal clothes and change into the simple garments of an ascetic as he prepared to leave for the forest where he would take samadhi and depart from this world, knowing his daughter was loved and safe with his brother's family.

At the gates of the palace, Airawat waited patiently for his master. He would accompany Devak to the forest and stay with him till the king's soul departed from his mortal body and ascended to Swarglok, to be united with his wife.

◆

Fourteen years passed.

Devki sat relaxing on a low couch. Three of her personal attendants were moving around the luxuriously set room, engaged in various activities to please their princess. A fourth one, dressed differently and looking unlike any of the other attendants, was busy rubbing scented oil in Devki's hair. Mandki was more of a friend and companion to the princess than an attendant. She had been with Devki ever since the latter had left her father's palace and came to live with Ugrasena's family fourteen years back. Devki had been three years old at that time and Mandki was eight. Devki's father was Ugrasena's brother and had been the ruler of Haripur while Ugrasena was the king of Madhuvan. After Devak took Samadhi and departed from the mortal world, Haripur and some of the neighbouring kingdoms that owed allegiance to Haripur also passed to Ugrasena. Ugrasena belonged to the Andhak dynasty of the Yedu clan. The Andhaks were one of the most respected families among the powerful Yedus at that time. The other prominent family among the Yedus was the Vrshni, with King Surasena as their head. Surasena ruled over Bateshwar. Both Ugrasena and Surasena were close friends and there was peace between the two powerful families.

'How does it feel to be the most sought-after bride in Bharat today?' Mandki asked jokingly, as she gave a final tug to Devki's hair.

'Feels like being a prized cow waiting for the right bull to come claim her,' Devki said with a wry smile. Mandki looked at her with a worried expression. Devki had not been her usual cheerful self for the past few days, ever since the incident with that vile warrior, Somdatta.

Devki had just turned seventeen, an age which was considered almost old for young princesses, if they weren't married by that time. It didn't matter that Mandki was five years older to Devki and still unmarried. After all, she wasn't a princess. It wasn't that Mandki didn't have her share of suitors. There had been several men who had tried to woo her and begged for her hand in marriage; but Mandki had been firm. She would not consider marriage till her best friend and mistress was married first. Devki had tried persuading her to tie the knot with one of the many handsome youth who had come to Mandki with earnest proposals, but this was the only thing that Mandki refused Devki, and the princess loved her even more because of it.

Ugrasena was always kind towards her and she received unrestrained love from her cousin Kansa. But, she didn't get along too well with the other sons and daughters. Neither was she particularly close to Kansa's two wives, Asti and Prapti, sisters of Jarasandha; the powerful King of Magadha. Lately, Ugrasena had started keeping unwell and she saw very little of him. Due to Ugrasena's illness, Kansa had become more involved in leading conquests over surrounding kingdoms, which had not yet accepted Ugrasena's dominion or who had moved their allegiance away from Madhuvan in the wake of the king's illness. Consequently, Devki didn't even get to see her favourite brother near as often as she would have liked.

Having Mandki with her made her feel she had a close companion. This was especially true in the past few days, considering the recent events. Somdatta's challenge to Vasudev filled her with dread. She didn't doubt Vasudev's courage, but she knew he didn't like to fight, unless there was no choice. Would he fight now? Would he fight for her hand? Would he win? Would he survive? She had scores of questions and no answer. And having so many unanswered questions bothered her.

'Where are you lost?' Mandki asked her. Devki shook her head in a futile attempt to dispel the disturbing thoughts. But Mandki knew what was bothering her friend.

'Vasudev can take care of himself, Devki. He will teach this upstart Somdatta a lesson in manners. And then he will come and ask you for your hand,' she said, holding Devki's face in her palms.

Devki nodded, trying to share her friend's optimism. 'I hope so Mandki. I hope so.' She hugged her friend and whispered, 'I don't want anything to happen to Vasudev.' Mandki held her tightly like she used to when they were both children and her friend was afraid of the dark. Only, it wasn't the dark Devki was afraid of this time. It was the fear of knowing that a ruthless Prince wanted to fight her beloved Vasudev, and the knowledge that if Vasudev lost, she would not only lose the one man she loved most in this world, but would have to marry his murderer, as the law of the time dictated.

◆

Vasudev paced pacing across the room, his hands folded behind his back and his head tilted downwards, as he tried to go over the events of the past few days in his mind. Everything had been going fine until recently. His father, Surasena, the king of Bateshwar, had spoken to Ugrasena and asked for Devki's hand in marriage for Vasudev. Ugrasena had whole-heartedly agreed. Surasena was his dearest friend and Vasudev and Devki had known each other for several years now, first as play mates during periodic visits of both families to each other's palaces, and later as young lovers, adoring each other from afar. Kansa had been elated at the news. Vasudev was a close friend. His character was known to be untarnished and Kansa knew Devki would be happy with him. In fact, just a month ago, Ugrasena had planned to announce their marriage. And then everything started to go wrong.

◆

King Vahlika, from the powerful kingdom of Bahlika had come to visit Ugrasena a few days back, and before he could announce that Devki's marriage was being solemnized with Vasudev, Vahlika proposed his son, Somdatta's name for Devki. Ugrasena had not expected this and he was caught off guard. He told Vahlika that it would not be possible for Devki to consider Somdatta's proposal as she intended to marry Prince Vasudev.

Vahlika nodded in understanding, but his son Somdatta who had accompanied him, was furious.

'You insult us Ugrasena. What does Vasudev offer that I don't? There is no warrior in all of Bharat Today, apart from Bheeshma or Jarasandha or your own son Kansa, who can claim to be my equal. And yet you stoop to give away Devki to that coward Vasudev; to a man who has never lifted a sword in the battlefield?'

'Vasudev loves Devki, and she loves him too,' Ugrasena countered. He was furious at Somdatta's words but he didn't want to get into a pointless argument. Somdatta was Bheeshma's cousin. Bheeshma was the most powerful warrior in Bharat and Ugrasena didn't want an unnecessary war.

'Let Vasudev demonstrate his love for Devki then!' roared Somdatta. 'If he is a man, let him fight for Devki's hand.'

Kansa had been sitting quietly thus far. At the latest insult to his friend Vasudev, he could control himself no longer. He got up and looked Somdatta in the eye. 'Devki is not an object Somdatta, to be betrothed to anyone who wins her in a war. She will marry the person she desires to marry and no one else. And if you have any disagreement with that, I would be happy to settle that for you right now, or on the battleground.' He towered above Somdatta, who was a massively built warrior and stood well over six feet in height. But he was no match for Kansa, who at about seven feet, was twice as wide as any other warrior of repute. However, Somdatta was afraid of no one, and he too got up and unsheathed his sword.

Ugrasena and Vahlika were horrified at the turn of events. Neither of them wanted war, and this was quickly turning into one. Vahlika took the initiative. 'Prince Kansa, no one doubts your courage, and your love for Vasudev and your sister Devki. But let's not get agitated. Let's try and settle this without a fight.'

Vahlika's words, said in a calm tone had a temporarily soothing effect on both Kansa and Somdatta. They sat down, with their hands still on their swords. Vahlika addressed his son, 'Somdatta, Devki's marriage has already been fixed with Vasudev. Can't you forget this and bless the two of them?'

Somdatta looked scornfully at his father. 'We came here with a marriage proposal. The announcement of Devki's marriage to Vasudev wasn't yet made public. How do I know that Ugrasena is not using this as an excuse to put us down and marry his daughter to that coward, Vasudev?'

Ugrasena's mouth tightened in silent fury. He looked at Somdatta with fire in his eyes. 'You doubt my words, prince?' he said in a tone that left no doubt about how infuriated he was with Somdatta.

'I don't doubt your words, great king,' Somdatta countered. 'However, the fact that we came here with a marriage proposal is known to all our kinsmen. If we go back empty-handed, it will be an insult for us, and our people will not be able to live with it. There will be years of animosity, which will not be good for either of our kingdom. It is better to settle this once and for all. Let Vasudev meet me on the battlefield. And if he wins, my kinsmen and I will accept his right to marry Devki. There will be no further wars; no long-lasting ill-feeling between two kingdoms.'

Ugrasena took his time to think over this. Finally he said, 'What if Vasudev refuses to fight? He doesn't have to, you know. Devki will marry him anyway. And Madhuvan is well equipped to fight Bahlika, if we need to.'

Somdatta's face lit up with an evil smile. 'Then let it be known that Vasudev was a coward who did not have the courage to fight Somdatta for the woman he claims to love. Let it also be known that the mighty Kansa allowed his sister to marry such a coward. And yes, if Vasudev refuses to fight, there will be war, but not one war. There will be a series of wars till either Madhuvan or Bahlika is decimated completely.'

Kansa interjected just as Ugrasena was about to say something. 'Devki will not marry a coward, for Vasudev is not one. Vasudev will meet you on the battlefield and he shall defeat you. And then the world shall know that Devki marries a man worthy of her.'

King Vahlika, who had been quiet all along, now spoke. 'I expected nothing less from you Kansa. But we need to be sure that you and your brother-in-law, Jarasandha, will not support Vasudev in this fight. For if you do, we will have no recourse but to call for my nephew Bheeshma's help. And if Bheeshma, Jarasandha and you participate in the battle, there will be a war among all the nations of Bharat. All of Bharat will be destroyed.'

Kansa nodded at Vahlika. 'Neither Jarasandha nor I will fight alongside Vasudev in this battle.' Then he glared at Somdatta. 'But know this Somdatta—if by any chance you do defeat Vasudev, I will personally fight you and grind your face in the mud before I allow Devki to be married to a man like you.'

◆

Vasudev paused in his pacing. The battle with Somdatta was scheduled one week from now. Somdatta was a mighty warrior who had won several battles against innumerable kings and princes. Some people had lately begun comparing his abilities to that of Bheeshma, the warrior who had once defeated the great Parshurama himself. His prowess was likened to Jarasandha, the undefeated King of Magadha and brother-in-law of Kansa, and his valour on the battlefield was comparable to the mighty Kansa.

But none of this scared Vasudev. Vasudev himself had been trained by the best gurus and he had full faith in his abilities. He could handle a sword as well as Kansa and he could ride a horse more swiftly and deftly than anyone else in Bateshwar. It was not the thought of being fatally wounded or losing the battle that bothered Vasudev. He was more worried about the soldiers on both sides, dying to satisfy the ego of one man, Somdatta. He had pondered over this matter for the last few days, ever since Kansa had apprised him of what had transpired in the discussion with Somdatta and King Vahlika.

Vasudev had also sought his father's views on it. Surasena's judgement had been clear. 'Fight Somdatta, defeat the upstart and bring Devki home,' Vasudev turned around as he heard the light tap on his door. Sini Yadav, his closest friend and confidante entered the war room and stepped around the huge table where Vasudev was standing. 'My prince!' Sini Yadav bowed slightly as a mark of reverance towards his future king and then smiled and embraced his dearest friend. Vasudev grinned back at him. He was glad he had called Sini. Merely having him around lifted Vasudev's spirits. Sini was not only his closest friend; he was also the most accomplished warrior in Bateshwar and the youngest senapati (commander-in-chief) of their army. He was about five years older than Vasudev and had been trained by the same guru in the art of warfare. But where Vasudev showed more interest in the philosophy of war, Sini was a natural warrior. He could kill without compunction as long as he knew he was fighting for the right side. Yet Sini would be the first person to concede that if and when Vasudev decided to enter the battlefield, the young prince of Bateshwar would prove to be a formidable warrior; because there is no one more fearsome than one who fights only when he has to fight, and then too only for the right cause. Such a man never breaks down in battle, and knows no fear once the decision to fight has been made in his mind. Sini Yadav knew Vasudev was one such man.

'Thanks for coming at once, Sini,' Vasudev said in his characteristic gentle voice. He knew Sini had been busy taking the entire army of Bateshwar through daily maneuvers, getting them prepared for the upcoming battle with Somdatta and the army of Bahlika. Even though Vasudev had not yet confirmed to Somdatta that he had agreed to the battle, Sini wasn't one to take any chances. Like the thorough senapati that he was, he had begun preparing the army as if the battle was already on.

'You called for me prince,' Sini said quietly. 'That was enough for me to come right away. Have you decided what you want to do?'

'I am still not sure,' Vasudev said softly. I love Devki as no man would love a woman but I don't want our marriage to be based on the slaughtering of thousands of soldiers from two different nations.'

Sini waited patiently. He knew Vasudev was talking more to himself, than to him; trying to come to a decision that he could live with, after everything was said and done.

'I wish there was some way of handling this without staking the lives of so many innocent people,' Vasudev sighed in frustration.

'What do you have in mind, Vasudev?'

'I want you to go to Bahlika and convince Somdatta to fight me in single combat, instead of engaging the two armies. That way no innocent lives need to be sacrificed.'

Sini sighed. He had expected Vasudev to come up with something like this. Surasena had also anticipated this and had discussed it with Sini. The senapati knew what he had to do and say. His voice was firm now as he spoke to Vasudev. It was no longer the friend and confidante speaking. It was the voice of the commander-in-chief of the army of Bateshwar; the second most powerful man in the kingdom after the king.

'Prince, I cannot allow you to fight Somdatta in single combat.' He lifted his hand to stop Vasudev from interrupting and continued. 'Your intentions are noble and I respect you for this, but this will set the wrong precedent for the future. What happens if tomorrow a powerful king covets the wife of another king? Will he not invite the weaker king in single combat? And once he defeats him, what happens to the hapless wife? Or for that matter, if a king envies the prosperity of another and invites him to single combat and wins over his kingdom? Are we to let one man decide the fate of an entire kingdom, Vasudev? This is not possible. Nations have armies so that they can protect the sanctity and sovereignty of the people from lustful kings and invaders. Today, even if a king is mightier than another, he thinks twice before he attacks a nation, because he knows his people will have to face an entire army. Even if they win the war, there will be massive casualties. And this prevents wicked rulers from waging unnecessary wars. If you agree to fight Somdatta in single combat today, you may defeat him, but what if other kings or princes elsewhere don't have your valour or your prowess? Can we afford to set up a precedent that will become a curse for other kings and their nations?'

Sini paused to catch his breath. Vasudev looked closely at his friend. He realized why his father had appointed Sini as the senapati of Bateshwar over so many other older veterans of war. Sini had exceptional insight and sensitivity that was rare not just in Bateshwar, but perhaps in all of Bharat. He smiled and for the first time in several days, it reached his eyes. His voice was firm as he spoke to his friend and senapati of Bateshwar. 'Prepare for battle Sini. Let Somdatta know we shall meet him at the crack of dawn seven days from now.'

Sini Yadav bowed to his friend and left the room. Vasudev sat down to study the battle formations Sini had suggested earlier. He knew what they had to do. They would win, and there would be minimum bloodshed.

◆

The battlefield looked like an ocean with waves of blue colliding against a mighty brown mountain. Somdatta and his Bahlika army were dressed in their conventional blue war dress. Sini was at the head of the Bateshwar army, all attired in their traditional brown. Somdatta had brought along a large force of ten thousand infantry, three thousand cavalry, eight hundred war elephants and fifteen hundred archers. Sini Yadav's army was miniscule in comparison and consisted of six thousand infantry, one thousand cavalry, and a little less than five hundred archers. His army had no war elephants.

The sun had barely crept up the horizon and the darkness of the night was just beginning to give way to a new day. Yet the heat was already suffocating. Rivulets of perspiration flowed down the faces of man and beast, alike. Flies had begun to settle on the stock-still bodies of the horses and elephants, and it wouldn't be long before they decided to bother the soldiers too. The battle had not started yet but the vultures had started hovering overhead, in sweet anticipation of the death that would surely follow. The armies waited for the sun to complete its journey to the tip of the horizon, so that the battle could be declared open. Slowly but surely, the ball of fire crept up, and then all at once the sun was over the horizon. Both sides simultaneously blew their shanks (Conches) and the two armies prepared for battle.

Somdatta was flanked on his right side by his trusted aide, Damodara. The two had fought alongside in more than thirty- two battles earlier and he had saved his prince's life on three occasions already. He was a giant of a man, almost as tall and heavily built as Kansa. Having Damodara next to him, made Somdatta feel better. Today, however, all the preparation they had put into this battle seemed wasted.

'Their force is less than half of ours, sire. They don't even have a single war elephant. What kind of a strategist is their senapati?' mumbled Damodara in his deep, halting voice. He didn't receive an answer, and looked at Somdatta, who seemed to be looking intently at the opposing army.

'What's the matter, sire?'

'I can't see Vasudev,' growled Somdatta. Damodara peered closely in the same direction.

He could see Sini Yadav standing at the head of the Bateshwar army but there was no sign of Vasudev.

'That coward has shown his true colours,' Somdatta gnashed his teeth in frustration. 'I was looking forward to cutting off his hands and legs and presenting it to his lover Devki, before I marry her. But that yellow-blooded rascal did not have the courage to show up. Never mind, we will destroy their army first and then decide what to do with him.'

Somdatta looked ahead and his expression grew grim as he saw that Sini Yadav had organized his forces in the Kamal Vyuha (lotus formation). This meant that archers were placed in the centre and the infantry and cavalry formed 'petals' around them for protection. This was the ideal formation for an army that did not have any war elephants. Somdatta would have used the same strategic arrangement for his own troops, but with his oversized elephants, the Kamal Vyuha was not possible. He instantly knew what he had to do. He indicated to Damodara to quickly get their entire force into the Matsya Vyuha (fish formation).

Damodara flashed an evil smile. He knew the Matsya formation was a deadly pattern and even large armies faced great difficulty in standing up to this particular arrangement. An army as small as Sini Yadav's would be completely routed. Moreover, the Matsya Vyuha was the best way to combat the Kamal Vyuha selected by Sini Yadav for his troops. Somdatta had chosen the formation well. As the name suggested, the Matsya Vyuha involved aligning the troops in the shape of a fish. The lighter-armed infantry would be placed in the centre of the formation and continue forward where they would give way to the cavalry, which formed the mouth of the fish formation. The sides of the structure would comprise the war elephants, and behind these huge beasts, the archers would hide and let fly their deadly arrows. The rear end again comprised the remaining infantry troops. Their fish formation would smash through Sini's lotus formation like an iron rod through a sheet of paper.

'Charge!' roared Somdatta standing at the mouth of the Matsya Vyuha, with Damodara by his side. The entire formation moved forward as one large entity and it was astounding to see thousands of men and beasts surging ahead as if bound by one invisible thread.

'Stand firm!' Sini Yadav shouted at the other end of the battlefield. His troops stood at their place, awaiting further commands from their senapati. The entire Bateshwar army resembled a gigantic lotus waiting for the mammoth fish-like structure rushing towards it in what seemed an attempt to completely devour it.

'Steady men, steady!' Sini said to his people, as he saw soldiers and animals getting nervous, waiting for the gigantic enemy force to hit them where they stood. The tension was palpable. It appeared that the Bateshwar soldiers had forgotten to breathe for a brief moment.

'If we stand still, we can handle their onslaught better,' Sini said turning to the archers in the middle of their formation. 'Aim for the sky. Make sure every arrow rains down from the sky and hits their elephants like a thunderbolt. That will keep them occupied for a while.'

His next command was to the cavalry. 'Spears at the ready, men. Keep them pointed towards the enemy.' All cavalry troops had arms of steel and the power of iron in their veins. They would impale the enemy's first charge on the tip of their spears, and they wouldn't waver. Sini knew this with the same certainty as he knew the names of each of his soldiers. To the infantry he instructed, 'Swords at the ready. Take down the first man to come in front of you. The rest will be easy.'

Sini wished Vasudev had been with him. His friend's presence had the same calming effect on him as his own had on his friend. But he had agreed with Vasudev's almost last-minute decision to not be with him at this moment. 'I hope you were right in deciding not to be here with me, my friend,' he thought grimly.

Meanwhile, Somdatta had not been idle. He knew the skill of the Bateshwar archers, and he realized that if he had been in Sini Yadav's position, he would have used his scant forces to try and wreak the maximum damage possible. *Our attack has to be swift and ruthless,* he thought grimly, as he ordered his soldiers arranged in the Matsya Vyuha to increase their speed. His cavalry rushed ahead with the speed of lightning. Somdatta's first charge resulted in the instant deaths of scores of his best riders as they were mercilessly impaled on the spears of the Bateshwar horsemen. However, by the time Sini's cavalrymen had recovered from the first onslaught and could re-arm themselves with another spear, the second wave of Somdatta's outsized cavalry was upon them and large patches of Sini's cavalry were cut down into pieces. The Bateshwar infantry tried their best to fight the enemy soldiers rushing over them on horseback, but their task was made difficult as they stumbled over the dead bodies of the fallen cavalrymen. The foot soldiers were no match for the high-perched cavalry of Somdatta's army and within moments, hundreds of dead bodies were scattered all around. Most of these soldiers were simply ground under the hoofs of the Bahlika steeds.

Sini's face was red with rage as he roared, 'Archers, let loose your arrows. Shoot without taking rest.' His archers had been waiting for the signal, and filled with the fury of watching their comrades being killed ruthlessly, shot their arrows in the air. The sky was covered with thousands of arrows, and the sound of the same arrows as they descended towards the earth was deafening. They rained down with the force of a thousand thunderbolts and created havoc in the ranks of Somdatta's army. Horses and men perished in the blink of an eye as long, deadly arrowheads pierced their armour and skin as if it were paper. Elephants were a different matter. Their thick pachyderm skin saved them from death, but arrows stuck in their eyes and heads made them go mad with painful rage. They ran amok and trampled their own soldiers under their huge feet.

Somdatta looked on in impotent rage as he witnessed his own elephants kill his soldiers and destroy the formation he had so skillfully executed just a few minutes back. He made his decision. 'Kill all the wounded elephants,' he shouted to the mahouts (the elephant drivers). In seconds, the riders of the wounded elephants drove the tip of their sharp rods into the relatively softer part of the elephants' neck. All mahouts were supposed to carry these iron rods, with the sharp tips laced with deadly Naga poison, in case of just such an eventuality. The wounded elephants tripped and fell, dead before they even hit the ground. Soldiers in the vicinity moved away quickly to save themselves from being trapped under the huge beasts. More than half of Somdatta's war elephants lay dead and a significant part of his Matsya Vyuha was in disarray. Somdatta signalled to Damodara, who quickly got busy trying to get the troops back into formation. Meanwhile, Somdatta ordered his archers to let loose their arrows, and the sky was once again filled with the deadly missiles, this time headed in the direction of the Bateshwar forces. The damage on Sini's side was also considerable as the arrows rained down on his troops. However, it was minimized as there were no war elephants to aggravate the chaos.

Sini rallied his troops as they now engaged the enemy in hand-to-hand combat. Damodara led the attack this time and Sini's soldiers fell in front of him like flies before a giant. Somdatta had sent Damodara up front with the sole purpose of taking hold of Sini Yadav and killing him. He knew once Sini was dead, the rest of the Bateshwar army would succumb in no time. Damodara slowly began making his way to where Sini stood commanding his troops. Meanwhile, Somdatta stayed back with the larger part of his army, keeping them in place. He knew they couldn't afford to lose their formation once again in this battle.

Sini saw Damodara advancing towards him. He was nowhere as large as Damodara, but there were very few men who were as good at sword fighting as Sini. Vasudev was one of those, but he wasn't here right now. He would have to fight Damodara himself. If he could kill Somdatta's right-hand man, it would be a big dent in Somdatta's armour. Sini Yadav rode ahead on his horse. Damodara saw him coming and smiled malevolently at him from a distance. He didn't want to fight Sini while he was on a horse, but he didn't have time to get a horse for himself. He waited for him to come close, and as Sini attacked Damodara with his sword, the latter ducked deftly, in a swift motion that belied his gigantic size. Before Sini could attack again, Damodara gave one mighty blow to the horse's head. The blow would have broken the back of a large man, but the horse only stumbled for an instant. This was, however, enough for Damodara as he used the moment to pull Sini off the horse and throw him to the ground. He walked slowly towards where Sini was sitting on the ground, shaking his head to regain his equilibrium. Damodara took out his sword, and gave Sini an evil smile. 'Welcome your death, senapati!' he mumbled softly. Sini held his sword up with one hand, trying to get up with the other. As per the rules of war, Damodara could attack him only when he was standing. Damodara eyed him carefully, waiting for the moment Sini would rise, so that he could finish him off with one swift stroke of his sword. Sini stumbled to gain his balance, just as Damodara rushed towards him with his sword held high.

At exactly that moment, the earth appeared to shake violently and sure enough, there was the deafening roar of what seemed like hundreds of elephants and horses galloping at breakneck speed. Over this disturbance, there was another sound, growing more clamourous by the moment. Both Damodara and Sini strained their ears to make out what the commotion was. And suddenly the din was audible. It seemed as if thousands of men were shouting,

'Bateshwar ki Jai...Rajkumar Vasudev ki Jai' (Praised be Bateshwar... Praised be Prince Vasudev). Sini Yadav smiled in relief in the same moment as realization dawned on Damodara. Damodara looked in Somdatta's direction for guidance, but he was preoccupied looking the other way, towards the rear side of his Matsya Vyuha, where there was major disorder. Damodara knew he had to make this decision alone. He turned to face Sini again, and charged at him. Sini had anticipated this move and he adroitly slipped down to his right knee, as Damodara's sword swooshed over his head.

Before Damodara could make another attack with his sword, Sini had sunk the tip of his blade right up to the hilt, in Damodara's abdomen. Damodara's eyes glassed over, and he toppled, crashing to the ground, even before he knew what had happened.

'You were a worthy enemy,' Sini sighed, as he looked at Damodara's lifeless body.

Though he was no stranger to death, and he would gladly fight anyone who threatened his nation, Sini always felt bad whenever a worthy opponent died at his hands. He quickly hopped back onto his horse to get a better view of what was happening at the far side of the battleground. He could see Somdatta waving frantically at his troops to break formation and turn around.

Sini knew the reason for Somdatta's confusion. Vasudev had attacked Somdatta's Matsya Vyuha from the rear. He had led the charge with the entire lot of war elephants at the disposal of Bateshwar. This was one of the main reasons he had asked Sini not to take the elephants with his troops. The chaos at the rear end of Somdatta's Matsya Vyuha was now evident. Vasudev's war elephants had completely decimated the tail end of the fish formation and a majority of Somdatta's infantry stationed at the back was crushed to pulp. The elephants rode over them and carried their onslaught right to the centre of the vyuha, trampling every infantry unit in their path. Meanwhile, soldiers perched on the elephants showered spears on Somdata's cowering archers. Vasudev's cavalry followed right behind the war elephants, finding it easy to find their footing as the elephants had literally cleared a path for them. His soldiers made short work of the remaining Bahlika foot soldiers. In a few minutes, the face of the battle had changed. Vasudev's well-timed attack from the rear end of Somdatta's forces had not only taken them by surprise and shattered the enemy's strategic formation, it had dealt such a crushing blow to the morale of the Bahlika army that the soldiers were finding it impossible to recover from the offense. Sini Yadav seized the opportunity to intensify the attack. Somdatta's forces were caught between Sini's troops in the front and Vasudev's fresh forces from the rear. It would have been a complete massacre if Vasudev had not blown his conch to halt the battle.

Sini's soldiers captured Somdatta's personal bodyguards, who were all killed right away. Somdatta was bound and brought to Sini, who placed the tip of his blade under Somdatta's chin and pressed it lightly, causing blood to trickle down his neck. 'I should kill you right away, you scoundrel,' he hissed. Somdatta ignored him as he looked around, as if searching for someone. 'Damodara,' he whispered. 'Where is Damodara?' he asked.

'Damodara is dead, you rascal,' Sini snapped at him. 'Dead... so that you could satisfy your ego,' he continued with contempt in his eyes, as he spat in Somdatta's direction.

'Sini!' Vasudev exclaimed in shock. He had just made his way to where they held Somdatta, and witnessed Sini spitting on the enemy's face, while the latter was held in chains.

'Vasudev,' Sini hugged his closest friend with love. 'Your strategy paid off. They were completely taken by surprise,' he grinned at Vasudev.

Vasudev, hugged his friend back, but Sini noticed he was not smiling. 'What's the matter, Vasudev? You don't look happy at our enemy's defeat,' Sini said with a tinge of disappointment in his voice.

Vasudev looked at his friend with a wan smile. 'No one is

happier than me that we have won, Sini. But at what cost?' He gestured towards the hundreds of soldiers lying dead on both sides of the battlefield. 'And is it right that you spit at a man bound in chains, in front of his own countrymen?' He looked at Sini with narrowed eyes.

Sini bent his head in shame. He knew he was wrong to spit at Somdatta while he was chained and helpless, but he couldn't control himself at the sight of the man who had been responsible for all this destruction. However, Vasudev was right. The ethics of war did not include insulting a man when he was already down and defeated.

'What do you want me to do prince?' he asked Vasudev with apology evident in his voice.

Vasudev glanced in Somdatta's direction. 'Ask your men to unchain him. And let his soldiers be free to return home. Tend to the injured on both sides of the battlefield, and then let us go home...to Bateshwar.'

Sini Yadav bowed to Vasudev and gave the command to unchain Somdatta. An unarmed Somdatta moved towards Vasudev. 'You have won my respect Vasudev, but not my friendship. I have lost too much today to ever be your friend, but I can promise that the next time we meet on the battlefield, I will not underestimate you. And I will have my revenge. But for now, you can tell Ugrasena and your father that you have won Devki from me.'

Vasudev clenched his jaw at Somdatta's last words, but he maintained his calm. 'Devki was never yours to give to me, Somdatta.' Then he smiled at his enemy, and there was steel in his gaze. 'But I look forward to meeting you again, in happier circumstances. You will get the invitation of my marriage with Devki.'

Somdatta looked at Vasudev with hatred in his eyes. But he refrained from saying anything. Sini shouted commands to prepare to return after tending to the wounded on both sides.

Vasudev mounted his horse and galloped back towards Bateshwar, followed by a team of trusted bodyguards. A chorus of 'Bateshwar ki Jai...Rajkumar Vasudev ki Jai' accompanied his departure from the battlefield.

Birth of a Demon Child

Kansa moved in his sleep. The nightmare was disturbing and it had been recurring for the past few days. Images of death... his death came to him in flashes. A little boy was running in the royal gardens, butter smeared across his face. He had the most innocent smile Kansa had ever seen. He moved surreptitiously towards the child so he wouldn't disturb the infant's unbridled frolicking in the mud. He bent down to see what the child was doing. He saw the infant shaping something out of the mildly wet mud; it looked like he was making a toy dagger. Kansa smiled indulgently at the toddler. At the age of three, he was already showing signs of being a true kshatriya (warrior). After all, he was the son of his beloved sister Devki and his valiant friend Vasudev. He had to be a warrior among warriors. The child had by now completed fashioning the dagger out of the wet mud and was waving it in an arc, as if parrying with an unseen foe. Kansa playfully tried to pull the toy dagger from the child's hands, but he resisted with a smile. Kansa laughed at this. The baby laughed too. But it seemed to Kansa that the child was not laughing with him; he was laughing *at* him. Suddenly, the child thrust the toy dagger in Kansa's direction and at that moment the toy weapon became real—a metal dagger with a lethally sharp end, pointed in his direction. Kansa barely escaped from getting hurt. Instinctively Kansa pulled out his own sword and just as he was about to plunge it into the child, Devki appeared out of thin air. She screamed, 'No, Kansa, he is my son...your nephew! You can't hurt him!' Kansa was shocked at what he had almost done.

He turned back to apologize to the child, but he was gone. In his place stood a fifteen-year-old youth with the same innocent smile the child had had. The young boy was holding the infant's dagger by the handle, but the tip of the dagger now rested in Kansa's abdomen, and Kansa could see more than feel the life blood pouring out of his body and on to the ground, making the mud even wetter. He looked at the boy, unable to understand. The boy laughed, and again it seemed as if he was laughing at Kansa. Devki came close to the boy and hugged him. Why was she hugging him? His beloved sister, hugging his murderer! And then Kansa heard the words that chilled his heart and made his blood freeze. 'Thank you my son!' Devki had just thanked the boy who had killed her brother.

Kansa got up from his nightmare, his angavastra drenched with perspiration. He felt sick. The dream had seemed so real; as if it were happening right before him. Devki's betrayal haunted him. Of all his brothers and sisters, she was dearest to him. What if she ever betrayed him? He shook his head vigorously to get the vile thought out of his mind. *She would never do something like this. This was just a dream!* he said viciously to himself.

What if it was not a dream? The hoarse and raucous voice came from somewhere inside his mind. Kansa jumped off his bed. His fighting arm instinctively reached to retrieve his sword from the other side of his bed. He looked around him trying to see where the voice was coming from.

You fool, you think you can kill me with your puny sword? the voice rasped. Kansa was familiar with the concept of ventriloquism. He knew there were people who could throw their voice in such a way that it appeared to come from one place, while the speaker would be at an entirely different place in the room. Somebody was using ventriloquism with him but to what purpose? Kansa decided he would find out. He walked stealthily towards the curtains on the other side of the room and with a swift jab he thrust his sword through the curtains. The sword passed through the cloth without meeting any resistance. He repeated this action with the curtains on all sides of the lavishly decorated room. He looked under the bed to see if the intruder was hiding there. Nothing! Kansa looked around the room bewildered.

You look in the wrong places for the wrong person, Kalanemi! The voice was mocking. Kansa put his hands to his ears trying to shut the hoarse voice out of his mind. *You can't shut me out by shutting your ears, Kalanemi!* The voice was gentler now; more appeasing. *I'm not your enemy...I'm your friend. The only friend you have.*

'Show yourself, you coward!' Kansa growled in anger. The voice in his head laughed mirthlessly. *You are not prepared to see me yet, Kalanemi. One day you shall, and then I will show myself to you. Right now you need to prepare yourself against your true enemies, Kalanemi.*

Kansa stopped searching around the room. He understood now that there was no intruder in the room. The intruder was in his mind. Someone was using cosmic telepathy to communicate with him. But who? And how? Only the three supreme gods or a brahmarishi could communicate through cosmic telepathy, and this voice was not God's. Who could possibly be doing this?

'My true enemies... What do you mean?' He growled.

Your closest friend and your loving sister...Vasudev and Devki...they are your true enemies, Kalanemi.

The voice in Kansa's head was even gentler now, as if sympathizing with him.

Kansa's mouth tightened in anger at the slander of the two people closest to him. Then another thought struck Kansa with the force of lightning. He spoke aloud, 'Why are you calling me Kalanemi?

Because that is your true name...that is who you really are...inside that mortal body that you inhabit.

The voice was softer now, gradually fading away.

'What? You are mistaken!' Kansa said in a mixture of confusion and anger. 'I am Kansa, son of King Ugrasena of Madhuvan.'

The voice in his head was almost inaudible now. *You are not Kansa, you are Kalanemi...the greatest demon king the world has ever known. And Ugrasena is not your father...*

'You lie, you coward. Show yourself to me so I may cut off your blasphemous tongue!' Kansa screamed with barely controlled fury. There was no answer in reply to Kansa's outraged scream, and Kansa thought the voice in his head had left him.

Then all of a sudden, it was back again, and with what seemed like a superhuman effort, it whispered, *Go ask Ugrasena who your true father is...* And with those words, the Dark Lord's voice disappeared, accompanied by his sad and hoarse laughter, even as Kansa struggled to come to terms with the reality of what he had just heard.

◆

Ugrasena was sitting on a diwan with Kansa on his right. Vasudev and Surasena sat facing them. They were meeting in the room meant for the guests of the royal family. A feast had been organized in honour of Vasudev's recent victory over Somdatta. Ugrasena planned to announce the news of Devki's marriage to Vasudev to the people of Madhuvan on the day of the feast. Kings and royal families from different nations in Bharat and other lands of Mriytyulok had been invited for the great feast. The main palace housed some of the more important guests like Surasena while other royal families were housed in various regal guest houses, adjoining the main palace structure.

'So Vasudev? How does it feel to be the man of the hour?' Ugrasena smiled affectionately at his future son-in-law. Vasudev looked respectfully at the king of Madhuvan. He was very fond of him and loved the way the old stalwart managed his kingdom. Firm like a ruler, but gentle like a father. *No wonder his people love him so much,* Vasudev thought.

'Where are you lost, young man?' Ugrasena asked laughing.

'I think he is missing Devki,' quipped Kansa, with a grin.

Everyone laughed.

Vasudev glanced at Kansa. His friend appeared fine on the surface but there was something bothering him that Vasudev could not understand. He didn't look his usual self. It almost seemed as if he was trying hard to look normal. *I must talk to him later and find out what is bothering him*, Vasudev decided.

'When is the wedding date fixed, Ugrasena?' Surasena asked. Surasena wanted to announce the ascension of Vasudev as the king of Bateshwar, on the day of his son's wedding and was looking forward to the date with anticipation. He had decided he was too old to continue as the ruler and was keen to enter the Vanaprasthashram, a stage where he would give up material comforts and go live in the forest, in search of a higher calling. He had waited so far to make sure Vasudev was ready to take charge of the kingdom. Vasudev's recent victory over Somdatta, and, more importantly, the manner in which he had conducted himself in victory, convinced Surasena that the prince was ready for his role as king of Bateshwar.

Ugrasena consulted the calendar given to him earlier by the court pandit. 'The most auspicious day for the marriage is three months from now, Surasena.' He looked at Vasudev and smiled. 'It will give us some time to prepare for the marriage, son.'

Vasudev nodded. He had been waiting to get married to Devki as far back as he could remember. They had been children when he first saw her, during a visit to Ugrasena's palace, years ago. He had known at first sight that Devki was the woman for him. Even though he had been living with Rohini for the past two years, Vasudev's thoughts had not once strayed from Devki. As if echoing his thoughts, Ugrasena cleared his throat a little self-consciously. He had been meaning to ask Vasudev something but hadn't got the opportunity so far. However, he had to know now, or it would be meaningless later. Still, he looked a little uncomfortable as he spoke to Vasudev 'How is Rohini taking all this? She can't be too happy with your impending wedding to Devki.'

There was silence in the room, Kansa, too, waiting for Vasudev's reply. Surasena would have liked to help his son but he knew this was something Vasudev had to handle on his own. Vasudev paused to decide how best to answer. Ugrasena had asked him a question that was of significant importance to him. His mind raced back to events in his recent past...

◆

Rohini Devi, fondly called Rohini by everyone, was the only child of Deodas. He was the chieftain of a minor province adjoining Bateshwar, and a close friend of Surasena. The two of them had planned Rohini's marriage to Vasudev when both Vasudev and Rohini were barely three years old. A few years after this, Rohini's father had been killed in a skirmish with an enemy. Rohini's mother too succumbed to illness shortly thereafter. Thus Rohini was brought up by one of her maternal uncles, a brahmin, and she received all her education on philosophy from the learned man. As she turned seventeen, it was time for her to marry. Her uncle, the Brahmin Shonalik, was aware that she was betrothed in principle to Vasudev. He visited Bateshwar to discuss Rohini's marriage with Surasena, who welcomed him, but shared with Shonalik that Vasudev was in love with Devki and intended to marry her. Shonalik was not angered as most people would have been. But he calmly told Surasena that no other man would come forward to marry Rohini, as it was common knowledge that she had been betrothed to Vasudev all these years. 'I understand your situation Surasena; I will let Rohini know that Vasudev can no longer marry her. She will spend the rest of her life as a spinster, but I know she is strong enough to accept this with grace.' Saying this, the brahmin blessed Surasena and departed for home to share the news with Rohini. Surasena was in dilemma, knowing he was breaking a promise made to his old friend, and also being unfair to Rohini who would be confined to a life of spinsterhood for no fault of her own. *But how can I ask Vasudev to marry Rohini when he clearly loves Devki?* he thought, and his perplexity and depression increased with each day. He knew if he shared his thoughts with Vasudev, his son would have no choice but to marry Rohini to honour Surasena's commitment to Rohini's father. Surasena didn't want Vasudev to be unhappy because of a commitment he had made when his son was too young to even know what had happened. Then a thought struck him and he decided to go and meet Rohini. On his arrival at Shonalik's modest house, he was welcomed as an honoured guest by the learned man. Sensing that Surasena wanted to talk to Rohini, Shonalik left them alone. No one knew what was discussed that day between Rohini and Surasena, but when Surasena returned to Bateshwar, he summoned his son and told him that he would be marrying Rohini in a month's time. While inwardly shattered at the thought of losing Devki, Vasudev quietly agreed to Surasena's request. 'Your wish will be carried out, Father,' Vasudev said softly. 'When may I go to Madhuvan to let Devki know that I won't be able to marry her?' he asked Surasena. Surasena looked with unabashed pride at his only son and hugged him. 'Did you think, Vasudev, that I would be so cruel as to not know that you can no more exist without Devki as the Earth without the sun?' Vasudev looked with surprise at his father, as Surasena continued speaking. 'You shall marry Rohini because I made a commitment to her father. However, when the time is right, you shall also marry Devki, because she is the one you truly love!' Vasudev found it difficult to hide his tears at his father's love for him, but he shook his head. 'I am afraid that won't be possible, Father. I cannot do this injustice to Rohini. She will never accept another woman as my wife. And I cannot let Devki feel second to anyone else either.' Surasena held Vasudev by his shoulder. 'Rohini understands that you love Devki, Vasudev. She has told me she will be happy if you can find happiness with the woman you truly love.' Vasudev looked unsure. 'But, Father...' he started to say. Surasena interrupted him with a slight wave of his hand.

'Rohini is a very wise woman, my son. And she has a large heart too. She will never want you to be unhappy.' Surasena paused for a moment before continuing. 'Love Devki my child...but honour Rohini too, at all times. You will have two wives and they will both be your strength. Mark my words, for you shall remember this someday.' Vasudev bowed to his father. 'Now go. Devki needs to know you are marrying Rohini. If she is as great a woman as I think she is, she will understand why you have to do this.' This was two years ago, and Vasudev had gone to Madhuvan and sought Devki's permission to marry Rohini. Devki was fifteen at that time, but with wisdom beyond her age.

She had quietly given her consent to Vasudev. 'Rohini is fortunate that she marries you today, Vasudev. Honour her as your first wife. I will wait till you come and ask for my hand, someday soon.' Vasudev left Madhuvan that day knowing in his mind that he was indeed one of the most fortunate men in Mrityulok, to have the love of a woman like Devki. Vasudev and Rohini were married in a quiet ceremony held at Bateshwar with only a few family members from Surasena's side in attendance. Shonalik was present from Rohini's side of the family, along with three brahmins, all of whom blessed the couple. In the past two years of marriage, Vasudev had given Rohini all the honours of being his first wife; but based on mutual understanding, neither of them had shared the conjugal bed. Rohini did this out of respect for Devki, and Vasudev was bound by his love for the only woman he had ever loved...Devki.

◆

Vasudev was brought back to the present by something Kansa had said. He looked blankly at his friend. Kansa realized Vasudev hadn't heard him. 'I know you love my sister more than anyone else, Vasudev. But I don't want her feeling second to Rohini. It is therefore important that we know how Rohini feels about your marriage with Devki.'

Though Kansa had reiterated the question, Vasudev looked at Ugrasena while answering. He knew the old king was anxious to know whether his niece, whom he loved like his own daughter, would find peace and love at Bateshwar. And though he loved Devki with all his heart and soul, at this moment he felt an unbridled sense of pride and respect for his first wife. 'Rohini sends this for Devki, respected king.'

Ugrasena extended his hand to take a carefully wrapped package from Vasudev. The parcel was covered in the most exquisite silk he had ever seen. But what lay cocooned inside the silk was even more exquisite. A necklace made of rubies and diamonds, each of them the size of a large grape gleamed with the brightness of the sun. Accompanying it were ten bracelets, made of the finest diamonds that competed to outshine the brilliance of the necklace itself. 'What...what is this?' he asked marvelling at the beauty of the jewellery.

'These are my late mother's jewels, handed down to her by her mother. They have been in our family for the past seven generations, and are given to the custodian of the royal family. Only the queen of Bateshwar may wear them, or in her absence, the bahu of the family,' Vasudev paused as his voice cracked with emotion. 'Rohini felt that only Devki could be the rightful custodian of these jewels, and she wanted Devki to know that she understands this and will always love her as her own sister.'

Tears flowed down Ugrasena's face and even the usually stoic Kansa was struck by emotion at the large-heartedness of Vasudev's first wife. 'Say no more my son!' Ugrasena got up to hug Vasudev. 'Rohini's gesture has more than answered my question. Prepare for your marriage to Devki in three months' time.'

Kansa shook his future brother-in-law's hands. 'Welcome to the family, brother.'

Exactly at that moment, the skies thundered. The rumbling was accompanied by what seemed like a hoarse and rasping scream from the depths of hell. But it was inaudible to everyone except

Kansa. He heard it and shivered with fear for the first time in his life. The rasping scream was the same as the raucous voice he had heard in his head, a day ago.

◆

'In the name of Vishnu, how many times do I need to tell you, you are my son!' Ugrasena shouted uncharacteristically at his beloved son. Kansa bowed his head, plagued by ambivalent feelings. His love and duty towards his father made him hesitant to probe further on this topic. Ugrasena had been devastated when Kansa had put forth the question, 'Who is my real father?' And for a fleeting moment, Kansa had thought of abandoning this quest that was hurting his father so much. However, he was driven by an inexplicably uncontrollable force, to persist in his quest for the answer. The Dark Lord's words had been haunting him for the past few nights and try as he might, he couldn't be his usual self.

'Father, there is something that you haven't told me. I have felt it all these years...in the whispers of Mother's closest attendants... whispers that stop as soon as they see me.' Ugrasena helplessly watched his son's tortured expression, and tried to imagine what the young prince would be going through in his mind.

'Mother never loved me the way she loved her other nine children. I learnt to live without her love because I knew you loved me more than any of my brothers and sisters. But sometimes I would catch her staring at me with such hate that the force of her loathing would make me want to die,' Kansa paused, his voice too broken to continue. Ugrasena waited with bated breath, hoping Kansa would not ask him what he knew now was inevitable. But he knew that Kansa was on the brink of asking the very question that he had been dreading all these years.

'And I always wondered what I had done to be the cause of such abhorrence from my own mother...' Kansa paused in mid sentence, making a superhuman effort to rein in his emotions. After what seemed like an eternity, Kansa seemed to calm down.

He looked at Ugrasena, 'Why did Mother hate me, Father?'

The pain and anger, lying buried in Kansa's soul for the past twenty-nine years of his life seemed to have erupted all of a sudden and it did not brook any easy answers. Ugrasena looked at Kansa closely, and for the first time he felt a sense of fear as he stared into the eyes of his son. He had always thought Kansa had soft, melting eyes, much like his mother. Today, those very eyes looked hard as steel. In that moment, Ugrasena realized with a shock that Kansa could probably hate with the same intensity with which he was capable of loving.

'It's a long story,' Ugrasena said softly, and motioned to Kansa to take a seat close to him. Then he held his son's hands as he prepared to tell him a story he had thought was buried in his heart forever.

◆

'Your mother was born to King Satyaketu of Vidarbha. They called her Shooraseni and she was supposed to have been the most beautiful princess in all of Bharat. Her beauty was so alluring that kings of different nations in Bharat and other lands in Mrityulok all desired to marry her. Even though her family and ours wanted her to be married to me, we knew some of the other kings might oppose, much as Somdatta did in the case of your sister. But I had the support of Vasudev's father, Surasena, and the other kings knew that if they had to battle the combined force of Madhuvan, Bateshwar and Vidarbha, they may not win. Finally, I married Shooraseni and brought her to Madhuvan. After marriage, I liked to call your mother Padmavati, the name given to her by my father.'

◆

Kansa listened to Ugrasena's every word, hoping that somewhere in those words, he may get to know the reason why his mother hated him so much. Ugrasena sipped some water before continuing.

◆

'Padmavati and I were very happy together. She loved me more than I had thought was possible and I realized that her external beauty was nothing compared to her inner loveliness. She was flawless. And she was devoted to me as few queens could ever be to their husbands. One day, we received a message from Padmavati's father. The king of Vidarbha was ill and wanted to see his daughter. I had to go out for a few days to quell some disturbance that was taking place in one of our outer provinces, and I suggested that Padmavati go and visit her father during that time. I told her I would join her there in a few weeks. Padmavati left for Vidarbha and I set out with a battalion towards the province where the unrest was happening.'

◆

Kansa looked at his father with concern. Ugrasena's voice was sounding increasingly strained and Kansa guessed that whatever Ugrasena had kept from him all these years was close to being revealed. A part of him wanted to ask Ugrasena to stop, but the other craved to know the truth. It drove him just as a moth feels drawn towards the flame, pulled by an uncontrollable force. Ugrasena continued with his story.

◆

'After Padmavati had been at Vidarbha for a month, her father began to get a little better, though his condition was still critical. Padmavati had not left his bedside for the entire time he had been bed-ridden. She was exhausted. Now that he was feeling slightly better, the old king asked her to take a break from nursing him and get some rest. I had sent a messenger to Vidarbha to let Padmavati know that I would be reaching in a couple of days' time to join her. Seeing her father's condition slightly improved, and on being goaded by him to take a break, she took few of her lady attendants to go to Puspavan. Puspavan was a beautiful mountain close to the king's palace and it was believed that the

Brahma kamal flower could be found there if you were fortunate enough to locate it. Your mother wanted to get the Brahma kamal for her father.'

◆

'The Brahma kamal?' Kansa said in surprise. 'But isn't the flower only found in Swarglok?'

Ugrasena looked at Kansa with a wan smile. 'Yes it is. But Puspavan is the only place in Mrityulok where the flower is believed to grow.' He looked forlorn as he said, 'And it was this very thing that led to all the tragedy later.'

'I don't understand,' Kansa said. 'Why did Mother want to get the Brahma kamal for grandfather?'

Ugrasena sighed. 'The flower is supposed to have magical life-giving properties. It is said that if you drink water poured over the petals of the Brahma kamal, it can restore life, or at the very least, make you stronger if you are weak. If you remember, when Lord Shiva attached the elephant's head to Lord Ganesha's body, his body gained life only after the Mahadev sprinkled water on his body. That water was sprinkled from a Brahma kamal.'

'I see,' nodded Kansa. 'So Mother thought if she could find the flower at Puspavan, she could restore grandfather's health by getting him to drink water poured from the magical flower?'

Ugrasena nodded. 'Yes, that's what she thought. Mind you, she was not sure that she would find the Brahma kamal at Puspavan. But she felt that it was at least worth a try. After all, various travellers from time to time had mentioned sighting the golden-white petals of the flower on the higher reaches of Puspavan. Padmavati thought if she could somehow get the flower it might restore the old man's health.'

'Did she find it?' Kansa couldn't contain his curiosity.

Ugrasena didn't seem to hear him. He was back to narrating the story.

◆

'Padmavati hiked up the mountain, accompanied by her attendants. Being an avid mountaineer from her early days, she easily walked ahead of the other women in the group. She was wearing the traditional silk dhoti tied around her with the loose end of the garment drawn in between her legs and hemmed in around her waist. Over that, she wore a conservative angvastram leaving her arms free to hack through the forest of Puspavan. It was a welcome break for her and out in the nature, she began to enjoy the scenery. The thought that I would be arriving in a few days buoyed her mood further. However, as it began to get dark, she realized that her companions had been left way behind, owing to the swift pace she had set for herself. She thought she would retrace her steps and meet up with her companions. They could put up camp for the night and the next day, they would start early to look for the Brahma Kamal flower. She turned around and tried retracing her steps. It took her a few minutes to realize that she had gone off track and was now completely lost in the forests of Puspavan. Padmavati was a very brave woman. She did not panic, as others in her situation might have. The forest was known to be inhabited by wild animals that ventured out at night. All her attendants were trained in martial arts, just as she was, and in a camp there would have been no cause for worry. However, alone in the darkness of the night, even a valiant woman like Padmavati would be hard-pressed to take care of herself if a particularly vicious animal were to attack her. Yet she kept her cool and weighed her options. She decided it might help if she were to shout for help. There was a chance that her companions might hear her and find her. She called out, but they had gone over to the other side of Puspavan to search for her, and they could not hear her.'

◆

'It must have been terrifying for Mother,' Kansa said, thinking of how Padmavati must have felt, alone in the night, with just her sword to protect her.

Ugrasena looked kindly at him and patting his hand, continued.

◆

'While her companions could not hear her, someone else did. A Gandharva was sleeping on the tree beneath which Padmavati was standing and shouting for help. His name was Dramil. While he was a Gandharva—a celestial being—he had the blood of an asura. In the world of Asuras, he was known popularly as Godhin. The vile Gandharva was instantly taken by Padmavati's unnatural beauty and he began to covet her. He knew Padmavati would never give in to his lustful desires of her own will. And he didn't want to force her as he wanted to enjoy her beauty in peace. So like the craven demon that he was, Dramil used his unholy powers to take my physical form. Having taken my form, he approached Padmavati. She was surprised at seeing who she thought was me at Puspavan, as she had been told earlier that I would arrive after two days. But Dramil was a cunning asura, and he told her that he had wanted to surprise her and arrived earlier than he had planned. He said that upon reaching Vidarbha, Padmavati's father had told him about her trip to Puspavan. Believing Dramil to be me, Padmavati naively believed all that he told her.'

◆

'But even if he took your physical form, did she not make out the difference in voice or the mannerisms?' Kansa was aghast at the possible consequences of his mother confusing an asura with his noble father.

Ugrasena, who had lived for years with the truth of what had happened that day, smiled sadly at his son. 'Gandharvas have the gift of not only being able to take the physical form of any person that they desire; they can look into your mind and fathom the slightest nuances of the person they want to impersonate—mannerisms, voice, tone—every other aspect of the person gets replicated to perfection. It's like they can look inside the deepest recesses of your mind. And whoever exists in your mind, anyone that you have ever known, is visible to them as if they were right in front of their eyes. Whatever interaction you have had with anyone can be seen by them as if its happening again in their mind's eye. And they can observe how a person talks, walks or otherwise conducts himself and can immediately clone those facets to masquerade as that specific person.'

Kansa was pale as the first glimmerings of what must have happened that day on Puspavan began to dawn on him. 'So Dramil looked into Mother's mind, and was able to see not just how you looked, but also the exact manner in which you behave with her?'

'Yes.' Ugrasena replied quietly.

'Oh God! Then what happened?' Kansa asked, gritting his teeth, fearing for the mother who had not once showed any love for him. Ugrasena continued with the story.

◆

'Thinking that her husband had arrived early to surprise her, Padmavati embraced Dramil. At her touch, he lost whatever constraint he may otherwise have had. Her beauty and the wild environment, coupled with the way she embraced him, made him lust for her even more. He held her close and during the night, the dastardly asura made love to Padmavati. When she got up in the morning, she found herself alone. Dramil was gone. That was the first inkling she had of something being wrong. She knew I would never leave her alone in the forest under any condition. After wandering around in circles, she finally met her companions, who had also been looking for her since the first light of dawn. She asked them if they had come across me. They were surprised at her question as all of them were aware that I was not expected back for another day. Padmavati kept her misgivings to herself but she was now very anxious. Her companions asked her if they should go deeper into the forests of Puspavan to look for the Brahma kamal. But she was impatient to get back to the palace. By now she had started having grave suspicions about whether she had really spent the night with me. She knew the answer lay in Vidarbha. If I was there, she could ask me why I had left her alone in the forest. If, however, I wasn't there... She didn't even want to think of what that would mean for her and for everyone else in the royal family. However, more than one tragedy awaited her when she reached the outskirts of Vidarbha. On their way, they were met by a group of the king's personal bodyguards sent to call them back urgently. The king had taken a drastic turn for the worse during the night. The royal vaid did not believe he would survive the day and he had sent the bodyguards to look for Padmavati and get her back before the king breathed his last. They had brought along a horse for her, in order that she made better time on the way back. For a brief moment, Padmavati forgot what had happened the previous night in the forest, as she desperately rode the horse, spurring him on to an impossible speed. By the time, she reached Vidarbha, the mourning in the streets told her that her father's soul had already departed his mortal body. A second shock awaited her. I was not at the palace, and as per the guards, I had not arrived yet. Padmavati collapsed before she could reach her chambers. The attendants thought it was the shock of her father's death but only she knew that wasn't the real reason.'

◆

Ugrasena paused to wipe a tear from his eyes. Kansa waited for the narration to continue, not daring to breathe as his mind struggled to comprehend what would have happened next.

◆

'I reached Vidarbha the next day, and upon hearing of the king's death, and Padmavati's condition, I rushed to her chambers. I was shocked at seeing her condition. She was pale as death. Seeing me, she took hold of my hand, and crazed with grief, she asked me, 'Did you come to Vidarbha yesterday? Say you were here...say it.' Not knowing what she meant, I shook my head as I told her I had just reached Vidarbha. At that she screamed once in unbearable agony and her body went into a series of terrible convulsions. I summoned the royal vaid, who arrived immediately and gave her some medicine to calm her and make her sleep. I sat by her side through the night. She was mumbling incoherently all through the dark hours. That made me increasingly concerned for her. More than once she maniacally mumbled the words "betrayed" and "revenge" in her sleep. It was all unclear to me and I was beginning to realize that there was something other than her father's death that was plaguing her. The next day, when she got up, she looked physically better but she seemed to have lost her natural effervescence. Despite my repeated entreaties, she refused to explain what was affecting her so acutely. After a few days, I too gave up and let her be. By now, I had been at Vidarbha for more than a month, and was keen to return to Madhuvan with Padmavati. The events related to King Satyaketu's last rites were also long done and there was no reason to stay there any longer.

'The night before we were to depart for Madhuvan, Padmavati's chief attendant came to me and told me the queen requested my presence in the garden. I was pleasantly surprised as Padmavati had not shown much inclination to talk to me or anyone else since my arrival at Vidarbha, and in the past one month, we had barely exchanged a few words. I quickly moved in the direction of the palace garden, excited to meet Padmavati and talk to her. She was sitting alone in the darkest corner of the grounds, and had her back towards me. I gently tapped her on her shoulder to announce my presence. She turned around in shock, as if she were expecting someone else. I was aghast at her appearance. Her hair was untied and she had a wild look in her eyes. Her normally lovely face was white as a sheet and every aspect of her persona exuded fear and some kind of revulsion that I couldn't quite understand. I was shocked at how she looked, and bending down on my knees, I took her hands in my own. "What's the matter, my love? What is troubling you?" I asked her gently. She looked me in my eyes then and seemed to draw some strength from deep within her. She whispered, "I am pregnant, Ugrasena." I looked at her. My expression was a mixture of surprise, happiness and confusion. "Are you sure, my queen?" I asked softly. Then, looking at her fearful expression, I said, "But that's great news, Padmavati. We are having a child." Her face betrayed her inner turbulence, but she quelled it in a final attempt to speak what had to be spoken. "This thing...it is not yours!" I stared at her, my mind a raging vacuum of bewildered thoughts. "But...how... why?" I managed to ask. She had a faraway look in her eyes, as she told me, in a monotone, what had happened that night in the forests of Puspavan. I listened in silence, my anger and disgust at the Gandharva's deceit growing with the passing of each moment. When she came to the point where she got up in the morning and found herself alone, believing me to have left her in the forest by herself, I couldn't hide my anger at the Gandharva's act. But my compassion for Padmavati overshadowed whatever anger I may have felt for Dramil in that instant and I held her in a close embrace. We stayed like that for a few minutes, till Padmavati's ragged breathing became a little normal.'

◆

'But how could Mother be sure the child wasn't yours?' Kansa asked embarrassed at discussing this with his father. 'I mean, couldn't she have conceived the child before...before she met Dramil that day in the forest?' he continued haltingly.

Ugrasena looked closely at his eldest son. He knew the next few moments would decide how Kansa viewed him for the rest of his life. He was torn between speaking the truth and hiding the reality between half-truths. In the end, his kshatriya upbringing that prevented him from prevaricating even in matters such as this, made him share the facts as they were. 'The last time Padmavati and I shared the same bed was just before she left for Vidarbha. That was a month before she met Dramil. After, I reached Vidarbha, for the entire period of a month that we were there, we did not have any physical relations, out of respect for her father's recent demise and also because she seemed very disturbed. The only time she was intimate with anyone in those two months, was with Dramil that night,' Ugrasena paused as he let his words sink in. 'No, the child was definitely born out of her contact with Dramil.'

'What happened after she told you about that event?' Kansa asked, his mind abounding with myriad confused thoughts.

◆

'We left Vidarbha the next day. Padmavati wanted to abort the child in Vidarbha but I felt it should be done in Madhuvan where we could keep the entire story secret. Immediately after reaching Madhuvan, I summoned the royal vaid and took him into confidence. The last several generations of his family had been in service of the royal family, and I knew I could trust him to keep the matter confidential. However, as fate would have it, when the royal vaid examined your mother, he announced that it was not possible to carry out the abortion without risking Padmavati's life. While Padmavati tried to persuade the physician to carry out the abortion irrespective of the danger, he was unrelenting and he told her it could not be done. I finally persuaded Padmavati to wait till the delivery was complete before taking any action. Eight months after we reached Madhuvan, Padmavati gave birth to a male child. The first thing she did when she woke up after the surgery was to ask for the child she had delivered. Her personal attendants quickly carried the baby to her bed and handed over the child to her.'

◆

'So Mother finally had some warm feelings for the baby?' Kansa asked quietly. Ugrasena ignored the question and continued.

◆

'Holding the newborn baby in her hands, she looked into his eyes. And then muttering something that to her attendants sounded like "revenge", she threw the child to the ground with all the force she could muster. The horrified attendants rushed to the child, dreading that he was dead with the force of the fall. But to their surprise and relief, the child lay on the ground unharmed, and alive. Padmavati tried snatching him away from the attendant holding it, but the other attendants, fearing their queen had gone insane, held her back. One of them rushed to me and told me what had happened. I hurried to where Padmavati was and upon reaching there, was greeted by a sight that I would never wish to see again. Padmavati held a sharp knife in her hand, a surgeon's knife, and she had an expression of such repugnant hate writ over her face that even I, who loved her so much, was shocked and scared at the malevolence exuding out of her. The attendant holding the child was cowering in one corner of the room, bravely trying to protect the baby, but fearing for her own life. I moved towards Padmavati, speaking gently to her to try and calm her. At the same time, I motioned to the attendant to leave the room, along with the baby. Padmavati hurled herself towards the retreating figure, but I held her in my arms while the baby was safely led away. Padmavati screamed and cursed with all her might, and then gradually, the rage ebbed as she sagged in my arms. Then she put her palms against my face and whispered, "Ugrasena...that thing...it is evil incarnate! Kill it...promise me it shall never grow up to deceive another woman such as I was deceived by its father!" Saying this, she fainted, lost in the effects of the rage and pain that had consumed her completely.'

◆

Ugrasena ended his story. He sat motionless and it seemed to Kansa as if his father's mind were somewhere else. Perhaps with his mother, who had died a couple of years back, leaving his father alone.

'What happened to that baby? He asked finally. Ugrasena was silent.

'Father! What happened to that baby?' Kansa pressed Ugrasena, wanting to know the fate of the hapless child born out of a lustful father and a vengeful mother.

'Did you kill the child?' Kansa asked, fearing his father's answer. Ugrasena's face was frozen and he sat motionless.

Kansa shook his father's shoulders to get him back to the present. 'Did you too feel like murdering the child?' he asked raising his voice. He couldn't explain why he felt such anger welling up from deep inside him.

'Did you?' he shouted.

Ugrasena shook his bowed head. 'No...no I didn't feel like murdering the child,' he whispered pleadingly.

Kansa knew his father was lying; lying for the first time in his life. But the lie didn't concern him. Right then, he wanted to know something else of far greater significance.

'Where is that child today? What did you do with him?' He looked at Ugrasena, his eyes penetrating into the depths of his father's soul.

Ugrasena looked up to meet his son's gaze, and his eyes were full of unshed tears. 'The child...he stands before me, my son!' he said softly.

Kansa heard the words he couldn't believe. And over the chaos caused by Ugrasena's statement, he heard in his head, the sad and raucous laughter of the Dark Lord, followed by his whisper, *Welcome to the truth, Kalanemi!*

The First Signs of Danger

Narada was possibly the most travelled demi-god. He made frequent visits to all the three worlds, including the dreaded regions within Pataal Lok. It was on one of his recent journeys to the netherworld that he had heard something that had made his feet turn cold with fear. He rushed back to Swarglok to share his findings with Brahma, his father and mentor.

'Are you sure your information is correct?' Brahma asked pointedly. He was aware of Narada's habit of exaggerating things.

'Father, I got this information straight from Devayam. He is Shukra's right-hand man!' Narada said petulantly, a little upset that Brahma was not taking him seriously.

'Hmm...that makes it different,' Brahma said softly. Shukra was the spiritual master of the asuras and a formidable personality. Even the mightiest asuras and the devas (demi-gods) held him in awe. Even though he was a mentor to the asuras, his morals were known to be unimpeachable, and on several occasions he had sided with the devas against the asuras when it came to matters of principle.

'Exactly what did Shukra's man tell you?' asked Brahma, with a great deal more interest than he had displayed a moment ago.

Narada's face showed his relief as Brahma finally gave him some attention. 'He told me that Shukra has been uncharacteristically worried since the past few weeks. And every time he has tried to ask him what is troubling him, Shukra has brushed his questions aside, deftly avoiding any direct answers.'

'What could be bothering Shukra?' Brahma said, more to

himself than to Narada.

'It seems there is a rumour that someone....some very powerful entity...is mobilizing all the asura forces. Every kind of asura...daityas, rakshasas, pisacas, danavas, bhutas, pretas, dasyus, kalakanjas, kalejas, khalins, nivata-kavacas, paulomas...all of them are being assembled under one banner in the form of the largest army ever seen!' Narada's voice trembled in fear as he narrated what he had heard.

'That is impossible!' Brahma roared. There is no asura left who wields the kind of power you are talking about. The only asuras who could have done this—Kalanemi, Ravana, Jalandhar—all of them are long dead.'

Narada nodded his head vigorously to show he did not disagree with the old man on this point. 'You are right, Father, but there is no doubt that an army the size of which has never been seen or heard of before is indeed being mobilized in Pataal Lok. And...' Narada's voice trailed off as he debated whether to share more with his father.

Brahma's eyes narrowed in impatience. 'And? And what?' he barked.

'Uh...nothing,' Narada stuttered, mentally kicking himself for having said more than he had wanted to. 'Speak up!' Brahma said impatiently. 'What is it?'

Narada sighed. He wasn't sure if what he had heard was true, and Brahma would have his scalp if he were wrong. But he couldn't keep the information away from him now that he had said as much.

'I picked up something else when I was roaming in the netherworld. It may not be anything important, but Devayam also mentioned that he had heard some senior members of the asura council saying that very soon they would be introduced to the potent power of Brahman...by being initiated into the powerful codes of Bal and Atibal...' Narada's voice trailed off as he looked at Brahma with concern.

'Father what is it? What's wrong?'

Brahma looked stricken, as though he had seen some terrible vision.

'That...is not possible,' he whispered, his expression resembling the face of a man who has seen or heard something impossible. 'It cannot be. Even Shukra doesn't wield the power of Brahman. It is known only to the Saptarishis....and...'

'And to you, and the Lords Shiva and Vishnu,' Narada automatically completed Brahma's sentence, echoing his father's thoughts. He looked questioningly at the man he feared and respected more than he loved. Brahma seemed to have become aware of Narada's searching gaze and made a herculean effort to calm his frayed nerves.

'Leave me alone, my son,' he said quietly. 'I need to meditate for a bit.'

Narada stared at his father with a feeling of growing unease. Brahma was definitely hiding something, but Narada was hesitant to question him. The last time he had gone against Brahma's wishes, he had been banished from Swarglok and had had to spend several years in Mrityulok as a mortal. He did not want to risk deportation, yet again. He bowed low and turning around, left the room.

Brahma looked at the retreating figure of his son, not really seeing him. His mind was fixed somewhere else—at a point in time more than two hundred years ago.

◆

The six boys were laughing at him, none of them even in their teens yet. And still they dared to mock him. Brahma's face contorted in anger. He looked around to see if their father was around to castigate them for their behaviour, but remembered that he was away for an extended period of meditation in some faraway land. It was then that Bahma noticed the boys' eldest brother standing at a distance. He was a handsome young man, wise beyond his years and Brahma's favourite pupil; the only person in the universe whom Brahma himself had initiated into the secrets of Bal and Atibal, the two codes key to using the potent force of Brahman. He had thought a hundred times before sharing the secrets of Brahman with the young man, but even Shiva and Vishnu had seemed to agree that the youth deserved the knowledge. Now he was the only one apart from the Saptrishis (the seven sages) and the Trinity (Vishnu, Shiva and Brahma), who knew how to control the universal force of Brahman. And yet he stood looking at his brothers making fun of his guru and did nothing! Nothing at all! Brahma's fury was terrible to behold as he glared at the young man. His curse was quick and the youth paled as he heard Brahma mutter the shocking punishment that would banish him forever from the place he had always thought of as home. He did not know what struck him till the Brahmashira hit him with the power of a hundred thunderbolts, hurling him down...and down...to the swirling depths of what was the lowest and seventh level within Pataal Lok. Brahma regretted what he had done in the instant that he pronounced his curse and let loose his most powerful weapon upon his dearest student. But it was too late. A few shreds of burnt flesh lying on the ground were the only evidence that the youth had once existed.

◆

'It can't be you!' Brahma whispered, his face still reflecting the agony of having done what he had done that day.

It is I, mocked a raucous voice, erupting suddenly in the middle of Brahma's head. While the harsh voice was almost indistinguishable from the soft and mellifluous tone of his former student, Brahma recognized it in an instant. It took him another second to realize that the voice was coming from inside his head. Someone was using cosmic telepathy with him. Someone who knew how to wield the universal powers of Brahman, along with all the associated abilities that came from the knowledge of Bal and Atibal, including cosmic telepathy.

'It...it is impossible!' he shuddered. 'You were...' Brahma couldn't complete his sentence.

Dead? hissed the voice in anger. *Yes, you almost killed me. But I survived. Not as I was earlier...before you cursed me and damned my soul for eternity into the netherworld; I changed...I had to change. You saw to that! But I'm stronger today, Gurudev...stronger than I ever was.*

Brahma controlled his tears as he heard the voice of the student he had loved the most once upon a time; more perhaps than his own sons. It filled him with happiness that the youth had survived. He had berated himself every day for the past two hundred years over what he had allowed his temper to do to the boy; believing all these years that he had killed him. It was a miracle that the boy had survived.

'I am happy that you are alive, vats' he said softly, using the traditional term elders employed for people younger to them.

No you are not! the voice was agitated now, reflecting the mental state of the person. *You are trying to manipulate me like you did in the past; and when I am off my guard you will try and destroy me again, finishing what you started two centuries back. But this time, I am not going to be caught so easily, Gurudev. This time I will be ready, and it will be I who shall strike. The only difference is I will tell you before I do.*

Brahma knew his former student was making a point; that Brahma had caught him off guard when he had unleashed the Brahmashira upon him. The former shishya was telling Brahma that when he would strike he would let his guru know that he was striking. The teacher in him was outraged at the disrespect shown to him. But the compassionate part within him knew that he had been unfair to the boy and it made him more tolerant.

'Come back, my child,' Brahma spoke with all the warmth that he could muster. 'You shall be granted all your lost glory...I promise you!'

Lost glory? Lost GLORY? the voice screamed in silent rage.

You imagine that I want any glory! I want justice. For having my soul damned for eternity into the depths of despair. For becoming what you made me...a demon! There was a moment of silence, and then the voice was back again. *No, Gurudev! I shall return you the favour you granted me. I shall convert the entire Mrityulok into a wasteland of demons, and then... I shall come for you...*

The voice in Brahma's head disappeared as suddenly as it had come. Brahma felt exhausted, as if the mere presence of the voice in his head had depleted him of all his vital energy. He willed his mind to dwell on the purifying aspect of the force of Brahman. Among its various powers, the force of Brahman was capable of lending its wielders instant energy and vital force, allowing them to continue for months without food or water or sleep. As soon as he focused on this vital force, Brahma felt his body grow stronger and his mind revitalized with renewed energy source.

He knew what he had to do, and it wasn't going to be easy. He commanded himself to take all thoughts of compassion for his former student out of his mind. The boy was no longer what he had been. Pain and the desire for revenge had made him evil. Evil had to be destroyed, and there was only one person who could be relied upon for it. He would need to seek out that person.

◆

Vasudev exchanged a quick glance with Devki. Both of them were worried about Kansa. The handsome and affable prince of Madhuvan seemed to have crawled into a shell of his own, and looked nothing like his old self. Kansa had shared the conversation he had had with Ugrasena with Devki and Vasudev. Both of them were taken aback, but more than anything else, they were concerned for Kansa's emotional well being. He sat there with them as a broken man.

'Bhaiyya, don't think this way,' Devki implored Kansa, calling him by the term she reserved only for her eldest brother. 'Father loves you...more than he loves any of us.'

Kansa looked through Devki. His eyes were glassy with untold pain. 'All my life I thought Mother hated me for some reason. But I was content knowing that father loved me more than anything else.'

He paused to look at Devki. 'Did you know Father, too, wanted me to be killed when I was a just a child?' His voice broke into a sob as he finally voiced the thought he had been hiding in his mind since the meeting with Ugrasena the previous day.

'That's not true, Bhaiyya. Father would never have wanted that,' Devki said emphatically. She felt Kansa's pain but even then, she couldn't bear to hear anything against the king who was her surrogate father.

Kansa smiled sadly at his sister. Her trust in his father—*I can't even think of him as my father any more*, he thought—was laudable.

'He did, Devki...he did. I looked into his eyes when I asked him if he too wanted me to be killed in my childhood. He lowered his eyes when he answered. And I knew that he was lying.'

Vasudev looked on helplessly as he saw one of his closest friends battling with his inner demons. But he knew it wasn't right for him to interfere. Kansa would have to figure this out for himself. The most important thing for a child was to know that his parents loved him unconditionally. It was the chain that bound a child's mind to its roots. To have found out that he was hated by his own mother and that the man he had looked upon as his father all these years was not his father at all, and had perhaps, even sought to have him killed at some point in his life, could destroy a man's belief in everything, including himself. Vasudev could understand what Kansa was going through. It didn't matter that Ugrasena had got over his initial hatred for the child and loved him as his own. The fact remained that he had once thought of killing him. Kansa had to decide for himself which side of the coin he was willing to give more importance to—that his father wanted him killed once upon a time, or that he had loved Kansa more than any of his other children. Vasudev hoped Kansa would give more importance to the latter; but he had no way of knowing what was going on in his friend's mind.

Devki was persistent, 'Even if I agree that he wanted to harm you as a child, hasn't he done enough after that, Bhaiyya? Hasn't he loved you more than any of us?'

'He couldn't look into my eyes Devki....even after all these years, he couldn't see into my eyes and tell me that he had wanted to kill me back then.' Kansa's voice broke as he continued. 'After all these years, knowing how much Mother hated me, he couldn't tell me the truth even now!'

'He could...' Devki started to say something but was interrupted by Kansa.

'When Mother died, he still didn't tell me the truth. You know he didn't allow me to touch her feet even as she lay on her bed, her praana having left her body forever...I always wondered why he wouldn't allow me to touch her then...I know now... he thought I would defile her body with my touch just as that Gandharva had done so many years ago.'

Devki's eyes filled with tears as she felt Kansa's pain. She hugged him tight, as Kansa's body shivered with a barely controlled emotional outburst.

'I love you, Bhaiyya. Vasudev, too, loves you like a brother,' Devki sobbed, her eyes mirroring Kansa's inner turmoil and pain. She continued to hold Kansa close to her, till she felt his breathing grow calmer and regular.

'My friend, you can't change the past,' Vasudev said gently, coming close to Kansa and Devki, becoming part of their circle of grief. 'But you can shape your future. And I will be with you all through.'

Kansa looked at his friend, next to his sister. He saw unadulterated affection on Vasudev's face. Devki's expression also showed her deep love for him. He drew strength from them and composed himself.

'I have only the two of you now. I love Father, but I can never be the same with him again. Being with him brings back too many memories of the past...recollections that I want to forget forever.'

He put one arm around Devki's shoulders and with his other hand he clasped Vasudev's arm. 'The two of you are the only reason I can carry on after what has happened,' he said quietly.

Suddenly he was reminded of the dream he had had a few days back—Devki's son stabbing him...Devki stopping Kansa from hurting the child...Devki laughing and thanking the child after he had killed Kansa—and his expression grew hard and grim.

'If the two of you forsake me too, I won't be able to handle it...you understand?' he whispered, his voice a confused mix of pleading and threatening.

Vasudev and Devki nodded mutely, both their expressions reflecting their confusion at what Kansa had just said and the manner in which he had said it. But they put it down to his current state of mind.

'I will never abandon you, Bhaiyya,' Devki said, putting her palm against Kansa's face. 'Nor shall I, Kansa,' Vasudev said looking his friend in the eye.

The three people, bound together by destiny, embraced even as the skies thundered with a promise of untold events. Kansa felt a tremour go up his spine as he heard the clap of thunder and the crack of lightning. Only he knew that the thunder would be followed by a raucous laugh. He was not wrong; but this time, it was the sound of an enraged shriek carried on the back of the thunder that raised the hair on the nape of his neck. Kansa trembled involuntarily as he felt the heat of anger in the sound that only he seemed to hear over the past few days.

◆

The Pisaca wriggled his body in excitement. The massive tentacles that served as his head shook of their own accord and were fearful to look at. The bonara and the kalakanja stood to one side, silently awaiting the latest instructions that the Dark Lord had sent through the pisaca. Both were miffed that the Dark Lord had chosen the pisaca to lead the attack on the mortal woman Devki. They were accomplished assassins with several celebrated kills to their credit. The pisaca had been newly inducted into the clan of the Zataka Upanshughataks (the acclaimed hundred assassins) of Pataal Lok. The bonara and kalakanja were taken aback that despite being amongst the most dreaded upanshughataks (assassins), they had been commanded to follow this new entrant to the clan. But they knew better than to go against the wishes of the Dark Lord.

'The Lord commands that Devki should die tomorrow,' hissed the pisaca. His voice betrayed the thrill he felt at the prospect of a kill. The tiny orifices that served as his mouth in each of the eight tentacles, dripped with putrid-smelling saliva.

'He wishes to see her decapitated head as evidence of her death, by end of the day, tomorrow,' he continued, filled with the importance of the task given to him by the most feared being in Pataal Lok.

The kalakanja shifted his feet uneasily. His intuition told him that this kill was of particular importance to their master. He found it difficult to understand why then, the relatively unknown pisaca was chosen to lead the mission. The other thing that bothered him was the urgency. Any upanshughatak worth his name knew that you had to stalk your prey and wait patiently for the right time to strike. Yet the pisaca said that they had been commanded to do the deed by the end of the next day. What's the urgency? he wondered.

The bonara felt the same way. But he was made differently. He could hide his feelings far better than any of the other upanshughataks and focus on what had to be done. This was one of the reasons he had survived more contract killings than any of the other members of the Zataka Upanshughatak tribe. He spoke softly to the pisaca. 'What is the plan?' he asked. The pisaca turned one of his tentacles towards the bonara, while with another one, kept the kalakanja in his sight. The other six tentacles looked around, scouring the area for any possible eavesdropper.

'I have observed Devki's movements over the past few days,' he said. 'She never steps out of the palace without her companions, and there are always a few guards close at hand.'

The kalakanja sneered as he interrupted the pisaca. 'Afraid, are we?'

One of the tentacles of the pisaca turned menacingly towards the kalakanja, but the other seven tentacles restrained the maverick limb. 'Not afraid!' he hissed. 'Just smart!'

'What's so smart about this? Can't we kill a couple of dozen guards and a few female attendants?' The kalakanja spat out the words.

'Of course we can,' the pisaca replied, a little more patiently now, as if he was explaining the basics of an assassination to a five-year-old. 'But when the three of us kill Devki in front of so many witnesses, there are bound to a be a couple of them who may escape in the middle of the bloodbath. Do you think the Dark Lord would be pleased to show his hand so soon?'

The mention of the Dark Lord subdued the kalakanja to some extent. Seeing him vacillate, the pisaca pressed his point. 'If anyone sees us and escapes, Ugrasena and everyone else in the kingdom will know that Pataal Lok has sent assassins. This is bound to come to the notice of Shukra. Once he knows of the Zataka Upanshughatak's involvement, how much time do you think he will take to connect the Dark Lord to us? Whatever the Dark Lord is planning, he was clear on one thing—Shukra should have no whiff of his involvement till the Dark Lord himself reveals it.'

The bonara looked at the pisaca with grudging respect. *The Dark Lord had chosen the right person to lead them in the plot to assassinate Devki.* he thought. 'Which is why we need to wait for Devki to be alone to kill her? Is that right?' he said aloud.

The pisaca nodded, glad that at least the bonara was in sync with him.

'But if Devki never comes out alone, how are we going to kill her without anyone else seeing us do it?'

The pisaca's body seemed to wriggle again; it seemed that he was laughing but there was no way to be certain, since the eight tentacles representing his face were almost impossible to read. 'Tomorrow she will be going to the Shiva temple to pray for her brother's peace of mind. The temple is on the top of a hill, a quarter of a yojana (one yojana being equal to eight miles) away from the main palace compound. If she is accompanied by any attendants, they will wait for her at the base of the hill since only the royal family goes to this particular temple. The soldiers, too, will wait there as the hill is supposed to be a holy zone. No mortal would dare to carry weapons on that hill, as a mark of respect for Lord Shiva.'

The bonara grinned malevolently as the full import of the pisaca's words struck him. 'So the soldiers would not feel it necessary to accompany the princess to the top of the hill, since they would believe it is a safe spot...it's a perfect time for the kill!' he exclaimed.

The pisaca nodded at the bonara, and then turned towards the kalakanja to see if he was in agreement with the plan. Under the combined gaze of his fellow assassins, the kalakanja nodded his consent reluctantly. He still wasn't happy being told what to do by the Pisaca but as a professional, he could see that the plan was perfect.

'Good!' the pisaca hissed in a pleased tone. 'We meet tomorrow at the top of the hill. May the dark force be with us,' he said, raising his voice and waving his extreme right tentacle in the air in salute to the Dark Lord. The bonara and the kalakanja too, raised their right arms in the air as their shouts filled the air, 'May the dark force be with us!'

A Prayer for Kansa

Brahma bowed to the magnetic individual sitting peacefully in front of him. The formidable personality reclined on the jagged rocks as comfortably as if he were sitting on the softest diwan in the universe. He looked like he had just come from a funeral— layers of freshly created ash were smeared in generous quantities over his body. The ash made his form appear grey; but on closer examination, one could see the light of Brahman emanating from all parts of the charismatic Being's sinewy body.

There was no sign of life or vegetation for hundreds of yojanas around this area. It seemed even the wind had trouble reaching this spot; yet there was a sense of peace and calm that prevailed here, which was difficult to discover even in the most favoured haunts in Swarglok. There were only two people in the entire universe that Brahma was in awe of, even a little scared of at times. He was standing in front of one of them right now. The last time he had angered the ash-clad person, Brahma had had to undergo untold mortification. But eventually, he had realized that this compelling person had helped him more with his castigation than he could ever have done through kind words. Today, Brahma hoped to persuade him for his help yet again.

'Aum-Num-Ha-Shi-Vai,' Brahma uttered the five-syllable mantra with a touch of reverence. It meant 'I bow to you, O Shiva', and he said this with a deep belief that Shiva epitomized the inner consciousness that dwelled in every living being.

Shiva smiled at the man standing in front of him, and wondered for the thousandth time how the youngest of the three supreme gods managed to look the oldest amongst them. Vishnu, and He, despite being older to Brahma by a few million years, still retained their youthful countenance, while Brahma had developed the façade of a much older persona almost within a few years of his birth. *It's probably because he is unable to control his senses,* Shiva mused to himself.

'I am yet to learn much, My Lord,' Brahma said with a humility uncommon to him, reading Shiva's mind through cosmic telepathy.

'Not much to learn Brahma...just a little more to apply,' Shiva corrected him gently. 'You have mastered the force of Brahman, and that gives you powers that a handful of people have in the universe. It also gives you infinite life.'

'Yes, My Lord' Brahma said meekly, not sure where this was leading.

Shiva continued, 'People die because their energy and vital force depletes as they age. Brahman represents the universal force and energy. If you have it inside you, you will never be short of the vital force that gives you life. You will live forever. That is how Vishnu and I have existed since the beginning of time...by carefully harnessing the force of Brahman inside us, where it now flows inside our bodies as if it were part of us. You yourself have done the same, haven't you?'

'Err...yes...but...' Brahma was totally confused now. *Why was Shiva giving him a lecture on Brahman energy,* he wondered.

Shiva interrupted him. 'Used properly, the force of Brahman keeps revitalizing your dead cells on an ongoing basis, which is why one never grows old. Have you wondered then, why you have steadily continued to age with time, despite having the knowledge of Brahman?'

Brahma was speechless. It was true that he had always wondered why it was that he alone had continued to grow older in appearance while Shiva and Vishnu still retained their youthful charm. He had put it down to the fact that they probably had more knowledge of Brahman than he had. After all, they were the ones who had a million years ago initiated him into the use of Bal and Atibal, the two defining mantras necessary to wield the vital force of Brahman. While he had grown older over time, he had been content that he still retained his energy levels and strength, while the devas, who only had recourse to amrit (life-enhancing nectar) had a life span of just a few thousand years. It was wrongly believed by some that the amrit could give you infinite life. It just extended your life by a few thousand years; that too since Vishnu had energized the potion with some of the force of Brahman before the devas drank it, ages ago. However, the presence of the Brahman force in the potion was not sufficient to give infinite life. This is why, once in a while, some deva or the other would grow old and finally die. But none of this still explained why Brahma was getting older with the years while the passage of time didn't affect Shiva and Vishnu in the least.

Shiva looked closely at Brahma as the latter did not answer his question. 'You understand the knowledge of Brahman...but your senses are not attuned to it in perfect harmony.'

Shiva held up his hand as Brahma attempted to interrupt him.

'Don't get me wrong, Brahma. You know as much about the theoretical aspects of Brahman as Vishnu and I do. But you have not prepared yourself to assimilate all that knowledge in the way it should be done. And that is why while you have benefitted from it, those benefits are nowhere as large as they could have been.'

'I don't understand, My Lord. What have I done wrong?' Brahma was completely nonplussed now. Shiva changed his tactic. 'Tell me what would happen if you tried to fill an empty bucket with water?'

Brahma arched his eyebrows. Much as he respected Shiva, he was beginning to feel that Shiva had been spending too much time alone in the sun. It was beginning to affect his mind, he thought.

Shiva laughed all of a sudden, and Brahma realized rather belatedly that Shiva had read his thoughts through cosmic telepathy. *Damn! Why do I always forget to shield my thoughts when I am with him?* Brahma mentally berated himself.

'No I haven't lost it, if that's what you are thinking,' Shiva smiled. 'But answer my question—what would happen if you tried to fill an empty bucket with water?'

Brahma sighed in resignation. 'The bucket would fill in sometime My Lord.'

'Absolutely!' Shiva said animatedly. 'Now if you were to poke multiple holes in the bucket, what would happen?'

Brahma shifted his feet uneasily, beginning to get a faint idea of where Shiva was going with this. 'The bucket would take a lot of time to fill...water would continuously need to be poured into the bucket, and yet, if the holes are too large, the bucket may never get filled completely. It would be a huge waste of water, My Lord.'

'Exactly! So what would you need to do to stop the water from being wasted?' He looked at Brahma with a twinkle in his eyes.

'It would make sense to put a stopper to all the holes immediately...,' Brahma stopped mid-sentence as he realized what Shiva was trying to tell him.

Shiva smiled benignly at the man that Vishnu and he had tutored close to a thousand millennia ago.

'So why aren't you plugging the holes in your system, my friend?'

Brahma looked down at his feet, as embarrassed now as he used to be as a child when Shiva or Vishnu would chide him for something he hadn't done well. Shiva got up and patted him on his shoulder.

'Your system is like that bucket we spoke of just now. And the force of Brahman flowing into your system is the water we mentioned. Ideally, your system should be full of the rejuvenating force of Brahman at all times, and you shouldn't age or lose your vitality with time. But your lack of control over your senses from time to time creates holes in your system...such large holes that even the vital force of Brahman is never enough to fill you entirely with vitality. And as a result, even though the presence of Brahman in you is enough to make you live infinitely, you age faster than Vishnu or I, because it is still not sufficient to keep your youth fully charged.'

Brahma gaped at Shiva, realizing his folly all these years. But he knew there had to be more.

'What is this lack of control that I suffer from?'

'Your temper...your ego...the yearning for things...for recognition...the list is endless,' Shiva paused before continuing. 'These things reduce the potency of Brahman in your system. They leave you weak and continuously needing to recharge your energies. You are never fully charged as a result.'

Brahma remembered how he had felt after hearing the voice in his head, the reason why he had come to Shiva in the first place. And he remembered how depleted he had felt of energy after that conversation with his former student. He saw Shiva observing him closely and knew that Shiva had telepathically read all the thoughts in his mind, including the reason that he had come to him for help. He saw Shiva's face tighten with emotion at what he had just read in his mind.

'You see, don't you, what your temper did to that boy two hundred years ago?' Shiva's voice was harder now. Gone was the soft tone he had been using with Brahma till now. The God had reverted to the role of a teacher, and Brahma was once again the diffident protégé.

'And it was your ego that made you curse the boy back then,' Shiva thundered, close to losing his legendary temper.

'My Lord...please....' Brahma's voice was a pleading whisper as he shuddered at the memory of what had taken place two centuries back. He had never been able to completely relive that event even in his mind. It was too painful. And to be reminded of it in the presence of Shiva was doubly agonizing.

Shiva took a deep breath to calm his inner self. He knew now why Brahma had come to him, and it repulsed him to know that he may need to be a part of this someday, even if in a passive role. *The boy had been good, almost too good. Damn it Brahma, why did you have to get us all into this mess!* he thought.

Brahma sighed in relief as he saw Shiva beginning to calm down somewhat. He knew he had not been fair to the boy by cursing him in the past. But that did not give the youth the right to put the entire universe at risk.

'My L-lord,' he stammered. 'That boy...he has become evil incarnate. He has to be destroyed.'

'Stop calling him "boy", dammit!' Shiva roared. 'He has a name, or at least had one before you made him a victim of your wanton temper.'

Brahma was taken aback with the force of Shiva's outburst. He had only once in his life seen Shiva lose his temper completely with him, and he didn't want that to happen again.

'B-But, My Lord...'

'Say it! Speak his name!' Shiva was unrelenting.

Brahma took a deep breath. He hadn't been able to bring himself to speak the name of his former student even in his thoughts, leave alone say it out aloud, all these years.

'A-Amartya,' he said diffidently.

'The full name!' Shiva goaded him.

'Amartya....Amartya Kalyanesu,' Brahma breathed out the name in anguish, desperately trying to control the emotions that were threatening to overcome him.

'Do you know the meaning of that name, Brahma?'

'Immortal goodness...' Brahma whispered, even as the cries of a half-burnt youth and the smell of scorched flesh from two centuries ago penetrated his memory.

◆

Devki was late for the prayers. She had to be at the Shiva temple by the first light of dawn. It was believed by her family that the first prayers of the day offered before the sun came up, were the most potent. She wanted to make sure that she was there in time to seek blessings for Kansa. Her mind had been deeply troubled after the last meeting with her brother. She wanted to do everything in her power to get him back to the way he had been before Ugrasena shared the secret of his birth with him. Ugrasena too had been closeted in his personal chambers ever since the fateful conversation with his son. She couldn't bear to see two of the most important men in her life, losing their zest for life with the passage of each day.

'Mandki, we are late!' she exclaimed, goading her childhood friend and companion to move fast. Mandki glared at her. She had been ready and waiting for Devki for the past half-an-hour. Devki gave her a sheepish grin, and put her left arm around her friend in an attempt to appease her. In her right hand she carried the puja thali, precariously balanced on the balls of her fingers.

'The horses are ready, My Lady,' Airawat nodded respectfully at Devki. Even though Airawat had addressed Devki, she noticed that his eyes were subtly observing her friend. Mandki seemed to be aware of the attention she was getting from the chief of Madhuvan's cavalry division. She suppressed a smile but consciously avoided looking in Airawat's direction.

'Thanks, Airawat. Are you going to be accompanying us to the Shiva temple too?' Devki smiled at the handsome man holding the reins to her horse.

'Yes, My Lady. I will be coming along,' he said in a soft and slightly self-conscious tone.

'Come on, Airawat. You don't need to call me "My Lady" and all that. You have known me since I was a child and you used to teach me how to ride a horse. You used to call me "little Devki" in those days.'

Airawat smiled at the memory of days gone by. He had been an ordinary cavalry man employed in King Devak's army. But more importantly, he had also been a personal bodyguard of the king and his favourite at that. When Devak's wife had died, he had been the one to ride all the way to Madhuvan to give Ugrasena the message from Devki's father. Later, he had also accompanied Devak to the forest where the king gave up his body to depart the mortal world. When he returned to Haripur, Devki and Mandki had already left with Ugrasena and his son Kansa, but there was a message awaiting him from Ugrasena at the palace. Ugrasena, who had been impressed with Airawat's loyalty to Devak, had invited him to Madhuvan to be a part of his retinue of personal bodyguards. As the king of the combined nations of Madhuvan and Haripur, Ugrasena wanted people he could trust, by his side. Airawat had been at the king's side for the past fourteen years. He had been a young man back then. Now he was almost thirty-three years old. While he had always respected Devki as a princess, he had developed a fascination for her companion, Mandki. Initially, he hadn't given her much notice as she was still a child. As the years progressed, however, he began to fall in love with her character and the nobility with which she conducted herself in everything, including rejecting the best suitors for her hand, because she did not want to leave Devki alone. It never occurred to him that Mandki was not just a woman with a flawless character. She was also possibly the most beautiful woman in Madhuvan, second perhaps only to Devki. Having said that, the brave soldier that he was, he had never been able to draw up the courage to declare his love to Mandki. He wasn't even sure if she had any idea about his feelings for her.

'Airawat...Airawat!' the sound of his name being called brought him out of his reverie. Devki was smiling at him, her eyes twinkling with mirth. Both Mandki and she were already saddled and waiting for him.

'I'm sorry, My Lady. I...I...' he stammered in confusion as he too, hastily saddled up.

'It's okay, Airawat. All of us have the right to get lost in our thoughts sometimes,' Devki grinned at him. Her keen insight told her Airawat was besotted with her childhood friend. *I wonder if Mandki knows how he feels*, she mused with a smile.

Devki and Mandki set off, accompanied by Airawat. A squad of twenty soldiers followed them at a respectful distance. Two pairs of watchful eyes observed their departure with satisfaction. They knew that the pisaca awaited them at the top of the hill. The branches and leaves on the trees rustled in fury as the two monsters raced from tree to tree in the direction of the Shiva temple.

◆

'Where is Devki?' Kansa asked as he poured himself some sherbet. He had come to bid farewell to Devki before leaving for Magadha. He intended to spend some time there with his brother-in-law, Jarasandha. The depression of the past few days had been weighing heavy on his heart and he felt it would help to get away from Madhuvan for a few days. His wives, Asti and Prapti, were also keen to meet their brother. They planned to be back in time for Devki's wedding. Kansa wanted to avoid meeting Ugrasena before he left, but he couldn't go away without saying goodbye to Devki.

'Where is she?' he asked one of the attendants hovering around him. 'She has gone to the Shiva temple, prince.'

'So early?' Kansa was surprised. He knew Devki loved her sleep and it was impossible to rouse her in the wee hours of the morning.

The attendant endeavoured to hide her smile. Everyone was aware of the princess' dislike for rising early. 'Princess Devki wanted to offer the first prayers of the day to Lord Shiva. She seemed somewhat rushed; in fact, she even forgot the fresh ash for the puja.'

Kansa rolled his eyes. *Mornings really aren't your time of the day, are they sister?* he thought to himself, both amused at Devki's penchant for being lost in the early part of the day; and full of affection, knowing that Devki would have got up early to offer prayers for him. He knew, however, that she wouldn't be able to do the puja without the fresh ash. It was a practice at this particular temple to put freshly created ash on the Jyotirlinga. The fresh ash served as a symbolic reminder that the only constant in life was death. Everything else could change any moment. 'Just like my life,' he thought to himself, the shadow of the past few days falling over his face.

'Who accompanied her to the temple?' he asked the attendant, making an attempt to shake off the depressing thoughts that plagued his mind.

'Mandki and Commander Airawat went with her, prince. They left half-an-hour back.'

'Hmm,' Kansa reflected for a brief moment. 'I shall carry the fresh ash for her myself.' *It will also give me a chance to meet her before I leave for Magadha*, he thought.

Carefully putting the urn of ash in the saddlebag, he mounted his mammoth steed and was off in a flash. He smiled slightly as he imagined Devki's expression when she would realize she had forgotten the ash behind.

◆

'O Shiva! I forgot to carry the ash!' Devki exclaimed morosely. Mandki and she had walked up, leaving their mounts at the base of the hill, where Airawat and the soldiers were waiting for them to return after the puja.

'Now what?' Mandki asked, her face mirroring her friend's distress. She knew how badly Devki had wanted to finish the puja before the break of dawn.

'I don't know' Devki sighed. 'Do you think someone could ride fast enough to the palace and get the ash in time? I won't need it till the end of the puja in any case,' she finished hopefully.

'Hmm, that's not a bad idea. Should I ask Airawat to ride back? He is the fastest rider in the Kingdom,' Mandki said with a shy smile.

'Yeah, why not? I'm sure he would ride for you till the end of the world' Devki joked.

Mandki, the woman who always seemed to have a hold on her emotions, actually blushed at the joke. *Ah! So she is aware of Airawat's feelings for her, and she isn't averse to liking him either it seems*, Devki mused with the hint of a smile on her face.

'Go now!' she playfully pushed Mandki. 'I'm starting the puja. You tell Airawat to come back with the ash, and then join me inside the temple compound.'

◆

The pisaca saw Mandki hurry down the hill. He couldn't believe his luck. He had thought they would have to kill both the women. Now, it was just Devki. They could finish her off and leave with her severed head before the other woman returned. He looked in the direction of the peepul tree on the far side of the hill. His uncanny powers of sight allowed him to see what no human eye would have been able to make out—the form of the bonara hiding amidst the upper branches of the tree, his sharp talons quivering with the excitement of a kill. The kalakanja was already inside the temple and he had been instructed to execute Devki quickly and quietly. She was to be given no chance of escaping the precincts of the massively built temple. The inner structure was built in such a way that once inside, the walls set at particular angles acted as natural barriers to any sound escaping outside. No sound could go out; and no sound could come in. *I hope the kalakanja doesn't botch up this job*, he thought. It was five minutes since Devki had stepped inside the temple compound. *He should have finished the job by now*, he thought with satisfaction.

◆

Devki bent down reverentially in front of the enormous Jyotirlinga. Inhabitants of the land of Bharat believed that there were twelve Jyotirlingas spread in different corners of the great realm. But citizens of Madhuvan knew that there was a thirteenth one; it was in Madhuvan itself. All Jyotirlingas looked like a normal Shivling, but were different; only a person who had attained a high level of spirituality could actually see the Jyotirlinga in its true form—as a pillar of flame arising out of the earth. The Jyotirlingas represented the infiniteness of existence—the fact that there was no end and no beginning to existence. The thirteen Jyotirlingas were believed to have been personally charged by Lord Shiva with his blessings and his formidable aura. The two Jyotirlingas closest in proximity to the one in Madhuvan were in the holy city of Kashi (Kashi Vishwanath Jyotirlinga) and in the snow-clad Himalayan town of Kedarnath (Kedarnath Jyotirlinga). They were about fifty-six yojanas and forty-four yojanas apart respectively from the one in Madhuvan. The Madhuvan Jyotirlinga was different from the other twelve, in terms of its sheer size. Standing at a height of one gavuta, it was almost four gavutas in circumference and was made of gleaming black stone. The sign of Aum was handpainted in red at the top of the Jyotirlinga, presumably by the pundit of the temple. A large trishul measuring five feet in length, with three sharp protrusions, lay behind the Jyotirlinga.

Devki wasn't interested in the history of the Jyotirlingas. All she knew was that she found a peculiar sense of peace whenever she was in the presence of the magnificent structure. And she had never come away unsatisfied after offering prayers at this temple. *Shiva, give my brother peace of mind*, she muttered to herself as she set about starting the puja.

She put the puja thali on the brass tray kept in front of the Jyotirlinga, and began chanting the mantras she had been taught while she was a child.

सौराष्ट्रे सोमनसथं च श्रीशैले मल्लिकार्जुनम् ।
उज्जयिन्यां महाकालमोङ्कारममलेश्वरम् ।।
परल्यां वैद्यनाथं च डाकिन्यां भीमशङ्करम् ।

सेतुबन्धे तु रामेशं नागेशं दारूकावने।।
वाराणस्यां तु विश्वेशं त्र्यम्बकं गौतमीतटे।
हिमालये तु केदारं घुश्मेशं च शिवालये।।
एतानि ज्योतिर्लिङ्गानि सायं प्रातः पठेन्नरः।
सप्तजन्मकृतं पापं स्मरणेन विनश्यति।।
ऐतेशां दर्शनादेव पातकं नैव तिष्ठति।
कर्मक्षयो भवेत्तस्य यस्य तुष्टो महेश्वराः।।
द्वादश ज्योतिर्लिंग स्तोत्रम्

As she approached the end of the mantra, she lit a set of thirteen dhupa battis (incense sticks) at the base of the gigantic Jyotirlinga. It symbolized that while she was praying at the Madhuvan Jyotirlinga, she was seeking the blessings from each of the thirteen Jyotirlingas spread across the great land of Bharat.

Having lighted the dhupa battis, Devki shut her eyes in prayer. Once in a state of deep meditation, she gradually became more aware of her surroundings, even with her eyes closed. She could hear the almost muted sputter of the burning dhupa battis. She was conscious of the night dew collected on the temple roof, falling as drops of water on the ground somewhere at the entrance of the temple door. The gentle breeze rustling through the inner corners of the temple sounded much louder as it caressed her face. Then her enhanced consciousness became aware of a malodourous smell, overpowering even the aromatic dhupa battis. *The smell...the awful smell...Oh God, what is that stench?* She thought to herself as she reluctantly opened her eyes.

Her attention focused on the Jyotirlinga in front of her. She thought she saw something reflected there, in the gleaming surface of the black stone. Her keen observation told her something was wrong, terribly wrong, even before she heard the maniacal cry of the creature behind her. Without thinking, she swerved and threw herself towards her left in one rapid motion. In the brief instant that she took to regain her balance and stand up, she saw the brass tray holding her puja thali sliced into half, by a huge sword held in the hands of a creature that didn't seem to belong to her world. *If I hadn't moved away, it would have been my head instead of that tray*, she thought, desperately afraid. And then, as the wind blew from the other side of the room, she caught the stink of the creature standing in front of her. She involuntarily turned up her nose in disgust. It was the stench of death; a putrid smell of defecation mixed with the disgusting odour of something rotten.

◆

The Pisaca smelt the wind through the fine orifices in his tentacles. It seemed the princess's companion was returning. He looked in the direction of the bonara, who too, appeared to have caught the smell of a human body. The pisaca made a hooting sound, too low for the human ear to catch, but to the bonara, it was as loud as if the pisaca had said something right in his ears. In a swift move, the bonara was off the tree and moved stealthily in the direction of the human smell. He hid behind a tree as he heard approaching footsteps. It was an old pundit, the keeper of the temple. The pundit was moving in the direction of the temple. The bonara looked towards the pisaca for instructions, who grimaced and made a slicing action with one of his tentacles. The bonara understood; he had to take out the pundit before he entered the temple, but it would have to be done swiftly so there was no chance of a scream or cry escaping the pundit's mouth that could alert the soldiers at the base of the hill. He waited for the old man to approach the tree, and just as he did, the bonara came up behind him. Sensing an alien presence, the Pundit turned around, but he was too late. The only sound that escaped his lips was a final prayer to his God, 'Aum-Num-Ha-Shi-Vai', as the razor-sharp talon of the bonara sliced through his neck like a knife cutting through butter.

◆

'Who are you?' Devki glared at the monster standing in front of her.

The kalakanja licked his greyish-black tongue, his sunken eyes shining brighter at this moment than they had in a long time.

'I asked...who are you?' Devki repeated her question, examining the monster closely. His emaciated body was all bone; whatever little skin was there, resembled dried up leaves. The veins were stretched tight all over the body. He stood towering at a height of three gavutas (eighteen feet). There was no sign of any clothing barring some tattered rags that were tied around his waist.

'I...am...your...death,' the kalakanja growled; the smell of fetid liquid gurgling in his throat almost gagged Devki.

A shiver ran down her spine. But she knew that if she gave in to the chilling fear that gripped her at the sight of this monster, she would surely die. She needed to buy time. Maybe some of the soldiers would come up the hill, looking for her if she didn't return soon. And Mandki would also be coming up anytime now... *Oh God! Mandki!* She thought as she realized that her dearest friend would be here at any moment, and would encounter the same danger. She had to warn Mandki before she entered the temple compound. And she had to save herself from this creature. Devki knew the only way her cries would be heard by the soldiers downhill was if she were able to get out of the temple. *I have to find a way of getting out of here*, she resolved.

The kalakanja saw the determined expression on her face and felt a shiver of excitement run through his decaying body. He hadn't had a woman in a long time, and she looked so desirable. Maybe, he could have some fun with her before he decapitated her. His eyes were drawn to the ochre-coloured blouse covering her breasts, and he felt his excitement grow.

Devki noticed the creature's lewd interest in her and she felt a fresh tremour of fear. She knew whatever the monster had planned for her would not happen now, not before the vile creature had satisfied his lust. She forced herself to go beyond her fear and focus on the fighting tactics Kansa had taught her, when she had become old enough to take up weapons. She looked around for something with which to defend herself but she could see nothing except the trishul lying behind the Jyotirlinga. That was too heavy for her to lift. She hadn't carried any weapon on her body either. Meanwhile, the kalakanja was circling her, taking his time, trying to trap her against the wall. But Devki knew what he did not; there was a small opening in the roof, on one side of the temple, about three gavutas from where she was standing right now. The wall adjoining the roof at that point had small footholds built into it. If she could somehow reach there, she could haul herself up the wall and climb through the enclosure to get outside. The towering kalakanja would not be able to crawl out through the narrow opening.

She started moving in the direction of the wall. At the same time, she deliberately took a deep breath so that her breasts would get pressed harder against her blouse. The ploy worked. Blinded by his lust, the kalakanja failed to notice her slow but gradual progress towards the secret exit. Less than a minute had passed since the kalakanja had attacked her, but it seemed like hours. By now, he was dangerously close. Devki realized with a feeling of horror that the creature may be on top of her before she had a chance to reach the wall with the footholds to the roof. She decided to risk taking a subtle look in the direction of the escape zone. It was now just a little more than one gavuta away. At the same time, the kalakanja too saw the footholds in the wall. In a flash he knew what she was planning. He snarled in fury. Abandoning all pretence, Devki turned and ran towards the wall. The kalakanja threw down his sword and darted after her, his hands outstretched. Devki felt the tip of his nails cut through her ankle just as she climbed out of the small enclosure in the roof. And then she ran with all the power she could muster.

She knew it wouldn't take the kalakanja much time to realize that he couldn't take the same route as she had. With his speed, he would still be out of the temple within the next few seconds. She jumped off the roof and hit the ground running, just as the temple door crashed open and the kalakanja hurled himself at her, snarling in fury.

◆

'My Lord!' Airawat bowed, surprised at seeing Kansa.

'How are you, Airawat?' Kansa smiled at the cavalry commander.

'I'm good, My Lord,' Airawat replied, his respect for Kansa evident in his voice. 'I was just going back to the palace. Princess Devki apparently needed something from there,' he said, not wanting to embarrass the princess by telling Kansa she had forgotten to carry the ash for her prayers.

Kansa looked at Airawat, and then at Mandki standing next to him. He laughed. 'Would she by any chance be looking for this?' he asked innocently, taking the urn filled with ash out of his saddlebag.

Mandki grinned sheepishly. Airawat stood looking discomfited. Kansa gave him a friendly slap on his back. 'It's okay Airawat... women do forget these little things from time to time.'

Airawat looked relieved, and returned a brief smile. Kansa looked at Mandki and asked her gently, 'Would you mind if I were to give this personally to Devki?'

'Not at all prince. I'm sure Devki will be delighted that you are here. Perhaps you could sit for the puja too...' she half-suggested, not sure whether Kansa would like her telling him what to do.

Kansa, however, did not seem to take offence. He smiled wanly, 'I don't think I will sit for the puja today Mandki, but I would definitely like to meet Devki and give her this,' he said pointing to the urn of ash. Mandki nodded.

'Let's go then!' he urged and started walking up the hill, too impatient to meet Devki to wait for Mandki. Mandki rushed behind him, trying in vain to keep pace with his large strides.

'My Lord!' Kansa turned around as he heard Airawat's startled exclamation. He looked inquiringly at the cavalry commander.

'My Lord...your sword,' Airawat pointed at the deadly weapon hanging at Kansa's waist.

Kansa chuckled. 'Ah yes...I forgot weapons aren't allowed on the holy hill. Hold this for me till I return, then,' he said handing over the sword, and continuing to walk up the hill.

Airawat struggled to hold the sword in his hand. *This thing must weigh three matras (forty-five kilograms) at least*, he mused, and wondered how Kansa wielded such a heavy blade.

Kansa and Mandki had almost reached the top of the hill when they heard the terror-struck scream. It was a hair-raising shriek that rooted Mandki to the spot. Kansa too felt his heart skip a beat.

'That's Devki's voice,' he choked. The warrior in him knew there was danger out there. He turned around and looked at Mandki. She was still standing frozen, completely dazed. Kansa shook her savagely, till she recovered from her shock.

'Listen to me,' he commanded. 'Run down and get Airawat and the soldiers. I'm going up now!'

Without waiting for her response, he dashed up the hill and felt his blood turn cold at the sight of what greeted him.

◆

The pisaca was startled when he saw Devki jumping off the roof. Before he had time to react, he saw the kalakanja barge through the temple door and hurl himself at her. *Damn you! What the hell were you doing inside? Why is she still alive?* A flurry of confused thoughts coursed through his mind as he saw the Kalakanja attack Devki.

Devki saw the towering creature heaving himself at her. In her terrorized state, she let out a bloodcurdling scream. And then, the years of training took over. She ducked just as the kalakanja jumped her. The momentum of the jump carried him over Devki's bent figure and he stumbled over, across the ground, far from her. This gave Devki the opportunity to start running downhill.

Devki's scream made it clear to the pisaca that the soldiers would arrive within a few minutes. *I will have to finish the job myself*, he thought viciously. In one gigantic leap from the tree he was hiding in, he crossed half the distance between Devki and himself within a flash. And that is when he saw the behemoth figure of Kansa emerge over the hill.

Kansa stopped in his tracks as he saw the half-serpent, half-octopus body of the pisaca, just a few feet away from his sister. Brave warrior that he was, this was the first time he was face to face with a pisaca; a creature he had just read about in books till now, as inhabitants of Pataal Lok were prohibited from trespassing in the world of Mrityulok. The hypnotic movement of the pisaca's tentacles seemed to lock up Kansa's muscles, against their own will. Then his gaze fell on the terrorized face of Devki and he saw the marks on her face where the kalakanja had inadvertently scratched her while jumping over her. The rage at his sister's state loosened the pisaca's hypnotic hold on him and he growled in fury. The pisaca did not want to get into a fight with Kansa; the Dark Lord's instructions had been explicit—kill Devki and get out of there with proof of her death. He calculated the distance between him and Devki, and decided he could reach her and yank her head off her body before Kansa would get to her. Kansa followed the pisaca's eye movements and realized what the monster was planning. In the very instant that the pisaca leaped towards Devki, his tentacles flexing to decapitate her, Kansa threw the heavy brass urn full of ash at the pisaca. The metallic urn found its mark and hit the pisaca in the centre of his head from where all the eight tentacles sprouted. The pisaca staggered in mid-air and landed on the ground, dazed. The ash had clouded his vision and he faltered. Seizing the opportunity, Kansa caught hold of him by his serpentine tail and dashed his body to the ground with one mighty heave. The pisaca lay motionless, his tail twitching involuntarily in pain and wrath.

Kansa held Devki in a tight embrace, half-sobbing in frustrated rage at seeing her in this condition. He knew, though, that the fight was far from over. The kalakanja was lumbering in their direction, his face contorted in anger. Kansa instinctively shielded Devki behind his body and got ready to battle the towering monster. He knew the kalakanja had the advantage of height and speed, but Kansa gauged from the monster's gait that he may not be able to turn around that fast. He balanced his body weight on the balls of his toes in the classical pose of a pugilist. He waited as the kalakanja approached him and allowed him the first punch. Kansa feinted to his left and at the last moment, moved his right hand in a deadly jab just under the kalakanja's abdomen. The blow would have permanently disabled a large mortal. But the kalakanja wasn't a mortal. The jab only served to halt him for a moment, and before Kansa could land a second punch, the kalakanja had lifted him up in the air with the ease of a full-grown man picking up a toy. However, this was what Kansa had been waiting for. He would never have reached the level of the monster's height on his own. As the kalakanja glared at him with a malevolent smile, Kansa dug both his thumbs, deep into the sockets of the monster's eyes. The kalakanja screamed in pain and instinctively let go off Kansa, clutching at his eyes in agony. Kansa balanced himself as he landed on his feet and in a sweeping motion, kicked the kalakanja behind his right ankle. The gigantic creature tripped and fell to the ground with a loud thud that reverberated throughout the hill.

Kansa was about to sit astride the kalakanja, with the intention of breaking his neck in the typical stratagem employed by wrestlers, when he saw an enormously built midget rushing towards him at what appeared to be an impossible speed. He stared, fascinated at the new monster, and tried too late to get out of its way. But the bonara was lightning fast. He rammed into Kansa before he could move and Kansa crashed to the ground in a nerve-jarring fall. The bonara seized the opportunity to slash at Kansa's neck with one of his sharply pointed talons. Kansa rolled away just in time to avoid the fatal blow, but the talon still scraped his chest. It was enough to rip through the steel mesh covering Kansa's torso. Kansa looked down at his chest; he was bleeding profusely. The blood was pouring out of his body at an alarming rate. He knew he only had a couple of minutes left after which he would not be able to move his limbs. The severe loss of blood would leave him in a state of temporary paralysis and the enemy would finish him off with ease. The bonara understood this too, but he knew there wasn't enough time to play with the mortal. The soldiers would be upon them any moment now and they needed to leave with Devki's head before that happened. Killing the giant mortal was not that important. He turned his attention towards Devki, who had rushed to Kansa's side. Devki felt a rage she had never felt before and looked at her impending death in the form of the bonara with a total absence of fear. The bonara raised a talon and moved in for the kill.

Just as he was about to bring down the talon to guillotine Devki, there was a chorus of 'Har Har Mahadev', and a spear flew through the air, chopping off the bonara's descending talon in half. He stared uncomprehendingly at the severed limb that served as one of his feet. All at once, the scene was full of Madhuvan soldiers rushing in the direction of the monsters. Airawat led them with a wrathful countenance. It was his spear that had chopped off the bonara's talon. But Airawat had underestimated the latter's strength and his evil purpose. Thinking that the bonara would not be able to balance himself on his remaining leg, Airawat ran towards him without defending his body with his shield. When he was within touching distance, the lethal creature heaved his body in the air, and in a swishing movement, slashed at him with his remaining talon. Airawat saw the talon coming at him and lifted his shield in defence, but it was too late. The talon sliced through the heavy shield and hacked off Airawat's left hand at the wrist. The bonara was about to finish him off when a bevy of soldiers rushed in to save their commander. The bonara's attention was diverted in killing the brave soldiers, who gave up their lives to save their noble leader. Airawat had by now lost consciousness and lay senseless on the ground.

Meanwhile, the pisaca got up gingerly. He was grievously injured from the beating he had received earlier from Kansa. He looked around in dismay at the kalakanja and the bonara caught up in trying to ward off the soldiers. His eyes searched for Devki; her death was the only thing of significance for him. He moved towards her. She was kneeling beside Kansa, trying to bandage his chest wound with cloth cut off from her sari. Devki saw the pisaca coming in her direction and she stretched her arm to grab the sword of a fallen soldier. The pisaca swirled his several tentacles in the direction of her face, each tentacle a deadly weapon. Devki was momentarily confused, and the pisaca seized the opportunity to knock off the sword from her hands. The next moment, his tentacles were wrapped around her neck, in an attempt to jerk her head off her body. Exactly at that moment, Kansa made a superhuman effort to lift himself off the ground and grabbing the sword Devki had been holding, he dug it in the middle of the pisaca's head, right up to the hilt. The attack on his head made the pisaca involuntarily pull back his tentacles to shield himself, releasing Devki's neck in the process. Exhausted with the severe blood loss and the energy he had spent to get up, Kansa staggered. For a brief instant, his eyes closed of their own accord. The Pisaca, with the last vestiges of his strength, pierced Kansa's exposed abdomen with the spike that lay hidden under his tentacles for close encounters with enemies. Kansa reeled back with the impact and fell to the ground, mortally wounded. The pisaca too tottered, swaying with the loss of blood from the head wound. Through a haze, he saw the bonara with his severed limb hard-pressed keeping the attacking soldiers at bay. The bonara was bleeding profusely from various cuts on his scaly body. The pisaca saw the kalakanja had killed more than ten soldiers but the large numbers attacking him from all sides would overpower him in a few minutes. The pisaca looked on helplessly, trying to decide what to do.

As if on cue, the raucous voice of the Dark Lord entered his mind. *Leave... Now!* the voice seethed, the rage in the voice unmistakable.

The pisaca trembled. They had failed their master. *He* had failed his master. The retribution would be terrible. He hooted in a low frequency, the sound audible only to the kalakanja and the bonara. The message was clear—they needed to leave at once. The three creatures from Pataal Lok focused at a point eight gavutas above the ground, equidistant from where each of them stood. The bonara and the kalakanja pointed one of their arms in the direction of that point, and the pisaca pointed one of his tentacles in the same direction. Before the others knew what was happening, an eerie green line of light emanated from the pointed limbs of each of the three creatures. It travelled upwards and seemed to culminate at the point above the ground, where the three of them were focusing their energies. As the three lines of light merged there was a simultaneous blast, eight gavutas up in the air. At the same time, there was a flurry of wind where each of the creatures stood, and what appeared to resemble a mini-typhoon hauled the swirling figures of the three monsters up into the air and disappeared along with them. The soldiers looked at where the three creatures had stood, just a moment ago. It seemed they had vanished into thin air. The mutilated and lifeless bodies scattered all around were the only evidence of the carnage that had taken place on the hill. Kansa and Airawat lay motionless, their life blood still ebbing out of their bodies.

Shiva Educates Brahma

'Where is he?' Ugrasena roared in pain as he ran in the direction of Kansa's quarters. A shell-shocked attendant had just informed the king that Kansa had been brought to the palace in an injured and unconscious condition. Devki had sent the attendant to urgently call him to Kansa's chambers where the royal vaid was administering emergency procedures to try and save the prince's life.

'Father!' Devki exclaimed as she hugged Ugrasena.

'Wh-What happened?' Ugrasena stammered as he saw the scratches on Devki's face and her bedraggled condition. Then his gaze fell on Kansa lying motionless on the bed, and he took a sharp breath. His chest and abdomen were bandaged all over and yet the blood had soaked through the layers. There was no visible sign of life, and it appeared that Kansa's soul had already departed his body. Ugrasena moved hesitantly towards his son and tentatively touched his forehead to smoothen the locks of hair covering Kansa's eyes. His lips were quivering with suppressed emotion as he sat beside the lifeless body of his son and took his hands in his own.

'Don't leave me, my son!' he whispered through a haze of tears, as he kept rubbing Kansa's palms. 'Don't leave me yet!' he repeated to himself over and over again.

'Your Majesty,' the royal vaid gently touched the king's shoulder. But Ugrasena was in a world of his own and did not respond. The vaid looked pleadingly at Devki. He was afraid that the trauma of Kansa's death would kill Ugrasena, who was already frail due to his prolonged illness.

Devki shook her head helplessly. She did not know what to do either. She couldn't believe her giant of a brother was dead. *It can't be, dammit! You can't die like this*, she thought angrily, as the dam broke and the tears threatened to drown her in her own sorrow.

'The wounds were too deep, my child. I'm sorry I couldn't do anything,' the vaid tried to sound professional but his voice choked towards the end of the sentence. He willed himself to regain his control, 'We will need to prepare the body...uh...the prince, for his final journey,' he said in an attempt to shift his thoughts to something that he could do in order to stop thinking about the young prince's death.

Ugrasena still sat mumbling to himself. But now his voice trembled with an unnatural excitement. Devki strained to listen to what he was saying. She froze as she heard the words.

'He is alive...he is alive. My son is alive,' Ugrasena was rambling incoherently.

Devki glanced in the direction of the vaid, who shook his head sadly. 'The king is in shock,' he whispered gently to her. 'It happens when one is faced with a trauma as big as this.'

Devki was only half-listening to the vaid. She was attentively looking at Kansa's body and suddenly caught an unmistakable movement of his arm. She wasn't sure whether Kansa had actually moved his arm or whether the king had shaken it unknowingly while rubbing her brother's palms. She walked towards the bed to take a closer look at Kansa's body.

And then it happened! Kansa opened his eyes and his pupils gleamed with a bright green light. Devki wasn't sure whether it was her imagination or she actually saw the flash of green. It was there for a moment and then it was gone, replaced by the brown pupils that she had always adored.

She turned around excitedly towards the vaid, 'He is alive... he opened his eyes just now,' she said exultantly.

The vaid rushed to the bed. The eyes were closed now. He gave Devki a confused stare, trying to decide whether she had imagined it, but Devki was pointing at Kansa's torso now. The vaid followed her gaze and his mouth fell open at what he saw. The bandages covering Kansa's wounds were beginning to dry up on their own. It was happening at an imperceptible pace but there was no doubt that it was happening. The vaid also noticed something else. He pointed at Kansa's arms to show Devki what he saw. The scratch marks on the prince's arms seemed to be vanishing before their very eyes. It was almost as if the skin surrounding the scratch marks was closing over to shroud the cuts, healing them completely.

'What sorcery is this?' Devki whispered in amazement, as she saw the cuts healing on their own, one after the other.

'Not sorcery, dear; in some people the cells replicate and grow back much faster than in others. This is why it takes some people a long time in having their wounds healed, while others heal much faster,' the vaid explained.

He examined Kansa's body more closely, 'But I must say I have never seen a man heal so rapidly in my entire life. The prince's cells seem to be replicating and growing back at a faster rate than any other case I have ever seen or heard about.'

'His heart has started beating,' Ugrasena whispered, still not taking his eyes off his son. The king was still in shock but he had regained some of his composure, now that Kansa showed signs of being alive.

'Your Majesty, I'm going to take his bandages off,' the vaid said motioning respectfully to the king to move aside.

'What? Won't that cause the wound to bleed again?' Ugrasena said in an unsure tone.

The vaid pointed at Kansa's torso, 'The bleeding has stopped, Your Majesty. The healing will be faster if I open the bandages and let the wound breathe freely.' For once in his life, he didn't wait for the king to give his concurrence, as he started to carefully remove the bandages.

'Wait!' Ugrasena commanded. 'How can the bleeding stop so suddenly?'

The vaid sighed 'I can't explain how, Your Majesty. This is the first time I have seen something like this. But I do know that the bleeding has stopped completely,' he said, putting the palm of his hand on Kansa's bandages and showing the king that his hand was dry.

Seeing Ugrasena's uncertain expression, he continued, 'Sometimes the body clots at a much faster rate. In the prince's case it has happened at an unprecedented speed. If I don't open the bandages now, the wound might start festering inside.' He waited impatiently for Ugrasena's reaction.

'Father, let him open the bandages,' Devki urged, as she patted Ugrasena's arm reassuringly. Ugrasena reluctantly nodded his agreement and the vaid proceeded to unravel the layers of bandages covering Kansa's torso. There was a loud gasp from the vaid as he undid the final layer. He motioned to Devki and Ugrasena to behold what he had just seen. The wounds on Kansa's torso, including the spot where the pisaca had pierced his abdomen with his deadly spike, had almost completely healed.

'Lord Shiva be praised!' Ugrasena breathed in relief as he kneeled down to thank the God. Devki mumbled her gratitude to Shiva too, as she gazed upon the now completely healed body of her brother.

The vaid shivered involuntarily. He knew what neither Devki nor Ugrasena knew. No mortal could have healed as fast as Kansa had just done!

◆

The cavernous room appeared even more sinister today to the three creatures than it had on their previous visit. The terracotta lamps shed their dim light around the room, making shadows appear out of nowhere. The windows were open; and outside the wind howled with a fury that was ominous in itself. The pisaca steeled himself to face the wrath of the Dark Lord. He knew he had failed him and would have to bear the consequences. His serpentine tail had almost recovered from the bruises received at Kansa's hands, but his head was badly wounded. The blood loss had been severe. In the haste to report to his master, he hadn't found time to get it attended to.

The bonara balanced himself on his lone taloned foot. The loss of his other limb hurt him sorely. It wasn't just the physical pain. His two talons had been his prime tools of imparting death to his enemies. The loss of one talon hit him psychologically. Yet at that moment, the bonara was more concerned about dealing with his master's rage at the failure of their mission than with anything else.

The kalakanja gingerly rubbed his eyes. They hurt where Kansa had dug his thumbs during their fight. His vision was still hazy and he had difficulty in focusing his eyes at one place for too long. He was as scared of the Dark Lord's anger as his other two companions, but he wasn't overtly perturbed. He knew their master's rage would be directed mainly at the pisaca as he was the leader of the mission. It was primarily his failure. *Poor bastard*, he thought. *The master is going to fry him alive*, he chuckled to himself.

The door to the room opened as the shrouded figure of their master glided in noiselessly. The deafening noise of the wind howling outside suddenly seemed subdued. As if on cue, the lamps began to burn with an eerie intensity. The only sound in the room was the crackling of the embers in the lamps, interspersed with the heavy breathing of the three creatures. They waited for their master to speak.

'You—failed—me,' rasped the Dark Lord. The voice was strangely calm. Yet that in itself made it all the more menacing.

'My L-Lord, it was m-my mistake,' stammered the pisaca, trembling in fear.

'Silence!' thundered the shrouded figure. The calm tone was gone. The pisaca cowered, his tail twitching involuntarily.

'You have both received grievous injuries,' the Dark Lord glanced from the pisaca to the bonara. The voice was devoid of emotion; it was a matter-of-fact statement. The two creatures lowered their eyes in shame. They were considered to be amongst the deadliest assassins of Pataal Lok and they had not only failed their master; they had also come back thrashed and mutilated by a bunch of mortals.

The Dark Lord moved towards the kalakanja, who too lowered his eyes at the approaching figure. 'You seem to be in pretty good shape,' he said softly.

The kalakanja gave a weak smile. He didn't know whether the master was praising him or being sarcastic. He shrugged his shoulders, 'I did my best, My Lord. I killed ten of the enemy soldiers.'

The shrouded figure nodded, reflecting some interest in what the kalakanja was saying, who was elated to have his master's attention. He continued proudly, 'I would have killed that mortal prince too, My Lord...had the soldiers not arrived at the scene.'

'Hmm, yes! You would have done that indeed,' he said softly. The kalakanja's chest swelled with pride.

'And is that why I sent you to Madhuvan in the first place? To kill those puny soldiers and that mortal prince?' The voice was a whiplash now and the kalakanja froze with fright. All his smugness evaporated in an instant as he realized his master had been toying with him.

The Dark Lord whispered some mantras under his breath. As the intensity of the mantras grew, the shrouded figure grew in size, till he was face to face with the towering frame of the kalakanja. The terrified creature stared into the piercing eyes of his master, and knew he would never forget this sight for the rest of his wretched life.

'You let your lust for that woman get into the way of killing her,' he rasped. 'You failed me.' The voice came from somewhere inside the kalakanja's head and he knew the master was addressing him specifically. The kalakanja wanted to tell the shrouded figure that it would never happen again, that he would make up for his failure, that he wanted to beg for one last chance to make his master proud of him. But he was unable to get a word out. His tongue twisted inside his mouth and his lips contorted in unimaginable agony. He felt his body lose control over his limbs as the blazing eyes of the Dark Lord continued to gaze at him. And when he thought it couldn't get worse, he felt his breath get stuck somewhere deep inside his throat and he felt the torture of suffocation drowning out all other sensations. In the last fleeting moments of the creature's miserable existence, the Dark Lord lifted his veil and showed the kalakanja the face that only a handful of people had been allowed to see in the past two hundred years. Even as the last breath of life escaped the kalakanja's mouth, he knew he would never see such a ravaged face as he had seen in his last moments. The memory of the disfigured face would haunt him forever in the lowest pit of hell, where he was being damned for eternity by his master.

◆

The bonara and the pisaca saw the kalakanja disappear from sight in front of their eyes. The Dark Lord still had his back towards them. He pulled the cloak around his head to cover his face again, and turned around to face the remaining two creatures. They shivered in anticipation of their own deaths as the towering figure of their master approached them. The Dark Lord stopped a few feet away from them and chanted another set of mantras. His body came down to its normal height.

He moved in the direction of the bonara, 'You fought bravely,' he said softly. The voice was calm again. His rage seemed to have been washed out with the kalakanja's death. He pointed his index finger in the direction of the bonara's severed limb and began chanting a mantra that the two creatures had never heard before. They realized it was a mantra from the Dark Lord's past, invoking some potent energy. A radiant blue light darted out of his index finger and enveloped the severed limb of the bonara entirely. As the passion of the mantra grew, the radiance of the blue light intensified. And before their very eyes, the pisaca and the bonara saw in awe as the severed talon was reconstructed out of thin air.

The shrouded figure gazed in satisfaction at the rejuvenated limb of the bonara. The midget monster flexed the reconstructed talon as if he still couldn't believe his body was whole again. Before he could thank his master, the Dark Lord had turned his attention to the pisaca. He repeated the mantra and the universal force of Brahman emanating out of his index figure sealed the mortal wound to the pisaca's head, leaving him completely healed.

'We won't get another chance to kill Devki for some time,' he said hoarsely. 'Kansa and Ugrasena will ensure she is never left alone again.'

The pisaca and the bonara waited patiently. They knew their master had something in his mind.

'We will need to try a different strategy,' the Dark Lord pondered, still lost in his own thoughts. An incongruous chuckle escaped the veil covering his face, as he decided what had to be done.

'You shall go to the kingdom of Banpur,' he commanded the Pisaca. 'And you shall proceed to the land of the Yavanas,' he said, instructing the bonara.

The two creatures looked enquiringly at their master, clueless about what they had to do once they reached their respective destinations. The Dark Lord motioned to them to come closer. As they neared him, he concentrated his mind to create a shield around the three of them. He didn't want Brahma or anyone else eavesdropping on their discussion through cosmic telepathy.

◆

'Was it necessary to kill the kalakanja, Amartya?' The middle aged man in spotless white clothes gently admonished the Dark Lord. He was the only person who could dare to call the Dark Lord by his birth name; the only man whom the he respected enough to seek his counsel.

'He failed me Bhargava,' rasped the Dark Lord, taking the omnipresent veil off his face. Bhargava involuntarily muttered some chants to calm his mind at the sight of the ravaged face. Irrespective of how many times he saw the mutilated face, he was still unable to control the revulsion that appeared unbidden to his mind. *How can he bear to see his face every day?* he thought.

'You could have given him another chance,' Bhargava persisted. 'Was it necessary to kill him? He was one of the Zataka Upanshughataks; it takes years of training to reach that level!'

'I would have forgiven him for his failure,' the Dark Lord paused, contemplatively. 'But he failed because he wanted to ravish that mortal woman.' He looked piercingly at the man called Bhargava. 'I can't allow one person's weakness to disrupt my plans...and...' he paused.

'And? And what?' Bhargava looked questioningly at him.

'My plans don't include the rape of innocent women,' the Dark Lord snapped in irritation.

Bhargava sighed. He knew he would never understand this man who had met him two hundred years back when Brahma had banished him from Swarglok. He found it okay to ask the assassins to decapitate Devki but he killed one of his best assassins because the man tried to rape the woman. Bhargava shook his head, realizing it was impossible to get to the depths of the complex man standing in front of him. At the same time, he was happy that the Dark Lord did not endorse the rape of an innocent woman. This knowledge made it easier for him to continue his covert support towards his friend.

'I saw how you reconstructed the limb of the bonara and the way you healed the pisaca,' he said hesitantly.

Turning his ravaged face towards Bhargava, Amartya Kalyanesu gave him a sharp glance. 'What do you mean?' he rasped hoarsely.

'I have always wondered why you don't reconstruct your own face,' Bhargava replied tentatively. 'I mean, you can obviously use the power of Brahman to make your face alright again. Why do you persist in carrying this caricature of a face when you have the power within you to change it in an instant?'

Bhargava hadn't intended to lose his control but he couldn't contain his outburst at his friend's apparent obtuseness to do anything about his ruined face.

Amartya Kalyanesu, the man feared and known in Pataal Lok as the Dark Lord, looked thoughtfully at Bhargava. Then he spoke quietly. 'This face...this caricature as you call it...reminds me every day of the injustice done to me. I will not alter it till I have done what I pledged to do two centuries back. It has taken me this long to set my plans in action. It won't take much longer now. With Devki's death, all possible hindrances to my plans will be removed forever.'

Bhargava nodded. 'And this decision to send the pisaca and the bonara to Banpur and the land of the Yavanas? This is part of the plan?'

'Yes,' Amartya Kalyanesu nodded. 'This will initiate the chaos necessary to put Mrityulok in a state of anarchy.' He smiled without humour, 'And when that is done, the stage will be set to show Brahma what happens when you create a demon out of a god!'

His raucous laughter filled with sadness reverberated throughout the cavernous room.

◆

'Amartya Kalyanesu has to be destroyed, My Lord!' Brahma said, in a brave attempt to persuade his former teacher.

'I agree I was unfair to him in the past,' he continued with a slight tremor in his voice. 'But that doesn't give him the right to put the entire universe at risk!' He looked defiantly at Shiva.

Shiva appeared calm, his initial anger at the memory of what Brahma had done to Amartya two hundred years back a little subdued. *He actually believes that destroying Amartya is the right thing to do*, Shiva thought, as he motioned to Brahma to sit close to him.

'Tell me Brahma...why do you think Amartya ought to be destroyed?' he asked him gently.

'Because he has become evil My Lord!' Brahma automatically replied.

'And why do you think he has become evil?'

Brahma looked incredulously at Shiva. *Is he serious?* he thought to himself. Then he caught himself as he realized that Shiva could easily read his thoughts.

'That boy...that creature...' Brahma corrected himself trying not to let his former affection for Amartya overpower him. 'He intends to share the secret of using the universal force of Brahman with the creatures of Pataal Lok...' He paused here.

'And?' Shiva looked at him enquiringly. 'I am sure there is something else bothering you.'

'The only reason he could have for sharing the powers of Brahman with those vile creatures is that he intends to launch an attack on Swarglok...on all of us,' Brahma blurted out.

'And that makes him evil?' Shiva asked gently. He raised his hand to halt Brahma from remonstrating.

'Haven't we too launched attacks on Pataal Lok from time to time in the past, Brahma? Does that make us evil too?'

Brahma gasped. 'We always had a good reason to attack them, My Lord. Are you comparing our reasons for attacking them with their justifications?' He looked in astonishment at Shiva.

'Reasons can always be justified Brahma. The biggest error in life is to believe that your reasons are right and the other person's reasons are wrong.'

'What...what are you saying?' Brahma's voice failed him.

'It is the purpose that matters. Reasons are not important. Reasons can be manipulated; purpose is constant. When we attacked Pataal Lok, it was with the purpose of ensuring all-round peace in the three worlds. Right now, we don't know what purpose Amartya has in attacking us.'

'Are you saying we wait quietly for him and his horde of demons from Pataal Lok to convert Mrityulok into a wasteland... and then to come for us and destroy Swarglok too?' Brahma allowed himself to express as much anger and disbelief as was possible without offending Shiva.

Shiva evaded the expostulation. 'Tell me Brahma, do you think Amarya was truly evil two centuries back, when you cursed him and banished him from Swarglok?'

Brahma was taken aback by the change in topic. But he answered without a moment's hesitation. 'No, My Lord. He wasn't evil then.'

Shiva smiled. 'Yet you attempted to destroy him. Today, you believe he is evil. How do you know that two hundred years from now, you may not find him to be good again?'

'My Lord, you are trying to confuse me!' Brahma protested. 'Amartya may have been good then, and I made a mistake in cursing him. But today he has indeed turned evil. And frankly, two hundred years from now, there may be nothing left for us to wonder whether he is good or evil any more. The three worlds as we know them today may cease to exist if he is allowed to live. He is evil, and evil has to be destroyed.'

Brahma paused, looking Shiva in the eye. 'You have to destroy him, My Lord!' Shiva's face was expressionless. 'What makes you think I will destroy Amartya?'

'Because you have always destroyed evil, My Lord!' Brahma was perplexed at Shiva's attitude. He had thought once Shiva knew of the danger Amartya posed, he would himself be keen to deal with him. But Shiva seemed totally non-committal.

'I have destroyed evil, when it has become too large to be accommodated any longer, Brahma. Never before that. And it has not happened yet!'

'But, My Lord...' Brahma rose from his seat to protest, but Shiva interrupted him.

'Remember when I destroy evil, everything along with it gets destroyed too. All the goodness too, will be decimated. This is why I come in only when evil has grown to such massive proportions that it justifies destroying the residual good along with the overpowering evil. Right now, the evil you speak of has not reached that stage. It doesn't warrant my coming in.'

Brahma looked in frustration at the being he respected more than anyone else in the world. 'Then there is no hope for us!' he sighed. 'Amartya will equip the demons in Pataal Lok with the force of Brahman and strengthened with the powers of Bal and Atibal, those vile creatures will convert Mrityulok into one vast graveyard. And then they...'

'It won't happen' Shiva cut him short.

'It...what?' Brahma stared uncomprehendingly at him.

'It won't happen,' Shiva reiterated. 'Amartya will not be able to infuse the demons with the force of Brahman.'

'You mean he may not remember the mantras of Bal and Atibal necessary to channellize the force of Brahman within the demons?' Brahma asked dubiously, knowing that Amartya's memory was unimpeachable.

'It has nothing to do with the mantras or with his memory, Brahma,' Shiva explained, reading his thoughts. 'For the power of Brahman to get activated within a person's body, there has to be a rare degree of goodness within that person. If that goodness doesn't exist, no mantra in the world can succeed in imbuing a person with the noble power of Brahman.'

'And that goodness doesn't exist in the creatures of Pataal Lok,' Brahma said exultantly.

'That's right,' Shiva nodded. 'But it goes far deeper than that. The demons are infused with the force of Aghasamarthan–a form of evil energy—not as potent as the force of Brahman, but still extremely forceful. Just as the force of Brahman pervades our being as a blue light, the force of Aghasamarthan fills up their consciousness with a green light. As long as the dark force of Aghasamarthan is in their bodies, they will be unable to accept the cleansing energy of Brahman. Their bodies will simply reject the energy, irrespective of any mantras that Amartya may use to infuse them with its powers.'

'Aum-Num-Ha-Shi-Vai,' Brahma bowed respectfully to Shiva. His mind was far more relaxed than it had ever been since his last meeting with Narada. 'What do I do now, My Lord?' he enquired.

'You said Amartya plans to lay waste to Mrityulok before he decides to attack Swarglok.' It was more of a question than a statement and Brahma nodded in agreement.

Shiva seemed lost in thought for a brief moment. Then he spoke softly, as if to himself. 'Amartya will try and use someone else to fuel his plans of creating chaos in Mrityulok. Yes, that's what he will do!'

He looked at Brahma. 'Is Narada still at home or has he left on his wanderings yet again?'

Brahma was caught off guard at the question. Then he smiled at the mention of his son who was famous for his nomadic roaming around the three worlds. 'He is still there, My Lord. But he plans to visit Mrityulok soon.'

Shiva nodded, 'Good. Tell him to do that. And ask him to keep an eye out for any strange occurrences. He should report to you, without the slightest delay anything out of the ordinary.'

Brahma looked questioningly at Shiva.

Shiva sighed. Brahma was a great man but he had never been a warrior in the true sense of the word. He had been too busy with the conceptualization of Mrityulok, to really focus on the wars that had been going on between the demons and the gods since the beginning of existence. That had been the job of the demi-gods, under the guidance of Shiva and Vishnu. It wasn't surprising therefore that Brahma found it difficult to think as a warrior would in these circumstances.

He explained to Brahma, 'When you want to take over an enemy land, you don't just attack them from the outside. That's too predictable and the enemy can always shield themselves against such an event. What you do therefore, is to create chaos and anarchy within the enemy territory.'

'How do you do that?' Brahma asked with interest. All this talk of military strategy was new to him, and he found himself strangely drawn towards it. It was as if after a lifetime of not picking up weapons, he seemed driven by some primal force to learn everything there was to learn about war in a single day. Shiva had once again donned the role of mentor and Brahma was yet again, the protégé.

Shiva understood this and smiled benignly at Brahma. 'What you do is plant a few of your trusted lieutenants in enemy territory. These people become your eyes and ears and give you vital information about what is happening there. A smart war strategist could also identify powerful allies within the enemy land and try winning them over to his side, or he could also exploit their weaknesses to get them to fight against each other and create chaos. In the resultant confusion, he will then attack and vanquish the enemy before the enemy even gets a chance to realize what is happening.'

Brahma stared in fascination as a hundred myriad thoughts coursed through his brain. But he knew there was more to be learnt here and he stayed quiet.

'Amartya Kalyanesu is going to do the same thing. He will send some of his trusted soldiers to Mrityulok to keep a tab on what is happening there, if he hasn't already done so. Let Narada check if any strange people or any unnatural incidents have been observed in key places across Mrityulok.'

Brahma made a mental note of this, as Shiva continued with his education on war strategy.

'Amartya will also pick a few of the most powerful kingdoms in Mrityulok and try and exploit the weakness of their rulers or he may try and pit one kingdom against the other in an attempt to create chaos. He may also try and woo some of these kings to see if they will ally with him in his attempt to take control over Mrityulok. Ask Narada to make it a point to visit all the influential kingdoms to assess if there is anything amiss with the behaviour of the rulers of those kingdoms.'

'I will do that, My Lord,' Brahma nodded. 'Those will include the kingdoms of Magadha, Madhuvan, Bateshwar, Bahlika, Vidarbha, Hastinapur, Madra and Gandhar, among others.'

Shiva nodded in approval. *He was always a quick learner*, he thought to himself, shielding his thoughts. He didn't want Brahma getting complacent with early praise.

Brahma rose to leave. He was elated at what he had achieved with Shiva. Even though he had refused to destroy Amartya, Shiva had still provided sufficient guidance to him. Brahma could now to do all that was necessary to pre-empt any move on Amartya's part to start his destructive vengeance.

'Brahma!' Shiva spoke softly as he saw him getting ready to leave. Brahma looked at him, expecting some last-minute advice on war strategy.

'Remember, when all your planning fails, there is only one person who can help you. Come to me when that happens and I will tell you who to go to.'

'Who is that, My Lord?' Brahma asked, confused. He had thought he could come back to Shiva for his help in case something went wrong.

Shiva smiled in response and Brahma noticed him dissolving in front of his eyes. The thought struck him that he had been talking to Shiva's projected image all this while. Shiva had never been here. He had just used his immense powers of concentration to create a holographic image.

And then another thought struck Brahma with the force of a thunderbolt that knocked all the breath out of his body. Shiva hadn't said '*If* your planning fails'; he had said,'*When* your planning fails'. That could only mean one thing: Shiva knew that whatever Brahma did, Amartya Kalyanesu would still succeed in doing what he planned; at least enough for Brahma to require coming back to Shiva to seek the help of someone that Shiva hadn't yet told him about.

The Seeds of Confusion Have Begun to Be Sown

The hills surrounding the powerful nation of Banpur reflected the shimmering light from the full moon. Banpur, nestled among the mountains of north-east Bharat, was ruled by the noble and formidable King Bana; one of the most respected and feared kings in the vast land of Bharat. Bana had taken over the reign of the nation following the death of Bali,. who wasn't just Bana's father, but also the man who had carved out the lush land of Banpur from the rocky mountains surrounding it. Bana took over from where his father left off and made Banpur a paradise on Earth; the most beautiful hill nation in Mrityulok. The country had not seen a war in the past twenty years, mostly because no ruler was foolish enough to take an army against King Bana. Not only because he was a great leader of men, but it was almost impossible to attack the hill nation, ensconced as it was amidst an armour of mountains. Hence, Banpur existed in peace, and the country prospered.

This particular night, the denizens of Banpur slept peacefully as the relative coolness of the dark night brought some respite from the unendurable heat of the day. A lone figure kept a wakeful watch on the royal palace. He was waiting for the guards outside the king's residential quarters to doze off before making his move. He did not have to wait much longer. Used to the uneventful and rather mundane routine of their duty, the guards dozed off one after the other, not bothering to adhere to the protocol of maintaining an active shift while the other lot slept.

The skulking figure of the pisaca crept out of its hiding place as he saw the last of the guards succumb to sleep. He had to get inside the king's personal chambers and do what his master had commanded. But he had to be surreptitious. The king of Banpur was a noble man but his physical prowess was legendary. Some said he was even more formidable than Kansa; the prince who had thrashed him so thoroughly during their attempt on his sister's life. The pisaca was in no mood to experience a similar fate tonight. He slithered noiselessly across the distance separating him from the palace entrance. He made it there without attracting any attention. Once there, he clambered up the wall to reach the zone forming the perimeter of the king's residential quarters. He made his way past the sleeping guards. Just as he reached the mammoth door that served as the entrance to the king's sleeping chambers, he saw one of the guards move in his sleep. The pisaca came to an immediate halt, waiting for the guard to settle down. The guard, however, seemed to be having a disturbed sleep. As the pisaca started again towards the door, the guard opened his eyes. For an instant, the pisaca thought of melting into the shadowy corners of the adjoining wall, but it was too late. The guard stared at him in a state of bewildered fear. Any moment and he could scream. The pisaca had no alternative. He surged ahead and one of his tentacles wrapped around the guard's face, stifling the guard's scream. Another tentacle swiftly found a particular nerve just under his ear, and pressed it hard for a couple of seconds. The guard's head rolled back, unconsciousness claiming him almost instantly. The pisaca propped him up against the wall, where he lay oblivious to his surroundings. He knew the guard wouldn't get up for at least an hour. That gave him more than enough time to do what he had come here for. When the guard would get up in the morning, he would probably think he had imagined seeing a creature in the night; maybe a nightmare. Either way, he would not mention it to his companions for fear of being ridiculed. And even if he did, there was no way anyone would know what had really happened.

The pisaca quietly entered the king's chambers. He could see the gargantuan form of King Bana, sleeping peacefully on his large framed bed. *This man must be at least seven feet tall*, thought the pisaca in stupefaction. The king's shoulders seemed like the trunk of a huge oak tree placed sideward—they were that wide. The pisaca now hoped more than ever that the king wouldn't get up and find him lurking in his room. He quickly scanned the enormous room, his eyes searching for something. He found what he was looking for in a far corner of the room. Keeping one of his several eyes fixed on the king, he slinked towards that side of the room. A large pot of water was kept on the shelf. The pisaca hissed in satisfaction, and carefully extracted a packet concealed under his tentacles. He opened the packet gingerly, and holding it above the pot, emptied its contents into it. The colourless powder dissolved instantaneously, blending with the water. The pisaca moved away and soundlessly exited the room, much in the same way as he had come in. The guards were still sleeping without a care in the world, as was their noble king. Only the pisaca knew that once the king drank that water, he would never be the same again. He would forever become a puppet in the hands of his master, dancing to his will like the several others who would soon lose their identity and be powerless. They would then do as the Dark Lord commanded them.

◆

King Bana got up in the middle of the night. He felt unnaturally thirsty and his throat was strangely parched. It felt as if an inexplicable voice in his head was telling him that he needed water. Bana shrugged off the feeling, attributing it to an overactive imagination. Nevertheless, he felt horribly thirsty. He swung his large frame out of the bed and ambled over to where the water was kept. He poured some of it into an earthen container and gulped down its contents. But the thirst seemed to be getting worse. He poured himself another measure of water and ravenously swilled that down too. To his astonishment, the thirst assumed burning proportions. Losing patience, he lifted the entire pot of water, and pulling his head back, he rapaciously drank from it. As the final drop of liquid entered his system, he felt a sense of relief, the indelible thirst finally in control. Bana sighed, feeling suddenly light-headed. He walked unsteadily towards the bed, and fell on it, losing consciousness before his head even touched the pillow.

◆

'The king is getting up,' exclaimed the attendant, excitedly motioning one of the guards to call for the royal physician. Bana was beginning to stir from his sleep, his eyes not yet open but his movements indicating that he would soon be up. The physician stumbled into the room in his haste to be at the king's side. He was relieved to see the king showing tangible signs of being awake. He pressed his thumb against the king's wrist and felt his pulse. *Oh my God, his pulse is racing at an unprecedented rate*, he thought. *It's almost as if he has been running for miles*, he reflected, the beginning of a frown creasing his furrowed brows. He shook his head in consternation. He didn't understand why the king's pulse was so high. And whatever he didn't understand bothered him.

King Bana stretched his arms with a big yawn and gradually opened his eyes. He lay immobile for a few seconds. All of a sudden, he became aware of the presence of people in his room. He turned his head and saw the physician looking strangely at him. He also noticed his chief minister, Bahusruta, standing at attention at the foot of his bed, worry and relief written large on his face. He got up slowly into a sitting position. He had never felt so good before. It felt as if he was several times stronger than he had ever been.

'What's the matter, pranapati?' he asked the physician, calling him by the name of his profession. 'Why are all of you in my room?'

The physician exchanged a furtive glance with the chief minister. The exchange of looks did not escape the alert eyes of king Bana.

'What is it, Bahusruta? he asked his chief minister. 'Why are you people acting so strangely?' Bana sounded miffed.

'Your Majesty, we are happy that you are okay now,' Bahusruta paused, unsure of how to continue. Bana's impatient look goaded him on. 'You...Uh...you have been unconscious for a while, Your Majesty, and...and we were rather worried about you,' he finished lamely.

Bana gave Bahusruta a surprised look and then looked quizzically at the physician. 'How long have I been unconscious?'

The physician shuffled his feet uncomfortably. He again looked at the chief minister.

'How long, dammit?' the king snapped uncharacteristically. Bahusruta cleared his throat, 'Twenty days, Your Majesty!'

King Bana felt his head spin. This was ridiculous. He felt as strong as an ox. If he had been unconscious for that long, he would have been emaciated by now. On the contrary, he had never felt as strong and energetic. Then another thought struck him and he looked sharply at the physician.

'If I was unconscious for twenty days, why aren't there any tubes in my body? How did you feed me all this time?' he asked, his eyes not leaving the physician's gaze even for a moment.

'Uh...we couldn't p-put any t-tubes in your body, Your Majesty,' the physician stammered in dismay. He pointed to a set of needles lying trashed in a container beside the bed. 'Every time we tried inserting the needle into your arm, it would bend and break...' He finished without completing the sentence.

The king stared contemplatively at the half dozen syringes lying in the container.

'How did you feed me then...all these days?' he asked finally. The physician wished he did not have to undergo this questioning any longer. His inability to explain any of what had happened in the last few days left him feeling desperately embarrassed and inadequate. He took a deep breath. 'We didn't Your Majesty...we didn't feed you at all these past twenty days!'

Bana took a long hard look at the physician and his chief minister. 'If I haven't been fed intravenously how did I survive all this while?' he wondered in astonishment. An inexplicable feeling of dizziness took hold of him, all of a sudden, and he held on to the edge of the bed to support himself.

Bana suddenly felt like being by himself. He waved his hand dismissively at the physician and Bahusruta motioning them to leave him alone. Bahusruta nodded respectfully and left the room. The physician hesitated for a moment, but decided he should leave too. He just couldn't comprehend why the king's eyes looked so green today. He shook his head as he left; there were a lot of things he didn't understand in this particular case.

Bana felt relieved as he saw them leave. He heaved himself off the bed, feeling his body lighter and more agile than ever, despite the recent bout of dizziness. He walked towards the shiny steel mirror at one end of the room. As he gazed at his reflection, his attention was drawn to an unnatural green light glittering in his eyes. He bent towards the mirror to take a closer look at the strange light reflected there. That's when he heard the voice in his head. It was a rasping kind of voice, inaudible, but there. Not being able to see anyone in the room, he stood confounded. He felt his limbs locked in an invisible stranglehold as the whispering voice grew more audible with each passing second. He strained to hear what the voice was saying. And then all at once, he heard it clearly, and the blood froze in his veins. *Welcome to the dark side*, the grating voice rasped. *You are mine... From now on, you will call yourself Banasura.*

◆

Beyond the north-western frontiers of the great land of Bharat lay a vast country feared for its ferocious fighters. It was said that the warriors in this land could shoot a flurry of arrows with deadly aim while riding a horse at unimaginable speeds. These were large men. A few amongst them were so intrepid and powerful that they could wrestle a grizzly bear with ease.

This was the land of the Yavanas, ruled by none other than the charismatic King Chanur. Even in his middle age, Chanur stood ramrod straight and looked healthier and stronger than most of the young warriors of the nation. He had once killed a tiger with his bare hands while protecting one of his soldiers. They had been pursuing a large tiger who had wreaked havoc in some of the villages of the kingdom. Chanur had pledged to end the life of this man-eater. He was accompanied by a group of bodyguards and soldiers.

They sighted the tiger after a frustrating chase lasting a little under two days. The animal was finally cornered, its back against an unyielding grove of trees, and surrounded on the other sides by the Yavana soldiers. Growling in barely suppressed fury, the tiger looked around helplessly for a way out. There was none. Chanur gave the signal to one of the soldiers to shoot the tiger down. The soldier, in an attempt to impress the king, pointed towards his sword, indicating that he wanted to kill the tiger with the long knife.

Chanur blinked in surprise at the foolhardiness of the soldier. This was no ordinary tiger. It was a man-eater, a very large one. And its senses were inflamed. For all his bravery, the soldier would certainly be killed if he went in with just a sword. Chanur hesitated. His instincts honed over a lifetime of war told him that he should tell the soldier to stand back and shoot the animal with an arrow rather than engage it in close combat. But he knew if he refused the soldier now, it would embarrass and humiliate the warrior in front of his fellow men. To a Yavana warrior, that would be a fate worse than death. The other soldiers stood looking at the king, waiting for his decision. Chanur made up his mind.

He took a deep breath and raised his right arm. Then slowly he pointed his thumb in a downward direction, giving the soldier permission to engage and kill the tiger. The young warrior smiled in relief, and bowed to the king. Then unsheathing his sword, he moved stealthily in its direction, watchful of every move the animal made. The tiger looked warily at the approaching soldier. As the warrior moved closer, it pulled back on its haunches and snarled. Two long saber teeth were visible as the tiger opened its mouth wide. When the soldier was about one gavuta away from the animal, the tiger went into a crouching position. The warrior knew this was an indication that the beast would jump at him any instant, and he primed himself for the attack, holding the sword in front of his body. But nothing in his past experience prepared the soldier for the speed and fury of the man-eater. The tiger was on top of him in one leap and the impact of its body crashing into him wrenched the sword out of his hand. The warrior went down with the animal still on top of him. The claws of the man-eater ripped out flesh and bone, and in a matter of seconds, the soldier's body was a wreckage of blood and torn skin. The smell of the warrior's blood made the tiger go insane with bloodlust, and it raised its head towards the sky and roared exultantly.

The other soldiers watched horrified, paralyzed at the speed with which everything had happened and the sheer fury of the animal. Chanur was the first to snap out of the hypnotic state the gory scene had put everyone into. In a flash he was off his horse and he lunged at the tiger in the same instant that the animal opened its gaping mouth to crunch the soldier's head between its teeth. If Chanur had been a second late, the soldier would be dead. Fortunately for the young warrior, the tiger's attention was distracted by Chanur charging towards it. Leaving the wounded soldier lying on the ground, the tiger turned its attention towards the new enemy. Chanur saw the tiger coming for him and he stopped, balancing his weight on the balls of his feet. As the tiger leaped at him, Chanur twisted his body in one graceful maneuver and as the tiger passed him, missing his body by inches, Chanur grabbed the animal by its torso. The weight of the falling tiger dragged Chanur down too, but he didn't let go of the animal's body. He landed on top of the tiger, and before the beast could find its bearings, Chanur jumped off lightly and stood facing the man-eater. The enraged tiger opened its mouth in a blood-curdling roar and attempted another jump at the king. But this time, the distance was too short and the tiger was forced to stand up on its rear legs to charge at Chanur, considerably reducing the impact of its attack. In one swift motion, Chanur gripped the tiger's open mouth with both hands, and held on with all his might. The veins in his arms were close to bursting with the strain, but Chanur was used to it, having fought with bears over the past several years. Just as it seemed that he wouldn't be able to hold on any longer, Chanur took a deep breath and let out a roar that was even more fearsome than the beast's. In one quick move, he snapped the tiger's mouth wide open, breaking the animal's neck in the same instant. The tiger's body went limp, collapsing to the ground like an empty sack. The warriors stood looking in shock at what they had just witnessed. They had heard about Chanur's strength and his battles with wild bears, but seeing him fight a large man-eater in front of their very eyes was a different experience altogether. The fight with the tiger had lasted a little over a minute. The spectacle of the battle had been so captivating that it had not occurred to any of the soldiers or even the bodyguards to shoot the tiger down during the fight. However, as they saw the man-eater crumple to the ground, their suppressed emotions erupted as one resounding shout of victory, in honour of their mighty King.

Chanur smiled, his body relaxing as the tension of the ferocious fight gradually left his body. He mounted his horse and looked on as a group of soldiers lifted the wounded warrior to rush him to the infirmary. This was Chanur, the leader of one of the most ferocious warriors in Mrityulok.

◆

Chanur was amongst the foremost warrior kings of his time, and was respected not just by his own kinsmen, but also by most of the other kings in Mrityulok. While the Yavana kingdom was farther from the others countries of Bharat than any other kingdom in Mrityulok, the influence of Chanur and the Yavanas was felt all around the great land of Bharat.

It was to this land that the Dark Lord sent the bonara. The midget monster knew that the pisaca had already done what their master had instructed him to do in Banpur with King Bana. The bonara was supposed to do the same with King Chanur. Strong and fearless as he was, the task still had him worried; because if Chanur caught him doing what he was supposed to, there would be no mercy. The Yavana king would surely kill him there and then. But more than the fear of Chanur, the Bonara was terrified of what the Dark Lord would do to him if he failed. The memory of the kalakanja dissolving in front of his eyes was still vivid in the bonara's mind. He did not want to invite the same fate upon himself by failing his master the second time. He recalled the Dark Lord's instructions. 'Wait for the dark before you enter the king's palace. Don't let anyone see you and don't kill anyone. Everything should seem normal when the day dawns.' And he remembered his master's final words, with a shiver of fear. 'Don't disappoint me this time, my friend.'

◆

The bonara crept out of Chanur's palace. His body was quivering with the excitement of having completed his mission successfully. It hadn't been as difficult as he had supposed. Getting into the palace had been ridiculously easy. The Yavana guards slept soundly and no one had heard or seen him slip inside the palace and then into Chanur's personal quarters. It had taken all of a minute to locate the jar of water in the king's room. Another few seconds and the colourless powder was emptied into the jar. Sometime during the night or the next day, Chanur would drink from that jar of water. *After that, the mighty Yavana king will no longer be his own master*, thought the bonara with a smug smile. He knew the contents of the powder would change Chanur in ways that were possibly not even completely known to him. Though he did know one thing with certainty: once Chanur drank that water, the potion mixed in it would render him powerless in the hands of the Dark Lord. One of the most powerful kings in Mrityulok would become a pawn in the hands of their master, just like King Bana possibly had by now, and like several others would, in days to come.

Madhuvan Has a Visitor

The frenetic activity at the royal palace in Madhuvan hinted at the fact that some major personage was expected. Even the normally staid and calm Ugrasena seemed a little hassled. He had already badgered Prasenjit, his external affairs minister, twice since morning, to ensure that everything was in order for the expected guest. The best carpets had been pulled out to adorn the pathway starting from the outer gates and leading up to the palace. The king's personal bodyguards had turned out in their finest attire; their wooden sandals brushed till they gleamed like steel. The swords and shields had been rubbed several times with oil to make them glisten with the brilliance of the sun. The ceremonial flag of Madhuvan, reserved only for the most influential visitors, had been taken out and was held up proudly by Airawat in his right hand. His left hand had been covered carefully to prevent people from staring at the severed limb.

'What's all the fuss about?' asked a young soldier who had been newly inducted into the legion of the king's personal bodyguards. 'Why is everyone so hassled?'

One of the older bodyguards, a veteran who had served Ugrasena for the past fifteen years, looked at him kindly. 'Speak softly, son. The king of Magadha is visiting Madhuvan.'

'The king of Magadha? You mean Jarasandha?' the young man was in awe, his voice louder than he had intended.

The veteran looked sharply at the young bodyguard. 'Sshhh!' he exclaimed roughly. 'It's King Jarasandha!' He looked around cautiously. 'Never repeat the mistake of calling him by his name, even when you are talking among friends. If he finds out, he will have you hanging from a tree before you even realize what happened. Many people have died in the past for lapses far less serious than this,' he whispered gravely.

The young man felt a shiver run down his spine. He had heard about Jarasandha's dark nature but had never believed most of it. It was said that Jarasandha had conquered more kingdoms than any other king of their time. But unlike most conquerors who let the vanquished rulers manage their kingdoms in return for a hefty royalty, Jarasandha didn't let any of the defeated kings taste freedom once he subjugated them. There were a horde of overthrown kings locked up in dungeons in his capital city. Some of them had already died in confinement and the ones who hadn't yet, wished they had.

'Wh-why did our prince marry Jarasandha...King Jarasandha's sisters, if he is so evil?' he asked the veteran in a shaken voice.

The veteran sighed. The young man would get him killed along with himself if he persisted with this chatter. He spoke in hushed tones, 'Our prince married King Jarasandha's sisters in order to form an alliance with the kingdom of Magadha. He knew the marriage would bind the king of Magadha to the kingdom of Madhuvan. King Jarasandha would never attack his own brother-in-law, you understand.' He looked at the young man hoping fervently that this would stop the naïve man from asking any more dangerous questions. He groaned as the young man opened his mouth to ask yet another question.

'But why would Prince Kansa be afraid of the king of Magadha? He is strong enough to fight anyone. And the army of Madhuvan can take on any nation.' There was unmasked pride in his voice as he spoke of Kansa and their army.

The veteran could not help admiring the younger man's faith in Kansa and in the Madhuvan army, but he knew his colleague didn't know Jarasandha well enough to have made that statement. He spoke gently, 'Son, Prince Kansa is a great warrior. Perhaps the greatest our land has ever given birth to. But you do not know King Jarasandha.' The veteran's voice dropped to an involuntary whisper, 'The king of Magadha has defeated various kings who were considered invincible till they fought with him. And the army of Magadha is ten times the size of our army. They can eat us for breakfast if they decide to fight us. King Ugrasena did well to marry our prince to King Jarasandha's sisters. We are safe now!'

The young man looked like he wanted to ask more questions. But the veteran gave him a tight-lipped glare that clearly indicated he was in no mood to entertain any more questions about the visitor from Magadha.

◆

Airawat bowed respectfully as Jarasandha passed him. The king of Magadha was just a little over one gavuta (six feet) in height. Airawat was no stranger to tall men. But Jarasandha was built like an ox. He had a crop of curly, short hair, unlike other kings who preferred to keep it shoulder length. There was a touch of grey around his temples but other than that, Jarasandha looked like a man in his prime. He exuded a strange animal force that was sufficient to cow down even the most intrepid warrior. His eyes, darkened with kohl, took in everything around him, including the one-armed Airawat holding the ceremonial flag of Madhuvan.

He smirked, as if laughing at a private joke. 'So Madhuvan has started recruiting handicapped men in their army now?' he commented sarcastically, pointing at Airawat's severed hand.

Airawat bristled in anger but he was careful to conceal his emotions. He wasn't afraid of Jarasandha but he did not want Madhuvan to get into trouble because of him.

Airawat's suppressed resentment did not escape Jarasandha's attention. He raised his eyebrows, 'Do you want to say something to me, soldier?' he sneered. He was sure this would provoke Airawat because the markings on his uniform clearly indicated that he was no ordinary warrior but the commander of the Madhuvan Cavalry.

Referring to him as a mere soldier in front of his subordinates might incite him into doing something brash, which would give Jarasandha sufficient cause to squash him.

But the Magadha ruler had misjudged Airawat's self-control. The commander took a deep breath to calm himself, 'No My Lord, I did not want to say anything. I just want you to know how honoured we are to have you here at Madhuvan.'

Jarasandha glared at Airawat, annoyed that he had not been given an opportunity to vent his anger. Airawat returned his stare unflinchingly, but took care not to let his defiance show in his expression.

'Hah!' Jarasandha snorted in disgust, and continued past Airawat to enter the palace, where Ugrasena and the other members of the royal family were waiting for him.

Airawat continued to stare at the back of the man some said was the most feared in all of Mrityulok. All of a sudden, a premonition that something terrible was going to happen gripped him. But he couldn't explain why he felt that way. All he knew was that it concerned Jarasandha and their beloved Prince Kansa in some way.

◆

Jarasandha and Ugrasena were seated in the latter's private court where Ugrasena met his personal guests. The minister of external affairs, Prasenjit, was also present. Jarasandha had told Ugrasena that he was here only to meet Kansa as he had heard about the near fatal wounds the prince had received recently. Ugrasena quickly filled him in on what had happened. Jarasandha's face was a mask of rage as he heard about the battle on the Shiva temple hill. He calmed down only when Ugrasena assured him that Kansa was almost recovered from his injuries and would be with them soon.

There was an uncomfortable silence as they waited for Kansa to join them. Ugrasena had never got along well with the king of

Magadha. He found the violent nature of Jarasandha revolting and
he had to consciously restrain himself from showing his disgust
at how Jarasandha was treating the several kings in his captivity.
Jarasandha was not too fond of Ugrasena either and he tolerated
him only because the old king's son was married to his sisters.
However, the main reason behind his hatred for Ugrasena was
that the old king had initially rejected Jarasandha's proposal of
marrying his sister Prapti to Kansa. Jarasandha's thoughts were
involuntarily pulled back into the past...

◆

Prapti had once been a beautiful woman but she had been involved
in an unfortunate accident where the right side of her face had
been irreparably burnt. Jarasandha had used a combination of
bribery and threats with various kings in order to persuade them
to marry his sister but nothing could persuade any of them. One
look at her charred face was enough to scare away any potential
suitor. Jarasandha made it a point to attack the kingdoms of all
the kings who had rejected his sister's hand. These vanquished
kings were currently languishing in his dungeons at Magadha. Yet,
even the spectre of being defeated and imprisoned by Jarasandha
was not sufficient to sway the kings to agree to a marriage to
Prapti. Jarasandha loved Prapti and he had been at his wit's end
about what to do.

Around this time, his friend Chanur, the king of the Yavana
kingdom, suggested that Jarasandha approach Ugrasena and seek
Kansa's hand in marriage for his sister. Chanur knew Kansa well
and had a feeling that he would agree to marry Jarasandha's sister.
The king of Magadha agreed to talk to Ugrasena, even though
he wondered why the dashing young prince of Madhuvan would
consent to marry his sister when he could have the most beautiful
princess in the land of Bharat as his wife. When Jarasandha
indicated to Ugrasena that he was keen to have Prapti married
to Kansa, Ugrasena was horrified. He emphatically rejected the

proposal. However, Chanur who had accompanied Jarasandha, diplomatically suggested that Ugrasena should at least talk to Kansa about it. While Ugrasena was not keen on doing this, he knew that an outright refusal to even discuss this with Kansa might enrage Jarasandha to the point of waging a war that would result in the death of thousands of innocent men and women. He told Jarasandha that he would talk to Kansa about the proposal only on one condition.

'What is the condition?' Jarasandha growled suspiciously.

'If Kansa refuses to marry your sister, you have to promise that you will not attack Madhuvan,' Ugrasena replied firmly.

Jarasandha was about to refuse this condition when Chanur intervened. 'Jarasandha will not attack Madhuvan. I guarantee it. Let Kansa take his decision without the fear of any reprisal.'

Ugrasena did not budge. 'I respect your word Chanur, but I would like to hear Jarasandha say the same thing.'

Chanur acknowledged what Ugrasena had said with a nod, and both of them looked at Jarasandha, whose face reflected his anger at Ugrasena and his own indecision on the condition. At last, he reluctantly nodded his head in agreement, 'Let Prince Kansa decide. Whatever his decision might be, I swear that I will not attack your kingdom!'

Ugrasena sighed in relief, sure now that there was no cause for concern. He called for Kansa, his mind comfortable in the knowledge that Kansa would never agree to marry the deformed sister of this evil king. When Kansa arrived, Ugrasena calmly told him about Jarasandha's proposal of marrying Prapti to him.

Kansa listened intently to everything that Ugrasena had to say. Then he turned his attention to Jarasandha. 'Does Princess Prapti give her consent to marry me?'

Jarasandha was stunned at this question. This was the last thing he had expected Kansa to ask. However, he recovered quickly and nodded. 'Prapti would be honoured to marry you, prince...that is, if you agree to marry her.' He paused and added, 'She...uh....her

face is badly disfigured. You should know that before you decide.'
Jarasandha looked expectantly at Kansa, hoping beyond hope.

Kansa nodded, acknowledging what Jarasandha had said. 'I understand that even if I refuse to marry her, you have sworn not to attack Madhuvan. Is that correct?'

Jarasandha's face fell. He nodded curtly, regretting having made the promise. He knew Kansa would decline his proposal and his sister would once again have to face the ignominy of rejection.

Kansa continued to look into Jarasandha's eyes. Despite his anger, Jarasandha could not help being mesmerized by the young man who exuded such confidence and strength.

'Then I agree to the marriage,' Kansa said softly, his eyes not leaving Jarasandha's face for even an instant.

'W-What?' Jarasandha was shocked. He wasn't sure if he had heard Kansa correctly. Ugrasena also looked bewildered.

'I said I agree to the marriage. I would be honoured to have Princess Prapti as my wife,' Kansa's tone left no doubt about his decision.

Ugrasena could not control himself any longer. 'But son, Jarasandha has promised he will not attack Madhuvan even if you refuse his proposal. You don't need to do this.' Ugrasena's unhappiness and perplexity at Kansa's decision was evident.

Kansa smiled for the first time since he had entered the room. 'Father, my decision to marry Prapti has nothing to do with the fear of Magadha attacking us. On the contrary, if the king of Magadha had threatened to attack Madhuvan, that would have been the only reason I would have rejected this proposal.'

Jarasandha embraced Kansa. 'You have won me over today, prince. From this day on your friends will be my friends; and your enemies shall have to face my wrath before they can hope to harm you.'

Ugrasena looked on helplessly. He still couldn't fathom why Kansa had agreed to the marriage. There were a multitude of thoughts racing through his head but his reverie was broken by something that Jarasandha was saying to Kansa.

'Noble prince, you are the first man who has agreed to marry my sister Prapti, and that too, without the fear of any threats. I have another request for you. Please grant me this favour too.' Jarasandha's voice was pleading, perhaps for the first time in his life. Kansa motioned him to continue.

'I have another sister,' Jarasandha continued haltingly. 'Her name is Asti. She is Prapti's twin sister and she is as beautiful as Prapti was before her face got burnt. Both of them love each other and have been inseparable from childhood. I have always been afraid that when they marry, they will be away from each other.' He paused to take a deep breath before going on. 'Kansa, I will not find a more noble man than you in all the nations of Mrityulok. Please do me the favour of marrying both my sisters, so that they can be together and have a man like you as their husband.'

Kansa was quiet for a moment. He did not believe in polygamy, unlike several other kings and princes who had more than one wife. But neither did he want to refuse his new friend his first request. More importantly, what Jarasandha had said about the bond between the two sisters helped him make up his mind. He nodded, indicating to Jarasandha that he would marry both the sisters.

A month later, Asti and Prapti were married at Magadha with a celebration the likes of which had not been seen in any part of Bharat for a very long time.

On the day of the wedding, Ugrasena couldn't control himself from asking something that had been bothering him ever since Kansa had agreed to marry Jarasandha's sisters. 'Why did you agree to marry Prapti when Jarasandha had promised he would not attack us, even if you rejected his proposal?'

Kansa smiled, 'You remember when Jarasandha mentioned the charred face of his sister?'

Ugrasena looked confused. 'Uh yes...what about it?'

Kansa looked intently at Ugrasena, 'I tried to imagine how Prapti would have looked; but try as I might, every time her face would metamorphose into Devki's features, half-charred and marked for life.'

Ugrasena looked like he wanted to say something, but Kansa continued as if he hadn't noticed, 'And as I stared into Jarasandha's eyes, I saw myself staring at my own face in the mirror, pleading to people to marry Devki...'

Ugrasena looked at his son with unadulterated love, as a trickle of tears poured out unbidden from his eyes. 'Devki is lucky to have you as her brother.'

◆

'My brother!' Jarasandha's reverie was broken as he saw Kansa walk into the room. He rose to grip Kansa by his shoulders, as the Prince returned his embrace with equal fervour.

Ugrasena smiled in relief to see the camaraderie between his son and Jarasandha. Over the last few years, he had reconciled himself to Kansa's marriage with Asti and Prapti. In all honesty, he had realized that Jarasandha's sisters were not at all like their brother. They were both extremely warm and affectionate and had won him over completely. Most importantly, they loved Kansa with all their heart. And the deep bond between the two sisters ensured there was no discord in their marital life despite being married to the same person.

'I'm so glad you could come down, brother,' Kansa smiled. 'I was on my way to Magadha the day the incident happened.'

Ugrasena looked at Kansa in surprise. His face reflected his hurt. He hadn't known that Kansa was going to Magadha. It pained him that Kansa had become so distant from him that he had planned on going away without even meeting him.

Kansa realized what Ugrasena would be feeling and he looked apologetically at his father, his expression a strange mixture of sadness and rebellion. 'I wanted to tell you, Father, but...but there was no time,' he commented lamely.

The exchange between Kansa and Ugrasena did not escape Jarasandha's vigilant eyes. He sensed there was trouble between the two but he didn't want to probe in Ugrasena's presence. He decided he would discuss it with Kansa later. 'So how are you feeling now, my friend?' he asked Kansa, deliberately changing the subject.

'As fit as a fiddle,' Kansa smiled at his brother-in-law, glad to talk about something else.

Jarasandha looked closely at Kansa. Something seemed different about the prince. Kansa's arms looked bigger and his shoulders, too, appeared broader than he remembered them. Warriors like Jarasandha noticed every little aspect of another warrior, especially one whose prowess they respected. And Jarasandha held Kansa in great esteem as a fighter. But it wasn't just Kansa's physical characteristics that seemed altered. Even his eyes looked different. For a moment, Jarasandha wondered whether it was his imagination or he actually saw a glimmer of green in Kansa's deep brown eyes.

The latter noticed Jarasandha examining him, and for some strange reason he felt uncomfortable. He too hadn't failed to notice the changes in his physique since his recovery. It wasn't just the speed with which he recuperated that surprised him. His muscles seemed bigger to him, and he felt as if he was several times stronger and agile than he had ever been. When he had questioned the royal vaid about this, the physician had seemed visibly disturbed and had not been able to provide a satisfactory answer. In fact, though Kansa could not be sure, he thought he had detected a hint of fear in the physician's eyes as he spoke to him. However, Kansa had put aside the physician's strange behaviour, seeing how happy his family, and especially Devki, were at seeing him fully recovered.

'Why don't you come with me to Magadha now?' Jarasandha said softly, interrupting Kansa's thoughts.

'I don't know if I should, brother,' Kansa replied hesitatingly. He saw Jarasandha's hurt expression and felt it necessary to explain.

'You see, we are still not sure why those creatures from Pataal Lok attacked Devki in the first place,' Kansa said thoughtfully. 'We don't have any animosity with those people...and they...they have never before appeared in Mrityulok unless there was a good reason for their presence here.' Kansa's face was tight with concern.

Damn, Jarasandha thought to himself. He hadn't expected this. He thought quickly. 'It's quite possible these creatures were thrown out of the nether world by the asura council.' he ventured, thinking aloud.

'It's happened in the past you know!' Jarasandha continued. 'From time to time, the asura council banishes some of their creatures out of Pataal Lok for not complying with the gruesome practices prescribed by the council members. The ousted demons know they can't go to the higher world because the demi-gods in Swarglok would kill them on sight. So these wretches prefer to seek refuge in our world. They know they are stronger than most mortals and can fight their way out even if their presence is discovered. However, most of the time, these vile creatures find a place to hide and stay out of sight of the mortals. They know the laws. If they are found on Mrityulok, it will mean instant death.'

Ugrasena who had been listening quietly till now chipped in, 'More than the fear of death, it is the knowledge that if their presence becomes known openly, some king or the other may decide to launch a full-scale campaign to unearth them out of their hiding places. That would hurt them far more than a few of their kind being put to death.'

Jarasandha glanced sharply at Ugrasena. He had not known that the old king too was aware of the presence of the creatures from Pataal Lok in Mrityulok. He had thought this knowledge was known only to him, and a handful of his close associates.

Kansa stared at Jarasandha and Ugrasena, 'Are you saying there are creatures from Pataal Lok in our world? That Mrityulok is full of these repulsive demons, and most of us are not even aware of their presence?'

Ugrasena nodded quietly, 'Yes, there are a lot of these creatures in Mrityulok. Over the past few years, hundreds of them have found refuge in our world.'

Jarasandha looked closely at Ugrasena. The truth was that the number of demons in Mrityulok exceeded a few thousand by now. But for Ugrasena to put the number even in a few hundred was surprising. *How much does he know?* Jarasandha wondered.

Kansa looked thoughtful. 'So you think those three creatures that attacked Devki on the Shiva temple hill were also among those people who have been banished from Pataal Lok?'

Ugrasena nodded again, 'Yes it's possible that they also belong to the group of exiled demons. They were probably hiding somewhere on the hill, and seeing Devki there, they may have panicked and attacked her, afraid that their presence might become known if she escaped.'

'Possible...even probable,' Jarasandha said, agreeing with Ugrasena.

Kansa's face contorted in anger at the memory of the attack on his sister. 'Vile demons. They should be thrown back into Pataal Lok.' he snarled.

'All demons are not repulsive or bad, my son!' Ugrasena said, looking at Kansa with an inscrutable expression.

'I am not a demon, Father,' Kansa said with suppressed anger. 'You don't have to make me feel good by saying all this.'

Ugrasena was taken aback at Kansa's reaction. He had not thought that Kansa would take the remark personally. He had only wanted to bridge the growing distance between the two of them. But his comment seemed to have pushed Kansa farther away.

Jarasandha did not fail to notice the latest exchange between father and son. He wasn't sure what all of it meant, but he resolved to ask Kansa about it later.

'So will you come with me, brother, or should I leave alone

for Magadha?' he asked Kansa.

Kansa looked undecided. He had wanted to go to Magadha to get away from his father and the troubling nightmares he had been having over the past few days. He had thought that being away for a while might allow him to get over the reality of his childhood and possibly bring back the feeling of love for his father. After the attack on Devki, he had decided against going away, fearing another attack on her. But from what Jarasandha and Ugrasena had just shared with him, it appeared that the attack on her had not been a planned ambush, but more of a reaction on the part of the creatures to keep their presence a secret. He looked around in frustration, still unable to decide whether to go with Jarasandha or stay back at Madhuvan.

Strangely it was Ugrasena who helped him decide. He went up to Kansa and held him by his shoulders. Looking into the eyes of his son, he whispered, 'Go...go to Magadha. I know you need to be away...from things...from me. But when you come back, come back to me as the son you have always been. And remember, I have always loved you as my own.'

Before Kansa could reply, Ugrasena had turned away and left the room with a curt nod to Jarasandha. Kansa looked at his father's retreating back, torn between the love he had for his father, and the pain of rejection he felt at the knowledge of his birth.

In the end, he willed himself to be strong and turned towards Jarasandha. 'We will leave in an hour. I want to say goodbye to Devki.'

Jarasandha nodded as Kansa made his way out of the room, in search of his sister. He was dying to know what had happened between Kansa and Ugrasena. But the thought that troubled him the most was how Ugrasena knew about the presence of the banished demons from Pataal Lok in Mrityulok. Ugrasena could upset all his plans. *I have to find out how much the old king knows,* Jarasandha thought, as his face creased into a frown.

A Walk in the Past

The Dark Lord moved in his sleep. It was rare for him to lie down at all. Sleep gave way to nightmares. Sleep brought back too many memories of his past life, ones that he had tried to bury over the last two hundred years. Sleep was an enemy!

But even he had to sleep occasionally. The force of Brahman running through his system kept his senses aware of what was happening around him at all times, so that even in his sleep no one could take advantage of him. But even the powerful energy of Brahman wasn't enough to prevent his unconscious mind from walking over the footprints of his past. There were always a few recurring memories that hounded him every time he lay down to sleep; the close relationship he shared with his guru, Brahma; the betrayal he experienced when Brahma banished him to Pataal Lok for no reason, almost killing him and ravaging his soul and mutilating his face forever; and the horror he experienced when he regained consciousness to find himself in the deepest pit of hell where Brahma had unfairly banished him for eternity.

The most feared figure in Pataal Lok lay curled up like a child in his sleep, his knees pulled up towards his chest, and his arms tightly hugging his legs. His disfigured face lit up with a smile, as his unconscious mind took him back to some happy moments from his past life...

◆

'Amartya, hurry up! Today is your initiation,' his mother bellowed from outside his room. Amartya grinned to himself. Today was the day when his guru, Brahma, would pronounce him to be a deva—a demi-god. At the age of twenty-two, this was an unprecedented honour. Yet it didn't stop his mother from treating him like a child. She was banging on the door and mumbling to herself, about how late he was for the initiation ceremony. It was still the beginning of the first prahar of the day. The ceremony was scheduled for the dvitiya prahar (the second period of the day, each day being divided into six prahars of four hours each). He decided he had enough time to perform his morning prayers and meditation, even though his mother was acting like he was already late.

Amartya focused inward on his energy centre, and willed himself to concentrate his energies on achieving a meditative state. He slipped into meditation with the ease of a person who had been doing this for the past twenty years of his life, since he was two years old and Brahma had pronounced him to be an extraordinarily gifted child. Time passed quickly as he sat in meditation. At last he came out of the state of concentration and got up to leave for the ashram where Brahma awaited him.

'You are so late, Amartya!' chided his mother as he stepped out of his room. She was busy trying to get her other six children ready for the day. Amartya was the eldest of her seven sons. The younger six also went to an ashram, but theirs was the regular gurukul where all the rishi's children went for their education in philosophy and other studies. Amartya was the only one singled out by Brahma in the past several millennia to be trained and educated under his own tutelage. A lot of Amartya's peers, including his own siblings, were not too happy at the special treatment Amartya received from Brahma. Amartya had discussed this with Brahma on several occasions, but Brahma had merely said, 'You are different, my child, and hence there will always be people who envy you. But you are meant for greater things; and one day all of them will know this!' Amartya had no idea what Brahma meant and what greatness he was destined for. But he had unshakeable faith in his guru and if Brahma said something, then it must be so.

Amartya touched his mother's feet as he prepared to leave for Brahma's ashram. As she touched his head with the palm of her right hand to bless him, he heard the barely suppressed giggles of his younger siblings. Amartya looked indulgently at his six brothers. He loved them even though he knew they envied him. All six were standing in a group giggling and chattering amongst themselves— Hansa, Damana, Suvikrama, Ripurvardana, Kratha and Krodhanta. Amartya walked up to them and patted Krodhanta, the youngest of the brothers, on his head. 'What's the joke, brother?' he smiled. Krodhanta looked away nervously, while the others still giggled. Amartya cupped Krodhanta's chin in his palm and raised his brother's face to look into his eyes, 'What is it, child? Tell me,' he coaxed.

Krodhanta looked up at him, undecided whether to share the joke with Amartya. Somehow, it didn't seem as funny as it had when he had been laughing with his other brothers. But he couldn't refuse Amartya, and he was compelled to lower his eyes at the intense gaze of his eldest brother. 'W-we were jo-joking about Brahma,' he stammered. Amartya unconsciously tightened his grip around his brother's chin, and Krodhanta winced in pain. Amartya didn't seem to notice. 'What was the joke?' he asked in a tight voice. Krodhanta looked miserable. He had realized by now that the joke wasn't funny at all, but he knew Amartya wouldn't let go till he had told him everything. He pointed at two of his older siblings—Hansa and Damana—and whimpered, 'Th-they were laughing at...at Brahmaji.'

Amartya's grip on Krodhanta's chin tightened further. 'Why?' he said quietly, his fury barely controlled.

Tears of pain sprang into Krodhanta's eyes, as Amartya's grip on his face intensified. 'They said Brahmaji married his own daughter...and that he....' His sentence was cut short by a tight slap from Amartya. Krodhanta ran crying to his mother, who looked on speechless at what had happened. She knew it was a sin to make fun of your elders, especially your teachers. And for that ridicule to have been aimed at Brahma himself—that was unforgivable. If anyone got to know about it...she shuddered to think what would happen. She understood why Amartya had slapped his younger brother so uncharacteristically. He was completely devoted to Brahma and to hear anyone ridiculing his guru would have been unacceptable to him.

Amartya hadn't moved. He stood rooted to the spot. Krodhanta's words rang in his ears: 'Brahmaji married his own daughter...' The giggling of his other brothers too resounded in his mind. But above all of this, he had a premonition of something that was about to happen, something that would change his life forever. For a fleeting moment, he saw a terrible vision of Brahma's face contorted in rage. But his guru's fury wasn't directed at his brothers...it was directed at Amartya.

◆

The Dark Lord groaned in his sleep, his breathing ragged and irregular, as if the events of his past life had happened in front of his eyes, yet again. He pulled his knees tighter against his chest, as if this action would enable him to ward off the disturbing thoughts. Gradually, however, his body relaxed and his breathing returned to normal.

◆

The ashram was decorated as Amartya had never seen before in all the twenty years he had been under Brahma's tutelage. Flowers of all possible species in the universe adorned the walls and the doors. Amartya had thought only Brahma and a few senior members of the ashram would be present at his initiation ceremony, but he hadn't imagined that there would be so many people. While he couldn't count all of them, it looked like there were at least fifty devas present at the function. Indra, the overlord of the devas, was also there, talking animatedly with Brahma. And then, Amartya stopped in bewildered shock. No...it couldn't be possible. Was he dreaming? He pinched himself to check if he was truly seeing what he thought he was. It took him a second to realize that this was indeed no dream. The two greatest gods in the universe were sitting quietly near the ceremonial fire, smiling at each other, their faces aglow with the knowledge that something spectacular was about to happen. Amartya felt his mouth go dry with excitement. This was the first time in his life he was seeing Shiva and Vishnu in their physical form. And it was perhaps the first time most of the devas present would have seen the three supreme gods at one place. The mightiest gods in the universe—Shiva, Vishnu and Brahma—all three present at his initiation ceremony.

Amartya hoped he hadn't done anything he was not supposed to. It was true that a ceremony to initiate someone as a deva (demi-god) happened rarely, perhaps once in a few hundred years. But did even such a ceremony warrant the presence of Shiva and Vishnu? Amartya was terribly confused. He stood in one corner of the sprawling ashram compound, unable to decide what to do, and whether to approach Brahma while he was still talking to Indra, or to wait for his guru to call for him. Also, he wasn't sure whether he was supposed to go to Shiva and Vishnu to seek their blessings or should he let Brahma escort him to them. 'There are so many protocols involved, and I am totally inexperienced in all this,' he thought to himself. In that instant, Brahma saw him and beckoned him with a broad smile. Amartya walked tentatively towards his guru, hoping fervently that he wouldn't make a blunder. As he came closer, he saw the powerfully built form of Indra, who stood a foot taller than Brahma and his body rippled with muscles. He was easily the largest person Amartya had ever seen. It never occurred to him that he himself was considerably bigger in size than even Indra.

'So this is Amartya!' Indra boomed in an affable tone. He appraised the young disciple of Brahma and admired the powerful build of the youth. But what struck Indra the most about Amartya was his face. He had never seen anyone so good-looking and innocent. Not even the Gandharvas, who were supposed to be the most beautiful creatures in the universe, looked half as handsome as Brahma's pupil. For a moment, Indra was envious of the youth, but he quickly controlled himself. His vanity had got the better of him on several occasions and he didn't want to make a fool of himself in front of the three supreme gods. 'You truly deserve to be a deva,' he said softly to Amartya. Amartya blushed, uncomfortable with the compliment. He had never gotten used to praise in the ashram. Brahma read Indra's mind and smiled, 'His looks don't do him justice, Indra. His heart is pure and his potential limitless. That is the only reason he deserves to be a deva...and more.'

Indra blinked in surprise. What did Brahma mean by 'more'? What could be more than a deva? Amartya too was surprised at Brahma's words but he remained quiet.

'Come...come, my lad,' Brahma held Amartya by his shoulders, and nudged him in the direction of the ceremonial fire. 'Today, you will meet the two greatest gods in the universe. They have been my teachers, and they shall teach you something too.' Amartya looked nervously at Brahma. Meeting Shiva and Vishnu was one thing. But learning from them, that was an entirely different matter. What if he proved to be a poor student? He couldn't bear to embarrass Brahma in front of the other two supreme gods. Brahma sensed his anxiety, and looked kindly at him, 'Don't worry, you will do fine,' he whispered.

Amartya bent to touch the feet of Shiva and Vishnu. The mere contact with their body was electrifying; the powerful force of Brahman coursing through their bodies was far more palpable than anything he had ever experienced earlier. He felt his fingers tingling even after the contact ceased. Both Shiva and Vishnu looked like mirror images of each other. For some reason, Amartya felt they completed each other. Both of them smiled and blessed him at the same time. 'Sit down, son,' Brahma instructed him.

Amartya waited for his guru to take a seat around the fire before sitting down himself. There were four mats placed around the fire, one on each side. Three of the mats were taken by the supreme gods. Amartya sat on the fourth mat. As if on cue, the multitude of conversations around them came to a halt. All eyes were fixed on the quartet sitting around the ceremonial fire.

Shiva and Vishnu glanced at Brahma, who nodded in understanding. He looked at Amartya and spoke in a soft, low tone. Such was the silence in the ashram that even his hushed tones carried to all those present for the ceremony. The only other sound audible was the crackling of the fire in the ceremonial pit. 'Amartya, you have been my student for the past twenty years, and during this time I have taught you all that was taught to me by Shiva and Vishnu,' he said, and paused, trying to decide whether to say what was in his mind, or just carry on. Finally, he decided to share his thoughts, 'It took you twenty years to learn all that Shiva and Vishnu taught me over a hundred years of my education with them. I don't know whether you are a better student or I was a better teacher.'

He paused as Shiva and Vishnu chortled in good humour. 'Obviously, you were a better student as I can't have been a better teacher than Shiva and Vishnu.' Brahma said with a deferential nod in the direction of the other two supreme gods. Shiva and Vishnu accepted the compliment and Brahma's humility with a polite shake of their heads. Amartya listened intently. All the praise was a new experience for him as Brahma had never bothered with compliments during his education.

'Today is your initiation ceremony...the day you were to be pronounced a deva,' Brahma continued in the same soft voice. Amartya straightened his back and tried to look suitably attentive as he felt the time of his initiation was near. He didn't want any of the gods feeling he wasn't paying attention.

'However, I regret to inform you that we cannot initiate you as a deva today,' Brahma said gravely. 'And both Shiva and Vishnu are agreed that my decision is correct.'

There was silence in the ashram at Brahma's words and Amartya felt his spirit crumple as he heard the ring of finality in Brahma's voice. He tried to recall what he had done to offend his guru...what he had possibly done to embarrass Brahma in front of the other gods. He looked up to see Brahma staring intently at him, and summoned his strength and bowed to Brahma before speaking, 'I apologize for letting you down, Gurudev. I am sorry that I couldn't honour you by being successful in my education. And I beg the forgiveness of the lords Shiva and Vishnu for disappointing them too.' He folded his hands in apology to all the three gods sitting around the fire. 'If you could grant me one more chance I would like to study harder and make you proud of me.'

Shiva and Vishnu exchanged glances. They looked at Brahma and both spoke at the same time. 'Our decision was right, it seems. He shouldn't be a deva, after all!'

Amartya willed himself to show a brave face. He had let down his guru, but he would make up for it if this were the last thing he ever did. His thoughts were interrupted by Brahma speaking.

'My son, we cannot make you a deva today,' he paused, 'Because we find that your potential exceeds that of a deva.'

Amartya gasped. More than a deva? What did Brahma mean?

'In the name of the Trinity, I ordain you, Amartya, to the order of a brahmarishi.' Brahma ended his sentence with a tilak on Amartya's forehead.

There was a collective gasp amongst the audience. Indra's face was pale. The other present devas looked bewildered too. Only Shiva and Vishnu appeared undisturbed.

'B-but, Gurudev, I am not worthy of this honour!' Amartya stammered. 'Why do you say that, Amartya?' It was Shiva who posed the question.

Amartya bowed before replying to the formidable personage, 'My Lord, a person becomes a maharishi after thousands of years of penance and meditation. And then if they are truly able to understand the meaning of life and all the mysteries of creation, they may be considered to attain the order of a brahmarishi.' Amartya dropped his voice a notch before continuing, 'My Lord, I am eternally grateful to all of you for this great honour, but I do not believe myself to be ready for such merit, yet.'

This time it was Vishnu who interjected. 'Amartya, do you believe that merit comes only with time?'

Amartya shook his head, 'No, My Lord, it is earned through one's actions and by the power of one's beliefs.'

'Exactly!' Vishnu exclaimed. 'Brahma learned from Shiva and me in a hundred years, what most brahmarishis take a few thousand years to understand. And you learned the same from Brahma in a mere twenty years! Does that not tell you anything?'

Amartya was silent, not geared to comprehend the greatness that the supreme gods wanted to bestow on him.

Shiva took up from where Vishnu had left, 'Learning is learning. It doesn't matter whether you become proficient in something in a thousand years or whether you gain competence in it in a mere twenty years.'

Amartya opened his mouth to say something, but Shiva stopped him, 'The very fact that you have learnt all there is to learn about life, death, karma and dharma in so short a time shows how different you are. It's nice to be humble, but don't confuse humility with self-doubt. It doesn't become you, Amartya.'

Brahma looked fondly at his student, aware that he would need a logical explanation more than anything else, at this stage. 'Amartya, when a person tries to learn on his own, he takes a long time; his learning follows a trial-and-error process. Learning under a guru can cut short the training period manifold. Most of the people who have become maharishis and brahmarishis have taken thousands of years to perfect their learning because they did it on their own. You took twenty years because every moment of those years, I was holding your hand and teaching you personally. Each day that you spent with me was equal to a hundred years of learning you would have managed on your own. Still...' Brahma paused before continuing, 'The fact that you picked up all the knowledge in a mere twenty years shows the extent of your potential. I, too, was taught personally by Shiva and Vishnu; yet I took a hundred years to learn all you did in twenty. That makes you very special and very different, my child.'

Amartya was silent for a moment. Part of what Brahma and the other two supreme gods had said made sense. But he knew he had to clear his doubts now, rather than later. The responsibility of being a brahmarishi was no mean task, and he had to be certain that he was up to it. He took in a deep breath and looked at the three supreme gods, sitting around the ceremonial fire. 'My Lords, Gurudev...in all the education I have received from Gurudev Brahma, I have heard about the spectacular feats of brahmarishi Vashishta and brahmarishi Vishwamitra. I understand now that I have learnt in a short while what others may have taken a much longer time to accomplish. But am I still ready for this? Brahmarishi Vashishta and brahmarishi Vishwamitra are capable of feats which even the devas find impossible to do. There is no weapon—human or celestial—that can destroy them. There is no magic in the universe that can charm them. They can lift mountains and alter the forces of nature with just the power of their thoughts...' Amartya paused mid-sentence as he saw the three supreme gods looking at him with broad smiles.

Brahma was the first to speak, 'You are right, Amartya. A brahmarishi can do all the things you just spoke about. And great brahmarishis like Vashishta and Vishwamitra can do even more because they are amongst the seven most powerful brahmarishis in the universe today. That is why they are called the Saptarishis.'

Amartya nodded. He knew about the Saptarishis, the seven most powerful and evolved brahmarishis who carried the responsibility of helping Brahma re-create the universe after every cycle of destruction. But Brahma still hadn't answered how he could do all the feats that the other bramarishis were capable of.

Brahma read Amartya's mind. 'Amartya, before the end of the dvitya prahar, this day, you will be endowed with all the powers that great Saptarishi brahmarishis like Vashishta and Vishwamitra possess. There will be no feat they can perform that you too will not be able to do. But in order for that to happen, we have to first imbue you with the powers of Bal and Atibal, which are necessary for you to harness the universal force of Brahman.'

Everyone's attention was suddenly drawn to Indra, as he let out a loud gasp. The lord of the devas was staring at Amartya with an expression that was inscrutable. But, the flaring of his nostrils and the ragged breath escaping unconsciously from his mouth clearly indicated that he was deeply upset at the initiation of Amartya as a brahmarishi. He had had his reservations when Brahma had invited him to witness Amartya's initiation as a deva and he had shared as much with Brahma. The lad was too young. But Brahma had sung paeans in favour of his disciple and Indra had given in. After all, as a deva, Amartya would have been subservient to him. But this...this was intolerable! How could Brahma exalt this youth to the order of a brahmarishi, when even he—Indra—had not yet been considered ready for such an honour? Would he now have to bow before this upstart? This was not acceptable! Even if Shiva and Vishnu had been blinded by Brahma's praise of his pupil, Indra would not be fooled by this.

'Is there a problem, Indra?' Brahma's voice was dangerously soft. Indra knew his behaviour was upsetting Brahma, and perhaps the other two supreme gods too. But he was in no mood to stay back to witness Amartya's initiation any longer.

'Something bothering you Indra?' Brahma asked again, this time not as softly. 'I...uh...I need to return to Indralok, My Lord,' Indra replied evasively.

Brahma raised his brows at the lord of the devas, 'What can be so urgent that you can't stay back for my disciple's initiation?'

Indra did not fail to notice the stress Brahma had put on

'my disciple', but he was too far gone to back track. 'I have something pressing to attend to, My Lord...something that requires my presence there.'

Indra turned towards Amartya, making a herculean effort to mask his outrage at the youth. 'But I wish you all the best, Brahmarishi Amartya. May you be the light that shines on all of us in the near future!'

Amartya couldn't help noting the emphasis Indra put on 'Brahmarishi' while addressing him. But his innocent mind supposed this was part of Indra's genuine feeling of happiness for the honour bestowed on him. He bowed towards Indra, even as Indra bowed to him and the other gods present, before leaving the ashram.

Brahma looked at Indra's departing figure. He shook his head and returned to sit down at the ceremonial fire. Shiva looked kindly at Brahma. 'Indra still needs to learn temperance, Brahma. Forget it. He will get over this as he has got over other issues in the past.'

Vishnu's face was a mask of hidden feelings. He disagreed with Shiva's assessment. He knew Indra wouldn't get over this particular issue that easily. For all of Indra's greatness, his vanity would not allow him to accept Amartya's elevation to a brahmarishi. But Vishnu decided to keep his reservations to himself. He didn't want to create any more discord during the event than had already happened owing to Indra's unexpected behaviour.

Brahma motioned to the devas present, as also the senior members of the ashram, to sit down in a circle around the ceremonial fire. Dusk was approaching and the initiation ceremony had to be completed before it was dark. Then he looked at Amartya who had been somewhat pensive in the wake of Indra's hasty departure. 'Amartya, your initiation as a brahmarishi will follow a three-part process.'

Amartya listened attentively. He may have been on the verge of becoming a brahmarishi—the most powerful order of people, just below the three supreme gods—but in his mind he still considered himself to be a student of Brahma.

Brahma was saying, 'Firstly, you will purify yourself with a dip in the holy waters of the river behind the ashram compound. As part of the purification process, you will perform the Acamana ritual. This, you will do alone while we wait for you to come back here. Once you return, Shiva and Vishnu will convey to you the two most potent mantras in the universe—Bal and Atibal. This will be part of your final formal education before you become a brahmarishi. After that, I will bind my mind to yours,' and share with you the secret of harnessing the universal force of Brahman.'

Amartya bowed to the three gods, who would together complete the formal education he had embarked on twenty years earlier. It was time for his purification.

Amartya doffed his angavastram and laid it neatly on the bank of the river. The water was ice cold but years of training his mind enabled him to wade into it, without any visible discomfort. When he was waist deep in the water, he stopped. In order to perform the acamana, he kneeled down till he felt his right knee touch the river bed. His left foot was kept flat and along with his right knee helped him maintain his balance. He filled the acamana-patra with water from the river, and cleaned both his hands by sprinkling them with water from the patra. Then holding the acamana spoon in his left hand, he poured a few drops of water into the right palm. While focusing his gaze on the water, he chanted the mantras of the sandhyavandana, the evening worship; simultaneously sipping water from the Brahma-tirtha (base of the right thumb). At the end of the acamana, he put both palms of his hands together in front of his heart, and chanted the final mantra:

> Aum tad visnoh paramam padam
> sada pasyanti surayah
> diviva caksur atatam tad

vipraso vipanyavo
jagrvamsah samindhate
visnor yat paramam padam

The entire Acamana process took the better part of an hour and by the time he was done, dusk was approaching. He waded out of the water, his mind and body, both feeling completely purged. He wore his angavastram and moved in the direction of the ashram, where everyone was waiting for him to return.

Brahma nodded in satisfaction as Amartya joined them around the ceremonial fire. 'It is time to convey the two mantras of Bal and Atibal to you now,' Brahma said, his excitement as great as if he were going through the process himself. He remembered how he had felt when Shiva and Vishnu had conveyed the potent mantras to him thousands of millennia ago. He thought he observed the same symptoms of anticipation and excitement on Amartya's face.

Shiva and Vishnu edged closer to the fire, as they were the ones who would lead this part of the initiation.

'Release your mind of all thoughts,' Shiva instructed.

'Focus your energy at the base of the fire,' Vishnu joined in.

Amartya did as he was instructed, his face aglow in the reflected light of the blazing fire. Brahma poured ghee in the pit to keep the fire burning with intensity.

'Observe my actions and perform the same body and hand movements that you see me doing,' Shiva guided Amartya. The two types of gestures were instrumental in the success of conveying the twin mantras. The body gestures were called the 'anga nyaasa' and the hand gestures the 'kara nyaasa'. In all there were six gestures and all six had to be executed while uttering the seed letters, called bijaksharas. The six bijaksharas accompanying each of the six gestures were klaam, kleem, kloom, klaim, klaum and klah.

'Repeat after me,' Shiva commanded as he started chanting the first part of the twin mantras.

Klaamityaadi shadanga nyaasah; Klaam angushTaabhyaan namah;
kleemtarjaneebhyaan namah; kloom madhyamaabhyaan namah;
klaimanaamikaabhyaan namah; klaum kanishTakaabhyaan namah;
klaah karatalakara prushTaabhyaan namah;Klaam hridayaaya
namah; kleem shirase svaahaa; kloom shikhaayai vashaT;
klaimkavachaaya Hum; klaum netra trayaaya vaushaT; klaah,
astraaya phat; Bhoorbhoovassuvaromiti digbandhah

'Now focus on the following thoughts and repeat after me,' Shiva's
voice was steady as he inducted Amartya.

Amrita karatalaardrau sarva sanjeevanaadhyaa avagha
harana sudkshau Vedasaare mayookhay, pranava maya
vikaarau, Bhaaskaraakaara dehau, satatamanubhaveham, tau
balaatibaleshau Om Hreem, maha deyvee, hreem mahabalay;
Kleem chaturvidha purushaarthe siddhi praday; Tatsavitur
varadaatmikay; Hreem varenyam Bhargo devasya varadaatmikay;
Ati baley sarva dayaamoortay Bale; sarva kshud bhrama
upanaashinee; dheemahi, dheeyo yonah jaateprachuryaa;
Prachodayaatmikey,
pranava Shirasaatmikay, Hum phat Svaahaa

Amartya felt his body and mind respond to the intonation of
the powerful mantras. A strange vitality filled up his being. A
power such as he had never felt or imagined before this day,
suffused his senses and he felt his chest would burst, with the
twin forces of Bal and Atibal beginning to dwell within him.
He controlled the feeling of panic gripping him as he felt his
entire being expanding with the power seeping inside him. It
took all his will to continue staring at the blazing fire and not
get distracted by the strange sensations. Suddenly he sensed that
Shiva had stopped chanting the mantras, and the steady voice of
Vishnu had taken over the final part of the process of conveying
the two potent mantras to him.

'Amartya, repeat after me, and feel the force of Bal and Atibal enveloping you all over,' Vishnu murmured gently, the soft tones of his whispers sounding eerily loud to Amartya in his current trance-like state.

Evam vidvaan kruta krutyobhavati, Saavitryaa Eva saalokataam jaayatee,ityupanishad Shanti paath:Om aapyaayantu mama angaani vaak praanashchakshuhu, shrotramatho,balamindriyaani cha sarvaani, sarvam Brahmaupanishadam, maaham Brahmaniraakuryaam, maa maa Brahma niraakarot-a-niraakarana mastu,a- niraakarana may astu. Tadaatmaani niratay yay upanishatsu, dharmaastay mayisantu tay mayi santu, Om shanti shanti shanti...

Amartya repeated the final three words of the mantra—shanti... shanti...shanti. (Peace! Peace! Peace!) The feeling of panic that had gripped him earlier was replaced with a sense of tranquillity. He flexed his muscles unconsciously. They didn't feel too different. His chest, which had seemed like it would burst during the chanting of the mantras, also felt the same now. In fact, he didn't feel any different apart from the feeling of serenity that enveloped him. It was then that he noticed his skin; it looked like it was shimmering with a bluish tinge. It was fascinating to behold. However, before he could dwell further on it, he was jolted back to reality by the voice of Brahma.

'Amartya, you are now imbued with the power of Bal and Atibal. From this moment on, you are no longer a mortal. You have all the powers of a deva and there is no feat of strength and valour that will any longer be impossible for you to perform. But in order to be a brahmarishi, you must now learn how to harness the universal force of Brahman. With Shiva and Vishnu's permission, I will now teach you how to do this.'

Shiva and Vishnu nodded their assent for Brahma to start the ultimate part of Amartya's induction as a brahmarishi. And

Brahma began the fantastic process that would change Amartya forever, making him amongst the foremost rishis of all time—a brahmarishi!

'Feel the force of Brahman around you, Amartya,' Brahma murmured softly. 'Brahman is everywhere....it is Brahman that makes the sun shine and give life to the mortals. It is Brahman that nourishes every living being in the universe, and Brahman that makes the water flow in the rivers and the air in the environment around you. Brahman is infinite...it carries within it the secrets of the past, present and the future. There is nothing in the universe that has ever happened, or will ever happen, that is a secret. All of it is contained within Brahman itself. Brahman is an advanced state of consciousness. When you are one with Brahman, you will be able to feel everything around you as you have never felt before; and be one with the infiniteness of existence. Since Brahman is infinite, when you control the force of its energy within your body, you will not grow old or sick or frail. You will continue to exist forever.

Brahma paused, seeking the mind of Amartya through his cosmic vision. He was astounded to see how receptive Amartya was to the understanding of Brahman. It was as if Amartya had left himself completely open to the desire for knowledge; to be one with the infiniteness of existence. That was the core of Brahman, and it was exceedingly strong in Amartya. Satisfied that Amartya was now completely geared to receive the secret of harnessing the force of Brahman, Brahma focused on the innermost root of his own consciousness and released at once the entire knowledge of Brahman from his mind into Amartya's consciousness. There was a sound like the clap of thunder as the knowledge of Brahman travelled from the guru to the disciple. A blinding spectrum of blue light enveloped Amartya, appearing to the devas present, as though it would consume the young man with its intensity. The scorching blue light raged around Amartya for a few seconds, till not even the outline of his body was visible, and then when it seemed that the young man had vanished, the blue light dimmed and entered his being through every possible pore in his body. Amartya the man was gone forever. In his place was the formidable and awe-inspiring aura of Brahmarishi Amartya.

'Open your eyes, Brahmarishi Amartya.' Amartya opened his eyes to see his former guru talking to him. It took him an instant to realize that Brahma's lips were not moving. Yet he could hear him.

'Yes, this is cosmic telepathy,' Brahma smiled. 'You will take a while to get used to your new abilities, Brahmarishi Amartya, but it will happen soon.'

'So how do you feel now Brahmarishi Amartya?' Brahma smiled as he continued to communicate with him through cosmic telepathy.

'I...I feel the same, Gurudev. I mean my mind feels more peaceful than it ever has and there are a lot of strange sensations I am experiencing right now, including hearing your voice in my head, without you speaking...but apart from all of that, I feel the same at a physical level,' Amartya looked embarrassed as if by feeling no different he was perhaps letting down Brahma and the other two Supreme Beings.

Vishnu laughed. 'Amartya, do you know that as of this moment, you are equal in strength and ability to Vashishtha and Vishwamitra—the two greatest brahmarishis of all time?'

Amartya was bewildered. He found Vishnu's words incredulous. Vishnu divined his thoughts. He was quick to make up his mind. He looked around the assembled devas, and his eye found the person he was looking for.

'Agni,' he called out to the deva standing at the far edge of the ashram compound.

Amartya looked at the deva Vishnu was addressing. Agni was considered amongst the most powerful devas in Indralok; almost on par with Indra. He had an athletic body that sparkled with the brilliance of a raging fire. Amartya knew Agni was one of the most accomplished destroyers of enemies in Indralok, and Indra used his services mainly when dealing with the most potent asuras. Very few people knew that Agni was Indra's twin brother, and those who were aware of this, also knew that Agni was possibly as powerful as Indra himself. He wondered why Vishnu had called for Agni, specifically at this moment. He received his answer in the next instant and it shook him to the core.

'Agni, I want you to attack Brahmarishi Amartya with your most powerful weapon, the Agneyastra,' Vishnu commanded.

Agni stood dumbfounded. Vishnu was asking him to attack a brahmarishi. Not only was this against the law but it could also be fatal for Agni. After all, brahmarishis were the most powerful beings after the three supreme gods.

Vishnu guessed Agni's dilemma. He sought to comfort him. 'Don't worry. I will not let anything happen to you,' he told Agni reassuringly.

Amartya watched speechless. He couldn't believe that Vishnu had just asked Agni to use the deadly Agneyastra on him. But what shocked him more was that Vishnu was speaking of protecting Agni rather than bothering about him. He looked at Brahma for guidance, who merely smiled and said, 'No matter what Agni throws at you, don't panic. Just focus on your inner core and weave the protective shield of Brahman energy around you.'

Meanwhile, Agni got ready to hurl the terrible Agneyastra at Amartya. The weapon appeared as though by magic in the hands of Agni, and to Amartya's amazement, the weapon started to grow in size. In a brief time, the Agneyastra had attained the size of a large spear, but it was at least three times thicker. A spark of fire emanated from the head of the Agneyastra. Amartya noticed Agni's lips moving softly as he chanted the mantras necessary to launch the deadly weapon. As if on cue, Amartya focused his mind on his inner consciousness and connected with the force of Brahman now dwelling inside him. Immediately, he felt an overpowering sense of calm as the Brahman energy enveloped him from all sides. He saw Agni hurling the Agneyastra towards him, and as the weapon heaved through the air, it gained intensity and all that was visible was a flaming ball of fire flying at great speed towards Amartya. Amartya forced his mind to stay focused on the shield of Brahman energy around him. He knew the Agneyastra contained fire of such intensity that it could not be extinguished by any means known to mortals, or even to devas. The flaming weapon hit Amartya just beneath his neck. Amartya braced for the impact, but there was none. The Agneyastra shattered into a thousand pieces at the same moment that it made contact with Amartya's body. The ball of fire was reduced to a few dim embers struggling to stay alive. Agni stared open-mouthed at the summary dismissal and destruction of his most powerful weapon. Then he bowed to Brahmarishi Amartya to show his respect.

Vishnu, meanwhile, was engaged in an animated discussion with Shiva and Brahma, both of whom were shaking their heads forcefully. It appeared there was a disagreement of sorts between the three supreme gods. Finally, Shiva and Brahma seemed to relent and Vishnu came forward.

'Devas!' Vishnu summoned the entire assemblage of demi-gods. All the devas present looked at Vishnu with some amount of trepidation. None of them wanted to face Brahmarishi Amartya after what they had just witnessed. Every deva present was praying fervently that Vishnu wouldn't pick them up against the newly inducted brahmarishi. However, Vishnu's next command left all of them shocked to the core. The difference was—they were not worried about themselves any more. They were seriously concerned for Brahmarishi Amartya's well being. They listened carefully as Vishnu repeated what he had just said; on the off chance that they had not heard him right.

'As I said, I want all of you to attack Brahmarishi Amartya... at the same time....from all sides.' Vishnu said, emphasizing each word. His eyes sought out the most powerful demi-gods from the group—Varun, Bhoomi Devi, Vayu, Surya, and Agni, who was standing some distance away from the rest of the devas. He motioned to the five of them to surround Amartya on all sides. The rest of the devas covered the space between these five potent demi-gods. In its completed form, the structure was made up of fifty devas circled all around Amartya, who stood in the centre of the ring.

Vishnu continued with his instructions in a calm voice. 'Use your most powerful weapons. Give him no quarter, and don't hold back. Attack the brahmarishi as if you were facing your most powerful adversary.

Agni glanced at Varun and Surya. He knew that alone, he had not been able to make any impact on Amartya. But this was insane! There was no brahmarishi in the universe, with the exception of Vashishta and Vishwamitra, who could withstand the combined might of so many devas, at one go. They might actually end up killing the young brahmarishi, thought Agni with alarm. Varun and Surya's faces mirrored his apprehension. Bhoomi Devi and Vayu had expressions that reflected the same thought—if they did what Vishnu had just commanded them to do, this could well mean the death of Amartya. And their hands would forever be stained with the blood of a brahmarishi. There would be no corner in the universe where they would find absolution after such a deed. But to refuse Vishnu's command would mean disrespecting one of the two most powerful gods in the universe. They were caught between a rock and a hard place.

Amartya looked around him and let his consciousness focus on each deva. The Brahman energy coursing through his body felt strangely familiar by now. It was as if he had been controlling this force forever. He felt his body and mind in total synchrony with the universal force. Amartya closed his eyes in order to better concentrate and realized with a jolt that even with his eyes closed he could sense the presence of each deva. He was able to feel their mind and read their thoughts as if they were an open book. He sensed their dilemma and their fear of hurting him.

And in that moment, he knew that there was nothing that they could throw at him that he couldn't handle. It wasn't arrogance; it was just the certainty of knowing that anything that they used against him came from the universe and by controlling the force of Brahman energy, he could control their weapons too. He smiled unconsciously, as he read Vishnu's mind and he knew that he had passed the test even before the test had happened. Vishnu knew it. Shiva knew it. In all probability, Brahma knew it too or he wouldn't have been standing silently while fifty of the toughest devas got together to attack him. He locked his mind with that of the three gods and read the same thought in each of their mind—'Brahmarishi Amartya has understood the secret of controlling Brahman energy.'

Amartya got ready. He knew the attack would begin any time now, and it did. Even though all the devas started the offensive at the same time, the extent of Amartya's concentration was so high that he was able to separate what each deva was planning as if their actions were happening in sequence and not simultaneously. He saw Varun release two deadly weapons. His right hand let loose a torrent of water with the force of a tsunami aimed directly at Amartya's chest. His left hand simultaneously heaved a giant noose with the intention of tying Amartya in a stranglehold from which not even the devas could escape once tied. At the same time, Bhoomi Devi, the keeper of the mortal world and the controller of the forces of nature, chanted a potent mantra that created an earthquake right at the spot where Amartya was standing. Vayu the mighty god of wind, let loose a gale that was powerful enough to lift an entire army of mortals off the ground. Surya shot out heat rays from his fingers that were scorching enough to dry an entire ocean. Agni's mantras sent forth a bundle of flames targetted at Amartya's body. The other forty-five devas too aimed their weapons of destruction at the brahmarishi.

The heat and flames created by Surya and Agni merged with the torrent of water released by Varun to form a mass of boiling liquid flying in Amartya's direction. The noise of the roaring earthquake created by Bhoomi Devi drowned out all other sounds. Vayu's swirling winds darkened out everything else, including the weapons of the other devas. For a brief instant, it appeared to everyone that Amartya had disappeared in the darkness and dust created by all the weapons aimed at him.

And then the noise of the earthquake dimmed just as suddenly as it had started. And the winds of Vayu were dispelled as if they were a mere breeze instead of a raging storm. The figure of Brahmarishi Amartya became visible to everyone. His eyes were still closed and he had the same smile he had had before the attack commenced. An aura of blue Brahman energy was visible all around Amartya that acted like a shield to protect him from all the weapons hurled at him. Then everyone saw what they would never get the chance to see again in their immortal lives. The earth that had split under Amartya's feet began to grow back again, even as Bhoomi Devi tried in vain to create another earthquake. The torrents of water released by Varun metamorphosed into vapour that was absorbed in the air where it originated from in the first place. Surya's heat rays were unable to penetrate the shield of Brahman and Agni's fire balls scattered all around as embers, yet again. Varun's other weapon—the deadly noose—was flung back and tied up all the Devas in a stranglehold. And at that moment, Brahmarishi Amartya opened his eyes!

There was a hush as the devas attempted to comprehend what they had just witnessed. What Amartya had done just now would perhaps have been impossible for even veteran brahmarishis like Vashishta and Vishwamitra. He had single-handedly defeated fifty of the most powerful demi-gods in Swarglok, without even attacking them. And all of it had taken less than a minute.

The devas expressed their respect for the youngest ever brahmarishi by chanting his name in unison. 'Brahmarishi Amartya...Brahmarishi Amartya...Brahmarishi Amartya...' Amartya acknowledged the sentiments of the devas with a slight nod of his head and a broad smile. He concentrated his energy on the noose that had tied up the devas. In the next moment, the rope unravelled and fell at the feet of the demi-gods, leaving them unfettered.

At that very moment, a bolt of blue edged lightning shot out of nowhere and struck Amartya in the centre of his chest. Amartya's body was thrown backwards and he flew in the air to land several feet away from where he had been standing. Everyone looked to see where the lightning bolt had come from. They saw Brahma standing there, the index finger of his right hand, where the lightning bolt had been fired from, still pointed at Amartya. Brahma stood immobile, his face a mask of horror.

Amartya got up dazed as Brahma approached him. 'I used the Vajra Astra on you just to show the devas that you can stand up even against my weapons. You could have stopped it with the same ease as you controlled the weapons of the devas. Why didn't you shield yourself?' Brahma asked him with a mix of bewilderment and anger. 'That lightning bolt could have seriously hurt you!' he seethed.

Amartya bent down to touch the feet of his former guru. 'How can I shield myself from you, Gurudev?' he said softly. 'Everything I know today, I have learnt from you. I know you would never hurt me. The thought of needing to protect myself against you never even entered my mind.'

Brahma brought the palm of his right hand down on Amartya's head to bless him. Amartya had picked up the secrets of Brahman energy in a fraction of the time that veterans like Vashishta and Vishwamitra had done; faster even than Brahma himself. His face reflected both, pride and love for his pupil who was now a brahmarishi.

Vishnu looked at Brahma and Amartya from a distance. But his mind was not on the affectionate expression on Brahma's face as he blessed his pupil. Vishnu's entire attention was riveted on the last thing Amartya had said to Brahma—'The thought of needing to protect myself against you never even entered my mind.' And Vishnu shuddered inwardly at the implication of that sentence. He knew in that moment what even Shiva had not guessed as yet. Amartya's blind trust in his guru would one day prove fatal for him; and what was worse, it would lead to events that might even bring about the destruction of the three worlds. He only hoped his fears would prove unfounded.

Meanwhile, Brahma was speaking to Amartya. 'Brahmarishi Amartya, you have now understood the entire secret of Brahman energy. From this day on, you will feel neither thirst, nor hunger; death will not touch you, nor will any enemy be capable of attacking you, unless you yourself decide to drop your guard like you did just now with me. Even in your sleep, your consciousness shall be alert to danger, and you will be able to perceive whatever transpires anywhere in the universe through cosmic consciousness and cosmic telepathy. You will be immortal and invincible as a god.'

As the devas and the senior members of the ashram raised their voices in honour of the youngest brahmarishi in the universe, Shiva looked kindly at Amartya and spoke, 'Brahma gave you all the reasons why you deserved to be a brahmarishi, Amartya. But he failed to mention the one reason that made me decide in favour of ordaining you as one.'

Brahma's face mirrored the confusion in Amartya's eyes, as he too waited to hear what Shiva wanted to say. Shiva smiled in his usual open-hearted manner as he continued, 'For me the thing that mattered most about you was the goodness of your heart...in the millions of years that I have been around, I am yet to see a heart as pure and as uncorrupted as yours.'

Amartya looked like he wanted to say something but Shiva didn't give him a chance. 'And for this reason alone, Brahmarishi Amartya, from now on you shall be known as Amartya Kalyanesu— immortal goodness!'

◆

The Dark Lord got up with a jolt. It was as if an iron rod had seared his heart. Shiva's words—*immortal goodness*—still rang in his mind. He had always wanted to be on the side of good. He didn't remember a time when he had hurt anyone or even thought of causing harm to anyone. But that was all in a different time; a past life that even he did not have the courage to think about, at least not when he was awake. Brahma's betrayal had changed that forever.

Brahma! The one person he had respected more than his own father; trusted with his life. And yet Brahma had turned out to be so fickle that he had called him a demon and banished him from everything that he held precious. Brahma had proven by his deeds that he was not worthy to be counted amongst the three supreme gods. Yet Shiva and Vishnu had done nothing about it. But then they hadn't done anything about Indra either. And Indra was the one responsible for Brahma turning against him. Even so, Vishnu and Shiva allowed Indra to continue as the lord of the devas. There was no justice in Swarglok. Corrupt and fickle people had been left to their pursuits, without being hauled up.

If Shiva and Vishnu were not willing to do what they had to, then he would do it himself. All Amartya had thought of in the past two hundred years was of how he would bring about the downfall of Brahma and Indra. Between the two of them, they had converted the entire Swarglok into a place of rot and corruption. If a few people had to die in order for him to succeed in his plans, then it was a necessary sacrifice. A little bit of evil was justified if it resulted in greater good. Still, it disturbed him every time he had to do something wrong, even now. On all these occasions he would seek out Bhargava—the one person who had saved him from insanity when he was thrown into the deepest hell within Pataal Lok. Bhargava could always be relied on to make him feel better about what he was doing.

I have to see Bhargava, he resolved, as he got up from the bed and changed his clothes. The man who was once known as Amartya Kalyanesu, covered his head and face with a cloak and walked out of the room.

Jarasandha Unveils Part of the Plan

Jarasandha sat alone in his room. It had been a day since he had returned to Magadha with Kansa, who had shared the painful secret of his birth with him while they were enroute from Madhuvan. Jarasandha had been shocked. He wouldn't ever have guessed something like this. All these years that he had known Kansa, he had not once heard even the whisper of the prince's controversial birth. With the exception of his sisters, there was no one Jarasandha cared for more than Kansa and he was genuinely concerned for his brother-in-law. However, he couldn't help seeing an opportunity now that had been eluding him for a long time.

This may be just the break we need, he thought to himself. The rift between Ugrasena and Kansa, and the fact that Kansa now knew he was no longer bound by blood to his father, may possibly make his task a little easier. The Dark Lord would be pleased. The only element of rancour was that the success of the overall plan depended to a large extent on Kansa's involvement. And Jarasandha wanted to avoid any potential pain to his best friend that could possibly occur due to that. Jarasandha shook his head in consternation. He would take things as they came. Right now, he had to have a clear head for his meeting with Chanur and Banasura.

◆

Jarasandha stared at the two powerfully built warriors sitting on either side of him. Both Chanur and Banasura were amongst the foremost warriors in the land of Bharat. When the Dark Lord had suggested that these two could possibly be involved in their plans, Jarasandha had thought they would never be able to convince them to join their cause. Yet the Dark Lord had proved again that there was nothing that he couldn't accomplish. Chanur and Banasura had somehow been persuaded to work along with Jarasandha to give the plan its final shape. Jarasandha looked closely at both the warrior kings. The two seemed different; their faces had an uncharacteristic hard expression and both appeared as if they were in some kind of a trance. As if their actions were being controlled by some third force—something much larger and powerful than either of them. Jarasandha recognized the Dark Lord's hand behind it all. Yet even he did not know how the uncrowned master of Pataal Lok had managed to bind these two valiant warriors to do his will.

'We need to smuggle another ten thousand asuras into Mrityulok,' Jarasandha said softly. 'And there is very little time to accomplish this.'

Chanur looked expressionlessly at his old friend. He had known Jarasandha since childhood and had been the one several years ago to suggest Kansa's hand in marriage for Jarasandha's sister, Prapti. But today he felt void of any feeling for either Jarasandha or anything else. The only emotion he was capable of feeling was whatever was dictated to him by an unknown force. He didn't know what that force was, but a strange power seemed to have caught hold of his mind and he felt compelled to do anything that he was mentally instructed to do. He looked at Banasura and recognized the same vacant expression on the king of Banpur's face that he had observed on his own several times over the past few weeks. 'Why do we need to smuggle the asuras into Mrityulok?' he mouthed the words in a mechanical tone.

Jarasandha nodded thoughtfully at the question, locking his eyes with both Chanur and Banasura, at the same time. 'It's a long story. Let me start at the beginning.'

The two warrior kings stared at Jarasandha, waiting for him to start.

'In the land of Pataal Lok, there resides a powerful Being... more powerful than anyone else I know. It is whispered that his prowess equals that of the three supreme gods and even the asura philosopher, Shukra, is in awe of this formidable person. No one knows who he is or his real name. It is not even known where he came from but a couple of hundred years back his presence suddenly started to be felt in Pataal Lok and since then, every creature—pisacas, bonaras, danavas, kalakanjas—every known form of asura in Pataal Lok is in mortal fear of him. No one knows why he hates the devas and Swarglok. But I know for certain that he has sworn to destroy the land of the devas. This person—this formidable force—is known in Pataal Lok as the Dark Lord!'

Chanur and Banasura blinked as they listened to Jarasandha. Jarasandha paused for a moment, deciding how best to continue.

'You are aware that in the past the devas have taken the help of mortals to defeat the asuras. And on every occasion, Swarglok with the help of mortals from Mrityulok, has been able to defeat the asuras. This happened before the time of Lord Rama when his father, King Dasarath, helped the devas to defeat the asura forces. And later, Lord Rama himself allied the forces of Mrityulok and Swarglok to defeat Ravana, the king of asuras.'

Jarasandha paused again. What he had to say next would come as a shock to both the warrior kings. He took a deep breath and continued, 'This time around, the Dark Lord wants to reverse the past. He plans to combine the forces of Mrityulok and Pataal Lok in order to wage a war against Swarglok.'

Banasura and Chanur blanched. Even in their trance-like state, what Jarasandha had just said, staggered both of them. Banasura was the first to voice his thoughts, 'But why would Mrityulok side with the asuras against the devas?'

Chanur was quick to add, 'The kings of Mrityulok would never fight against the devas.'

Jarasandha nodded as he heard the two kings speak. He didn't know the extent of the Dark Lord's influence over their minds yet but he hoped it was enough to make these two warriors go along with the plan. Else, everything he had achieved till now would be lost.

'You are right. Most of the kings in Mrityulok would never side with the asuras in a fight against the devas. But the Dark Lord doesn't need all of them to side with him in any case. All he wants is for a few of the most powerful rulers to be on his side. Once that is done, the smaller kingdoms will be compelled to go along with them. The ones who do not agree will be executed.'

Banasura and Chanur jumped out of their seats at the same time, the trance that held them in its power temporarily broken. Both of them were outraged at what Jarasandha was suggesting. For a brief moment, Jarasandha contemplated that they might physically attack him. He flexed his muscles for a possible assault.

And then it happened! A bright light shot out of the ground, apparently out of nowhere. Chanur and Banasura were enveloped within the eerie glow that eclipsed everything else in the room. The two warriors initially appeared to fight against the ball of light surrounding them, but gradually their bodies grew limp and their efforts waned at thwarting the force that engulfed them. Their eyes once again took on the vacant expression they had had when they first entered Jarasandha's room. The Dark Lord had them back in his power.

The intense light that had surrounded Chanur and Banasura began to dim and was soon gone. The room seemed to return to its normal state. Jarasandha looked at his two powerful former friends who were now reduced to puppets in the hands of the Dark Lord, shuddering involuntarily. He waited for Chanur and Banasura to settle down. Chanur was the first to resume his seat.

Banasura looked around, his expression a mix of confusion and fear. Like Chanur, he too had been feeling for the past few weeks that a strange power appeared to have him in its hold.

But he couldn't figure out what it was. Every time he felt he had control of his senses, the invisible force would take over his mind and he would again feel powerless to do anything of his own volition. He shook his head, trying in vain to shake off the feeling of being out of control. But the action did not seem to help. He could feel and see everything as he used to, but the conscious part of his mind that dictated what he must do or should do, seemed to be dead. He felt like a zombie. He looked at Chanur, and saw the same vacant expression in the Yavana king's eyes.

Jarasandha resumed talking. 'As I was saying, the Dark Lord wants to ally the forces of Mrityulok and Pataal Lok in a fight against the devas. In order to do this, he wants to be certain that he has the support of the most powerful kingdoms of Mrityulok. I have already pledged the support of Magadha to him. He wants to know whether he can rely on the Yavana kingdom and the kingdom of Banpur.' Jarasandha looked pointedly at Chanur and Banasura as he said this.

Chanur and Banasura nodded mutely, pledging their support to Jarasandha, in favour of the Dark Lord. Jarasandha gave a satisfied smile and continued.

'The next step will be to gain the support of the other major kingdoms—Madhuvan, Bateshwar, Hastinapur, Panchaal, Bahlika, Chedi, Gandharva, Madra, Kishkindha, Saka, Salwa—all of them need to be spoken to and brought over to support the Dark Lord in his plans. If any of these kingdoms do not agree to join our plans, we will need to find other means to persuade them.'

'Kingdoms like Hastinapur and Panchaal will never agree to join this plan, Jarasandha,' Chanur said skeptically.

'Neither will Madhuvan or Bateshwar. And they are too strong to be threatened or destroyed,' Banasura muttered mechanically, under his breath.

Jarasandha smiled. He had anticipated these sentiments from the two kings. If they hadn't reacted this way, he would have felt they had lost their strategic wisdom. He decided it was time to explain the rest of the plan to them.

'Those kings who do not agree to support our plan will be dealt with in a different manner,' Jarasandha said softly.

'Differently? How?' Chanur asked bemusedly.

'It is very simple,' Jarasandha answered. 'The kingdoms we feel are agreeable to our plan of supporting Pataal Lok in the fight against the devas will be told the entire plan and will begin training their armies for the war that is inevitable. Those kingdoms that are not in line with our plan and are weak will be crushed in battle by us in the next few months. We will then take control over their land and their military.'

Jarasandha paused before continuing, 'We will, however, use a different strategy for kingdoms like Hastinapur, Panchaal, Bateshwar and the others that are not agreeable to our plans but are too large or powerful to subdue.' His eyes glittered as his two companions waited expectantly. 'If they can't be with us, they shouldn't be against us. If they are kept busy handling their internal issues, they will not get the time or opportunity to meddle with things that are happening outside their kingdom's boundaries.'

Chanur interrupted Jarasandha, 'So you mean we keep them so busy trying to resolve internal matters that their entire attention is focused on getting things right within their own land rather than focusing on what we are doing!'

Jarasandha smiled. Chanur was smart, even in a situation where his thinking abilities were under the Dark Lord's control.

'Yes Chanur. In the time that they are resolving their own matters, we would be able to assemble most of the kingdoms in Mrityulok under our banner. We will then be prepared to join our forces with Pataal Lok. By then even if there are a few kingdoms in Mrityulok that do not support us, we will be able to subdue them with the might of our combined forces.'

Banasura still had a confused expression. 'I don't understand how we are going to keep these kingdoms busy in their internal matters. Exactly what did you mean by that?'

Jarasandha flashed him a triumphant smile as if he had been waiting for this very question. 'Over the past few years, more than a hundred thousand asuras have been smuggled into our world from Pataal Lok. There are only a handful of kings who know about this, including me. Those kings who are aware of this are my vassals; their lands are ruled by my generals and they are under complete control of Magadha. Majority of the asuras have been brought in to Mrityulok through Magadha and we have allowed this to happen surreptitiously. Once these asuras enter Magadha, my confidantes ensure they are scattered around different parts of Mrityulok, so that they mingle freely amidst the people of various kingdoms. The asuras then take on any work or profession they can manage to, without too much difficulty. Here too, my confidantes and close associates help the asuras to secure jobs that do not attract too much attention. As we speak, these hundred thousand asuras have infiltrated almost every nation in Mrityulok.'

Banasura and Chanur stared at him in disbelief. 'Are there any asuras in Banpur too?' Banasura asked incredulously.

While the question had been asked by Banasura, Jarasandha knew the answer would interest Chanur too. He referred a scroll of paper that had a series of numbers and codes written on it in a certain order. His fingers traced a pattern on the paper as if searching for something. Finally, he smiled as he looked at the two warrior kings seated in front of him. 'As of today, there are three hundred and sixty-nine asuras in Banpur, and...' he turned his attention to Chanur, 'one hundred and seventy-three of them in the land of the Yavanas.'

Chanur and Banasura couldn't believe what they had heard. Their border security was thoroughly professional, very unlike the patrols within the kingdom. It was almost impossible for anyone to breach the security checks there. Yet, Jarasandha had somehow managed to smuggle in a large number of asuras into their respective countries without them being any the wiser.

Jarasandha knew what they were thinking. He decided it would help to explain. 'The numbers in your lands are actually very low. I smuggled only a few of the asuras into your kingdoms as a test. I knew if I could smuggle them into your land, I wouldn't have too much of a problem getting them into other nations in Mrityulok.'

'The other kingdoms...they have a larger penetration of asuras?' Chanur asked hesitatingly.

Jarasandha nodded, 'Yes, most of the other kingdoms would each have an average of a couple of thousand asuras inhabiting their lands currently.'

Banasura took in a sharp breath, 'What are these asuras going to do within these kingdoms?'

'Right now, nothing!' Jarasandha replied evenly. 'However, at my command, they will start wreaking havoc within each kingdom. Each of these asuras is a trained assassin, accomplished at killing. At first it will be minor offences—robberies, looting and other forms of vandalism. Gradually, the tempo will step up as they begin to commit murders of innocent people and start harassing the citizens. In some cases, they may dress up as soldiers of a neighbouring country and attack the towns of bordering nations. At other times, they may commit offences in the name of the king himself. Whatever they do, the end result will be confusion within these kingdoms, and in some cases, misguided wars between neighbouring countries.'

'And all of this will keep these kingdoms busy with either internal strife or in fighting with their neighbours,' Banasura finally nodded in understanding.

'Yes, and it gives us enough time for what we have to do.' Jarasandha smiled. 'What are the next steps?' Chanur questioned.

'We have to get a final lot of ten thousand asuras into Mrityulok, and this needs to happen over the next two months,' Jarasandha said quietly.

Chanur nodded as he began to understand the dilemma Jarasandha must be facing. 'You cannot smuggle in so many asuras from Magadha alone in such a short time, right?'

Jarasandha nodded. His respect for Chanur went up a notch higher as he realized Chanur had figured out his problem without his even mentioning it.

Chanur was thoughtful, 'So you would like to smuggle in some asuras through my land and through the country of Banpur too!' It was more of a statement than a question but Jarasandha nodded in acquiescence.

'But even if Banasura and I allow the asuras to enter through, we will still not be able to smuggle in such large numbers without making it an open secret. Therefore, you need to have the immediate support of a few more kingdoms that can help smuggle in the asuras. Am I correct, Jarasandha?'

Jarasandha smiled, 'You have got it my friend. We will need at least five to six kingdoms helping us in this effort, which will be difficult if not impossible to manage in such a short time.' He paused for effect. 'Or we can smuggle in a majority of these numbers from one country alone!'

'Madhuvan!' exclaimed Chanur as he finally understood what was in Jarasandha's mind.

Jarasandha slapped his thigh with enthusiasm. Chanur had understood the plan to perfection. 'Yes, it has to be Madhuvan!' he said excitedly. That is the only kingdom in Mrityulok whose borders spread out the most. There is no other kingdom through which we can get in such large numbers without raising suspicion.'

Banasura snorted, 'But Ugrasena will never allow the entry of asuras through his land!'

Jarasandha smiled and this time, his smile was full of meaning. 'You are right, he won't. But Kansa will!'

This time both Chanur and Banasura were so shocked that the only response they could offer was blinking their eyes in utter confusion.

'Kansa?' Banasura said in disbelief.

'Kansa would never get involved in this, Jarasandha,' Chanur said quietly, recovering quickly from the shock. 'Especially not after a bunch of asuras almost killed his sister!'

Jarasandha took a deep breath before replying. He still wasn't sure if he should be involving Kansa, but the stakes were too high now to be ambivalent. 'That's exactly why he will help,' he said softly. 'He has been told that the asuras being smuggled into Mrityulok are actually inhabitants of Pataal Lok who have been banished from the netherworld by the asura council because they were not willing to conform to the evil practices laid down by the council members.'

'So he doesn't know that these asuras are actually trained assassins who are going to create destruction in Mrityulok?' Banasura was incredulous.

Jarasandha nodded. 'No, he doesn't know that. At least not yet. When the time is right, I will tell him, but he is not ready yet for that truth.'

Chanur still looked unconvinced. 'Even if he believes that these asuras are unfortunate creatures who have been banished from their world because of no fault of their own, the fact still remains that three of these creatures tried to kill his beloved sister and almost killed him too. Knowing that, why would he support the entry of more asuras into Mrityulok?'

Jarasandha sighed. For all his inherent evil, he still wasn't comfortable with what he was doing to Kansa, and talking about it only made him feel worse. It was like admitting that he was willing to risk his best friend's happiness for his own selfish reasons. But there was no choice. The Dark Lord had offered him too high a reward for helping him in his war against the devas.

Jarasandha shook his head. He knew Chanur was waiting for an answer. 'Ugrasena unwittingly helped us in this matter. The old fool seems to know a little about the asuras being smuggled into Mrityulok. But I don't think he has any idea that they are actually trained assassins infiltrating our world with the purpose of causing death and chaos at a later date. He seems to believe the story that the asuras have been banished by their council members for not adhering to the practices set by the netherworld. He told Kansa that the Asuras who attacked Devki possibly did so because they panicked at their presence being exposed.'

Chanur shook his head, slightly irritated. 'I still don't understand why Kansa would help smuggle these people in.'

Jarasandha nodded patiently. 'From what Ugrasena told Kansa, he believes that the attack would never have taken place if the asuras had not panicked that their presence being exposed might lead to their persecution by people in Mrityulok. He feels that if the asuras in Mrityulok can be assured that no harm will come to them, they will also not resort to attacking mortals. And it will prevent any occurrence like the one that happened with Devki.'

Chanur felt a little better after hearing this. But something still bothered him. 'How much does Ugrasena really know about the asuras? And how?'

This was a question Jarasandha had been asking himself too, ever since he realized Ugrasena knew something about the asuras entering Mrityulok. But he kept his reservations to himself. 'I don't know how much he knows. Perhaps with time, we will get to figure it out. For the moment, lets focus on what we *can* do.'

Banasura looked a little unconvinced. 'What you said about Kansa sounds good. But will Ugrasena also be in favour of allowing so many asuras to come in through the borders of Madhuvan? I mean, if he believes that the asuras entering Mrityulok have been banished from Pataal Lok, wouldn't he also realize that they can't be so huge in number?'

Chanur seemed to agree with Banasura. 'That's right. Once he sees a few thousand asuras entering through his land in a short period of time, he is bound to realize something is not right. He is not a fool you know!'

Jarasandha grunted, 'We don't have to bother about Ugrasena. He won't be king for long. If everything goes as per plan, he will be deposed from the throne soon.'

Chanur gave a start. The thought that Ugrasena would no longer be king seemed incredulous to him, even in his current state. 'Who...who will depose him?' he asked haltingly.

Jarasandha smiled, his eyes like two balls of fire, 'Kansa!' He paused for effect. 'Kansa will depose the old king. I just need to work on his mind a little before that.'

Chanur and Banasura tried to absorb what Jarasandha had just told them. Their troubled thoughts were interrupted by a noise like the screeching of a banshee that raised the hair on the nape of their neck. Jarasandha recognized the sound for what it was. The Dark Lord was laughing, but it sounded more like the howl of a wild animal caged for centuries and yearning to get out. For the first time that day, Jarasandha too shivered in fear and the expression on his face mirrored the feelings of the two warrior kings sitting next to him. He knew he couldn't fail the Dark Lord.

The Plot Begins to Unravel

Vasudev sat under the gigantic banyan tree, which was the pride of the royal garden of Madhuvan. It was just under an hour that he had been waiting for Devki to appear. Most young men would have given up by now or would be fuming with anger at being kept waiting for so long by their lady love. But Vasudev was different. He had waited for several years to marry Devki and waiting an hour for her while she beautified herself didn't bother him at all. He gazed in wonder at the mammoth roots of the tree. Like most tropical trees, the banyan was a 'strangler' tree. The seeds of banyans are dispersed by fruit-eating birds. They then germinate and send down roots towards the ground, which frequently envelop part of the host tree, giving the banyan the popular name of 'strangler fig'. The 'strangling' growth habit is common in banyans as its several roots compete for light.

The banyan is so much like the kshatriya race, mused Vasudev. *A king lovingly brings up several Princes and then the heirs fight amongst themselves in order to survive and win the crown; at times not just destroying themselves but also the source of their existence.* Vasudev sighed. He had seen numerous examples where aggressive and blindly ambitious princes had destroyed everything their forefathers had built. In some unfortunate cases, a son would wantonly kill his father in order to usurp the throne. Vasudev shuddered. Patricide was the most shameful act a person could commit, and yet so many warriors did it every now and then. He was glad there was no case of pitrhanta (patricide) in his family or in Devki's clan. In fact, Kansa loved his father Ugrasena just as much as Vasudev loved his own father, Surasena.

He shook his head to shake off the depressing thought of patricide from his mind. He glanced at the overhead sun to make out the hour of the day. Dusk would be at hand in another hour. Devki would possibly take that much more time to get ready. He smiled at the thought. He loved the fact that she was always excited about meeting him, enough to take the trouble of getting dressed for him; even though he loved her in her simplest attire, devoid of any make-up.

Let me make something nice for her, he thought with the sudden enthusiasm of a child. The philosopher- warrior unhooked his scabbard and kept it gently, with the enclosed sword, on the ground. He didn't want any encumbrance as he bent down to find what he was looking for.

He searched for the freshest-looking leaves. The banyan tree leaves were large, leathery, glossy green and elliptical in shape. The leaf bud is normally covered by two large scales. However, as the leaf develops the scales fall off. The young leaves left behind have an attractive reddish tinge and are extremely soft to touch. Vasudev finally selected four large red leaves and clubbed them together to form a kind of funnel. He took out a small curved knife from his inner pocket and gently grazed it in a downward motion against the bark of the tree. A thin layer of the bark was stripped off and acted as a natural rope with which he tied the four leaves so that they would hold together like a bouquet. Then he searched for the best lilies in the garden and plucked out a dozen of the most beautiful white flowers. The stem of the lilies was dug into the surface of the banyan leaves, with just the flowers showing on top of the red leaves. In a moment, a beautiful bouquet of flowers mounted on the attractive banyan leaves was ready. Vasudev raised the gift he had prepared for Devki at eye level in order to admire his handiwork. *She will love this one,* he decided with relish, his teeth gleaming in a smug smile.

'So, the foremost warrior of Bateshwar has turned into

a gardener, I see!' The voice was loud and full of mischief. Startled, Vasudev turned around and was mortified to see Devki accompanied with her attendants, laughing uncontrollably at the sight of him holding up the flowers. His face turned deep red, and he swore under his breath. Devki was quick to notice his discomfiture.

Dismissing her attendants, she went up to him. 'My warrior prince,' she cooed lovingly. 'I always knew no one could wield a sword like you. But you never told me you had this talent too.' She smiled as she raised herself on her toes to kiss Vausdev on his lips. Vasudev was slightly taken aback. She had never displayed affection in public before this day, even though they had had their share of intimate moments in private. Vasudev returned Devki's kiss tentatively at first. And then lost in the fervour of her emotions, he allowed his own restraint to relax too. They kissed passionately for what seemed to be a lifetime, but were in fact, just few moments. Finally, Devki pulled gently away from Vasudev's tight embrace. 'Easy, my love, easy!' She smiled as she looked up into the eyes of the only man she had ever loved. 'There will be time enough for this after we are married.'

Vasudev sighed as he relaxed his hold on Devki. He loved her in a way that was difficult for anyone to comprehend. She was the one thing that made complete sense in his life. Marrying Rohini had been the most difficult decision for him, and he would not have been able to do it if Devki herself hadn't coaxed him to do it for reasons that were beyond both their control. But while he had the highest regard for Rohini, his love was entirely reserved for his childhood beloved, Devki—the woman who made his life seem complete in every way.

'I can't wait to be married, my love,' he said, his voice heavy with a strange amalgamation of desire and deep affection.

Devki giggled. 'I know you can't. All you men are the same!' Vasudev's face fell, and he gave Devki a hurt look.

'Oh, come on,' Devki was instantly repentant. 'I was only

playing with you. I can't wait to be married either. I have waited so long that it feels when the day comes, I won't know how to react.'

Vasudev impulsively took her in his arms, 'Don't worry. You will do fine. Just be yourself. I love you that way!' He kissed her lightly on her forehead.

There was a coughing sound behind them. 'Can you two lovebirds leave each other at all?' Mandki was grinning from ear to ear.

Devki glared at her friend. She rarely got any time with Vasudev, and he had come to Madhuvan for the first time after their marriage date was fixed. And here was Mandki, interrupting even those few precious moments of her time with him.

Vasudev, however, was chivalrous as always. He bowed slightly to Mandki and smiled at her. 'How's your soldier doing, Mandki? I heard he got hurt in that fight with the asuras.'

Mandki struggled to hold back her emotions as she remembered holding Airawat while he lay unconscious, his left hand cut off by one of the demons he was fighting with. And then later, when he regained consciousness in the hospital. She had looked into his eyes and sensed the sadness there.

Devki realized her normally stoic friend would break down any moment and she went up to Mandki and hugged her close. Vasudev looked kindly at her. 'He is a tough man, that soldier of yours. Losing his arm is not going to keep him down. I believe King Ugrasena has retained him as his cavalry commander. That was a sensible decision. He is still the best man in the Madhuvan army.'

'He...he said you spoke to him in the morning. Thank you. It was very kind of you,' Mandki murmured.

'You don't need to thank me,' Vasudev laughed. 'I was trying to see if I could persuade him to join the Bateshwar army as our cavalry commander. But he is too loyal to Devki's father to leave.'

Devki and Mandki both laughed at this. The clouds of sadness were momentarily dispelled and Mandki seemed to relax somewhat. Then all of a sudden, she remembered why she had come there. 'Prince, the king requests your presence in his personal chambers. He said it won't take too much time but it is urgent.'

Vasudev looked uncertainly at Devki. He didn't want to disrespect Ugrasena's request but neither did he want to put down Devki. He knew she had been looking forward to spending some private moments with him for a long time.

Devki nodded her head, 'Go,' she said. 'But come back soon. I will be waiting near the lake.' She seductively fluttered her eyelashes at him, hinting at the possibility of some more play at the end of his meeting with her father. Vasudev grinned and strode off quickly towards the palace.

◆

'But this is incredulous!' Vasudev exclaimed. What Ugrasena had just shared with him had astounded him beyond words. 'Are you sure, tatatulya?' he persisted, hoping he had perhaps misunderstood Ugrasena. The use of the term tatatulya (meaning 'like a father') was sub-conscious and it was the first time Vasudev had used it for Ugrasena.

Ugrasena looked closely at his future son-in-law. He knew he had shocked Vasudev. The prince of Bateshwar looked every bit as alarmed as he himself had been when he first got to know about the truth behind the asuras entering Mrityulok.

'I am sure!' Ugrasena replied softly. 'Narada himself told me about it.'

At the mention of Narada, Vasudev's face grew grim. He had been hoping Ugrasena's source might have made a mistake. But knowing Narada, he would have verified everything before sharing his fears with Ugrasena.

Vasudev was lost in thought. Then something struck him. 'When did Narada tell you about this?'

'Last night!' Ugrasena looked at Vasudev's astonished expression, and said evenly. 'Yes, he is still here. He appeared dressed as a traveller at the palace gate late last night. The guards were about to shoo him away but he asked for Airawat. He knows from the past that I trust Airawat completely. He had a brief chat with him after which he handed Airawat an enclosed message for me. Even Airawat didn't know it was the venerable Narada standing at the gate. After I read the message Airawat brought me, I told him who it was, and asked him to bring in Narada without letting anyone else know his identity. I had guessed by then that Narada must have some grave reason for coming in disguise.'

'I met Airawat today morning. He didn't mention this to me,' Vasudev said thoughtfully.

Ugrasena patted his hand. 'He wouldn't, Vasudev. He is bound to me and despite knowing your relationship with me, he will still not disclose confidentialities unless he is told to. That is what makes him so trustworthy.' There was a note of pride in Ugrasena's voice. He obviously had a soft corner for Airawat.

Vasudev nodded. He had shared the fact with Ugrasena not as a reaction to Airawat's behaviour but more as a matter-of-fact statement. However, his respect for Airawat went up as he realized just how loyal the man was to his king.

'Would you like to meet Maharishi Narada?' Ugrasena suggested. 'When I told him you were here he was keen to meet you before leaving.'

Vasudev's face lit up. 'Of course I would love to meet him, tatatulya.' A meeting with Narada was always refreshing as the Maharishi was known for his lack of pretentiousness and his straightforward nature.

Ugrasena nodded and went himself to escort Narada from his room. Vasudev waited in Ugrasena's personal quarters. He had only met Narada once when he was a child and the sage had come to Bateshwar to meet his father, Surasena. He remembered Narada then to have been a young rishi with a great sense of humour. It would be invigorating to meet him again, as an adult this time. Vasudev only hoped that what Narada had to say would be far less serious than what it seemed at the moment. If what Ugrasena had just shared with him was true, then there was grave danger for everyone in Mrityulok.

◆

'This is wonderful news, Mandki,' Devki shrieked in delight.

Mandki smiled a little self-consciously, but her happiness was apparent. She had not been certain how Devki would react to her news, and she was glad that her childhood friend was so obviously joyful for her.

'Does anyone else know? Has Airawat told anyone yet? When did all this happen?' Devki inundated Mandki with a volley of questions.

'Whoa, girl, take a break!' Mandki laughed, putting up the palms of her hands. 'Let me answer one question at a time,' she smiled.

'I don't have the patience for all this,' Devki interrupted her. 'Tell me everything quickly, you naughty woman,' she playfully teased Mandki.

Mandki sighed. Devki had never had the patience to wait for anything in her life; and definitely not when she was as excited as she was now. She took a deep breath, 'No one else knows yet,' she said quietly. 'I...I proposed to Airawat yesterday!'

'*What!*' Devki exclaimed disbelievingly. 'Why didn't you wait for him to propose, Mandki?'

Mandki didn't respond at first and Devki thought for a moment that perhaps she hadn't heard her question. But then she spoke, a little haltingly at first and then more purposefully as she collected her thoughts. 'In the beginning I thought I wouldn't let him know that I love him...have loved him ever since the day he got us both to Madhuvan from your father's palace. You were a child then Devki, but I was old enough to be in awe of his fine character and his selfless nature. Later, as several young men proposed to me I turned them all down, because I wanted to wait for you to get married first. I used to notice Airawat getting tense every time some young man from the palace decided to propose to me. Every time I would reject their proposal, I would observe Airawat sigh in relief. But he never once proposed on his own. I guess he was waiting for the right time to do that; perhaps after your wedding when he thought I would be open to getting married too. I had decided I would wait for him to come to me, as I knew he would one day soon. I knew he loved me too; I had seen him look at me in a particular way. I would still not have proposed to him or let him know what I had in my heart for him. But then...' And here Mandki faltered, her lips quivering with suppressed emotion.

'But then what Mandki? Then what happened?' Devki persisted.

'Then he lost his arm, Devki!' Mandki sobbed. 'And for a kshatriya warrior like him, it hit him hard. I have seen him struggle for hours in the training pit, trying to practise fighting with one arm. I have seen his frustration at not being able to balance his body weight with the sword in those complex manoeuvres these warriors use. I have felt his frustration and his rage in my heart every time he has failed in his attempts. He feels he is no longer the man he was. I realized he would never propose to me on his own because he feels he is somehow lesser now than he used to be.'

Mandki paused to regain her breath and composure. 'I couldn't let him destroy both his life and mine, Devki. I had to tell him that he is still the most wonderful man ever. And that I can't think of a life without him...' Mandki's voice faltered, overcome by the emotions she had pent up in her heart for the past few weeks.

Devki instinctively put her arms around her best friend. 'I am so happy for both of you,' She gazed into Mandki's eyes, 'Airawat is truly a rare man and he will keep you very happy. And he is the luckiest man in the world to have your love.' She hugged Mandki tight, just the way they used to hug when they were children.

'Have you fixed the date for your wedding?' Devki asked, moving away from her friend at last.

Mandki shook her head, 'No,' she said quietly. 'Both Airawat and I wanted to wait till after your marriage.'

Devki began to say something, but Mandki cut her short. 'No, Devki, I will not leave your side till you are married to Vasudev and you leave for Bateshwar with him, as his bride.'

Devki was shocked at her words. It had never occurred to her that a day could come when Mandki and she would no longer be together. But she knew Airawat would never leave her father and go to Bateshwar, and Mandki would never be truly happy without Airawat. She took a deep breath, 'I will miss you in Bateshwar, Mandki.'

Mandki smiled through a haze of tears. Their childhood was behind them. Marriage and love beckoned them. The past was gone and the future was uncertain. But both of them were loved by men who would do anything for them. If that wasn't being fortunate, then nothing else was.

◆

Vasudev looked like he had been hit by a thunderbolt. Narada had just turned his world upside down. The maharishi had told him in great detail all that he had shared with Ugrasena the night before. There was no longer any doubt in Vasudev's mind. There was grave danger to everyone in Mrityulok.

Ugrasena looked at his future son-in-law. Vasudev resembled his father, with the same cogitative look on his face whenever he was greatly perturbed. Ugrasena started to say something but Narada made a subtle gesture for him to stay quiet. Vasudev was trying to absorb whatever he had just heard and it was important that he be given some time to clear his head before they started discussing any action plan.

Finally Vasudev spoke, and his first words were addressed to Ugrasena. 'You mentioned that you have known about the asuras entering Mrityulok for quite some time now!' Ugrasena nodded his head in agreement.

'Forgive my asking you this, tatatulya...' Vasudev seemed to hesitate for a moment. 'Why didn't you put a stop to it after you got to know about this? And why didn't you share this with any of the other kingdoms? Even Father is not aware of this!' The last words carried an unspoken accusation and Vasudev squirmed as he spoke the words. He knew he was putting Ugrasena on the spot and it pained him to do so. But the gravity of the situation did not warrant any subtleties.

Ugrasena cleared his throat. He was aware of the effort it must have taken Vasudev to ask him this question, that too in front of Narada. 'About two years ago, our border security forces captured a group of five asuras while they were trying to sneak into Mrityulok through Madhuvan. They looked a lot like mortals and they might have passed undetected had one of the border security men not heard them talking. They were speaking in the asura tongue and this particular security man happened to be familiar with their dialect. When the demons were captured, they tried to bluff their way out by saying they were traders coming from Magadha. The security forces checked their passports and personal ID papers. They seemed to be fine but when the documents were subjected to rigorous checking, the papers were found to be forged. They were fantastic fakes but there was no doubt about the forgery,' Ugrasena's voice exuded pride at the commitment and alertness of his border security.

'Then what happened?' Vasudev prodded him.

'The asuras were brought to me and I met them along with General Atharva, the head of the Madhuvan Border Security Force. They broke down under interrogation and confessed that they were indeed asuras who were trying to enter Mrityulok illegally. Atharva was of the opinion that we should give immediate orders for their execution and I supported his view, even though as a principle, I am against capital punishment.' Vasudev looked like he wanted to say something here, but Ugrasena put up his hand to stop him. 'Just as I was about to sign the order for their execution, one of the asuras spoke up. He said he wanted to confess something else.'

'What more did he want to confess?' Vasudev wondered aloud.

'What he said astonished me. And I think it was his confession that put me on the wrong track in the first place.'

'Ugrasena, get on with it,' Narada said gently, but with a touch of impatience. 'You don't have to justify your decision to us. You did what you thought was right, at that time. Just tell Vasudev what happened.'

Ugrasena nodded apologetically at Narada and continued. 'The asura told us that it wasn't just the five of them who were trying to enter Mrityulok illegally. He said a few hundred of them had breached the borders of various kingdoms over the past few years.'

Vasudev was shocked. 'What! Why would he tell you all this?' he said incredulously. 'Wouldn't it give away their plans? After all, you had no idea about this till then.'

Ugrasena nodded. 'That's what I thought. But hold on. Listen to what happened next. When I asked him the reason for the asuras entering Mrityulok, he said that these people had been banished from Pataal Lok by the asura council because they had offended the council members by refusing to follow the gruesome practices prescribed by the council.'

'So they made it look like they were actually aggrieved people who had been thrown out of Pataal Lok because they didn't want to participate in evil practices?' Vasudev said contemplatively.

'Exactly!' Ugrasena exclaimed. 'And they said that once they were banished from Pataal Lok, the only option for them was to either travel to Swarglok or to enter Mrityulok. They would have been instantly spotted in Swarglok given the tight security there, and the devas would have put them to death given their zero tolerance for asuras. Therefore, the only alternative open to them was a surreptitious entry into Mrityulok through various bordering kingdoms. The asura said that all they wanted was to quietly settle down at some place in Mrityulok, and live out the rest of their miserable existence in peace. He said he had told me everything and by confessing to me he had put in danger the lives of all the asuras who had over the years settled down in Mrityulok.'

'Wow!' said Vasudev softly, marvelling at the ingenuity of the asura. 'So he told you all that in order to gain your confidence and make you feel that he trusted you completely. He knew even if he didn't tell you this, you would have considered the possibility of other asuras having entered Mrityulok, on your own in any case.'

'That's right,' Ugrasena conceded. 'I didn't realize the asura was feeding me half-truths. His confession made me believe that he was being completely honest with me. And it also lent credibility to the rest of his story about the asuras being banished from Pataal Lok by the asura council.'

'It wasn't your mistake, tatatulya,' Vasudev said quietly. 'Anyone with a heart would have believed the asura and done what you did. But what happened after that?'

'I...I conferred with General Atharva and we both decided that these asuras had already faced a lot in their homeland and we should help them settle down in Mrityulok. We let them go, with the injunction that they should find a quiet place to settle down and keep themselves out of sight of the mortals. At that time, I genuinely believed that their secret was known only to General Atharva and me, and I had given them my word that I would not divulge the secret of their presence on Mrityulok to anyone else. This is why I did not share this with anyone, including your father.'

Vasudev and Narada were quiet. They knew the king hadn't said everything that was bothering him yet.

Finally, Ugrasena exploded in a mass of rage and pain, 'I trusted these bastards. And then a bunch of asuras attacked my daughter...and...and almost killed my son. Even when that happened, I thought it must have been the work of some asuras who panicked at their presence being discovered and attacked Devki. But what Maharishi Narada told us gives everything an entirely different colour.'

There was an uncomfortable silence as Vasudev and Narada waited for Ugrasena to calm down. Then something occurred to Vasudev. 'Tatatulya, have you spoken about the asuras entering Mrityulok with anyone else?'

Ugrasena's face grew suddenly grim as he recalled the last conversation he had had with Kansa in Jarasandha's presence, just before they left for Magadha. He quickly narrated to Vasudev and Narada the entire discussion. Narada listened tight-lipped as he heard what Jarasandha had told Kansa about the asuras' presence in Mrityulok, and Vasudev whistled in astonishment.

◆

Devki looked at the sun settling down in the west. She couldn't decide whether it was the impending darkness or the eerie silence in the garden that made her feel the first symptoms of sadness and imminent danger. It had been several days since the attack on her at the Shiva temple, but she could still feel the fetid breath of the towering kalakanja on her neck, as he chased her. The thing that was making her more restless was she had a premonition that it wasn't over yet; that the worst part was yet to come. And that in some way, whatever was going to happen involved Vasudev and her, and perhaps even Kansa, the person she loved second only to Vasudev.

She shook her head. The memory of how Kansa had risked his life to save her was difficult to forget. And the images of his bloodied form lying lifeless on the ground would be impossible to take out of her mind, ever. *Kansa is so alone, so anguished after what Father told him about his birth. I wish I could make everything right for him*, she thought poignantly. *If only he would talk to Asti and Prapti, he might feel better.* Kansa had not allowed anyone, including both his wives or even Devki, to discuss how he felt after Ugrasena had told him about his birth father and his mother's feelings towards him. Devki knew the inability to voice his feelings was suffocating Kansa inside and would in time change him as a person if he didn't let people in.

She heard a twig snap under someone's feet behind her. She turned around with a smile, expecting Vasudev to have returned. But her face fell as she saw it was Mandki. Normally, she loved to spend time in the garden, alone or with Mandki. But today she had looked forward to being with Vasudev. His long absence irked her. She was peeved at her father for calling him to a meeting today of all days, and with Vasudev too, for not returning soon. But a closer look at Mandki's face made Devki forget her anger momentarily. 'What's wrong, Mandki? You don't look too good,' she said with concern.

'Something's not right, you know,' Mandki mumbled. 'I was with Airawat when a messenger from your father came in and whispered something to him. I couldn't hear what he said and Airawat obviously wouldn't tell me, but he excused himself immediately and rushed off to the king's chambers. The only thing he said was that it might be a while before he returned.'

Devki was thoughtful. 'But isn't Vasudev too with Father?'

Mandki nodded her head. 'It looks like the king wanted Airawat for the same meeting'

'Hmm. I wonder what is going on,' Devki mused. 'You know, last night I couldn't sleep for some reason. I was standing in my balcony and I happened to see the lamps on in father's room. I found this strange as he usually sleeps quite early. I strained to see what he was doing, since his room is a little farther down the hall from mine. I saw him talking to someone in his room. It was a man, but he had his back towards me. Father seemed to be reading something the man had given him. After a while, I saw him speak to the man, and the man turned to leave. You know who this man was?'

Mandki looked confused. She shook her head.

'It was Airawat,' Devki said slowly.

Mandki looked surprised, 'What was he doing in the king's room at that hour?' she wondered aloud. Devki nodded and continued. 'It isn't just what he was doing there at that hour. What happened later was more intriguing. After he left, I saw Father pacing in his room. He seemed very agitated, as if something bad had happened or he was expecting it to happen.'

Mandki looked at Devki. All of this sounded rather odd.

Devki continued, 'In a few minutes, I saw Airawat return with another man. I couldn't see this man's features as his face was covered with a cloak. It looked like he was taking pains to hide his identity. What surprised me the most was that Father bent down to touch this man's feet as soon as he entered his room. The man blessed Father and took a seat. Father drew the curtains after that and I wasn't able to see anything further. Airawat left the room after a couple of minutes. I stayed in the balcony to see if the other man would come out, but after waiting for a long time, I gave up and went to bed.'

'This is bizarre,' Mandki muttered. 'Why didn't Airawat tell me about this today?'

Devki smiled. 'He wouldn't. You know how loyal he is to my father. And since Father hasn't told me or anyone else about it, he would have obviously asked Airawat to keep silent on this.'

'Well, it would seem that your father is sharing this with Vasudev too,' Mandki said in an even tone.

Devki slapped her forehead, 'Of course!' she exclaimed. 'No wonder Vasudev is taking so long. It must be something really serious then,' she said with a worried expression on her face.

'Don't worry. At least Vasudev will tell you about it when he returns from the meeting,' Mandki said trying to cheer up her friend.

Devki snorted, 'You don't know Vasudev then. He would

never allow his love for me come in the way of his duty. And if my father tells him it is confidential, Vasudev will die before divulging any secrets, even to me.'

Mandki smiled wanly. She was already used to Airawat's penchant for keeping state secrets and she understood Vasudev was no different. 'I just hope everything is fine,' she said.

'It will be,' Devki assured her. But while she sought to comfort Mandki, she knew deep down that something was happening; something that neither she nor anyone else may have control over. She prayed fervently that her premonitions were wrong. But even as she prayed, she felt the cold finger of fear run down her spine.

◆

'Wow, so Jarasandha too knows about the asuras entering our world,' Vasudev exclaimed.

'And his story seems to match the one they gave Ugrasena when they were captured by the Madhuvan border security,' Narada said completing Vasudev's thought.

'I wonder how much Jarasandha really knows,' Ugrasena said quietly. 'Is it that he too has been fooled by the asuras or does he actually know more than whatever little he told Kansa and me?'

Narada took charge of the discussion. 'Let's not bother ourselves yet about what Jarasandha knows. I will find that out through my sources. Right now, we need to focus more on how to tackle the issue I have told you and Vasudev about.'

Vasudev sighed. He had come to Madhuvan to spend a couple of days in peace with Devki. It didn't look like he would get any time with her now. What Narada had shared with Ugrasena last night, and with him now, required immediate attention.

There was a knock on the door, and Airawat entered the room. Vasudev glanced at Ugrasena, who nodded, 'I had sent for Airawat. I think you are going to need his help.'

Vasudev smiled. It would be interesting to have Airawat by his side. He genuinely liked the quiet man. He knew there was a ton of substance behind the calm exterior.

As Ugrasena motioned for Airawat to take a seat, Narada spoke. 'Vasudev, why don't you share with Airawat what I have told you and Ugrasena.'

Vasudev hesitated. Protocol suggested that the king of Madhuvan should share the plan with Airawat, since he was a soldier of Madhuvan.

Ugrasena realized Vasudev's dilemma, and tried to make him comfortable, 'Vasudev, you have to lead the action on this one. It's best that you are the one to share the plan with Airawat.'

Airawat maintained a poker face as he waited for Vasudev to tell him what was going on. He had known since last night that something was amiss. But he hadn't wanted to question his king till he was told what to do. The soldier in him, however, was ready for anything that spelled trouble for his motherland.

Vasudev started in a low voice that gained strength as he continued. He told Airawat about the asuras entering Mrityulok and how Ugrasena and Atharva had let the ones they had captured go free. Airawat raised his eyebrows only once at that, but almost immediately controlled his reaction at the mention of his king's kindness towards the captured asuras.

Vasudev paused for a moment. He had told Airawat everything. Except what Narada had shared with Ugrasena and him. He wanted to ask for Airawat's thoughts on whatever he had been told till now before he went any further. 'Any questions so far Airawat?' he asked.

Airawat shook his head. The warrior in him told him the main part of the story was yet to come.

Vasudev persisted. 'I am sure you must have some questions.'

Airawat sighed. 'Prince, it is a fact that I do not hold any love for the asuras. In the past, they have done enough harm to mortals. And most of their previous endeavours have been aimed at hurting the people of Mrityulok. However, in the last couple of centuries, there doesn't seem to have been any incident where they have openly done anything to injure us.'

Vasudev made an encouraging motion for Airawat to continue.

Airawat looked towards Ugrasena, 'Therefore, if the king let those asuras go, I don't think he did anything wrong. They were clearly being persecuted by their own kind and had nowhere to go. By allowing innocent asuras to settle down in our land, the king has merely demonstrated that people of Mrityulok don't turn their back on anyone who needs our help.' He paused, 'However, I am sure that there is something more than what you have already told me; something which may make me change whatever feelings I just shared with you.'

Vasudev grinned despite the seriousness of the situation. He was sure now that Ugrasena had chosen the right man to work with him on this. Airawat was nobody's fool; his mind was razor sharp and his ability to interpret a problem was uncanny.

He addressed Airawat directly and this time his voice was firm and clear, 'You are right. There is more than I have told you already, and it is going to make you change your feelings about the asuras.' Airawat tensed involuntarily as Vasudev continued.

'The asuras who were captured by the king lied to him. They were honest in that they were not the first asuras to enter Mrityulok illegally. But they lied when they said that only a few hundred of them have breached our borders over the last few years.'

'How many have come in?' Airawat couldn't help asking.

'They number in the thousands, and they have spread out all over the kingdoms of Mrityulok. They are everywhere, disguised as mortals, engaged in different kinds of work and trade,' Vasudev answered in a soft voice.

Airawat had a horrified expression on his face. 'This is incredulous!' he exclaimed. 'What is their purpose?' he managed to ask finally.

'Maharishi Narada tells us that all the asuras who have entered Mrityulok so far are trained assassins. They have been under training in Pataal Lok for the past hundred years, or perhaps even more than that. It is quite possible that they have been entering through various border kingdoms into Mrityulok for the past several years, in small numbers. Their documents and ID papers are done to perfection and from what we know, the only time they were found out was when a Madhuvan border guard recognized their language and their documents were subjected to more than a routine check.'

Airawat's face was pale as he spoke. 'Why would Pataal Lok send so many assassins into our land? This is bizarre.'

'Think! Why does anyone send spies into a country Airawat?' Vasudev asked in a quiet voice. 'Because they want to keep a tab on that country's activities,' Airawat answered almost immediately. 'Correct. But that can be done with a handful of spies. Why would someone send in thousands of spies, who also happen to be trained as assassins?' prompted Vasudev.

'By Vishnu!' exclaimed Airawat as the full realization of the asuras' plans dawned on him. 'They want to create anarchy within all the kingdoms of Mrityulok.' His voice faltered towards the end of the sentence.

'Yes, and they are waiting for the right moment to do just that,' Vasudev completed the thought that had begun to take shape in Airawat's mind.

Airawat struggled to control his panic as the thought seeped in completely. Gradually, years of training his mind succeeded in helping him think clearly. 'The only purpose an enemy has to create anarchy within someone's country is to keep them so busy handling their internal conflicts that they wouldn't be ready to face an attack from outside. This would mean that Pataal Lok has plans to launch an attack on Mrityulok. The question is when... when would they do it?'

'It could happen any time, Airawat,' Narada finally spoke. 'Even as we speak now.' He looked at the grim faces of the people around him and sought to reassure them. 'But I don't think it will happen that soon. Before the attack starts, there has to be sufficient chaos in every kingdom. That stage hasn't been reached yet.'

Vasudev chipped in. 'My feeling is that they will need more asuras in every kingdom before they can create that scale of mayhem in Mrityulok. This means we can expect a lot more cases of asuras trying to breach borders of various kingdoms to enter Mrityulok. Maharishi Narada has compiled a list of the main kingdoms that have borders with Pataal Lok. This includes kingdoms like Madhuvan, Magadha, Banpur, Yavanas, Hastinapur, Bateshwar and a few others. The maharishi is going to meet up with the kings of all these countries to caution them against the threat. Meanwhile, King Ugrasena is going to step up the security at the Madhuvan borders. If we can control the flow of asura assassins entering Mrityulok, we can indefinitely delay their plans and perhaps even destabilize their intentions completely.'

'But...' Airawat started to say something. He was interrupted by Vasudev who hadn't finished yet.

'While the maharishi will try destabilizing the asura plan by cautioning the border kingdoms, we need to take care of the other important issue,' Vasudev paused to clarify his thoughts in his own mind, before continuing, 'Since we can be certain that Pataal Lok will not attack us until there is significant anarchy on Mrityulok, our focus should be on controlling their efforts at creating that anarchy.'

'How will we do that?' Airawat questioned.

Vasudev had anticipated this question. 'Each of the kingdoms in Mrityulok will need to create a task force whose objective it will be to look out for signs of rebellion or lawlessness in their own country. The moment they observe any activities that could lead to uncontrollable mayhem, they will address it immediately. If we are able to get each country in Mrityulok to build such a task force, and if Maharishi Narada succeeds in getting the border kingdoms to control the entry of any more asuras, we will be in a much stronger position.'

Airawat seemed lost in thought. He spoke at last. 'It's a good plan, prince. But whatever you have told me till now is all part of a defensive strategy. The maharishi will caution the border kingdoms, and that is a good way to prevent entry of new assassin teams from Pataal Lok. The task forces in all the kingdoms will keep track of any anarchist activities and that is also a good defensive strategy...but that is all it is...a defensive strategy.'

Vasudev looked closely at Airawat. He wondered if Airawat would say what he hoped.

Airawat took a deep breath. 'I suggest we do all of that. But we need to take the battle to the asuras. We should be creating a covert operations team in every kingdom that will only have one task—to hunt down the assassin asuras hiding in their respective kingdoms. Let's take the problem out by its roots!' Airawat finished with a low growl.

'Bravo!' exclaimed Vasudev. 'That's exactly what we are going to do Airawat. But I wanted to hear this from you. I am certain you are the right man for this job. I am not sure if the other kingdoms will agree to do this right away, at least not until Maharishi Narada has discussed the whole problem with them. But Madhuvan and Bateshwar will definitely get cracking on this. And you are going to help me build the team for both our kingdoms.'

Airawat seemed to hesitate. Ugrasena and Vasudev exchanged glances.

'What is it, Airawat? Is there a problem?' Ugrasena stared at him quizzically.

Airawat still hesitated, and Vasudev spoke up, 'Speak up man. If there is a problem, I need to know now. I need you with me totally—mind, body and soul. There can be no room for any doubt once we are started.'

Airawat looked apologetically at Ugrasena. He seemed to ignore Vasudev and directed his words at his king. 'My Lord! Prince Kansa...have you spoken to him about this? He should be here to lead the task force for Madhuvan.' Airawat bowed his head, dismayed at having questioned his king's command for the first time in his life.

Vasudev looked like he wanted to say something but Ugrasena stopped him. This was something he had to do himself, or Airawat would not agree. 'Airawat, Prince Kansa needs to be away for some time.'

'He...uh, he has some things he needs to work out in his mind, and he has asked to be left alone till that happens. Much as I love my son, I respect his need to be away till he is comfortable coming back and taking his rightful position at Madhuvan as the Crown Prince. But this danger from the asura assassins that we have spoken about cannot wait till my son returns. Therefore, I have asked Vasudev, the prince of Bateshwar to lead the task force for both Bateshwar and Madhuvan until Kansa comes back. In the interim, I am sending a confidential message for Prince Kansa today itself, informing him about the danger and asking him if he would like to return to lead the Madhuvan task force. If he comes back now, you will work under his command at Madhuvan while Prince Vasudev will take care of the danger in his own country at Bateshwar. Do you understand?'

Ugrasena's last words carried the full command and authority of his position and were not lost on Airawat. He bowed to his king and nodded.

'Good then, you will start working with Vasudev on building the task force for Madhuvan. If Kansa comes back, you will be under his command, or else you will report directly to Vasudev. Meanwhile, Vasudev will travel to Bateshwar immediately and share the plan with his father, King Surasena. Whether he stays there to lead the task force at Bateshwar or returns here to lead the Madhuvan task force too, will depend on Kansa's decision to return. The maharishi will be leaving tomorrow to travel to all the border kingdoms.'

Ugrasena stood up to indicate that the meeting was over, at least as far as Airawat was concerned. Airawat bowed low to his king, and nodded respectfully to Vasudev. He went over to Narada and touched his feet to seek the blessings of the venerable sage, before exiting the king's chambers.

Vasudev looked at Ugrasena, 'I need to meet Devki before I leave. She won't be pleased that I have to return to Bateshwar so soon, but I will explain it to her. If all goes well, Kansa should be here soon. Else, I will return after starting the task force in Bateshwar. In case I have to be here, Sini Yadav is more than capable to handle the team at Bateshwar.'

Ugrasena nodded. 'Let me know how things go, Vasudev. Tell Devki I am sorry for taking so much of the time that you meant to spend with her. But she will have you all to herself after the marriage in a few months, anyway.'

Vasudev grinned at the king's subtle joke, and seeking the blessings of both Narada and Ugrasena, he, too, left the chamber in search of Devki.

Narada and Ugrasena were left alone. Narada held the old king by his shoulder. 'I know you have Kansa's interests in your heart Ugrasena. But put pressure on him to return. He shouldn't feel left out that you have asked Vasudev to lead the Madhuvan task force too.'

Ugrasena shook his head. 'He won't feel that way. He loves Vasudev as a brother. And Vasudev is going to lead the task force only if Kansa does not return. But I know he will return. I am going to request him as his father to come back to save his country from this danger. He won't refuse me.'

Maharishi Narada was quiet. His capabilities were not as advanced as that of a brahmarishi, but he was still able to pick up parts of what would happen in the future from the energy flowing through the universe. And whatever little he was able to read of the future, he knew one thing for certain—Kansa would not return to lead the task force.

Signs of the Future

The Dark Lord paced the room. Every pore of his being exuded a state of severe agitation. Bhargava sat quietly watching him, with a concerned look on his customarily placid face. It was unusual for his friend to show signs of being extremely disturbed. He knew that Amartya was consumed with pain and impotent rage, but he seldom allowed his feelings to be observed by anyone. *Something big must have happened for him to be so visibly agitated,* mused Bhargava. He badly wanted to know what, but he knew better than to disturb his friend, when he was in one of these moods. He waited patiently.

'They know. They know everything!' Amartya shouted in frustrated rage.

The explosion of anger was so sudden and uncharacteristic that Bhargava positively leaped out of his seat. 'What's wrong, Amartya?' he asked in concern. 'I have never seen you express your anger this way.'

The Dark Lord clenched his teeth. 'Don't call me by that name. Amartya Kalyanesu is dead! I am just a shell of my past self.'

Bhargava gave him a sad smile. 'It's not that easy to shake off our past, Amartya. And definitely not something that a man of your abilities should do.' He gazed at the broken man standing in front of him. 'You are still a brahmarishi, my friend. And nothing that happened to you or will ever happen to you can change that truth. But forget all that for now. What's bothering you?'

The Dark Lord met Bhargava's gaze, who was compelled to look away. 'They know what we are planning. Narada has told

Ugrasena the truth behind the asura assassins entering Mrityulok. There is a leak in your camp, Bhargava.'

'Impossible!' Bhargava exclaimed in shock. 'That cannot be. The only people who knew about the plan apart from you and me are all part of the asura council. The others who know the plan are the assassins who have been sent to Mrityulok. All of them are mercenaries and are aware that they stand to earn a great deal of wealth if they help the plan succeed. None of them could have betrayed us.'

'It is obviously not impossible, Bhargava, since it has already come to pass. Someone has to have told Narada what we are planning.'

Bhargava grew silent. He knew Amartya was right. Someone had told Narada about the plan. But the question was who? Who in Pataal Lok would have risked the wrath of the Dark Lord? And to what purpose? Then a thought struck him and his face shone with excitement.

'Amartya, you have the power of tapping into the universal energy that allows you to read whatever happened in the past or will possible happen in the future. Can't you use that to find out who the traitor is?'

Amartya Kalyanesu suppressed his impatience. 'Do you think I have not tried that already?'

Bhargava stared at his friend. Amartya was uncharacteristically short-tempered with him today. He had never shown signs of impatience with him before this. *He must be really troubled*, he thought.

'So what happened?' he asked. 'What did you find out?'

'Nothing!' Amartya Kalyanesu sighed in exasperation. 'Someone has created a protective shield over the traitor. Someone who knew I could use my powers of cosmic telepathy to find out who betrayed us.'

'But can't you breach the shield?' Bhargava queried.

Amartya shook his head, 'No. The shield is made up of

potent Brahman energy. It protects the thoughts of the person being shielded in a way that no one except the person who has created the shield can breach it.'

'Who could have the power to do this?' Bhargava wondered aloud.

'Only a maharishi, a brahmarishi or one of the three supreme gods could have created such a shield,' Amartya replied quietly. Since Narada knows about our plans, it is most likely he who created the shield around the traitor before speaking to him.'

'So there is no way we can find out who the person is?' Bhargava asked with grave concern.

'It's unlikely,' replied Amartya quietly.

Both of them were silent for a while. 'What do we do now?' Bhargava asked gravely.

Amartya spoke and his voice was deathly calm. There was no sign of the agitation and anger that had been there just a few moments before.

'The fact that they know our plan will definitely go against us,' he said, then paused. He seemed to weigh his words before continuing. 'But they still don't know the details. Our assassins are spread out all over their land. By the time they warn the kingdoms they think will listen to them, we will send in more assassins through kingdoms like Magadha and Madhuvan... especially Madhuvan.'

'Why Madhuvan?' Bhargava quizzed him.

'Madhuvan has the largest border with Pataal Lok. Even if they mount the strongest security around their borders, we will still be able to send in more assassins through their kingdom than through any other land.'

'Hmm,' Bhargava said thoughtfully. 'But won't Ugrasena set up measures against such a plan? And don't forget his son Kansa is a powerful and intrepid warrior.'

'Kansa will not oppose us, Bhargava. The asura blood of his birth father runs within him. And the demonic tendencies of his birth legacy were activated when he was almost killed by my trio of assassins during the attack on his sister.'

Bhargava looked confused. 'I don't understand. What do you mean?' he asked.

'Kansa has within him the blood of a mortal and a demon. His mortal side comes from his mother, Padmavati, and the demonic part is inherited from his birth father, who seduced his mother. Since Kansa spent his entire life with mortals, his demonic side never got a chance to exert itself. And truth be told, his mortal side has been so dominant that it would have been impossible for his other half to have ever come up on its own.'

'Then...' Bhargava started to interrupt but was stopped by Amartya.

'During the attack on his sister, Kansa was fatally wounded by two of my assassins, a bonara and a pisaca. He was in a precarious state when the Madhuvan soldiers carried him back to his palace. The royal vaid there tried his best to save Kansa but by then it was impossible for anyone to have salvaged his life. His mortal half was not strong enough to fight the grievous wounds he had received. A normal mortal would have died at this point. But Kansa is different. When his mortal side gave up, his demonic half, which had lain dormant in his system for so long, took over automatically. His body started to produce more of the demonic life cells, and it was this that eventually saved his life.'

Amartya paused to scratch the burnt part of his face. It always itched more when he allowed his emotions to get the better of him, even temporarily. 'In time, as the demon cells inside his system start replicating themselves, whatever little of the mortal is left within him will disappear. His demonic side will take over completely.'

Bhargava tried to assimilate this new information. 'How long will it take...for his demonic side to take control, I mean?'

'It might take days, or it could be months before it happens,' Amartya replied. 'Kansa is an unusually noble man, and in spite of the demon cells growing within him, his intrinsic goodness will fight against the latent evil struggling to erupt inside him. The only thing that can possibly accelerate his complete transformation into a demon will be if he faces some severe trauma during this period.'

'What kind of trauma?' Bhargava probed.

'Anything. Any major emotional or psychological upheaval in his life could push him over to the dark side completely and irrevocably.'

'And if and when that happens, how would he change?' Bhargava asked.

'He will go completely insane and unpredictable. Remember he is not a pure demon. Someone who is raised as a demon may not have any qualms of doing what they have to do, no matter how evil they may have to become. In Kansa's case, while his conscious behaviour may eventually mirror a demon's, his mortal side will always keep surfacing to confuse him. Over a period of time, he will become a paranoid schizophrenic. And this could make him more dangerous and evil than any other demon would otherwise be.'

Bhargava was quiet. He was a man of principles and had never hurt anyone in his life without cause. He had the greatest respect for people like Kansa. It pained him to know what lay in store for the noble prince but there was nothing he or anyone could do now. What had to be done would be done. The destruction of Kansa, if necessary, would need to be tolerated for the greater good. But there was something else that had been bothering him for many weeks and he needed to know the answer to it now.

'Amartya,' he looked at his friend. 'Why is it necessary to kill Devki? What has she done to us?'

Amartya returned Bhargava's gaze with equanimity. He had an inscrutable expression on his face. 'Nothing!' he said softly. 'She has done nothing to us...yet.'

Bhargava did not miss the emphasis on the last word. But his face told Amartya that he had not understood his meaning at all.

'Devki can be the greatest stumbling block to our plan in the future, Bhargava,' Amartya said haltingly.

'How can she...' Bhargava stopped mid-sentence. 'Did you see something in the future?' he asked, suddenly, his eyes betraying his anxiety.

Amartya sighed. It never ceased to surprise him how other people—even people as evolved as Bhargava—thought that a brahmarishi could see the future with ease. 'Let's just say that I saw something that indicates Devki could be a danger to our plan in the future.'

Bhargava shook his head in exasperation. 'What does that mean? You either saw her being a danger or you didn't! Why the confusion, then?'

'Bhargava, people like me and the other brahmarishis can see the past with clarity. Because what has already happened is completely certain and without any ambiguity.' He paused, reflecting how to explain the dilemma to the only friend he had had since he was banished to Pataal Lok by Brahma. 'The future, however, is uncertain. It changes every moment. At best, we can see possibilities of what could eventually happen. There are so many possibilities that one can never be completely sure of what will really happen.'

Bhargava stared uncomprehendingly at Amartya. 'Are you saying that not even the three supreme gods can see with certainty what will happen in the future?' he asked incredulously.

Amartya nodded silently.

'By Shiva and Vishnu!' Bhargava exclaimed. 'Then how in the name of everything holy can you be so sure that Devki will pose a danger to us in the future?'

Amartya frowned unconsciously. But his answer was quick, 'Because every possible scenario that I am able to pick up from the energy flowing in the universe shows Devki as the one person who can ruin everything we have planned.'

'How can a mortal woman undo what you and I have planned? You are amongst the most powerful brahmarishis and I...I have some powers too!' Bhargava spoke with an air of disbelief in his voice.

Amartya smiled. He knew Bhargava was being humble in voicing his own abilities. The unassuming man who had befriended him so willingly two centuries back was perhaps amongst the most powerful asuras in Pataal Lok. But he had the soul of a brahmarishi. *Perhaps even more than that*, Amartya thought to himself.

'You didn't answer me, Amartya. How can a mortal woman upset something that you and I have planned with such care over the past two hundred years?' Bhargava sounded impatient and this was rare for him.

'Devki will not ruin our plans directly,' Amartya said almost in a whisper. 'But it is through Devki that our designs could come to nothing.'

Bhargava looked even more confused. 'What does that mean? Stop talking in riddles!'

Amartya bent close to his friend. And when he spoke, his voice had a note of despair that cut through Bhargava's heart. 'Devki will have a son with Vasudev. Every vision of the future that I have been able to foresee shows only one thing. Her son will undo everything that we have planned till now. Once he is born, it will be almost impossible to use the support of Mrityulok in the fight against the devas.'

There was an uneasy silence as Bhargava tried to take in what Amartya had just said.

'Is this why you sent your three upanshughataks to kill Devki? So that her marriage with Vasudev never comes to pass, and that... that child is never born?' Bhargava's voice was unsteady but his mind was clear.

'That's correct,' Amartya nodded.

'So what happens now? She is safe and will possibly marry

Vasudev in the next few days.'

'She will marry Vasudev. This became a certainty when the pisaca and the other two upanshughataks failed to kill her that day.' Amartya paused, scratching the side of his face again. 'But her child will not be born. At least not if I can do anything about it,' his voice had a strange faraway tone, as if he was there and yet not there.

'How will that happen Amartya?' Bhargava said, clutching at some possibility of reprieve.

Amartya looked him in the eye. When he spoke his voice sounded different, almost sad. 'Kansa will kill every child she brings into this world. Her son will never be born.'

Bhargava blanched. His soul recoiled at the very thought of infants being murdered in cold blood. For a moment, he was tempted to forsake all the plans Amartya and he had so meticulously laid down over the past several years. *Was revenge worth this carnage?* he thought with anguish. *Was anything worth this?* But then he remembered his mother lying in a pool of her own blood, her head severed from her body. The thought helped him steel his mind against any thought of abandoning their plan. He would have his revenge on Indra and the rest of the devas. And Amartya would have his revenge on Brahma, and Indra too. *Yes, it was definitely worth it!*

Training of the Asura Assassins

It was nearing dusk. Five dozen newly inducted asuras were being trained in various deadly arts, including close-combat manoeuvres, archery and duelling with swords. They had been handpicked by Ugra, the Chief of the Zataka Upanshughataks. Ugra had joined the upanshughataks clan two hundred and thirty years back and had quickly made a name for himself as one of the foremost assassins in Pataal Lok. His services were not only sought by some of the most fearsome asura kings but also by some of the rulers of Mrityulok from time to time, when they wanted to execute a particularly dangerous enemy without wanting to indulge in a full-scale war. Ugra was massively built and had more kills to his credit than any of the other Zataka Upanshughataks. His favoured weapon of death was the axe and he wielded it with a skill that was both fearsome to behold and hypnotic. Ugra owed his allegiance only to one person—Bhargava.

◆

Several years ago, Ugra had been justly accused of assassinating one of the asura council members and had suffered the misfortune of being caught in the act. It was the first and the only time he had been trapped while fulfilling a contract and the other council members had bayed for his blood. At this point in time, Ugra hadn't yet become the chief of the Zataka Upanshughataks—the dreaded tribe of the hundred assassins—and he did not wield significant influence amongst the clan. In fact, there were a lot of his tribesmen who seemed happy to be getting rid of him, none more so than their chief, who saw Ugra as a threat to his power. Consequently, the asura council did not have any fear of the upanshughataks taking revenge on them for sentencing one of their kind to death.

Ugra was supposed to be hanged upside down over a burning cauldron of oil and left to die a slow and torturous death as the flaming oil would swallow him bit by bit. The thing that infuriated him most was that the person who had given him the contract for killing the asura council member was also present amongst the people who voted for his death. Ugra could have implicated the man and perhaps got a lighter sentence. But it wasn't in his nature to squeal on a client. And he knew that the other council members would probably not even believe him even if he decided to betray the man who had handed him the contract. He kept silent, even as he was tied and hauled up with his head facing the ground. As the first blast of oil fumes from the cauldron hit him in the face, he saw a slightly built man staring strangely at him, from amongst the first row of onlookers who had gathered to witness his punishment. The man was dressed in white and had long flowing hair. He was obviously someone who commanded great respect among the council members, even though he didn't look like an asura. In fact, Ugra couldn't help wondering even in that moment that the slightly built man could possibly pass off as a mortal. As the fumes grew stronger and the heat became unbearable, Ugra noticed this man in animated conversation with the asura council. A heated discussion seemed to be taking place between the man in white and the key council members who had voted in favour of Ugra's execution. Then, as suddenly as it had started, the discussion stopped.

Ugra noticed the chairperson of the asura council motioning hastily to one of the soldiers. And just when Ugra was certain his head was going to be boiled while he was still alive, the soldier, accompanied by his colleagues, removed the cauldron from where it stood. The relief from the scorching heat was beyond description.

Ugra felt he could breathe again. Someone cut him loose and he fell to the ground, unhurt but a little dazed with the ordeal of the past few minutes. As he was led away by the soldiers, he happened to pass the man in white. Just as he crossed him, the man bent over and whispered something to him. Ugra nodded and moved on. From that moment on, he was forever indebted to Bhargava, the man in white, the man who had somehow persuaded the asura council to let him go free. Ugra never found out how Bhargava had managed the miracle, and Bhargava didn't find it important to tell him. But a debt had been placed on him, and Ugra was not a man who forgot to pay his debts.

◆

Ugra rose to become the chief of the Zataka Upanshughataks within a few years of this incident. The former chief had been found with his head cut off, lying in a gutter outside the city walls. The modus operandi of beheading his victim's head was known to be Ugra's and the other upanshughataks knew this. Yet such was the fear inspired by Ugra amongst his clansmen that none of them dared to voice their suspicions, even amongst themselves.

Ugra took over as the chief upanshughatak without any incident. The first thing he did was to instill a sense of brotherhood amongst his men. Till now, the hundred-odd assassins in the clan operated more as individuals and there were recurring instances of territorial fighting and petty disputes over available contracts. With Ugra taking over as the chief, the upanshughataks were assembled like a mini army with one general—Ugra himself. Everyone took their orders from him and he was careful to ensure that he was fair to each of them, without any favourites gaining ground as had happened under the former chief. Ugra made it clear to the assassins that they were a family and would have to look out for each other, irrespective of any personal differences. Any petty dispute would be resolved with a heavy hand. No one person could gain precedence over the whole tribe. The rules he laid for his clan ensured that they operated as a tightly knit team, with their loyalty only to one person, Ugra.

Unlike when Ugra had been captured and sentenced, now if any of the upanshughatak clansmen were captured by the Pataal Lok officials, the tribe would launch an offensive of such magnitude that no one would dare to meddle with their affairs in the future. There were a few random incidents where some overenthusiastic official would arrest an upanshughatak for questioning. The result was always the same. Before the day was through, the official's body would be found decapitated, and the captured upanshughatak would be freed by the other clansmen. In time, no one dared to arrest or cross the way of the upanshughataks. Even the asura king, Vrushaparva, did not dare to carry out an offense against Ugra and his assassin army.

In order to ensure that they did not provoke the Pataal Lok government to take serious steps against them, Ugra made it a point to have his tribe settle some distance away from the main city, and his men were instructed to avoid any incidents unless there was a contract to be fulfilled or one of their members had been captured and had to be freed. The upanshughatak tribe grew in fame and strength. Once in every few years, a clansman would flout a major rule and go against the ethos set by Ugra. The result was instant death. A new recruit would take the place left vacant by such an event. The number of upanshughataks never exceeded a hundred, including Ugra, and each of the assassins belonging to this tribe were the best in Pataal Lok. They included different categories of asuras—pisacas, bonaras, bhutas, pretas, kalakanjas and several other forms of the Pataal Lok inhabitants. But each of them had only one identity. They were known as a Zataka Upanshughatak.

◆

One day, a few years after he had saved his life, Bhargava came to meet Ugra. This was the first time that Bhargava had met him after he had rescued Ugra from certain death. He complimented the latter on how he had disciplined his men. Ugra accepted the praise, wondering all the time why Bhargava had come to him after so many years. But more than that, he was curious to ask him the question that had been left unanswered so many years ago: 'Why did you decide to save my life that day, My Lord?'

Bhargava smiled at the huge man standing respectfully in front of him. He had known Ugra would ask him this question. Truth be told, he had asked himself the same question multiple times over the last few years. Bhargava had no love for assassins and it had surprised him that he had used all his goodwill with the asura council to persuade them to let this man go that day. After all, the man was a ruthless assassin. Why had he saved him? However, his answer when he spoke to Ugra, did not reflect any of the self-doubt he felt within him, 'I saw you look at the man who had given you the contract. He was one of the council members who voted against you and handed you the death penalty. Yet you did not betray the man. You could have turned him in and got a lighter sentence, but you kept the truth to yourself.'

Ugra looked flabbergasted. 'How did you know that man had given me the contract to assassinate his rival in the council? No one knew about it apart from him and me.'

'There are very few things I am not aware of Ugra; as you shall realize in time to come,' Bhargava spoke softly but Ugra did not fail to notice the steel in his voice.

'W-who are you, My Lord?' the chief of the Upanshughataks whispered, his voice reflecting the awe he felt for the slightly built man.

'My name is Bhargava, and that is enough for you to know for now, Ugra,' Bhargava stared at the man in front of him, and it hit him in that very moment why he had saved the assassin's life.

'I saved your life because I saw that you kept your honour as an upanshughatak, even when you realized that the very man who hired you was one of those sentencing you to death.' Ugra stared incredulously at Bhargava, who continued speaking, 'Yes, I am aware of the code of the upanshughataks. Once you take on a contract, you take an oath that you will not compromise the confidentiality of the contract, or the person who gave it to you, under any circumstances. And you did just that! Even after the man sentenced you, you did not break your oath.' Bhargava paused briefly. 'And that makes you a rare man, Ugra. Anyone who would maintain loyalty to his oath, in the face of death, is a man worth respecting...and worth saving!'

Ugra felt a strange sensation as he heard Bhargava speak. He knew the middle-aged man spoke from his heart. And there was such truth and openness in Bhargava's voice that it touched him to the core. 'With these words, you have bound me to you for life! What do you want me to do, My Lord?'

Bhargava allowed himself the luxury of a slight smile and proceeded to tell Ugra exactly what he wanted him to do. He would need an army of thousands of trained asura assassins, and he wanted Ugra to handle this task. Ugra did not ask Bhargava why he wanted him to do this. The fact that Bhargava had asked this of him was enough.

◆

It had been almost two hundred years since Bhargava gave him the task, and Ugra had trained thousands of asura assassins during this period. He made sure that the discipline in his tribe of Zataka Upanshughataks did not go down, despite the enormous amount of time he had to spend away from his clansmen.

Bhargava had told him that he was working for the Dark Lord. Ugra had never met the Dark Lord personally but he had heard of him. He had become a legend in less than two hundred years. Some said he was a god who used the power of Brahman, and others said that he was the most powerful asura the netherworld had ever known; that Ravana and Kalanemi were like children compared to his abilities. Ugra had no time for legends or myths.

He didn't believe there was a Dark Lord, and if there was one, he wouldn't respect him till he had seen his powers with his own eyes.

As far as Ugra was concerned, he was doing what he was doing solely for Bhargava. He didn't owe the Dark Lord anything. And the fact was that in the last couple of months, he had been furious with the Dark Lord. The man had killed one of his Zataka Upanshughataks, a kalakanja. This particular one had been one of his oldest assassins and the fact that an outsider from the tribe had killed one of his men made Ugra furious. He had told Bhargava that he would kill the Dark Lord for what he had done, but he was surprised at Bhargava's reaction; he had laughed uncontrollably as if Ugra had just made a joke instead of threatening to kill the Dark Lord. After his laughter subsided, Bhargava gently said, 'You can't kill the Dark Lord, Ugra. You can, however, seek his blessings.'

This had enraged Ugra even more than the death of the kalakanja. He couldn't understand why the one man he respected so much seemed to be in awe of a mere legend; of someone he wasn't sure even existed in the manner people talked about him. 'Why do you seem to be afraid of this man, My Lord? Give me permission and I will bind him and drag him to you.' This time Bhargava's reaction shocked Ugra even more than before. The usually calm face and dreamy eyes of the scholarly man flashed fire at Ugra and his expression was full of anger as he spoke: 'How dare you speak about the Dark Lord in such a deprecating manner, you fool?' Bhargava was breathing heavily in rage. 'And who told you I am afraid of him? I respect him, for if there is one man in this universe who should be respected, it is him!'

Ugra was speechless. The man he had heard people refer to as the Dark Lord was someone to fear; not respect. *What does Bhargava mean?* he wondered.

Meanwhile, Bhargava had calmed down. 'You will learn to respect the Dark Lord in time, Ugra. Till then, don't make the mistake of speaking lightly about him in my presence. Am I clear?'

Ugra nodded thoughtfully. The message was clear. He would not offend Bhargava again by talking disparagingly about his friend, at least not in his presence. In his own mind, he still hated the Dark Lord for having killed one of his men.

◆

Ugra's attention was suddenly attracted to a young asura using a long sword. The asura was one of the five dozen new recruits that were being trained under him for Bhargava. The asura was using a blade that was almost one gavuta in length and was made of such fine metal that it fluttered in the wind like a paper sword. The only difference was that this blade could slice through a pachyderm with ease. The young asura was using the blade incorrectly and would possibly end up killing someone with it while training; most likely himself.

'Hey you!' Ugra shouted in anger. The asura with the sword looked at him in trepidation. Ugra was notorious for his temper.

'That's not how you use this type of sword, you moron!' Ugra growled in anger. 'Let me show you how to use it,' he said, grabbing the sword from the young asura's hands and clipping him on the head with his palm, as a rebuke.

'Here, take this sword,' he growled, handing him a conventional sword with a rigid blade, slightly shorter than the sword he had just been using. The asura held the new sword with trembling hands. His legs were shaking and he was finding it difficult to stand straight.

Ugra noticed the young recruit's fear and softened a little. He knew he wouldn't be able to teach him anything as long as the kid was scared to death. 'What's your name son?' he said in what he hoped was his kindest voice, but was actually only a little better than a snarl.

'G-ghora, sir,' the young asura stuttered, still scared of the man he knew was the deadliest assassin in Pataal Lok.

Ugra burst out in laughter. Ghora, the young asura looked

at him, his expression a mix of a scowl and fear.

'Do you know why I am laughing, Ghora?' Ugra asked him trying to stifle the laughter that threatened to overpower him yet again.

'No sir, I do not know why you are laughing!' Ghora sounded peeved and a significant portion of his fear seemed to get replaced by a sense of growing indignation at his teacher.

Ugra noticed the change in Ghora's mood. *Ah! You have more spirit in you than you know yet son*, he thought to himself. 'Do you know that your name and mine mean the same thing?' he asked, smiling.

Ghora looked perplexed. This was the last question he had thought Ugra would ask him. He shook his head. He had no idea what his own name meant, leave aside what his teacher's signified. Both his parents had been killed in a violent fight with a neighbouring tribe and he had been raised as an orphan. Delving into the meaning of his name had been the last thing on his mind all these years.

'Ugra means "fearsome",' Ugra said softly, interrupting his thoughts. 'And Ghora is another word with the same meaning.'

Ghora's eyes widened. He hadn't known this is what his name meant. For some inexplicable reason, he felt his chest expand with pride as he listened to Ugra explain it to him. It was as if merely knowing what his name represented was giving him a newfound power—a greater sense of confidence.

'Come, let me show you how to use this sword now,' Ugra brought his pupil back into the present with a lightly aimed jab at Ghora's abdomen, who squirmed in pain as the tip of Ugra's sword nicked some skin off his abdomen. The wound was very minor but the learning was clear—'Don't lose your focus when you are in front of the enemy.'

Ugra extended his sword arm in the air and with a quick move, covered the entire space between Ghora and himself, in a series of sword movements. The weapon hissed through the air with such speed that it seemed as if there were multiple swords covering different points of the space between the two duellists. Every time Ghora tried to jab and cut at Ugra with his own sword, it was met with a steel barrier created by the continuous movement of Ugra's swirling sword. And then suddenly, Ugra bent down and in a sweeping horizontal motion, brought in his sword from Ghora's right towards his feet. To all those watching, it seemed as if the sword had sliced through Ghora's feet. Ghora fell down, and there was a moment of speechlessness amongst all those present. He looked at his feet with shock, and was amazed to see they were still attached to his body. Like all the spectators, he too had thought that Ugra's sword had sliced through his feet when he brought his sword in the direction of his legs. His amazement grew as he realized with a jolt that Ugra had used his sword to cut through his sandals. Such was the precision that only the sandals had been ripped off, causing Ghora to fall because of the impact of the sandals being knocked off.

He got up gingerly, still not able to believe that his feet were intact. Finally, he bowed to Ugra. 'That was incredible, sir! I didn't realize what was happening.'

Ugra smiled and gave Ghora a friendly slap on his back. 'Now you know what you can do with this word, eh?' he smiled broadly.

Before Ghora could reply, Ugra heard a grating voice from behind him, 'That's not the way to use this sword, my friend.'

Ugra turned around in fury, his face, a mask of rage. The friendly demeanour disappeared from his face, as if the light banter with Ghora had never happened. He was ready to duel and kill whoever had dared to challenge his skill with the sword, that too in front of his trainees.

He was surprised to see Bhargava standing there. But the man who had dared to challenge him was someone else. That person stood next to Bhargava, attired in black. Had it not been for Bhargava's presence, and the fact that the person who had challenged him was accompanied by the man he most respected,

Ugra would have attacked the challenger by now. As it was, he bowed respectfully to Bhargava. 'My Lord, it is an honour to have you here,' Ugra said, studiously ignoring Bhargava's companion, the man who had dared to challenge him in front of his students.

Bhargava smiled benevolently, 'I heard you were training a new batch of recruits. I thought it would be interesting to see how you transform a bunch of greenhorns into professional assassins.'

Ugra had an inscrutable look on his face. Much as he respected Bhargava, he was not happy that he had brought a stranger to his training camp. And he was still seething at the audacity of this stranger, who had challenged his skill in front of his men. *If he dares to question my abilities again, I will break his neck,* he thought savagely.

At exactly that moment, the stranger accompanying Bhargava spoke again, and this time his tone carried a hint of mockery. 'As I was saying just now, that's not how you use that particular sword, my friend.'

Ugra had had enough. His dark face took on a purple hue and his eyes looked as if they would pop out of their sockets any moment. 'Why don't you put your money where your mouth is, stranger,' he snarled. 'Let me show you how this sword is really used, then,' Ugra almost spat out the words.

Bhargava tried to intervene. 'Calm down, Ugra. My companion is just saying there could be a better way of using the sword. It's his opinion. You don't need to get upset about this, really.'

Ugra shook his head. He wasn't in any mood to let this stranger get away so easily. Not after he had been fool enough to challenge him twice. 'My Lord,' he looked at Bhargava. 'I demand that this man prove the truth of his words. He has challenged me in front of my men. Either he apologizes now or he should get ready to duel with me and prove that he knows how to use this sword better than I do.'

Before Bhargava could say anything else, the stranger cut in, 'Ugra is right. Since I have questioned his skills, I should also prove the same.'

'B-but he is the chief of the Zataka Upanshughataks...' Bhargava started to say.

Ugra smiled. *Now this man is going to shit in his clothes. He obviously didn't know who I was before he shot off his mouth*, he thought malevolently.

The stranger looked in Ugra's direction. 'Oh, I didn't know who he is,' he said softly.

Ugra's smile grew wider. *Now he is going to apologize; the snooty bastard*, he mused to himself.

'But now that I know who he is, it is even more important to teach him how to use that sword,' the stranger completed his sentence.

Ugra gaped at him. *This man is a fool*, he thought viciously. *After he knows who I am, he is still being obnoxious. He won't go home alive today*, he resolved in rage.

'Prepare yourself!' Ugra shouted at the stranger as he threw him one of the swords with the long blade, before grabbing one for himself. The stranger caught the sword thrown at him in one neat motion.

Ugra walked towards the shrouded figure taking his time, clearly enjoying the thought of what he was going to do to him. Then suddenly his face grew grim. He looked beyond his adversary at the figure of a bhuta creeping up silently behind the stranger. The bhuta had a curved knife in his hand and it was evident that he was going to try and slice the stranger's neck from behind. As the bhuta crept closer to the stranger, Ugra recognized him as one of his Zataka Upanshughataks. He understood what the bhuta was trying to do. As part of their tribe's rule, if any one of them was in danger from an enemy, the tribe would attack the enemy without asking any questions. Ugra realized that the bhuta must have seen the stranger carrying a weapon against him and thinking he was in danger was planning to take out the enemy from behind.

Ugra opened his mouth to stop the bhuta at the same time that it jumped towards the stranger, the curved knife held tightly in its hand. Ugra watched horrified. He didn't want the stranger to die in this manner. He wanted to kill him after defeating him in fair battle.

What happened in the next instant horrified Ugra even more. The stranger turned around with a speed that was impossible to behold. He pointed the palm of his left hand in the direction of the bhuta. There was a sound like the clap of thunder and a blue light shot out of his hands and hit the bhuta in the centre of his chest. The bhuta's body seemed suspended in mid air for a while, and then fell, dead even before it hit the ground.

There was complete silence for the next few minutes. The sun went down without anyone noticing. The five dozen new recruits who were being trained by Ugra huddled closer to each other. Bhargava looked at the stranger with an inscrutable expression, as if unsure of the latter's next move. Ugra was still dazed. Bhutas were the most dangerous of the Pataal Lok monsters, and considered virtually indestructible. Yet the stranger had destroyed him as if he had been a mere child and not one of the deadliest assassins in the netherworld.

Ugra looked closely at the stranger. He wondered why the man kept his head and face covered with a cloak. He wanted to look into the eyes of the person who had just killed one of his tribesmen.

'Who are you?' he asked, his voice a mixture of rage and curiosity.

The stranger looked in his direction, his face still veiled. 'They call me the Dark Lord!' he said softly, his voice a hoarse rasp.

◆

Ugra stared uncomprehendingly at the cloaked figure facing him. *This can't be*, he thought to himself. *The Dark Lord actually exists!* All these years, the chief of the Zataka Upanshughataks had disdainfully rejected the legend of the Dark Lord as the fancy of easily awed men. He hadn't thought that a man with the powers ascribed to him could exist in reality. Yet here was this cloaked figure who had demonstrated a small part of his powers in the ease with which he had destroyed the bhuta.

Ugra felt his heart beat faster with the knowledge that he had challenged this man to fight him. *If the bhuta hadn't appeared when he did, I would be the one lying dead now*, he thought with a slight shudder. Ugra wasn't afraid of any man. But the person standing in his presence was not a man. He was death incarnate. Disgusted at the fear threatening to paralyze him into inaction, Ugra vigorously shook his mane of matted hair; as if by that action he could also shake off the feeling of dread that was rapidly overpowering him.

'So are we going to duel today or are we not?' the Dark Lord asked in a genial tone.

Bhargava finally intervened. 'But Amartya, this is the chief of the Zataka Upanshughataks. If you kill him, who is going to train the assassins to enter Mrityulok?' Bhargava hesitated. What he had to say next was difficult for him. But he said it nonetheless, 'And...and Ugra is my friend. I can't have you kill him!'

Ugra's heart warmed to Bhargava. He had always considered the old man his friend, ever since he had saved his life. But he had never thought that Bhargava may look upon him as anything more than a tool to train the assassins. Hearing Bhargava calling him his friend filled the big asura with a joy he had not known till now. He also realized now why Bhargava had told the Dark Lord that he was the chief of the Zataka Upanshughataks earlier. He had done it so that the cloaked figure would refrain from hurting him. Ugra mentally kicked himself. *And I thought Bhargava was trying to scare this man by telling him who I was. He was actually pleading with him not to kill me*, he reflected with embarrassment.

The cloaked figure was laughing; it was a hoarse laugh, but a laugh undoubtedly. 'Who said I am going to kill Ugra? I just want to teach him how to use that damn sword.'

Ugra felt his anger rising again. It helped subdue the fear he felt in the Dark Lord's presence. 'It is easy to fight anyone when you use magic. Try fighting me without your tricks and I will show you how to use that sword.'

The cloaked figure chuckled. 'This is not magic, son. It is pure Brahman energy; the very force that moves the universe.' He paused, his veiled face lost in thought. 'But you have a point. I will not use this with you. It wouldn't be fair. I will fight you as a normal person, without the use of anything but my skill.'

Ugra relaxed. Irrespective of how powerful the Dark Lord was, Ugra had unshakeable faith in his own skills as a swordsman. He knew there was no one who could use a long blade like him. He got ready to duel. But the cloaked figure stopped him.

'While I will fight you without using the force of Brahman energy, would you want me to use some magic to get your bhuta back to life?' He chuckled again, while emphasizing the word 'magic', thinking to himself how anyone could confuse Brahman energy—the oldest form of power—with something as crude as magic.

Bhargava was astonished at Amartya's light-hearted mood. He hadn't heard him chuckle or joke in the past two hundred years, ever since he had known him. *Maybe getting him out of that bloody room of his is good for his mind*, he thought to himself.

Ugra and the other asuras watched dumbfounded as the Dark Lord pointed his index finger at the lifeless bhuta. A cloud of blue light enveloped the dead monster's body and the incredible power of the Brahman energy could be felt by all present, even at that distance. The asuras looked on amazed, as the bhuta started showing the first indications of regaining life. It started with the faint almost imperceptible movements of his extremities, and then transformed into more visible signs of life creeping back into his form. The bhuta stirred and finally opened his eyes with a jolt. He looked around and saw the dazed eyes of other asuras staring at him. Gradually, he realized that he was sitting on the ground, and he jumped up with a scream. Bhutas dreaded any contact with the earth as overexposure to it could reduce their potency.

'Welcome back, Nisata. You scared the living daylights out of me,' Ugra said exultantly, hugging the bhuta. 'I thought you were gone forever.'

Nisata gently extricated himself from his chief. He floated in the direction of the Dark Lord. Ugra tensed, concerned that the bhuta might again try and attack the cloaked man, and this time the Dark Lord may not be so merciful. But his anxiety was misplaced. To his utter amazement, Nisata prostrated himself in front of the Dark Lord. 'Forgive me, My Lord, I thought you were going to hurt my chief. I didn't know who you were.' His nasal voice was full of respect for the man who had brought him back to life.

The Dark Lord motioned to Nisata to rise. He was aware from his initial days in Pataal Lok how painful it was for a bhuta to be in contact with the ground and he wanted to spare it any superfluous pain. 'You were doing your duty, Nisata. I forgive you. Go now. Your chief and I have work to do!'

Nisata looked from the Dark Lord to Ugra, unsure what to do. Ugra nodded at him and the bhuta floated away into the darkness.

Ugra looked uncomfortably at the cloaked figure. He found it difficult to comprehend this man people called the Dark Lord. He had killed the kalakanja and sent him to the deepest recesses of hell, and yet just now, he had brought back to life the bhuta who had tried to kill him. The contradiction bothered him. But what perplexed him even more was that he was beginning to respect the man, perhaps even like him. Two things that were not easy for a man like Ugra to do.

'Uh...I-I wanted to thank you for bringing the bhuta...uh, Nisata...back to life,' Ugra mumbled in a low tone.

'It's quite okay. You don't need to thank me for that. I took his praana and I gave it back to him. It is inconsequential. You can, however, thank me later for teaching you how to use that sword,' the Dark Lord's voice was mildly mocking again, but this time, Ugra didn't find it within himself to react.

'It would be an honour to learn from you, My Lord!' he said softly.

◆

Ugra looked with satisfaction upon his latest batch of trained assassins. This was possibly the best lot amongst all the men he had trained so far for Bhargava. A few weeks had elapsed since the Dark Lord and Bhargava had visited the training arena, and their coming had provided a huge impetus to the enthusiasm of the new recruits. Seeing the Dark Lord instruct the fearsome chief of the Zataka Upanshughataks in the finer aspects of sword play, had made them even more enthusiastic about excelling in their training.

Ugra smiled with unbridled affection at Ghora, the boy who had grown to become a leader of men in a short time. It had been difficult at first. Ghora had too much kindness in his nature to become an assassin. But he was a natural hunter. Despite his youth and his disarming charm, he was now amongst the foremost warriors that Ugra had ever known. His prowess in the art of fighting exceeded even the best of the Zataka Upanshughataks. More importantly, however, he had shown an incredible talent for leading men. It was this particular trait, more than his fighting prowess, that convinced Ugra to announce Ghora as the commander of the assassin module being sent to Hastinapur. New recruits were being dispatched to the city of Hastinapur and the young boy would now lead these men when the time came.

Ghora's unit got ready to leave. They would enter Mrityulok through Magadha and surreptitiously make their way to Hastinapur. Ghora spoke to his men, and made his way towards the man he had begun to view as his father.

'Pranaam, Gurudev,' he kneeled down in front of Ugra, who blessed him and in a rare display of public affection, hugged the young man. He looked closely at Ghora and sensed that something was bothering the boy.

'You look troubled, son. What is the matter?' he asked quietly.

Ghora shuffled his feet uncomfortably. He had passed all the tests with remarkable ease, and Ugra had been more than vocal about his potential and bright future. But there were questions that plagued him, made him get up in the middle of the night, drenched in sweat.

'What is the matter with you?' Ugra repeated his question, more forceful now.

'Gurudev, why are we doing this?' he asked in a strained voice. 'Why do we want to kill innocent people in Mrityulok? What have they done to us?'

Ugra's face tightened. Since he had begun to think of Ghora as his adopted son, he too had begun to question his purpose in life. He had frequently considered leaving with Ghora to move to a new place, away from Pataal Lok, and start a fresh life somewhere else. But the debt he owed to Bhargava precluded any other preferences he may have otherwise had about leading a different life.

He looked now at Ghora and spoke firmly. This time, the voice was that of the chief of the Zataka Upanshughataks, and not that of the adoring mentor. 'It is not for us to question why,' he said his voice heavy with regret. 'Bhargava demands my loyalty and I demand yours. I have already offered Bhargava mine. Will you offer me yours?'

Ghora did not fail to sense Ugra's pain as he forced himself to say the words to his favourite pupil. He hung his head, ashamed at having questioned his teacher. The greater part of his soul still recoiled from what he knew he had to do when he reached Hastinapur. But the other part of him that was mortgaged in loyalty to Ugra, made him nod his acquiescence to his teacher.

'I will do what you have commanded me to do, or else I will not return with a head on my shoulders.'

He quickly walked back to his men, ready to leave the only land he had ever known as home.

Svapnasrsti

Jarasandha shifted his body impatiently. He had been standing, gazing through a carefully concealed peephole that gave him an unrestricted view of Kansa's bed chambers from his own room. The peephole had been built in such a way that it was virtually impossible for anyone in the guest room to notice. The acoustics of the adjacent room were architected in a manner that even the slightest whisper from the guest room could be heard in Jarasandha's chamber, but sounds from his room would be completely inaudible in the guest section. This had been done to enable Jarasandha to spy on the activities and conversations of specific guests that came to Magadha. In this case, it was being used to keep a tab on Kansa's movements, and this was not something that Jarasandha relished. It bothered him that he was making Kansa an unwitting player in his deal with the Dark Lord. But the stakes were too high. The Dark Lord had promised to make him, Jarasandha, the undisputed lord of all of Mrityulok if he helped him. Once he ascended that ladder over all the other powerful kings of Mrityulok, he intended to make Kansa his heir. This thought made him feel less guilty about what he was doing to his closest friend and brother-in-law.

The king of Magadha sighed. Power was such a strange experience. It didn't matter how much of it you had, you always wanted more. He was already one of the most powerful kings in Mrityulok. Most of the rulers in Bharat and the other lands of Mrityulok bowed to him. But to be the Lord of all of Mrityulok! That was a powerful dream indeed; a dream that only the Dark

Lord could help him achieve. And it would be his, if he supported the Dark Lord in his plans.

Jarasandha noticed Kansa move in his sleep in the other room. He was suddenly alert. It had begun! The Dark Lord had told him that he would be using the art of svapnasrsti on Kansa. Svapnasrsti was the ability to enter a person's mind and create a dream that would seem so vivid that the person dreaming it would be haunted by the reality of it, even after waking up. Frequent doses of svapnasrsti administered to a person could make them lose sight of what was real and what was imagined. This had already happened with Banasura and Chanur. They were now completely in the power of the Dark Lord, not knowing most of the time whether they were taking their own decisions or being prompted by some powerful external force.

There was a sudden gasp from Kansa, and Jarasandha watched him writhe in agony on his bed. Kansa's face reflected pain of such proportions that even the battle-hardened Jarasandha shuddered. And in that instant, he saw Kansa leap up from his bed, his hand clutching his heart. 'He killed me Devki...your son killed me,' he screamed in anguish, sobbing hysterically. His face reflected his betrayal and his torment.

◆

Ugrasena completed writing the letter to Kansa. His quill hovered over the page, unsure how to end the note. He wanted to write 'Your loving father' at the end of the message, but he didn't know how Kansa would react to it in his current frame of mind. Instead, he just wrote 'Your father' and hastily folded the letter in a scroll that would be carried by a messenger to his son in Magadha.

'Hand this to my son when you reach Jarasandha's court,' Ugrasena instructed the messenger. Rabhu nodded in understanding and turned to leave.

'And Rabhu...' Ugrasena called after the messenger. 'Hand it over only to the prince. No one else must know the contents.'

Rabhu nodded gravely and gave Ugrasena a final bow. The king's words and tone left him in no doubt about the importance of keeping the message confidential. He would make sure it reached the right hands.

◆

I have assembled a task force of fifty, My Lord!' Airawat said in a matter-of-fact tone. 'Another fifty will be ready in the next few days. These are the toughest men I could find in Madhuvan. Some of them are from the army, but majority are mercenaries who will fight anyone if the price is right.' He saw Ugrasena's cogitative expression and decided to explain.

'The mercenaries may not have the same code of ethics as our army, My Lord. But they are fearless and their fighting tactics are unconventional. I believe we will require people like those to fight the asura assassins.' Airawat waited for some reaction from his king, which was not long in coming.

'But how predictable will the mercenaries be? And will they be amenable to being instructed?' Ugrasena seemed to hesitate before continuing. 'We can't afford any chances when fighting with the asura insurgents, Airawat.'

Airawat had anticipated this argument. 'My Lord, the mercenaries practice the same discipline as our army personnel; perhaps even higher. That won't be an issue. And don't forget, while the mercenary will do anything for a price, they too are born of the same land as we. The only thing they hold dearer than money is the love for their country. They will give their life for Madhuvan...for the safety and honour of all the lands of Mrityulok' There was pride and conviction in Airawat's voice.

Ugrasena nodded his assent. 'That's good then. What are the next steps?'

'Special training for the task force has already commenced, My Lord. We should be ready in a month's time.' He paused, unsure of his next question.

Ugrasena, however, noticed his hesitation. Airawat had been too long with him for the king to miss these strategic pauses. 'You wanted to ask me something, Airawat?' he prodded gently.

'Uh yes, My Lord...I was wondering...would Prince Kansa be joining us? Vasudev is held in awe by everyone, especially after he defeated Somdatta so decisively. But the men would be happier to be led by their own prince.'

Ugrasena looked hard at him. 'And you, Airawat? Would you also be happier to be led by Kansa?'

Airawat looked away. He didn't know what answer the king expected. Hence, he spoke from his heart. 'My Lord, I am a soldier. I will follow any general as long as he is worthy of respect and has the welfare of the country close to his heart. Both Vasudev and Kansa meet these criteria. But the rest of the team...I think they would be more motivated if they were led by their own Prince. And the fact is that there is no general in this land who inspires the best in these men as Prince Kansa does.'

'Hmm!' Ugrasena mumbled softly. 'Then for your sake and the sake of your men's motivation, let us hope that Kansa returns to Madhuvan soon. I have written to him and if I know my son, he will be here soon.' Ugrasena smiled at his cavalry commander.

Airawat's face reflected his happiness at the news. Like most people, he hadn't failed to notice the growing strain between the king and Prince Kansa in the recent past. But he was relieved that Ugrasena had called for his son. Airawat, too, felt confident that Kansa would return to lead the Madhuvan task force. And with the valiant Kansa leading them, they would break the back of the asura assassins.

◆

Jarasandha took the letter from Rabhu's hand. He was glad he had spies on his payroll in every major kingdom including Madhuvan. He asked Rabhu to wait while he took the letter with him to his anukta kaksha. He wanted to read it in peace and without anyone else watching. He took the letter out of the scroll, and his hands trembled with excitement as he began to read what was written:

My son,

I hope you have found the peace you were searching for, when you left your home. I sincerely hope so, because I haven't had one moment of peace in my life ever since you left. I know you feel I have let you down somehow. And perhaps I have.

You asked me a question the other day when I told you about your birth. And I did not answer the question. Perhaps my inability to give you an answer made you imagine things differently than how they were. Your question was whether I, too, like your mother, ever felt like killing you when you were a baby. I couldn't answer this question that day because it breaks my heart to even think of such a thing for you. The truth is that the first time I laid my eyes on you, as you huddled close to that attendant while your mother was trying to kill you, I loved you in that instant. It didn't matter that you were born from another man. I accepted you as mine...as a gift from the gods. I gave you all my love and you returned more than I ever gave you. It saddened me sometimes that I couldn't give the same love to your other brothers and sisters because all my love went to you and Devki. But your affection and regard for me, more than made up for everything else.

I am writing this letter to you today, because I need your help. Madhuvan and its people need their Prince to return. And no one desires that as much as I do.

I would not be exaggerating if I said that the entire land of Bharat and other lands in Mrityulok are in danger. There is a conspiracy afoot. Pataal Lok has sent asura assassins that have breached the borders of several kingdoms and spread all over key locations in Mrityulok. These assassins are lying in wait for a signal from their commanders in Pataal Lok. At the first indication, they will start spreading chaos all over our world. And then...we believe that when the chaos reaches its zenith, Pataal Lok will launch a full-scale attack all over Mrityulok. We don't yet know why they are doing this. But Maharishi Narada—yes, Narada himself told me all this—believes that this attack could happen anytime in the future.

We need to defend ourselves against this imminent danger. Narada is personally travelling to various kingdoms to caution them and advise them to assemble special covert task forces to search out these assassins and destroy them. Airawat has already started preparing such a task force at Madhuvan and both he and I are looking forward for you to come and lead this as the Madhuvan commander-in-chief. Meanwhile, Vasudev has gone to Bateshwar to ask Sini Yadav to build a similar task force there. I mentioned to Airawat that Vasudev would lead the Madhuvan task force till such time that you return, but I know that won't really be necessary. Because I have no doubt that as soon as you read this letter, you will take the swiftest horse available in Magadha, and return to your father and your home.

Meanwhile, do not mention any of this to Jarasandha. I know he is your friend and brother-in-law but he could be involved in this conspiracy.

Come back soon my son. Your motherland and your old father both need you here.

While I know you will come as soon as you can, do send me a brief reply about your arrival through Rabhu, the messenger I sent along with this letter. I will accordingly let Airawat know when he can welcome back his commander-in-chief at Madhuvan.

Your father,
Ugrasena

Jarasandha's eyes gleamed with a strange fusion of anger and elation as he finished reading the letter. He was furious and perturbed that Ugrasena knew about the Dark Lord's plan, and that Narada was already on his way to caution other kingdoms. But he was delighted that he had confiscated this letter before it fell into Kansa's hands. The implications of Kansa reading this letter were not lost on Jarasandha and he shuddered at the consequences. Not only would it have pitted Kansa against him, but reading this letter would have ensured his immediate departure for Madhuvan. The fact that the letter would have also brought a reunion between the father and son was an additional concern. Jarasandha couldn't afford any of this.

I have to destroy this letter, he decided. It was too risky to have it lying around, waiting to be discovered by someone, especially Kansa. Jarasandha looked around the anukta kaksha. The fire place had not been lit in days. He debated whether to call one of the attendants to start the fire, and then decided against it. Jarasandha never ever asked for the fire to be lit unless it was extremely cold, and the weather right now didn't warrant one. It would unnecessarily make the attendants suspicious. But then he didn't need a full-fledged fire to burn the letter, he considered. Jarasandha walked towards his table, his eyes intent on the exquisitely shaped lamp kept there. The flame from the lamp would be sufficient to incinerate the letter completely. Jarasandha rolled it up like a pipe and held it at one end, careful not to burn his hand. For a brief moment, he faltered at the thought of destroying the one thing that could provide peace to Kansa's tortured mind. But the thought of compromising the plan and risking everything that had been done till now made him steel his mind and ignore whatever scruples he may have had.

Jarasandha watched the flame leap up from the lamp to consume the letter. In the blink of the eye, the note was reduced to cinders. The words from Ugrasena that could have rescued Kansa from certain disaster were lost forever; scattered as ashes, a sign of death and destruction that was bound to occur as a result of events beyond human control. Destiny was playing out its hand.

◆

Jarasandha found Kansa sitting by the lake adjacent to the palace. The prince of Madhuvan seemed oblivious to Jarasandha walking towards him. His eyes looked glazed as if he was lost in his own world, where reality and dreams had ceased to exist separately. He jumped with a start as Jarasandha touched him lightly on his shoulder. The fear in his eyes was palpable and he looked like a caged animal who knew he was trapped in a prison from where there was no escape. He stared, blinking rapidly at Jarasandha and his body seemed to relax a little as he saw who it was. 'You startled me!' he said softly, trying to sound natural, but his voice had lost its gentle quality. Somehow, it sounded strained and harsh.

'I am sorry, brother; I didn't mean to come up on you like that. I didn't realize you were lost in your thoughts,' Jarasandha said, trying to help Kansa in making his reaction appear normal.

Kansa looked confused. 'I wasn't lost in my thoughts...' he started to say, and then stopped. 'I...uh...I don't recall how I reached here. I remember waking up and then...nothing else...' His voice trailed off, uncertainty and puzzlement evident on his handsome face.

Jarasandha looked anxiously at his brother-in-law. He badly wanted to be the undisputed master of Mrityulok but not at the cost of anything happening to Kansa. He didn't want his sisters hurt either; he knew they couldn't live without him. Moreover, Kansa in this state wouldn't be of any use to him to do what needed to be done in the days to come.

'Brother, you need to get a grip on yourself,' Jarasandha said in a gentle tone, hating himself for what he knew he was going to do next.

'I am trying,' Kansa said in a whisper. 'But I don't know what's wrong with me.' He hesitated, as if unsure whether to share his fears with Jarasandha, then continued. 'I keep getting these dreams...more like nightmares, where I am being killed...by a child...born of Devki.' He paused, a stricken look was on his face, 'And every time the child kills me, Devki just stands there laughing...and thanking the child for killing me!' Kansa's voice broke as he choked on the last few words.

The svapnasrsti used by the Dark Lord is beginning to affect his mind, Jarasandha thought to himself. 'It's nothing, brother. It's just your mind playing games with you,' he said aloud, trying to make light of the whole thing.

'No it isn't. It seems so real. When I get up, it feels like my chest is actually gushing out blood...where that child had pierced my torso with his sword. And Devki's reaction...that, too, feels so real...as if it was happening right in front of me,' Kansa shivered as a wave of nausea swept over him.

Jarasandha held him by his shoulders. 'Look, all this is because you are away from home. And...' He paused, knowing he had to put this in the right manner for Kansa to take the bait. '...and also because lately you have been having issues with your father.'

'What does that have anything to do with my nightmares?' Kansa snapped.

Jarasandha kept his voice calm. 'You are feeling isolated because of the strain your relationship has undergone with your father. And you are away from home, so you probably feel that others in your family—like Devki—have also forsaken you.' Jarasandha waited for this to sink into Kansa's mind before continuing, 'And this is affecting your psychology; making you feel as if those closest to you don't care about you. Your nightmares are an exaggerated manifestation of the stress you are going through.'

Kansa seemed to take in all of this. Then the same look of helplessness covered his features. 'What do I do? What do I do, dammit? This is driving me insane!' he uttered a muted scream, full of agony.

Jarasandha knew Kansa might never be so vulnerable again.

This was the time to strike. 'I think you should write to Ugrasena. Let your father know how you feel. I think writing to him and opening your heart to him will make you feel better. And who knows...perhaps he will write back to you and things will be better between the two of you,' Jarasandha said in as casual a voice as he could muster. It was imperative that Kansa did not suspect his intentions.

'You think that will work? Kansa looked uncertain. 'I don't see how it will stop all the nightmares. And what if Father says something that will take us further apart?'

Jarasandha shook his head impatiently. 'What is there to lose in this, Kansa? I think it will help your mind to share what you are feeling with your father. At least try it. Anything is better than just sitting around like this!' He spoke the last words with greater feeling than he had wanted to, worried that Kansa may decide against writing to Ugrasena. It was imperative that he did.

After what seemed like an eternity but was no more than a few seconds, Kansa seemed to make up his mind. 'Alright! I will send him a brief letter,' he said. To his surprise, he suddenly felt a lot better, just having decided to do this. *Maybe Jarasandha is right. Perhaps I will feel better after sharing my feelings with Father*, he thought with a weak smile.

Jarasandha was ecstatic. 'Wonderful!' he exclaimed. 'Write a letter to him now, and I will personally make sure it reaches him before the day comes to an end tomorrow.'

Kansa hugged Jarasandha with warmth. *I am blessed to have you close to me, my friend*, he thought to himself. He failed to notice the triumphant smile on Jarasandha's face.

◆

'Get me Upadha,' Jarasandha said curtly to his personal attendant. 'And make it quick,' he snapped.

The attendant speculated why his master was so edgy today. But more than that, he wondered why Jarasandha had asked him to summon the foremost forger in Magadha, and that too in such haste.

◆

Pranaam Pitashree,

I realize I have caused you much pain in the past few days. Perhaps, I was so shocked at what you told me about my birth that I found it difficult to accept that I was someone else's son, and not yours as I always believed. And I lashed out at the only person whom I could in that instant—you!

I want you to know that I may be a demon's son by blood, but I will always remain your son by virtue. And no fact about my birth can ever change that.

I have been a self-obsessed fool these past few days; and in being so I have gone far away from you when instead I should have been with you, taking care of you at this time. But I will change this!

I intend to leave Magadha in a couple of days and return home to you and my family. In the meanwhile, I am sending this letter to you so you have my apologies and my love even before I reach Madhuvan.

I would have liked to leave for home tomorrow itself but Jarasandha would feel slighted if I left in such haste.

I feel as if I am alive again after an eternity. Pranaam,

Your loving son,
Kansa

Jarasandha smiled smugly as he finished reading the letter Kansa had given him to send to Ugrasena. The plan had worked.

He looked at the tall, unsmiling man standing courteously in his presence. Upadha was a forger with an almost miraculous talent for copying anything he set his mind to. He had been in

Jarasandha's service for several years, and it was he who had been given the onerous task of forging the documents for the asura assassins who were being smuggled into Mrityulok over the last several years. With the exception of the five asuras caught by the Madhuvan border security, there had been no other case of the forged documents having been discovered. The man was perfect for the job Jarasandha had in mind for him.

Jarasandha handed Kansa's letter to Upadha. 'I want you to study this handwriting carefully. And then you will write a different letter—one that I will dictate to you!' he said with a gleam in his eyes.

Upadha bowed, his face expressionless. This was his job, and there was no one better than him. It would be done.

Tamastamah Prabha

Bhargava watched the unmoving figure of the man he had grown to respect and love over the past couple of centuries. Amartya Kalyanesu appeared lost to the world, his eyes closed in a state of deep meditation. The cloak that always covered his head and a large part of his burnt face had been taken off and placed neatly on the ground, next to him. It was important to take off the hood because the energy of Brahman harnessed from the universe would enter the body through the crown of the head, at a point known as the Sahasrara Chakra. The cloak would obstruct the flow of energy entering Amartya's body. In most people, the energy flowing through the Chakra would be too feeble to be visible. In Amartya's case, however, the flow of Brahman energy was so strong that it almost appeared as if a shower of blue light was pouring through the Sahasrara Chakra into his whole being. Amartya's body seemed clothed with the blue radiance.

He looks so peaceful sitting like this, Bhargava thought, sighing to himself. *It is almost as if he was still in Swarglok, before Brahma cursed him.* Bhargava clenched his teeth in anger as the memory of what had been done to Amartya flashed through his mind. It wasn't just that Brahma had wrongly banished him from his world, almost killing him in the process. What was worse was that he had thrown him into the deepest pit of Pataal Lok—the seventh level, also called the Tamastamah Prabha. And someone like Amartya who had only practised goodness in his life hadn't been prepared for what awaited him in that dreaded region.

The horrible part was that for the first seven days that Amartya spent there, he had none of his brahmarishi powers. Brahma had used the most powerful weapon in Swarglok—the Brahmashira—on Amartya, which was four times more powerful than the dreaded Brahmastra. Used on any deva, it would have killed a demi-god instantly. On a brahmarishi like Amartya, its effect was that it took away from him all the power of Brahman energy for a period of seven days. Seven days that Amartya was totally powerless, left to survive in Tamastamah Prabha where no outsider could survive for more than a day.

Bhargava shuddered as he recalled Amartya's experience in the hell of hells for those seven days...

♦

Amartya felt himself falling from the skies, sucked into a vortex of air that was impossible to break out of. He found himself powerless as his body swirled in the whirlpool of energy created by the Brahmashira. Amartya felt himself being pulled through different planes of existence of the three worlds. And then just as he thought that he was trapped in the air bubble for eternity, he saw the landscape around him begin to change dramatically. There were no lakes or seas or oceans in this land. He realized with a jolt that the air bubble carrying him had entered Pataal Lok—the lowest of the three worlds. As he was carried further, he remembered from his earlier study of the three worlds, that Pataal Lok had seven levels—Ratanprabha, Sharkaraprabha, Valukaprabha, Pankkprabha, Dhoomprabha, Tamahprabha and Tamastamah Prabha, the seventh and most feared plane of existence. With the exception of Ratanprabha, none of the other six levels had any mountains or oceans or any manner of habitation. The width of each level of existence in Pataal Lok increased as he passed from one plane to the next. Tamastamah Prabha, the seventh and the final level within Pataal Lok, was the largest in breadth and the most barren—and the place where he realized he was headed.

Amartya braced himself for the inevitable impact as the air bubble carrying him raced towards the surface of Tamastamah Prabha. When the impact came, surprisingly he felt nothing. The bubble had disappeared and he found himself lying on the ground. He looked around him. The surface of this region was covered with jagged stones, of a dirty brown hue. The land stretched for yojanas around him and he was unable to see any protrusion on the surface. There were no trees, no mountains and no water body as far as his eyes could see.

Amartya suddenly felt exhausted and drained of energy. He hadn't felt this way even once after his initiation as a brahmarishi and he wondered why his body felt bereft of the force of Bal and Atibal. Part of his mind was still reeling under the shock of Brahma's sudden attack and his final words as he hurled the Brahmashira at him. What was it that Brahma had screamed in rage? Amartya tried to remember and his soul recoiled as he recalled the exact words Brahma had hurled at him before he unleashed the Brahmashira upon him: 'A man who cannot respect his guru is not a man, and definitely not a brahmarishi...he is a demon of the lowest order and should be relegated to the lowest pit in hell where demons reside.'

Amartya sagged to the ground, his mind tortured as the words of his former guru finally sank into his head. Brahma had called him a demon of the lowest order. Why? Try as he might, he couldn't comprehend why Brahma had punished him in this way. It wasn't he who had insulted his guru. It was the others. Yet Brahma had done this to him. The pain in his mind threatened to consume him. It was in that instant that Amartya became aware of the searing pain on the left side of his face. He brought the palm of his hand to touch the face, and recoiled in horror. His hand had gone through the side of his face and he could feel his fingers inside his mouth. The skin on that side had been burnt completely and what little remained was hanging limply on the side. Amartya choked, partly in shock at the ravaging of his face, but mostly owing to the agonizing pain that had taken hold of him. The pain grew in mounting proportions, and despite his struggling with it, he found himself falling to the ground in a swoon. He lost consciousness even before his head hit the stony ground with a thud.

It had become dark when Amartya woke, still dizzy with the agonizing pain. He felt weak with hunger and the thirst was gnawing at him. Once again, he wondered why he was feeling the symptoms of a mortal, when the powers of Brahman bestowed on him should have protected him from symptoms of pain, hunger and thirst. He shook his head in pain and frustration, trying to decide what to do next. It was then that he became aware that he was not alone. He couldn't make out anyone else's presence, but he was certain that there were others besides him, and not too far from where he stood.

It was an eerie feeling; knowing that someone was there, and not being able to see them. Time passed slowly, too slowly. He stood where he was, not daring to move. A strange fear had him in its grip; he hadn't felt anything like this since he was a child and afraid of the dark. As his eyes started to adjust to the growing darkness, he began to get a better sense of his surroundings. He still couldn't see anyone distinctly, but he noticed some activity, a little ahead of where he was. He willed himself to walk towards the source of the movement. The forms grew more distinct in appearance as he reached closer. And then Amartya gasped in terror. More than a dozen serpents were feeding on something that looked like a corpse of an asura. The serpents lay so close together as they feasted on the cadaver that it was impossible to distinguish the snakes from each other. Amartya stared at the frenzied feeding, mesmerized by the sight. Suddenly, one of the serpents turned away from the corpse and looked at where he stood, watching them. Its eyes gleamed yellow and it seemed as if they were on fire. As if on cue, the other serpents too turned to stare in Amartya's direction. Twelve pairs of eyes spitting fire bored into his mind. The snakes appeared almost human in the way they looked at him, their forked tongues flowing out of their mouth and curling in a smile of anticipation. They found the man standing in front of them more enticing than the corpse they were feeding on. Amartya watched in horror as the serpents moved away from the dead body and slithered towards him. When they were within spitting distance of him, they raised themselves on their tails till they were at eye level with him. He wanted to scream and run but the hypnotic eyes of the snakes held him rooted to the spot, and he found it impossible to tear his gaze away from them. Then all of a sudden, their gleaming eyes registered a fear of their own; and as suddenly as they had approached him, they vanished, gliding away into the darkness. Something had scared the serpents. Amartya did not know what, but he felt his heart beat gradually return to normal as he saw them retreat.

He took a deep breath to calm himself; as he took in the lungful of air he sensed the foulest smell he had encountered in his life. It was the stench of decayed flesh, putrified over scores of years; and it came from somewhere behind him. Even before he could turn around to see what it was, he felt something soggy and scaly enter his ears. He turned to find himself face to face with a human-like creature. But this was no human. The creature had sunken eyes, mummified skin and narrow limbs. Its gigantic belly contrasted starkly with its slender neck. The creature had a host of maggots coming out of its ears and nose. Amartya instinctively brushed the side of his head with his hand, and a maggot that had entered his ear dropped to the ground. He looked at the maggot-infested creature standing next to him with a mix of fear and disgust. This was the first time he had come face to face with a bhuta. He realized now what had scared away the serpents. Bhutas were considered the most dangerous creatures in Paatal Lok and their hunger and thirst were impossible to quench irrespective of how much they ate or drank. Normally, bhutas inhabited the three levels of existence above the Tamastamah

Prabha and rarely ventured into the seventh level. This one had probably been banished or had somehow lost his way into the hell of hells.

The bhuta looked greedily at Amartya. He waved at the maggots covering his face in an attempt to dislodge them and several of them fell to the ground. The ones remaining buzzed in anger and huddled closer to each other. The hypnotic effect from staring into the snake's eyes was over and Amartya tried to calm himself. He took a step back, away from the bhuta, and concentrated his mind to harness the universal force of Brahman. As he watched the bhuta approach him again, Amartya extended his arm to unleash the Brahman energy, just enough to repulse the creature. To his utter amazement, nothing happened. Amartya focused his mind and tried again; this time trying to invoke a larger quantum of energy. Again...nothing happened! It was as if he had never had the ability to control the force of Brahman. The monster grinned malevolently and leaped towards him. Amartya screamed in terror as he felt the fetid breath of the creature on his face. The momentum of the bhuta's jump and his weight knocked Amartya to the ground. He struggled to push it away but the creature seemed to be possessed of supernatural strength and in the absence of his brahmarishi powers, Amartya found his efforts to wrench free of the creature were rendered futile.

The bhuta started to bite off the pieces of flesh that were hanging limply from Amartya's face. Amartya screamed as the already unbearable agony of his wound reached unimaginable proportions. Time seemed suspended as the bhuta bit off pieces of his flesh, bit by bit. The only sounds to be heard were the tearing off of the flesh and the disgusting munching noises coming from its mouth. And then Amartya gradually became aware of another sound. It started like the wind blowing on the surface of the ground, as if from a great distance. However, in a matter of a few seconds it gained intensity and it was as if a thousand banshees were screaming in fury. The bhuta heard it too and he paused his munching. The screaming held more meaning for him than for Amartya, it seemed. In the next instant, the bhuta leapt off Amartya and began running away. Amartya watched his retreating back. Even in his current state, he marvelled at the sight. The bhuta looked like he was gliding in the air, his feet barely touching the ground. Amartya recalled from his days in Brahma's ashram that bhutas shirked any contact with the ground as it depleted them of their supernatural strength. This bhuta was moving at an incredible speed. The screaming sounds had by now turned into a roar. Amartya didn't have to know what was happening to figure out that there was imminent danger. Instinct told him to head in a direction away from where the bhuta was going, because whatever was coming from afar definitely involved the vile monster. He got up and started running diagonally away from the bhuta. After he had placed what he thought was sufficient distance between the bhuta and himself, he paused to look back. The roaring noises had by now reached a crescendo. Amartya watched stupefied as the ground along which the bhuta had moved began to turn black. He wondered at this and then it hit him! Thousands of serpents were slithering in the direction of the fleeing bhuta. The deafening noise was a result of so many snakes moving together on the gravelly surface and their collective hissing and spitting. Amartya guessed the serpents that had been scared away by the bhuta must have got their own kind to come seek vengeance. Tamastamah Prabha was the land of the serpents. The bhuta was an outsider for them. As much as Amartya himself was. But then Amartya hadn't snatched away the food from the serpents as the bhuta had, which made it a prime enemy; it had to be taught a lesson so that other outsiders wouldn't dare to come into the region of Tamastamah Prabha and challenge the true inhabitants of the land—the serpents.

Only the fittest survive! Amartya thought to himself. *It doesn't matter if you are strong. There will always be someone stronger than you. Unless...unless you can be stronger than everyone else...*

The epitome of immortal goodness that was Amartya Kalyanesu clenched his teeth to master the agony that threatened to subdue him yet again. The anguish and pain he felt at Brahma's betrayal of his trust began to give way to the initial symptoms of anger and resentment He turned his back on the sight of the serpents chasing the bhuta, and slowly started walking in search of a place he could lie down and find some semblance of peace.

◆

Bhargava's reminiscence was interrupted by the screeching notes of an owl. He looked around him. It had begun to turn dark. Amartya was still immersed in meditation, his concentration unbroken. Once again, Bhargava was thankful for having found Amartya. He wondered how different his destiny would have been if he hadn't gone to Tamastamah Prabha that day...

◆

Bhargava had spent the last few hours in the most desolate stretches of Tamastamah Prabha. His quest for a specific medicinal herb had been futile so far. He was looking for a particular plant that was to be found only in the land of the serpents. The leaves from this plant, when mixed with other concoctions that he had evolved, would provide him the cure he was looking for.

Bhargava was an udbhividyak (ethno-botanist) of the highest order and the medicines and panaceas he had developed over the years had served as palliatives and magic cures for several diseases and ailments. But there was one particular ailment that had been eluding even him. Over the past few months, a lot of asuras had been complaining of severe headaches, dizziness and eye infections. Bhargava had initially thought these were separate ailments and had treated them accordingly. However, as none of the standard cures worked, and the number of sick asuras drastically shot up, Bhargava was compelled to believe that these were not isolated symptoms but the result of a single virus.

Months of study indicated that the only plant that could cure these symptoms was to be found in the seventh level of Pataal Lok, in the dreaded Tamastamah Prabha. This plant had mallow leaves, which when ground to a fine paste and applied around the eyes and forehead of a person, would prevent the infection causing the symptoms. The mallow plant was edible in nature and the only non-fleshy product that the serpents in Tamastamah Prabha fed on. It had fruits that were round and shaped like cheese wedges, which gave the plant its nickname. The mallow plant had immense curative properties.

Bhargava had almost given up on his search and was about to leave when he heard an uproar from a distance. It seemed like a scream; the only difference was that the shriek sounded almost mortal. And it had a petrified note to it. The intensity of the cry told Bhargava he didn't have a moment to lose if he had to save whoever it was. He rushed in the direction of the commotion. The scuffling and disturbance was emanating from inside a cave. Bhargava entered the cave, chanting the mantras he had learnt from childhood, to give him strength. What he saw left even him horrified.

A pair of pisacas were attacking a mortal. One of the pisacas had punctured the mortal's abdomen with its spike and the other one was feeding on the face of the hapless man. Pieces of flesh and bone had been torn asunder and the mortal was bleeding profusely. Bhargava concentrated his mind to focus on his innermost core. And he began to chant the mantra he had sworn never to use on anyone.

It was the most potent mantra known only to a few of the most powerful practitioners in Pataal Lok. Once invoked, it would unleash the force of Aghasamarthan, the opposing force of Brahman used by the Gods. Like the force of Brahman, the Aghasamarthan also harnessed energy from the universe, but unlike the former, the Aghasamarthan energy fed on all the evil forces present in the universe. And Aghasamarthan was quantum times less controllable than the force of Brahman.

A person using it could get so caught up in its evil influence that he would find it impossible to break out of it. After a time, the user ceased to control the evil force. The force of Aghasamarthan controlled the user. Bhargava had invoked the force only once before in his life and the experience had convinced him never to use it again. But this occasion was an exception. He couldn't allow the brutal murder of a mortal in Pataal Lok.

'Stop!' Bhargava shouted at the pair of pisacas. The two creatures turned around from their prey to see who had dared to disturb their meal. There was a flicker of recognition as they saw Bhargava. The udbhividyak was a known man within all the seven levels of Pataal Lok and was held in awe by even the most powerful asuras and council members. But the pisacas were beyond reason by now. Their blood lust and the taste of live flesh made them disregard the note of warning in Bhargava's voice. They turned their backs to him and went back to eating the mortal. It was a mistake they wouldn't live to regret.

Bhargava finished chanting the deadly mantra, and his body began to turn a green hue as the evil forces of Aghasamarthan rushed in from all over the universe to become a part of him. Then when it seemed that the energy building within him would burst through every pore of his existence, he emitted a low sigh that emanated from the pit of his stomach. In the same moment, he extended both his index fingers in the direction of the pisacas. The intense green light that burst out of his fingers reduced them to ash in the blink of an eye.

The mortal, barely alive, stared at Bhargava. The udbhividyak looked fearsome, his eyes burning a fiery green and his body too enveloped in the green shower. Bhargava chanted another set of mantras in order to control the Aghasamarthan force that threatened to consume him. Gradually, the green force surrounding him began to wane and his eyes reverted to their natural colour. He looked closely at the mortal he had just saved from certain death. The left side of the man's face was completely burnt. The charred flesh was hanging loosely on the side. Most of it had been eaten away by the two pisacas he had just saved the man from. His abdomen was a wreck of blood and gore, where one of the pisacas had buried his spike inside his gut. Yet with all the wounds he had, the man was still alive. *He is strong beyond belief*, Bhargava thought in amazement. He wondered who the mortal was and how he had landed in the hell of hells.

'Who are you?' Bhargava asked in a soft voice as he felt for the wounded man's pulse to gauge whether he would live. The man returned his gaze unblinkingly. He was alive but it seemed to Bhargava that something in him had died forever.

After what seemed like an eternity, the man replied and his voice, when he spoke was rasping and hoarse, no longer the one he had been born with. 'Amartya Kalyanesu...ordained as brahmarishi by Vishnu and Shiva...cursed by Brahma to remain forever in this hell.'

Bhargava stared incredulously at the man he had just saved. News of the man who had been initiated by the supreme gods as the youngest brahmarishi in the history of the universe had travelled to Pataal Lok. Bhargava had heard about it. He couldn't believe he was standing next to the same man who he had heard had single-handedly defeated the combined forces of all the devas after his initiation as a brahmarishi.

Bhargava fell down on his knees and bowed in respect to Amartya. 'My Lord, I would be blessed if you accompany me to Ratanprabha—my house, as my honoured guest.'

Ratanprabha was the first and the highest level within Pataal Lok where the royalty and the mightiest of the asuras resided.

Amartya nodded weakly as he raised his hand to bless the man kneeling before him. He did not know yet that the effects of the Brahmashira would wear off in a few hours' time and he would regain his brahmarishi powers before the sun would set that day. The white-haired Bhargava and the grievously wounded brahmarishi walked alongside each other. It was not only the beginning of the seventh day of Amartya's banishment to Pataal Lok; it was also the start of a friendship that would endure for a lifetime. Bhargava hadn't found the mallow leaves he had come in search for, but he had found something that was far more important to him...the one person who could help him seek revenge on Indra and the rest of the devas.

◆

Amartya opened his eyes, his meditation finally over. As he bent to pick up his cloak from the ground, he became aware of Bhargava sitting close by, watching him.

Amartya smiled at him, but his disfigured face made it look more like a grimace. 'Have you been waiting long, Bhargava?' he asked gently.

'I had come to talk to you,' Bhargava replied returning his smile. He took a deep breath, 'I just had word from Jarasandha. Narada has started his campaign of cautioning various kingdoms about the presence of our assassins on Mrityulok. Some of these kings have started preparations of their own against this danger, while others have decided to play the wait-and-watch game.'

Amartya nodded. The meditation had calmed him and he did not react to Bhargava's report. 'What news of Kansa? How is he doing?'

At the mention of Kansa, Bhargava's face grew grim. 'Kansa has started showing signs of delusion and paranoid schizophrenia,' he said and paused. 'It appears your svapnasrsti has worked its effects on him faster than we thought. Maybe because his mind is in a vulnerable state these days.'

Amartya nodded again. There was no joy in his expression. 'Kansa will become completely schizophrenic in the next few days,' he said tonelessly. 'Once his dark side takes over, he will do whatever his inherent nature compels him to do.'

The two men sat quietly as the night turned darker and the

shadows grew heavier. Finally Bhargava spoke. 'Are we doing the right thing, Amartya? Do the means justify the end?'

Amartya coughed hoarsely. He knew this was not the first time Bhargava was suffering from self-doubt, and it wouldn't be the last time either. 'In the end, there is only the end...not the means. Swarglok has to be cleaned of the corruption that people like Indra have pushed it into. Nothing that we do in order to root out that corruption is unjustifiable, Bhargava. Not the destruction of Kansa; not even the death of other innocent mortals. The bigger evil lies elsewhere and if the supreme gods will not do anything about it, then someone has to.'

Bhargava listened quietly. He knew Amartya was right. Indra had committed every form of debauchery and depravity over the past few centuries. Yet, neither Shiva nor Vishnu had taken him to task. *The vile man rules over all the devas and is steeped in sin... still no one says or does anything,* Bhargava fumed in silent fury. Images of his mother's body lying in a pool of blood clouded his vision, as they always did whenever he remembered the trauma of his own past.

Time crept on as the two men sat lost in their own thoughts; each one consumed by his private hell and thinking what the future had in store for him. Meanwhile, the wheels of destiny kept rolling. They stopped for no one; not even for a brahmarishi.

Turned over to the Dark Side

Jarasandha finished reading the letter he had dictated to Upadha. *The forger has surpassed himself. Ugrasena will never know the difference*, he thought with satisfaction.

Jarasandha had worded the letter to Ugrasena with great care. It was imperative that the old king of Madhuvan did not realize that this particular letter was not written by Kansa. Jarasandha had already destroyed the original letter written by Kansa to his father, but not before Upadha had scanned Kansa's handwriting in order to forge the duplicate letter dictated by Jarasandha.

Jarasandha had crafted the letter in such a way that it would appear as a reply from Kansa in response to Ugrasena's letter. *This should break the umbilical cord between father and son forever*, he thought with a devious smile. He dismissed the forger with a significant reward for his services and asked his attendant to call for Rabhu—the messenger sent by Ugrasena.

Rabhu materialized almost immediately. It had been a few hours since he had handed Ugrasena's letter, meant for Kansa, to Jarasandha; and he had been wondering what he had been up to. He knew the Magadha king would not have given the letter to Kansa; that much was clear to him. But how would he explain to Ugrasena that he had returned without a reply from Kansa? This petrified him. If Ugrasena got to know he had not handed the letter to Kansa, the punishment would be instant death.

'Here, take this letter and give it to your king,' Jarasandha commanded handing the same scroll to Rabhu that he had carried from Madhuvan.

'B-but, My Lord,' Rabhu stuttered in fright. 'What do I tell the king?'

Jarasandha looked contemptuously at the man standing in front of him. He hated traitors, even though Rabhu had deceived his master for his own benefit. 'Let Ugrasena know you gave his letter personally to Kansa...and tell him that the prince has sent his reply.'

Rabhu wavered. He wasn't sure about this. 'But, My Lord, I gave the king's letter to you. Has the prince replied to that letter?' His voice faltered as he saw the look of fury on Jarasandha's face.

'Listen to me, you dog!' Jarasandha growled, shaking Rabhu roughly by the neck. 'You will tell Ugrasena exactly what I have told you. You gave Kansa the letter Ugrasena sent through you, and the prince has sent back this letter in reply.' He let go off Rabhu's throat. 'Now do you understand this or should I break your neck for you?'

Rabhu cowered in fear. Words refused to come out of his mouth and he was barely able to nod his head in understanding.

'Now get out of my sight,' Jarasandha snarled.

As Rabhu hastily turned to leave, Jarasandha called after him, 'And remember my friend...Ugrasena might forgive your betrayal if you tell him what happened. But I will find you out from the deepest corner of Mrityulok and cut you into a thousand pieces if you betray me!'

Rabhu nodded and rushed out of the palace, the scroll containing the letter clutched in his hand. He wanted to put as much distance between him and Magadha as was possible.

◆

'You gave the letter to Kansa?' Ugrasena questioned Rabhu when they were alone in the King's personal chambers.

'Yes, My Lord. I personally handed it over to the prince,' Rabhu hoped his voice sounded firm. Despite the long ride from Magadha, the dread of Jarasandha was still starkly vivid in his mind.

'Hmm!' Ugrasena murmured to himself. 'And how did the prince look? Did he seem well?'

Rabhu wondered what reply he should give. 'He seemed well enough, My Lord.' He seemed to hesitate. 'He read the letter and then asked me to wait while he wrote a reply for you.'

Ugrasena did not seem to notice that the messenger's voice quivered unnaturally as he spoke the last sentence. Nor did he observe the shifting of his feet or the other symptoms that should have told him something was wrong. He was excited that Kansa had sent him a reply and was eager to dismiss the messenger and read the letter in peace.

'Thank you, Rabhu. You have served me well in this,' Ugrasena said and took off his necklace and handed it as a gift to the messenger. 'Go rest now; you must be exhausted!'

Rabhu accepted the gift quietly. It was far more valuable than the few gold coins he had sold his soul for, to Jarasandha. But it wasn't the value of the gift that made him question his principles, perhaps for the first time in his life. Even in the excitement of receiving the letter he thought his son had sent him, Ugrasena had still shown consideration for Rabhu. *Very few people would do that...and definitely not a king!* Rabhu thought to himself. *Oh God, what have I done?* He castigated himself for having betrayed his king.

For a brief moment, he hesitated at the door. He wanted to confess to Ugrasena his betrayal. He wanted to tell the king that the letter he was holding in his hands was not from the prince but most likely a forgery done by Jarasandha. But in that instant, he recalled with trepidation the final words of Jarasandha—'Ugrasena might forgive your betrayal if you tell him what happened. But I will find you out from the deepest corner of Mrityulok and cut you into a thousand pieces if you betray me!' And with the memory of that warning threatening to suffocate him, he found he just didn't have enough courage to tell the truth to Ugrasena. He bowed to the king and left the room. The last thing he saw was Ugrasena lovingly extracting the letter from the scroll and beginning to read...

Pitashree,

As I go through your letter, I am struck by a few things, and I wonder how I did not realize the extent of your selfishness even when I left home.

You claim you loved me since I was a child, but you also stress the fact that I am not your son by blood. Furthermore, you appear to be burdened by too much sadness that in taking care of me, you couldn't give enough love to your other children—those sons and daughters that were born to you of your own blood!

However, what strikes me most about your letter is that you didn't call me back because of some newfound love for me, but because you want me to return to fight a bunch of asura assassins.

It's interesting that you don't want any of your blood children to fight these so-called deadly invaders; possibly because you do not want to risk their precious lives, whereas it is easy to risk mine.

At the end of your letter, I observe that you do not call your son back, but the commander-in-chief of the Madhuvan army.

My answer therefore to you is this—ask one of your precious children to protect your motherland; assuming that any of those weaklings can actually lift a sword to defend even themselves. Maybe then you will realize that there is no Madhuvan without Kansa.

I wish you and your children the best in what you need to do.

Kansa

Ugrasena stifled a moan as he finished reading the letter for the second time. He couldn't believe Kansa had sent this reply to him in response to the loving letter he had written. *He has twisted everything I wrote*, Ugrasena thought with anguish. He read the letter a third time. And slowly but perceptibly his grief turned to anger as he read and re-read the provocative words etched on paper. The royal rage mounted as he read the last line—'I wish you and your children the best in what you need to do.' In one sentence, Kansa had estranged himself from the entire family.

Ugrasena took a deep breath. His mind was made. He took a sheet of royal stationery and began to write a brief reply for Kansa.

◆

'You called me, My Lord?' Airawat stood at attention as he entered Ugrasena's chambers.

'Yes,' Ugrasena replied in a tired voice. 'I want you to leave for Bateshwar immediately. Tell Prince Vasudev that I want him to come to Madhuvan at once.'

Ugrasena paused. He knew his next words would be especially tough on Airawat. 'Tell Vasudev he will be leading the Madhuvan task force against the asura assassins.'

Airawat blanched. 'But, My Lord...Prince Kansa?'

'The prince will not be returning to Madhuvan for some time Airawat,' Ugrasena said quietly.

Airawat stared uncomprehendingly at his king. 'Won't be returning to Madhuvan? But how is that possible? Haven't you told him the danger we are in?' Airawat's voice rose unintentionally as he strove to understand the meaning behind Ugrasena's words.

'I have told him everything. He has still decided to forsake his family...and his country,' Ugrasena snapped uncharacteristically.

Airawat bent his head in grief. He had not had any doubt that Kansa would return to Madhuvan as soon as he knew what was happening here. But it seemed the prince ascribed more value to his rift with his father than he did to his love for the motherland. 'When do you want me to leave for Bateshwar?' he said in a monotone.

'Right away!' Ugrasena commanded. 'And send Rabhu to me.

He needs to carry a letter back to Kansa today itself.'

Airawat nodded and left the room. He couldn't believe Kansa had forsaken them in their hour of greatest peril. He hoped this was not a portent of worse things to happen in the future.

Ugrasena watched the retreating figure of Airawat. He rolled the letter for Kansa and inserted it in the royal scroll. He hoped Rabhu felt rested enough to make another trip to Magadha, today itself.

◆

Rabhu handed over the latest letter from Ugrasena to Jarasandha. He was half-dead from the exhaustion of making another trip to Magadha, without a break; Ugrasena had insisted that he leave immediately with the letter.

Jarasandha took the letter from Rabhu's hand. He extended his hand to give the messenger a purse laden with gold coins as payment for his services. Rabhu did not make any move to accept the reward.

'What's the matter with you, you scoundrel?' Jarasandha roared in anger. 'This payment isn't enough for you now? Being greedy are we?' he snarled threateningly.

Rabhu shook his head. He felt strangely detached from the situation. It was a moment of truth for him. All these years, he had been selling out vital information to Jarasandha and the king of Magadha terrified him, like he did everybody else. But right now, Rabhu did not feel afraid of anyone, not even Jarasandha. He hadn't felt this way when he was riding back to Magadha with Ugrasena's latest letter in his possession. He had simply thought this was the last time he would serve Jarasandha. But now that he was face to face with the king of Magadha, he felt a strength he had never known before. He knew he could have pleaded exhaustion and requested Ugrasena to send someone else with this letter. But there was a high possibility that whoever else Ugrasena would have sent to Magadha might have also been in

Jarasandha's pay.

'You have given me enough in the past, My Lord,' Rabhu said softly. 'You don't need to pay me for this service.'

Jarasandha looked disbelievingly at Rabhu. *Birds don't change their feathers*, he mused to himself. *Why is this man not accepting compensation for this job?* He shook his head in consternation. But he decided to keep a close watch over the messenger while he was in Magadha.

'I am not going to offer you this money again,' he said gruffly. 'Have you changed your mind?' Rabhu shook his head. 'No, My Lord. As I said earlier, I don't want any payment for this.'

'Get out of my sight then and wait till I summon you,' Jarasandha snapped impatiently. He wanted to read the letter quickly to see what it contained; and to gauge whether he would need to call Upadha to forge yet another letter for Ugrasena on Kansa's behalf.

Rabhu bowed to Jarasandha and left for the waiting quarters reserved for messengers, presumably to linger for Jarasandha's summons till the king was ready to call him again. But he had no intention to wait there. He wanted to look for Kansa to tell him the truth of Jarasandha's betrayal. He realized Jarasandha would kill him for this, but the feeling of detachment he had been experiencing lately seemed to keep the panic at bay.

◆

Jarasandha hastily pulled out the letter from the scroll. He couldn't wait to read Ugrasena's response to the forged note he had sent on behalf of Kansa. His face lit up as he read the letter from Madhuvan. *I won't even need to alter this*, he thought with malevolent glee. The reply Ugrasena had sent for Kansa would sever the father-son relationship completely.

He carefully placed the letter back into its scroll and re-sealed the lid. Then, humming a tune under his breath, he went in search of Kansa. He couldn't wait to see his brother-in-law's reaction to the letter.

◆

Airawat gaped in admiration as he reached the outskirts of the Kingdom of Bateshwar. The last village he crossed ended half a yojana (four miles) before the main city started. The road leading from this village up to the gates of Bateshwar was cobbled and was extremely narrow. Airawat guessed the width of the road was no more than one-and-a-half gavuta (nine feet). Normally, the road leading up to any city's gate was almost always broad and expansive, in order to give visitors a sense of largeness. The military commander in Airawat understood however, why Bateshwar had purposely kept this road so narrow. Any enemy attempting to attack the main city would find it hard to bring the full force of their army into the city at one time.

The road was so narrow that it would make it impossible for more than four cavalrymen to ride alongside. And the cobbled road would render it difficult for the horses to move fast. The horses and their riders would make ridiculously easy targets for Bateshwar soldiers mounted on top of the city gates.

The gates themselves were a sight to behold. They stood at a majestic height of ten gavutas (sixty feet) and were intricately carved with figures of Shiva and Vishnu in various martial postures. The depth of the gates was almost half a gavuta and they were made of saag wood, considered even tougher than iron. It would have been impossible for any battering ram to break through this barrier to the city. Airawat wondered what mechanism Bateshwar had in place to operate the opening and shutting of such massive gates. He made a mental note to check this before he left the city. As he rode closer to the gates, he noticed the guards standing at the entrance grow perceptibly alert. Their hands were placed lightly on the handle of their swords even though they kept them sheathed. Airawat had to consciously restrain himself from reaching for his own sword. The atmosphere at the gates seemed charged with tension. A large man, presumably the captain of the guards, approached him even before Airawat had dismounted.

'Identify yourself before you dismount, traveller.' The captain was polite but there was a taut note in his voice that bordered on curtness.

Airawat felt the first stirrings of irritation. He wanted to meet Vasudev and return to Madhuvan as soon as he could. The excess security and the barely concealed curtness of the captain made him impatient. He took out his passport and personal ID papers identifying him as the cavalry commander of Madhuvan and handed it over to the captain.

The captain's eyebrows shot up as he saw the documents. When he spoke, his voice was gentler than it had been earlier, 'My name is Hitarth, and I am captain of the guards. I apologize for holding you up, Commander Airawat. But I will need to have these documents verified before I can allow you to enter. Also, I will need to know the purpose of your visit to Bateshwar.'

It was Airawat's turn to raise his eyebrows. He felt his instincts go on high alert. It was customary for documents of even senior visiting officers to be checked at the city gates of any kingdom, but the security officers would do that after they had at least allowed the visiting officer to dismount and sit in the waiting room. This kind of behaviour was unprecedented. But Airawat was a man who respected processes, and if this was how things happened at Bateshwar, he would play along. He wondered, however, what had happened to warrant such tight security.

'I have come to meet Prince Vasudev on a matter of great urgency,' Airawat said quietly. 'You can verify this directly with the prince, Captain Hitarth. Meanwhile, I will wait here till you check my documents.'

Captain Hitarth gave a smart salute to Airawat and turned back towards the entrance gate. Airawat saw him pass his documents to someone on the other side of the city gateway, through a small opening. 'Run this through the lab for me, and make it double quick,' he snapped the instructions to a guard on the inner side of the city walls.

'Give me a few minutes, sir,' a voice replied from the other side.

Airawat looked in surprise at the source of the voice. He couldn't fathom how the voice could be heard so clearly on this side, through the thick wooden partition. He looked closely at the gates. He was able to see a small box perched at shoulder level, just above the opening where the captain had passed the documents to the other side. It seemed like a contraption through which guards on either side of the city walls could communicate with each other. *Ingenious,* reflected Airawat to himself.

Captain Hitarth paced impatiently as he waited for Airawat's documents to be verified by the lab on the other side. There was a crackling sound from the box mounted on the gate and the voice of the guard from the other side could be heard clearly, 'The documents are fine captain.' In the next instant, the papers were returned through the same opening.

Captain Hitarth whispered something through the box that Airawat couldn't hear. Before he could figure out what was happening, the mammoth gates of Bateshwar started to open. The captain mounted his own horse and moved in Airawat's direction. 'Once again, my apology for holding you up, Commander Airawat, but it was necessary to do the verification.'

Airawat nodded absent-mindedly. All he wanted now was to meet Vasudev and convey Ugrasena's message to him.

'Follow me, commander. The Prince is with the commander-in-chief right now. He has asked for you to be taken to him immediately.' *About time!* Airawat mumbled to himself, as he goaded his horse to keep pace with the captain of the guards.

◆

Airawat couldn't help being impressed by the architecture of the city. Bateshwar was different from any other city he had seen in bharat, or any other land in Mrityulok. The capital city seemed to have been built at three levels.

At the lowermost level, there were the pit-dwellings. These were constructed at a depth of eight gavutas (forty-eight feet) below ground level and extended over the entire breadth of the city. It was like having a second city under the main one. Pit-dwellings had houses that were kept vacant during peace time but could be used to shelter women and children in the unfortunate event of an enemy breaching the city walls. They were akin to a veritable city with their own roads and provisions for medical treatment and emergency supplies. Architects and city planners had constructed air ducts at vantage points to allow a constant supply of fresh air into the pits. The pit-dwellings had not been used since they were built, as the city walls had never been breached. The city council, however, ensured that the lower level of the capital city was kept clean and tested for efficacy in the event of an unforeseen emergency.

The ground level of the city comprised the lion's share of the population. The drainage systems were the same as in other kingdoms of Bharat. The only difference was that there was not a single sewer or drain that was left uncovered. A row of immaculately pruned hedges extended on all sides of the expansive streets. Flowers of different varieties adorned the sidewalks. What was interesting was that all houses seemed to have been built almost similarly. The basic architecture remained the same, even if some houses were bigger than the rest. A majority of the population, including the traders, the workmen and the warriors, resided at this level within the city.

As Airawat's mount cantered behind the captain of the guards, the cavalry commander of Madhuvan couldn't help noticing a steep road leading up a hill. This was the road Captain Hitarth chose to take as Airawat followed close on his heels. It was impossible to see what lay on top of the hill as the road veered every now and then. After a ride that lasted for a few minutes, the climb gradually became gentler and more linear. Airawat almost stopped in his tracks as his gaze fell on the scene in front of him. The third level of the city was constructed on top of the hill. Even before they reached the pinnacle, he noticed heavily fortified encampments on the sides of the knoll. Even though it was impossible to see inside the encampments, he guessed they were occupied by hundreds of armed soldiers. Gradually, the fortified encampments gave way to larger, more aesthetic dwellings which Airawat guessed were the residences of the ministers and senior officials of the court. These too were fortified, but despite the natural security provided by the architecture, each of these residences had a group of soldiers stationed outside for good measure. In most cases, there were two to three platoons outside each residence.

Airawat marvelled at the brilliance of the architecture and the planning of the city. The pit-dwellings ensured security for the city denizens during an emergency. The ground level was aesthetically built with every imaginable facility, to make life comfortable during peace time. The top-most level of the city was constructed all over the hill to provide the Bateshwar soldiers a strategic advantage over any enemy approaching from ground level. It also ensured the safety of key members of the royal family and the other court members.

Finally, Captain Hitarth came to a halt. They had reached the last building at the end of the steep road. It was balanced on the edge of the hill. *It would be ridiculous to call this a building,* chuckled Airawat. The structure was magnificent and was a perfect example of a parvata durga (hill fortress). The only difference was that Airawat had never seen a hill fortress such as this one.

Normally, there were three types of hill fortresses. The prantara durga was built on the summit of a hill. This was the most common type and most kingdoms in Bharat had such forts. The giriparshva durga had both, major civilian structures and fortifications extending down the slope of a hill or mountain, to include the strategic civilian population within the defence system. In the third type of hill fortress—the guha durga—the residential quarters of civilians were situated in a valley surrounded by high, impassable hills. The hills housed a chain of outposts and signal towers connected by extensive defensive walls.

The beauty of the Bateshwar defence system was that it included the best features of all the three types of fortress formations. In fact, the entire city of Bateshwar resembled a veritable fort, surrounded by hills on all sides, with the royal palace itself being housed on the top of the hill.

Captain Hitarth had a hurried conversation with his counterpart at the fortress gate. The captain of the guards outside the hill fort looked like a twin of Hitarth, both in physical form and in the efficient and cool way that he appraised Airawat. He nodded to Hitarth and barked an order to one of his minions to open the gate to the fort. Captain Hitarth motioned to Airawat to follow him and the two men entered the palace fortress.

Airawat had always considered Madhuvan to house the most beautiful palace in all of Bharat. But the royal palace at Bateshwar simply took his breath away. The residential quarters of the royal family were on the east side of the fort. They were separated from the rest of the area by a running stream of water, five gavutas in width. A cobbled road led in a direction away from the residential area and ended in a large field, big enough to contain a thousand warriors without appearing cluttered. This was the place where Sini Yadav and Vasudev were training the task force to take on the asura assassins. Airawat's jaw dropped in incredulity as he saw the number of warriors assembled on the field. At least five hundred of the toughest men he had ever seen were engaged in various forms of exercises and manoeuvres. They were supervised by a tall broad-shouldered man, with long hair that reached beyond his shoulders. He carried himself with the air of a military man born to war. His chest plate was full of decorations he had received in countless battles over the years. Airawat recognized the stripes on the man's shoulders and realized he was looking at the commander-in-chief of the Bateshwar army, Sini Yadav.

Sini Yadav's attention seemed to be focused at the moment on a group of warriors fighting a solitary figure in their midst. Airawat noticed that Captain Hitarth too had reined in his horse and stopped to observe the intense sparring happening at a distance. Six men were attacking a masked man. The masked man wore a spotless white robe, loosely wrapped around his body. He had a lean form but each part of the warrior's body seemed to ripple with an unnatural strength. What struck Airawat with particular interest was that he was not wearing any armour and held only a wooden sword in his right hand. The other six fighters wore heavy armour protecting every part of their body and each of them was armed with a gleaming metal sword.

'This is crazy!' whispered Airawat. 'The odds are too unfair, and that man is not even armed properly'.

Hitarth gave Airawat a perfunctory look. 'Watch!' he said softly, his eyes intent on the scene unfolding in front of them.

The masked man crouched low, his torso leaning forward, the left arm extended in front of him and the hand holding the sword pointed backwards in an iron grip. His aggressors circled him carefully; it was as if they were trying to bring down a fearsome opponent and they knew they couldn't afford any chances. Each of the attackers was looking for an opening, a chance to get through the strategic stance adopted by the masked man. The ragged breathing of the six attackers was the only sound in the vast field. The masked man seemed to be perfectly calm, his concentration unbroken even as the others continued to circle him.

One of the attackers had tiptoed noiselessly behind him. And another one on his right had slowly but gradually moved closer to their target. The masked man didn't seem to show any signs of having noticed either of them approaching within his safety zone. Sensing an opportunity, both men attacked; the one from behind focused on the lower back of the masked man and thrust his sword in that direction. The attacker on the right simultaneously made a sweeping motion with his sword in an attempt to hack off the man's head.

Airawat forced himself to stand still at what he thought was the end of the white-robed figure. Just when it seemed that the sharp metal from both attackers would seal the fate of the masked man, he suddenly bent lower till his body was almost parallel to the ground. The attack from the rear passed over his head with inches to spare, and the other sword circled harmlessly in the air above him.

And then, the masked man made his move. In a lightning thrust, he extended his sword arm backwards in an upward motion, catching the man behind him in the middle of his abdomen, just where the armour ended. The contact made the attacker behind him double up in pain. A simultaneous rear kick to his head finished off the man and he dropped unconscious to the ground. In the same instant, the masked man circled his sword arm and caught the aggressor on his right just behind the knee. The attacker stumbled and his face made a shattering impact with the elbow of the masked man. The second attacker staggered and fell to the ground. It had only taken a few seconds. There were now four aggressors left. They looked at each other, grim faces reflecting both fear and awe at the prowess of the man they were attacking. But these were hardened warriors and had been handpicked by Sini Yadav. They would not let a single man humiliate them in front of their commander-in-chief. They looked in the direction of Sini Yadav, who smiled encouragingly at them. This appeared to make them more determined to defeat the masked man.

The men seemed to reach an unspoken decision as the remaining attackers realigned themselves around their target. There was now a man on each side of the faceless man. Airawat realized with a jolt what they were planning; this time the attack would be from all sides. He watched spellbound. The masked man had changed his stance too. He was no longer crouching but stood erect, facing the man directly in front of him. He seemed oblivious to the other three on his sides and the rear.

Time stood still. Everyone present on the field forgot to breathe as they paused their activities to watch the next stage of the duel. For a moment, it looked as if no one wanted to make the first thrust. The remaining four aggressors seemed to be waiting for the masked man to make his move and decide their response accordingly. The masked man, however, seemed unfazed. He looked like he was cast in stone, as he stood unmoving, unblinking. The warrior standing in front of the masked man exchanged a quick look with one of his partners on the left of the target. *It is a signal*, thought Airawat, his excitement and apprehension for the lone fighter mounting. The same quick look was exchanged between the remaining warriors. The fighter in Airawat noticed that the attackers had tightened their grip on their swords. They had stopped breathing, too. It was a certain sign that they would attack in the very next moment. Airawat tensed as he waited for the inevitable assault from all sides.

When the assault finally came, Airawat was not the only one shocked. The masked man turned around in an unpredictable move to face the man who had been behind him. Even before the attacker had time to register what had happened, the masked man punched him hard under his chin. The man's head rolled back revealing the whites of his eyes, and he crashed to the ground. A lighting kick caught the second man behind him in his groin and felled him. The third warrior on his left had regained his composure by now and brought his sword down on the masked man with all the might he could muster. The latter did not attempt to step out of his way. He dropped down on one knee and gripped his opponent's wrist, twisting it in one quick motion. The aggressor's sword clattered to the ground and he screamed in agony as he felt the bone in his wrist break. He was no longer a threat. The fourth man snarled and throwing all caution to the wind, charged towards the target who was still on one knee. The masked man observed the attacker's shadow, and in a calculated move, waited for him to come within striking distance. As the warrior reached closer, the masked man drove his sword backwards. It hit the attacker on his inner thigh and stopped his charge. He then got up and turned to face the last aggressor, who stood clutching his leg. The wooden sword had connected hard with his femoral artery, located within the inner thigh to the side of the man's genitilia. If it had been a real sword, it would have sliced through, leading to fatal loss of blood, followed by paralysis and then death. In this case, it had only incapacitated the man temporarily. The masked man touched the debilitated warrior on the head with his wooden sword, and the man bowed low in respect.

Airawat watched as the man with the broken wrist also bowed to the masked man. The other four aggressors struggled to get up from the ground and approached the man who had single-handedly defeated six of the best warriors chosen by the commander-in-chief of Bateshwar. They didn't know the identity of the white robed man wearing the mask; but they were kshatriya warriors, and they respected only one thing—a man who could defeat them in fair battle.

Sini Yadav moved his mount in the direction of the masked man. When he came close, he jumped off the horse and stood face to face with the mystery figure. 'Maybe you should fight those bloody asura assassins, all by yourself,' he joked, smiling at the masked man.

Airawat watched closely as the masked man patted the shoulders of the commander-in-chief. A muffled voice spoke from behind the mask covering his face. 'I wouldn't mind fighting them alone, but I don't see the point of you training these men if you are not going to use them,' he laughed.

Airawat recognized the voice of Vasudev even before the prince of Bateshwar had taken off the veil covering his face.

◆

'What news have you brought from Madhuvan, my friend?' Vasudev said smiling at Airawat. He gripped the Madhuvan cavalry commander by his shoulders in the standard greeting favoured by warriors. While he waited for Airawat to reply, he doused his head in a large pan filled with cold water to wash away the grime and sweat accumulated during the duel. The blend of rose petals and lime slices mixed in the water rejuvenated him and whatever little fatigue he may have felt as a result of the recent sparring left his body.

'I'm afraid the news is not so good,' Airawat said in an uncharacteristically pessimistic tone. 'Kansa has refused to return to Madhuvan.'

Vasudev couldn't believe his ears. 'Does he place his differences with his father above the safety of his motherland?' he asked incredulously.

Airawat was quiet. He did not feel the need to respond to the outburst and he knew that Vasudev didn't expect an answer either. He had just expressed the same sentiment that Airawat himself had felt when Ugrasena had told him about Kansa's refusal to return.

Vasudev shook his head sadly. 'This is not the Kansa we know. This is a different man...' He let his words hang in the air. Airawat and Sini Yadav waited for him to speak but Vasudev seemed lost in thought.

The training behind them continued unabated as Sini's task force practised various fighting techniques amongst themselves. Loud cheers erupted every time a warrior would defeat a sparring partner in a particularly spectacular fashion. Vasudev remained oblivious to all the cheering and shouting around him. Finally, he appeared to come out of his self-imposed reverie, and when he spoke, his voice was firm. 'Sini, you will lead the Bateshwar task force against the asura assassins. Give them no quarter. Let them feel the heat of our metal so that no one dares to attack our motherland again.'

Turning towards Airawat, he spoke softly, but the resolve in his voice was unmistakable. 'I will return to Madhuvan with you. You will lead the team under my command. Together we will dig out the asuras from wherever they are holed up.' Airawat bowed to Vasudev, acknowledging his instructions. This time, there was no hesitation in his mind as he kneeled to Vasudev, accepting the prince of Bateshwar as his new commander-in-chief.

◆

Jarasandha handed Kansa the scroll containing the letter from Ugrasena. He watched as Kansa excitedly opened the lid of the scroll to extract the letter. In his excitement to read the letter, Kansa did not even notice that the seal on the lid had already been broken once. He had not expected a reply from Ugrasena so soon. *Father must have been really happy to read my letter*, he thought to himself as he unfurled the letter, spreading it out in front of him. *I'm glad I wrote to him*, he smiled, his brown eyes twinkling with genuine happiness after a long time.

Kansa started reading the letter. It was very brief. Jarasandha, who stood close by him, felt that he read the letter several times. Kansa's body stiffened perceptibly as he continued to stare at the letter he held in his hands. Tears poured down his face as he stood, unmoving, and all of a sudden, his huge shoulders slumped as if they no longer had the courage or the strength to carry his weight. Even as Jarasandha looked on, Kansa staggered, his legs buckling under him as he crashed on his knees to the ground. He held his face in his hands, willing to tear the eyes that had made him read the words he would never forget...or forgive. And from within the depths of his soul, a scream erupted that reverberated throughout the palace walls and raised the hair on Jarasandha's neck. It was a primal shriek that carried all of Kansa's pain and rage closeted within his heart. Jarasandha moved tentatively towards his friend, fearing that Kansa might hurt himself, but more fearful for his own safety. The man who sat screaming on the floor was not the Kansa he knew. That man had changed in a way that was difficult to comprehend.

Jarasandha held Kansa by his shoulders, in a vain attempt

to help his friend get up. Kansa, still in the throes of a powerful emotion, pushed him away and the mighty Jarasandha found himself hurled through the air as he landed on his back a few feet away. It took him a few moments to gather his senses and get up, still shocked at the inhuman strength with which Kansa had thrown him. He stared with trepidation at his friend's back, but this time, did not venture near him. Gradually, Kansa's body seemed to slacken and without turning around, he held out the letter in his hands, towards Jarasandha.

Jarasandha had already read the letter, and he knew Ugrasena had written this as a reaction to the letter he had sent on behalf of Kansa. But he had to make a pretence of reading it again, as if he were seeing it for the first time.

> Kansa,
>
> *I have read your letter. You do not need to return now, or ever again to Madhuvan. If Devki wants you to attend her marriage, I will need to bear the fact of your presence here, but I will do so for her sake.*
>
> *When I die, one of my 'true sons' will take over as king of Madhuvan. And if none of my blood sons is deemed capable of handling the throne, I am going to decree Vasudev as the future ruler.*
>
> *I have considered at length before writing this letter to you. But in the end I am compelled to believe that you have more of your birth father's instincts in you than you have of your mother.*
>
> *I too wish you the best in what you need to do.*
>
> Ugrasena

Jarasandha looked up from the letter and stared at Kansa, who had his back towards him. 'This...this is disgraceful,' he said, in an attempt to add fuel to the fire. 'On the one hand he calls you a demon's son and then he tries to use that as a reason to disinherit you and have some wimp sit on the throne that belongs rightfully to you!'

'What do you think I should do?' Kansa said in a whisper, his voice eerily soft.

Jarasandha thought quickly. The letter from Ugrasena had already turned Kansa irrevocably against his father and also planted the seeds of distrust against his closest friend Vasudev. If he could somehow turn that distrust into a deep-seated hatred for Vasudev, it would be an invaluable step forward for his own plans. *And if somehow Devki could also be alienated...that will be like having your cake and eating it too,* he thought. And then it struck him exactly how he could turn Kansa against both, Devki and Vasudev.

'The throne belongs to you after Ugrasena's death, Kansa,' Jarasandha said carefully. 'But there is time for that. I think you should talk to Devki and see how she feels about all of this.'

Kansa nodded slowly, his back still towards Jarasandha. 'Yes, I will talk to Devki. She is perhaps the only person who really cares for me. But I will not go to Madhuvan to meet her Jarasandha... not right now...not after this letter.'

Jarasandha struggled to conceal his smile. He had been apprehensive that Kansa might go to Madhuvan and the truth of the forged letters might come out if he met Ugrasena. He now addressed Kansa in the gentlest tone he could muster, 'I will send Asti and Prapti back to Madhuvan with a message for Devki. Don't worry, you will not need to go to Madhuvan right now. Devki will come to meet you here.'

'Thank you, my friend' Kansa said, turning around for the first time since he had read the letter, to face Jarasandha.

Jarasandha gasped. Kansa's eyes glittered bright green and his face shone with an energy that was not mortal in nature. The fire of Aghasamarthan burned in his eyes. *He has already turned over to the dark side,* Jarasandha muttered to himself. He handed the letter he was holding back to Kansa and hastened to leave the room. He wanted to ensure his sisters left immediately for

Madhuvan. And after that, he was keen to know what his spies had found out about Rabhu, the messenger from Madhuvan who no longer wanted payment for betraying Ugrasena.

◆

Rabhu heaved a sigh of relief as he saw the two spies trailing him pass within inches of where he was hiding. He had realized he was being followed when he had seen the same pair of men behind him even as he kept changing direction. And any doubts he may have had about being trailed were dispelled as he saw them increase their pace whenever it appeared that he was moving too far away from them.

Rabhu had decided to share with Kansa his fear that the first letter Ugrasena had sent for him might not have been given to him, and that Jarasandha had probably forged the letter that he had carried back to Ugrasena. Rabhu still wasn't certain why the Magadha king had done what he had, but he was sure that it didn't augur well for Kansa or his father. Having left Jarasandha with Ugrasena's second letter, Rabhu had gone to the aaram kaksh (waiting room) meant for the messengers, just as he had told Jarasandha he would. But he did not linger there. Instead, he had slipped away in search for Kansa, hoping he could meet him before Jarasandha became aware of his absence. It had been the end of the dvitiya prahaar when he had left the waiting room. It was now well into the tritiya prahaar and he knew beyond a shadow of a doubt that Jarasandha would have figured he was up to something. The presence of the spies tailing him confirmed any doubts he may have had in this matter.

Rabhu had seen Kansa ride out on his horse a few minutes after Jarasandha had left with the letter in his hand. The prince had seemed like a changed man as he rode his horse savagely out of the palace gates. Rabhu had tried to follow him on his own horse but Kansa had been too fast for him to keep pace with.

Finally, Rabhu had left his horse in a corral outside a crowded tavern, where he knew his horse would be inconspicuous among the scores of others tied there by the visitors to the pub. He preferred to be on foot while he waited for Kansa to return to the palace. It was on the way back that he had noticed the spies tailing him and he had been forced to move in an opposite direction in order to lose them.

Now it was getting late, and Rabhu knew there was no way he could go back to the aaram kaksh and explain his absence to Jarasandha. He would somehow need to meet Kansa and then leave for Madhuvan surreptitiously. There was no doubt in his mind what Jarasandha would do to him once he found him. He looked around him to make sure he had eluded his pursuers. Then he started walking back in the direction of the palace.

◆

Jarasandha watched with satisfaction as he saw his sisters leave for Madhuvan with an armed escort to keep them safe on the way. He had no doubt that Devki would return with Asti and Prapti as soon as she received the message that her brother was unwell. Asti had raised her eyebrows in surprise when Jarasandha had told them to convey the message of Kansa's illness to Devki and get her to Magadha. And Prapti had wanted to meet Kansa before they left. But both the sisters were too much in awe of Jarasandha to argue with him. His instructions had been explicit and firm—they were to leave immediately without meeting Kansa and they would return with Devki.

Now that one part of his plan was set in motion, Jarasandha turned his attention to the other task at hand. He wanted to know what the spies had found out about Rabhu. The scoundrel had not been in the aaram kaksh as he had instructed him to be, and Jarasandha knew Rabhu was up to something. The spies would tell him what it was. But first he had to meet Chanur and Banasura, who were leaving for their kingdoms today.

◆

Banasura and Chanur waited patiently while Jarasandha shared with them the transformation of Kansa. There was silence as Jarasandha finished his story. He had carefully refrained from mentioning the role the Dark Lord had played in the entire episode, and had only told the two warriors what had transpired between Kansa and Ugrasena. Jarasandha was one of those people who did not believe in his right hand knowing what his left hand was up to. He didn't want to share any information with these two warriors that could help them break out of the Dark Lord's power, or be used against him in the future.

Finally Chanur spoke. 'Ugrasena cannot just disinherit Kansa and make Vasudev his successor. The prince of Madhuvan won't take this injustice lying down.'

Jarasandha weighed his words carefully before responding. 'Kansa is not thinking about the throne of Madhuvan just now. He is deeply troubled and he feels betrayed from all sides. Ugrasena has alienated his son and his letter has planted the seeds of distrust between Vasudev and Kansa. The only person he trusts at the moment is Devki. I have sent my sisters to get her here, and they should return with her in the next three days.'

Banasura appeared puzzled. 'But why have you asked Devki to come here at this time? I thought the idea was to turn Kansa against Ugrasena and Vasudev so he could ally with us. Now that he is finally coming around to our side, wouldn't a meeting with Devki be a risk?'

Chanur nodded his head. 'I must say I agree with Banasura. I don't understand this either. There is a possibility that Devki might be able to convince Kansa that all of this is just a big misunderstanding between her father and brother. What if Kansa agrees to return to Madhuvan with her and everything you have done so far is rendered futile?'

Jarasandha had anticipated this risk when he had suggested to Kansa that he meet Devki once. But it had been a calculated one. Jarasandha knew there was a high probability that Kansa might himself, at a later date, want to meet Devki. And it could be at a place where Ugrasena too might be present. Or worse, by then, Kansa might have had enough time to reflect on Ugrasena's letter and wonder why his father had sent him such a harsh letter in response to his own. Right now, Kansa was too emotionally strung to even begin to think rationally. More importantly, there was another angle that neither Banasura nor Chanur had understood yet. But then, they hadn't been students of buddhir brahmi (psychology) as Jarasandha had been from a very young age.

'Who do you think is the most important person in a young woman's life?' Jarasandha asked softly. While he was looking at Chanur, the question was meant for Banasura too. The two warriors looked at each other in perplexity.

Chanur was the first to answer, 'It depends,' he said. 'It could be either the mother or the father, depending on who the woman is closer to.'

'Or it could be a sister or a brother,' Banasura added.

'Quite right,' Jarasandha nodded patiently. 'Actually, both of you are correct...but only up to a point. The family is definitely the most important thing in a woman's life.' He stared at both the warriors sitting in front of him and chose his next question carefully. 'But what happens when the same woman falls desperately in love with a man? Will the family still remain the most important factor in her life?'

Chanur, as usual, was the first to get his drift. He said excitedly, 'No, the man she loves gradually gains more significance in her life than even her family.'

Jarasandha's eyes gleamed, 'And when that woman has been in love with a man ever since she was a child, how much more important would that relationship be for her?' He left his question hanging.

'Like Devki and Vasudev,' Banasura joined in the excitement.

'She has been in love with Vasudev since she was a child.'

Jarasandha got up from his seat. 'Yes, when Kansa meets his sister, he is bound to share his reservations about Vasudev with Devki. In his current state of mind, he may even go further and say things about Vasudev that he normally wouldn't. As much as she loves Kansa, I don't believe she will allow even him to talk ill of the man she loves more than anything else in the world.'

'And that is bound to create friction between brother and sister!' Banasura exclaimed softly.

Jarasandha nodded. 'Yes, enough friction perhaps for Kansa to feel that he has not just lost a father and a close friend, but the one woman he cares for the most...his sister Devki.' He waited for his words to sink in before he continued. 'Kansa is already close to losing his grip on his past. The break with Devki will finish off whatever ties hold him back from uncovering his intrinsic nature.'

Banasura and Chanur were quiet. Jarasandha's last words had struck something deep inside them; as if they were already going through what lay in store for Kansa. Like the prince of Madhuvan, they, too, had lost all connection with who they were in the past. Right now, they were only puppets dancing on a string manoeuvred by a powerful force in Pataal Lok.

They were brought out of their reverie by something Jarasandha was saying. They looked blankly at the king of Magadha and he repeated his instructions to both of them. Jarasandha had just commanded them to unleash the asura assassins within their kingdoms. Both warriors nodded and left the room to go to their respective countries.

Jarasandha stood alone, lost in his thoughts. The chaos on Mrityulok was about to begin. It would start from the Yavanas' kingdom and from the land of Banpur. Over the next few days, Jarasandha's generals, in charge of other vassal kingdoms would instruct the asura assassins hiding in those lands too to start the carnage. Madhuvan would be next as soon as Kansa came over to their side in totality. Jarasandha sighed as a wave of ecstasy swept over him. The day wasn't far when the Dark Lord would take over the mortal world and make him—Jarasandha—the supreme lord of all lands in Mrityulok, including the great nation of Bharat.

◆

The two spies shook in fear as they waited for Jarasandha to explode in anger. They had lost Rabhu somehow. And they still had no idea where the messenger was. Jarasandha glared at both of them; but he was in a magnanimous mood today. This meant the spies could expect to be pardoned instead of being thrown into a dungeon for the rest of their miserable existence.

'You say you saw him riding after Prince Kansa?' Jarasandha asked one of the spies.

'Yes, My Lord,' The spy nodded vigorously as if by doing so he could somehow make up for the blunder of losing the messenger. 'I saw Rabhu riding in hot pursuit of the prince. He even shouted above the din of the horses to try and attract the prince's attention, but the Lord Kansa seemed caught up in his own prince's thoughts as he rode and he did not hear Rabhu calling after him.'

'Hmm,' Jarasandha digested this new information. *So that is what that scoundrel is planning…he wants to tell Kansa about the letters.* His brow furrowed as he tried to control his rage at Rabhu's intended betrayal. *You will die a dog's death, you rascal*, he resolved to himself.

The spy who had spoken earlier now looked at his king. 'What are our orders, Lord? Should we try finding the messenger, in places we have not searched yet?'

Jarasandha shook his head, 'No, he will return here. We will wait for him to show his vile face, and then I will deal with him.'

He motioned to the spy who had been quiet all this while, 'You keep watch at the palace gate. He is bound to come from there. He probably knows what you look like so make sure he doesn't see you.'

To the other spy he said, 'Send Upadha and Vikrant to me. Ask them to come here without delay.'

Both spies left and Jarasandha laughed unrestrainedly, alone in the room. Rabhu had unwittingly given him the opportunity to make Kansa's meeting with Devki even more volatile. The fact that Rabhu would die before that happened was incidental...but necessary.

Jarasandha sighed contentedly as he sat down on the diwan. *Now if only Upadha and Vikrant do what needs to be done*, he thought.

◆

Upadha used part of his angavastram to wipe the copious sweat flowing down his face. He had spent the last hora (one hour) in the royal archives section, trying to look for any communication from Bateshwar to Magadha. He had systematically looked through the previous two years of correspondence between the two kingdoms. There were hundreds of letters from Surasena and from the prime minister of Bateshwar. However, there was no letter from Vasudev. It was imperative that he get his hands on any form of correspondence from the prince of Bateshwar or he would not be able to do what Jarasandha had asked of him. Upadha's desperation grew with every passing minute. His hands moved faster and his eyes fervently scanned the mounds of correspondence for any sign of a letter from Vasudev.

Just when he was ready to give up, he noticed a letter from the prime minister of Bateshwar. It was written and signed by him, but was copied to the king and the prince too. At the end of the communication, both Surasena and Vasudev had signed their names.

Upadha peered closely at the letter. *By Shiva! What a stroke of luck*, he chuckled to himself. While Surasena had merely signed his name as an acknowledgement of having read the letter, Vasudev had not just put his signature to the letter; he had also added a brief comment for Jarasandha. Upadha looked at it closely. It was a scribble and there were scant words written there to be able to analyse Vasudev's writing pattern with perfection. But it would be enough for someone with Upadha's enormous capabilities.

Upadha gave a satisfied smile. The work Jarasandha had entrusted him with would be done!

◆

Vikrant was perched on top of a tree that overlooked the entrance to Kansa's quarters within the royal palace of Magadha. From this vantage point, he could see not only the door leading up to Kansa's accommodation; he also had a clear vision inside Kansa's inner chambers. Jarasandha's instructions had been clear. Vikrant was to wait for a man called Rabhu to appear. One of Jarasandha's spies stood at a distance, camouflaged perfectly to all intents and purposes. It would have been impossible even for Vikrant to know where the spy was hiding if he hadn't been told beforehand. The spy's job was to identify Rabhu as and when the messenger made his entry. When that happened, the spy would give a prearranged signal to Vikrant.

Vikrant had been told that Rabhu would make an attempt to enter Kansa's quarters to meet the prince. His job was to ensure this did not happen. This part did not bother Vikrant much. He was a master archer, one of the most proficient in his art in Magadha. It was the other part that disturbed him; the part where he would need to shoot one of his deadly arrows at Kansa.

It had been two horas since the master archer had climbed the tree. The branch where he sat was not big enough for a man of his size, and he was balanced precariously on his haunches. The impending darkness served to keep him hidden from prying eyes, but it also meant that the mosquitoes would come out in hordes any moment. The buzzing of the insects had already started and Vikrant felt the pinpricks all over his body as the mosquitoes fed freely on his motionless figure. He controlled the growing urge to swat away the insects. It was imperative that there were no signs of his presence on the tree. He tried to feel his limbs; he had lost nearly all sensation in his legs as the blood settled at concentrated spots in his lower body. The position was unbelievably uncomfortable and if it hadn't been for his intense training, he might have yielded to the overpowering desire to adjust his body weight. Yet it was necessary that the growing cramps in his muscles didn't interfere with the accuracy of his aim when he would be required to shoot at his target. Vikrant took a deep breath and with his eyes open, began to chant a mantra taught to him by his master. It served to calm his frayed nerves and miraculously made his muscles feel more relaxed. Gradually, the cramps appeared to leave his body and he felt reinvigorated. He moved his right hand lovingly over the mighty bow he held in the other hand. The action always made him feel more in control of any situation. He picked out an arrow from his quiver. The touch of the quiver felt different and uncomfortable; it was the first time he was using it to carry his arrows. He wondered why Jarasandha had insisted that he use this particular quiver instead of his own, but decided that the king must have had a valid motive for doing so.

The mantra had heightened his senses significantly and his entire being was attuned to his surroundings. He stiffened as he saw from the corner of his eye, the spy signalling to him. It meant Rabhu had entered the palace compound. He would be approaching Kansa's quarters any moment now. *Why can't I see him?* Vikrant thought in consternation, as he tried to scan every part of the compound from atop the tree. And then he saw the messenger. Rabhu had wrapped a dark blanket across his body, which made it difficult to sight him in the darkness of the night. But as he drew closer to the entrance to Kansa's accommodation, the light from the night lamp made it easier to spot him.

Vikrant picked up an arrow and placing it meticulously against the bow, he strung his lethal weapon. He knew his aim had to be unerringly perfect in order to produce the desired result. His shoulders ached with the strain of pulling the bow and holding it in that position, but he wasn't ready to let loose the deadly arrow yet. Kansa wasn't in sight.

Rabhu eyed his surroundings cautiously as he gingerly approached the entrance to Kansa's quarters. He knocked on the door, timidly at first and then with greater intensity as he realized the knocking might not be audible to Kansa inside.

'Who is it?' Vikrant could barely hear Kansa's strained voice from where he was. The prince's tone reflected the anguish he was going through.

'A messenger, prince! I need to talk to you...it's urgent.' Spurred at the sound of Kansa's voice, Rabhu had abandoned all caution by now, and his voice carried clearly in the openness of the compound.

'Wait, I am opening the door,' Kansa answered from inside; his voice perceptibly expressing his confusion at the words of the messenger.

Rabhu's face lit up as he heard this. His excitement was palpable as he waited for the door to open. Rabhu was not a very tall man, and the door's length was almost one-and-a-half times his height. Almost adjacent to the door was a window, which was open. Kansa apparently did not believe in keeping the windows barred; not that there was any reason to. It was virtually impossible for any intruder to reach the palace compound without being caught by the security at the gate. The only reason Rabhu had been able to get this far without being caught was because Jarasandha had ordered the security detail to be deliberately slackened in order to allow Rabhu easy entry; unknown to Rabhu, a squad of security guards were hidden close by, waiting for the right moment to pounce on him.

Vikrant focused his attention on the open window. He knew Kansa would have to cross the window before he reached the door, outside which Rabhu waited anxiously. The lamp inside the living quarters reflected myriad shadows of the prince as he approached the window. The archer tensed, pulling back the arrow as much as his strength allowed. And then as Kansa moved across the open window, he came in full view of Vikrant. His arrow was pointed in the direction of Kansa's broad chest. He gently exhaled as he released the arrow, which flew with lightning speed towards its target.

The archer who had not once in his life missed a target, watched calmly as his arrow dug itself in Kansa's shoulder instead of the prince's chest. Even as he watched Kansa roar and fall back with the impact of the arrow, Vikrant jumped from the tree and ran towards Rabhu.

Rabhu heard Kansa's cry of pain at the same time that he saw Vikrant leaping off the tree and running in his direction. For a brief moment, he thought Vikrant was going to attack him, but the archer simply dropped his bow and the quiver filled with arrows at Rabhu's feet as he ran past him without breaking speed. In a few seconds, the archer had exited the palace gates.

Even as Rabhu struggled to make sense of the situation, he heard a bellow from near the palace gate. A squad of heavily armed security guards rushed at him, the razor-sharp edges of their spears pointed directly at him. And in that moment, Rabhu understood exactly what had happened. But it was too late. By the time Kansa would open the door and come out, everything would be over for him, and perhaps for the prince. Rabhu closed his eyes. He offered a prayer to his clan deity, Shiva, for absolution for his soul. A part of him sensed the soldiers approaching closer, but the other part of him was already in a different world. He did not feel any pain as the glinting spears sank into his body from all sides, and his corpse fell to the ground, the sharp weapons still stuck in him.

Unseen by anyone else, the captain of the guards bent down and placed the note that Upadha had given him in the inner pocket of the dead messenger's waistcoat.

◆

The door to Kansa's quarters was almost taken off its hinges as an injured and enraged Kansa stormed out. A rivulet of blood poured out of his shoulder where the arrow had lodged itself, and the viscous liquid had soaked through the prince's white angavastram, turning it scarlet. Kansa's eyes fell on the guards standing outside his door, before his attention was drawn to the lifeless body of Rabhu lying at their feet. The messenger lay sprawled and his face reflected a peculiar calm, as if in death he had finally made peace with himself.

Kansa examined the quiver containing the arrows. He was familiar with the different varieties of quivers used by archers in different nations. He himself preferred a bow quiver, where the quiver could be attached directly to the bow's limbs, the arrows being held steady by a clip. It made it easy to carry around without the encumbrance of carrying the bow and the quiver separately. But this quiver was different. It was what was commonly referred by warriors as an arrow bag, and was a simple drawstring cloth sack with a leather spacer at the top to keep the arrows divided. When not in use, the drawstring could be closed, completely covering the arrows so as to protect them from rain and dirt. Some had straps or rope sewn to them for carrying, but many were either tucked into the belt or simply set on the ground before battle to allow easier access.

Kansa's eyes narrowed—this type of quiver was most commonly used in the kingdom of Bateshwar.

He took out an arrow from the quiver. It was a powerfully structured projectile, with an incredibly sharp tip. It was impossible to ascertain the provenance of the arrow, though; it could have been from any of the several nations in Mrityulok. He tried comparing it to the arrow stuck in his shoulder, but was unable to see the latter properly since it was beyond his line of vision. Losing patience, he used his other hand to grip the arrow at the centre, and with one immense heave, he pulled it out of his shoulder. Splintered pieces of bone and cartilage were carried along with the blood that erupted out of the cavity. Oblivious to the excruciating pain, Kansa compared the arrows. They were the same. His mind raced with feverish intensity as he tried to reconstruct what had happened. *The man called out to me and said he wanted to discuss something urgent. It was probably a ploy to get me to come to the door. He must have known I would need to cross the open window to reach the door. And when I did...that's when he shot that arrow at me. My scream must have alerted the guards to the presence of an intruder, and they attacked the assassin.*

Kansa was about to question the captain of guards when the enormous figure of Jarasandha came charging through the gate.

'Where is the assassin? Take me to the bastard who dared to attack my brother!' he raged. The captain pointed at the motionless figure of Rabhu prostrate on the ground. Jarasandha kicked the corpse viciously on the head, and there was a snap as the cervical vertebrae cracked. If Rabhu hadn't been dead already, the savage kick would have finished him anyhow.

Jarasandha, still fuming, glowered at the guards. 'Out of my sight, all of you!'

The captain of the guards nodded at his men to leave, while he stayed back. He knew Jarasandha hadn't played his final card yet and his presence was required till that was done. Jarasandha bent down, pretending to look closely at the dead man. He gasped and even the captain of the guards was impressed by the charade put up by the king.

'This...this man. I know him,' Jarasandha appeared to splutter in perplexed fury.

Kansa stared at his brother-in-law. 'Who is he? How do you know him?'

'This man's name is Rabhu. He is the messenger from Madhuvan who brought the letter from Ugrasena today,' Jarasandha paused for Kansa to absorb the full significance of his words before he spoke further. 'I had told him to wait in the aaram kaksh just in case you desired to send a reply for your father. Later, when I realized you didn't want to respond, I sent an attendant to fetch the messenger. I was told this vile man had not even been to the aaram kaksh. I remember thinking that was very strange behaviour for a royal messenger.'

The captain of the guards spoke up, 'He must have slunk away, My Lord; with the intent of assassinating the prince. It's possible he was hiding here in the compound right after he left King Ugrasena's letter with you. Since the prince has been out for the past few horas, the assassin must have bided his time till it was dark and he considered it safe to venture out of his hiding place.

Kansa was visibly shaken, and it was not because of the pain. He wondered why his father's messenger had tried to kill him. *Father has already disinherited me. Why would he send an assassin? And why is this man carrying a quiver that is from Bateshwar?* he deliberated with mounting frustration.

Kansa picked up the quiver yet again to examine it closely. There was no doubt about it.

'This quiver has been made in Bateshwar. It's the type their warriors use,' he said quietly. Then he pointed towards the top of the quiver. 'Look at this,' he said indicating the leather spacer. It was made of the most exquisite leather they had ever seen. 'And observe the quality of the cloth,' he muttered, running his hands gently over the fine material of the arrow bag. 'This particular quiver is of the highest quality. Only a connoisseur who has the money to back his passion would own such a quiver.' Kansa shook his head. 'This is not an assassin's arrow bag; it reeks of wealth...of royalty! *But why Bateshwar?* he whispered to himself.

Jarasandha exchanged a quick look with the captain of the guards. It was time to bring down the curtain on the last scene of this act.

The captain took his cue from the king. 'My Lord, with

your permission, can I carry out a search on the assassin's body, before he is taken away?'

Jarasandha nodded and the captain went through the motions of going through Rabhu's clothes; he knew what he wanted was in the inner pocket of Rabhu's waistcoat, because he had himself put it there, unseen by the other guards after Rabhu was speared by his men. After he had completed the farce of going through the rest of the clothes, he gingerly dipped his hands in the pocket containing the note that Upadha had handed him, and drew it out with a flourish.

'My Lord, there is a note here!' he exclaimed, as he handed it to Jarasandha. The king extended his hand to take the note and started reading it. His eyes gleamed as he saw the contents. *Upadha is a genius. I must remember to reward that man handsomely for this,* he thought.

'What does it say, Jarasandha?' Kansa's voice was weary with pain. Jarasandha turned to look at him. 'It is a very brief note,' he said hesitatingly.

'What does it say?' Kansa repeated his question more forcefully. His features were drawn in a tight line.

Jarasandha cleared his throat, 'It says—"Finish the job while Kansa is still in Magadha".' Jarasandha paused. 'There is some more,' he said finally.

Kansa's heart skipped a beat as he waited for Jarasandha's next words.

Jarasandha stared at the note. When he had instructed Upadha what to write in the letter, he had been certain this would turn Kansa forever against Vasudev. But he wondered now, if he had perhaps gone too far in the wording of the note. *Will Kansa be able to take the shock?* he wondered

'Read the rest to me now!' Kansa said softly, the menace evident in his tone.

'"The demon's son should not return to Madhuvan alive,"' Jarasandha emphasized each word of the remainder of the note.

A low growl started from the base of Kansa's throat as he snatched the paper from Jarasandha's hand. The snarling, inaudible to the others at first, turned into a hair-raising howl as Kansa recognized the handwriting on the note.

Each word on the letter had been inscribed in Vasudev's patent style.

◆

Devki was in a foul mood. Asti and Prapti had arrived with the news that Kansa was unwell. On the way, Asti had developed severe abdominal pains and the two sisters had decided to wait at Madhuvan till such time that Asti got better. Meanwhile, Devki left for Magadha as soon as she heard about Kansa's illness. In the process, she had her first ever altercation with Ugrasena.

'Why do you want to go and meet that man?' Ugrasena shouted uncharacteristically at her. Devki was taken aback with the sheer intensity of his emotions. She couldn't understand what had come over her father. The king, who had loved Kansa even more than he loved Devki, seemed now to be totally against his son.

'Why shouldn't I meet him?' Devki retorted. 'He is my brother; your son. What's wrong with you, Father? Why are you acting so strangely?'

Ugrasena's face was red with anger. 'That man you call your brother has forsaken us. He is no longer the boy I cherished or the elder brother who showered love on you. He is an insensitive prince who won't even lift a finger to protect his motherland!'

Devki walked away in anger, on hearing her father speak thus about Kansa. She told him there was nothing that could stop her from meeting her brother, especially when he was unwell. Ugrasena stared after his daughter, knowing well that her impetuous nature and her love for Kansa would not allow her to stay back at Madhuvan, just then. This was the first time she was going away without his blessings. It was also the first time that Ugrasena had no desire to meet his son.

◆

Devki sensed there was something wrong even before she entered the palace compound. Sentries were posted everywhere and security seemed to be tighter than what would be normal in peace time. She had been to Magadha earlier with Kansa, within the first year of his marriage to the twin sisters. She got the feeling that the city had changed a lot in the last few years. Somehow, it seemed darker and murkier. Devki shook off a feeling of dread as she entered the palace. *Something is wrong*, she thought to herself. She could feel it in her bones. Devki was endowed with an enhanced level of perception. She could usually sense when things were not right, like she had in the Shiva temple before the kalakanja had attacked her. This was one of those occasions when her senses screamed a sentiment of discord in the elements around her.

She asked to be taken directly to Kansa's chambers. The attendant within the palace escorted her to her brother's room, and left her at the threshold. Devki knocked gently at the door. There was no answer from within. She knocked harder. As she waited for a response, she heard what sounded like a snarl. It emanated from inside her brother's room. All her senses were now on high alert. Not knowing what the snarling sound signified, and afraid for Kansa's safety, Devki pushed open the door and barged inside. The sight that met her eyes left her shaken. Kansa sat on the floor. His lips were moving as if he were talking to someone but there was nobody in the room. The snarling sound seemed to be coming from Kansa as he breathed harshly. His personal appearance seemed greatly altered too—from his usual impeccable grooming to his current slovenly state. His long hair appeared dishevelled and fell in irregular waves across his face. His lips were curled up in a warped smile as he stared blankly at Devki. His flat, expressionless gaze raised the hackles on her neck.

'Bhaiyya!' Devki exclaimed in alarm. Kansa appeared not to hear or heed her. His gaze seemed to pass right through her.

'Kansa!' she screamed at him. Her raised voice served to jolt the prince out of his trance-like state and he looked around him, dazed, as if wondering what he was doing sitting on the floor.

'Devki?' he whispered. 'Is that really you or is it my imagination?'

Devki rushed towards Kansa, bending down on her knees to hug him as she used to when she was a little girl. She lovingly pulled back the hair covering his face and looked into his eyes. It shocked her to see the pain reflected there. 'What's wrong Kansa? What has happened to you?' Her voice was full of anguish.

Kansa did not answer immediately. He had felt the warmth of love after days and he was loath to let go of the feeling. He basked in Devki's love as she held his hand and made him feel wanted.

'Tell me, Bhaiyya, what's wrong?' Devki persisted after a while as she saw Kansa grow calmer.

'Our father has disinherited me,' Kansa said finally. 'He said I have more of my birth father's demon traits than my mother's characteristics within me.' There was an edge to Kansa's voice that Devki had never heard before.

'That is insane!' Devki said incredulously. 'He can't do that. Who could be better than you to take over as king after Father steps down?'

Kansa smiled. 'Vasudev,' he said softly. 'Father is going to decree Vasudev as the king after he retires.'

'What!' The words gagged in her mouth as she struggled to come to terms with this news. She had had no idea that things had turned so sour between her brother and her father. Ugrasena's anger at her coming to Magadha to meet Kansa had seemed strange to her, but this was unbelievable.

'It's okay, Kansa,' She said soothingly. 'There's obviously been some major misunderstanding between you and Father. I will talk to him. And Vasudev will also speak to Father. He will never agree to sit on the throne of Madhuvan while you are there!'

At the mention of Vasudev, Kansa's face contorted. Then

he laughed. The maniacal laughter baffled Devki. She looked questioningly at her brother.

Kansa suddenly stopped laughing. The change in his mood was staggering. He lowered his voice conspiratorially, and leaning closer to Devki, whispered, 'You are right. Vasudev will never agree to sit on the throne of Madhuvan while I am alive.' He paused to gather his strength. 'This is precisely why he wants to have me assassinated!'

Devki recoiled at the words. *Vasudev? My Vasudev? It can't be,* she told herself. *Kansa has to be wrong.*

'You are mistaken, brother. Vasudev would never do what you are suggesting.' Devki bit her lip to keep herself from crying. 'He would gladly give up his own throne if that could save your life.'

Kansa gave her a sad smile. 'It's you who are mistaken, little sister. Vasudev did try to have me assassinated. Two days back his assassin shot an arrow at me. He probably meant to aim for my heart but the arrow struck me on my shoulder. If he hadn't missed, I would be dead by now.'

Devki gave Kansa a quizzical look. She couldn't see any visible signs of an injury on either of Kansa's broad shoulders.

Kansa followed her gaze and strived to explain. 'The bone in my right shoulder was crushed and I lost a lot of blood. But the wound healed in a few horas just as it did when I was wounded fighting those monsters on the Shiva hill.'

Devki remembered how Kansa's wounds had miraculously healed before her very eyes even as he lay unconscious. She didn't doubt that someone had shot at Kansa as he said, but she was equally sure that Vasudev had had no part to play in it.

She shook her head, 'You are wrong, Kansa. Vasudev would never do what you are saying he did,' her voice was gentle but firm.

Kansa's eyes flashed like lightning. In another swift change of mood, he snapped at her, 'You lay more store by that man's credibility than your brother's words? That vile man who married another woman, despite claiming to be madly in love with you!

Has love made you completely blind, you little fool?'

Devki gaped at Kansa in astonishment. He didn't look or sound one bit like the brother she had known since childhood; the man who had lifted her in his arms when she was leaving Devak's house forever, or the brother who had risked his own life saving her from those monsters. The man in front of her now had none of the sensitivity or love she had always felt flowing from her brother. This man looked and spoke like a stranger. And he looked every bit as dangerous as the creatures he had fought to save her from just a few months ago.

She involuntarily took a step back. Kansa noticed her fear and he softened his tone. It was almost as if there were two personalities struggling within him, each of them trying to dominate the other.

'Look at me, Devki,' he implored her. 'Vasudev is not who you think he is. He has already betrayed my trust by trying to kill me. I will not tolerate it if he tries to harm you.' His voice was gentle now and Devki's heart went out to him.

Then as suddenly as it had disappeared, his other persona took over yet again and he snarled, 'Vasudev will die. He will not harm you or me ever again!' Kansa's eyes glittered green as the malevolent side of his nature exerted its full force over his senses.

'You will not harm Vasudev, Kansa!' Devki's voice trembled as she stood up to the towering figure of her brother.

The voice that answered her was not that of her brother. It had a harsh quality to it and it seemed to sneer at her. 'And what will you do if I do harm him, you foolish woman?' The face staring at her seemed to taunt her, daring her to react.

'I will kill you, you monster!' The words were out of Devki's mouth before she could even comprehend what she had said. Enraged as she was with Kansa, she immediately regretted her choice of words.

In the same instant, Kansa's malevolent half left him and his softer mortal side took over. He sagged visibly at Devki's words. The green light that shone in his eyes dimmed and his brown eyes stared at her in an embodiment of pain and rejection.

'Yes, I know you would kill me, Devki...I know that now.' He took one long look at her. 'I just didn't think you too would consider me a monster, like your father.'

Devki felt like holding him and telling him how sorry she was. She wanted him to know that she loved him and all of this was just a mistake, a horrendous mistake. But words failed her as she saw Kansa metamorphose into his malevolent self again. He felt it too, and he shouted at her in one final attempt to fight the monster growing within him and threatening to take over him completely, 'Go...go away from here right now. Leave *now!*'

Devki didn't want to leave him in this state, with so much unsaid. But the urgency in his voice told her she needed to get out of the room and away from Magadha as soon as she could. Perhaps, there would be another occasion when they could sit and talk, like they used to as children.

She ran out of the room, just as Kansa's body was wracked with the shock of multiple convulsions. The force of the seizures virtually lifted him off his feet and threw him on the floor, his entire body engulfed with an agony such as he had never known.

As his conscious mind switched off, he heard the gentle voice of the Dark Lord guiding his sub-conscious mind. Kansa felt himself being propelled through a never-ending dark tunnel, the sides of which were lighted, reflecting the several past lives he had undergone. As he neared the end of the tunnel, he reached a stage in his past lives that the Dark Lord particularly wanted him to see. In front of him, he observed a vast field. Assembled there was the largest horde of warriors he had ever seen. Every kind of asura was visible, and at their centre, stood a powerfully built warrior. Everyone seemed to be in awe of this demon they called Ravana. And then there was a sound like the stamping of a huge army, and every asura present grew silent and went down on their knees. The one they called Ravana also looked in the direction of the commotion. It wasn't an army marching towards them. It was an asura whose size dwarfed everything else in the vicinity. As he approached closer, Ravana, too, kneeled in front of him and bowed his head. The gigantic asura touched Ravana's head with the palm of his hands and lifted him up to hug him. He was Ravana's maternal uncle, the king of demons, the one they called Kalanemi!

◆

Kansa regained consciousness with a jolt. The Dark Lord had taken him back to his past life and allowed him to see who he was. Kansa had changed forever; metamorphosed into something that even he didn't fully fathom at the moment. His mortal past as a noble warrior now lay submerged somewhere deep within his consciousness. In its place remained the towering frame of the greatest demon king the world had ever known—Kalanemi!

But more important than seeing his several past lives, the Dark Lord had also shown Kansa the face of the person who was destined to kill him in this birth. The face had belonged to a beautiful boy, no more than fifteen years old, and the eighth offspring of Devki and Vasudev.

Kansa smiled. He knew what he had to do.

Bhargava Shares His Secret

'It is done!' the Dark Lord said quietly. 'Kansa has been turned.' He stood in the centre of Bhargava's room. There was no trace of joy or satisfaction on his face at Kansa's metamorphosis of Kansa; just the barely perceptible indications of being resigned to what had happened.

'What are my instructions?' Bhargava murmured. His face, too mirrored Amartya's lack of pleasure at Kansa's transformation.

Amartya seemed to mull over his thoughts before responding. Then appearing to make up his mind, he addressed Bhargava firmly, 'Send a messenger to the king of Magadha. Ask Jarasandha to spread the word to the asura assassins hiding in every part of Mrityulok. The time has come for them to start the work they have been trained for.'

Bhargava looked astounded, 'Already? Isn't it too early Amartya?'

Amartya shook his head, 'No. It is time!' he said, taking a deep breath. 'Narada has already spoken with various kings and while most of them have listened to him with disbelief, some of them have started building task forces to flush out the assassins. It's a matter of time before the countries content to sit on the fence today begin establishing similar groups to seek out our men. We need to strike before that happens.'

Bhargava nodded. He knew, looking at Amartya, that there was more. He didn't have to wait long, before the Dark Lord shocked him yet again.

'Ask Ugra to speed up the training for the last batch of

assassins. I want all ten thousand of them trained and ready to be sent into Mrityulok in the next three saptakas (three weeks). Now that Kansa is on our side, a significant part of these men will make their entry through the Madhuvan border. The remaining can enter Mrityulok through Magadha.'

'Kansa may have come on our side Amartya, but Ugrasena is still the king of Madhuvan. How do you think thousands of our men are going to enter his land without Ugrasena taking any action? Bhargava sounded agitated at what he sensed was a big loop hole in Amartya's strategy.

Amartya was staring at Bhargava but his mind seemed elsewhere. The latter realized that Amartya was focusing his energies on seeing what the future heralded. Eventually, Amartya seemed to come back to himself and his eyes blazed with the power of Brahman, 'Ugrasena will not be king for long. His cub has transformed into a lion and it will not be long before Kansa will return home to claim Madhuvan!'

Bhargava began to say something, when Amartya held up his hand to stop him. The light of Brahman that blazed in his eyes now enveloped his whole being and filled the room with its blue iridescence. Amartya's eyes were fixed on the door that led to Bhargava's chambers. He raised his finger towards the door and it opened on its own, revealing the figure of a man eavesdropping on their conversation. The man stared into the blazing eyes of the Dark Lord and he trembled in fear. Then, as he turned his head to look at Bhargava, he gasped, his face reflecting an expression of complete bewilderment.

◆

'Shukra Acharya!' the man exclaimed in disbelief.

Bhargava looked calmly at his right-hand man. While Amartya and he had tried to conceal his involvement in their plan right from the beginning, Bhargava had always known that some day, his participation would be discovered. Apart from Amartya, Ugra and his assassins, no one knew Bhargava's true identity, but now his closest aide knew too.

'Devayam!' Bhargava spoke softly to the man who still stood staring at him in bafflement. 'Come in and close the door behind you, my friend.'

Devayam looked at the man he had worked for and admired for the past several years. Shukra Acharya, the best-known philosopher and ethnobotanist in all of Pataal Lok; the man whom even the Asura king Vrushaparva and his council members looked up to when they needed advice on matters of politics, administration and occasionally even on war. *This is the same man who had the moral fibre to admonish asura kings when he thought they were wrong. And now, he takes the side of the most feared man in Pataal Lok—the Dark Lord himself!* Devayam's expression told Bhargava how confounded the young man was.

Amartya was able to read Devayam's thoughts with ease, but he did not want to intervene. He knew this was something Bhargava had to handle himself.

Bhargava—the man known in the three worlds as Shukra Acharya—smiled at Devayam, in an attempt to make him comfortable. He patted the diwan and motioned for Devayam to take a seat next to him. 'You look disturbed, Devayam,' he said gently. 'Tell me what is bothering you.'

Devayam struggled to form words. The feeling of incredulity had gradually given way to a slowly simmering anger that threatened to erupt any moment. It was only his respect for the greatest philosopher in Pataal Lok that kept his temper in check. He had avoided looking in the direction of Amartya all this while. Now he glared at Bhargava, and pointing towards the Dark Lord, he said accusingly, 'How can you connive with a man like this against your own people?'

Bhargava's face reflected his considerable surprise at the question. 'Connive against my people? What do you mean by that?'

'I heard your conversation. You plan to send assassins into

Mrityulok,' he stared rebelliously at Bhargava. 'There have been rumours that an army is being assembled in Pataal Lok. King Vrushaparva and his council members have maintained total silence on this. I thought you knew something about it and that's why you have been perturbed the past few days. I mentioned this to Narada when he was here a few days back. I didn't know then that you not only knew about the army being assembled, you are probably the one behind it all, along with this man they call the Dark Lord!' He finished in rage, pointing a finger at Amartya.

Bhargava struggled to remain calm. Devayam's disrespect for Amartya was gnawing at him. 'There is no army being assembled... yet! There might be at some time in the future. It's difficult to say right now,' he paused. 'But how does this make me connive against my own people, as you said just now?'

Bhargava's calm tone had its effect on Devayam. He grew visibly less antagonistic. 'Acharya, if we raise an army such as is being rumoured, the only purpose of such a force would be to attack one of the other two worlds. In either case, people are going to die in vain. The last time Pataal Lok waged a war under Ravana against Mrityulok, millions of our people died just to satisfy the ego of one man.'

'I just told you, we are not raising an army right now. If we do, it will be because that will be the only option available to us.' Bhargava looked benevolently at his aide. 'You know I would never encourage unnecessary bloodshed, Devayam.'

Devayam struggled with his feelings. He found it impossible to question the man who had taught him everything he knew till now. But there were other questions that he had to have an answer to. He bowed his head. This time, his tone was much softer. 'What about the assassins being smuggled into the mortal world, acharya? How do you explain that? Won't that action beget a much larger reaction from Mrityulok? What do we gain by doing this?' His voice reflected his anguish at the grievous possibilities and more so, the role his mentor was playing in it.

Bhargava sighed. 'Everything is not done for a gain, Devayam.' He shook his head, 'Anyway, do you have faith in me?' His tone demanded an honest answer and Devayam squirmed under his mentor's gaze.

'I have complete faith in you, acharya,' he said slowly. 'But I do not trust this man!' he pointed belligerently at Amartya.

'If you have faith in me, then know this—I have complete belief in the great man you point your finger at,' Bhargava finally snapped at the constant insults to Amartya.

Devayam was taken aback at Bhargava's sudden anger. 'I-I don't understand, acharya. Why are you with this...this man?' he stammered in confusion.

Bhargava stood up and went up to Amartya. Under Devayam's astonished gaze, he prostrated himself on both knees in front of Amartya, who placed his right hand on the acharya's head and blessed him. Bhargava felt a shiver of energy pass through him as Amartya's hand connected with his Sahasrara Chakra. He got up, his face alight with his fidelity for his friend. Pointing towards Amartya he said, 'This man you call the Dark Lord is Brahmarishi Amartya Kalyanesu, a brahmarishi in the category of Guru Vashisht and Guru Vishwamitra, perhaps even more. Will you dare to question the moral fibre of a Being such as him?'

Devayam gaped at Amartya and he noticed the aura of blue surrounding him. He felt compelled to bow to the man he had only recently raged at. But Amartya read the doubts in his mind, and said, 'You bow to me, Devayam, but there are still unspoken questions in your mind. It doesn't befit a man of your integrity to bow to me till those questions have been answered.'

Devayam looked at Amartya, beginning to understand somewhat why his mentor respected this man so much. 'Why are we training assassins to kill innocent people, My Lord? Is this not evil? What could possibly justify something like this?'

Amartya gazed at the man who displayed such intense self-belief in questioning not just his own mentor but also a brahmarishi. And he mentally lauded the young man. Aloud he said, 'Perhaps you could call this evil. But sometimes, it is justifiable to commit a relatively minor evil in order to eradicate a larger one.'

Devayam looked helplessly at Bhargava. His expression told the acharya that he had not been able to comprehend the meaning of Amartya's cryptic words.

'Let me tell you a story, Devayam,' Bhargava said, making up his mind. At the end of it, I would like you to tell me if you noticed any evil in it.'

Devayam nodded with some relief. All of Shukra Acharya's students knew his penchant of explaining concepts through stories. In any case, it would be easier to understand the point through a story rather than to try and make sense of the brahmarishi's enigmatic statement.

Bhargava indicated for Devayam to take a seat and he started his story.

◆

'In the land of Kambhoja, almost three hundred years ago, there lived a simple sage. He had built a hermitage far away from the city, and lived there with his wife, Kavyamata. Aware of the sage's reputation, several kings and other well-known rishis had sent their children to be taught at his ashram. Assisted by his wife, he transformed the staid hermitage into a sanctuary of learning. While most of the other sages and rishis favoured the devas at the expense of the asuras, this person was above these petty biases and he was respected equally, by both, the devas and the asuras.

'One day, when the sage had gone out to meditate atop a mountain adjoining the hermitage, a group of asura children came rushing through the gate of the ashram. Most of them were less than ten years old and the others had barely touched adolescence. As soon as they entered the ashram, they fell at the feet of Kavyamata, the sage's wife. Kavyamata asked one of her shishyas (students) to get them some water. After the children had calmed down somewhat, she asked them the reason for their terrorized entry into the ashram. The children said that they were from a nearby asura colony, and had gone to the forest for a picnic. As they ventured deeper into the woods, they came upon a large group of armed men. Seeing the children, the armed men attacked them, without provocation, and killed some of their companions. The children who survived the assault tried to run back to their colony to save their lives. In their confused state, they lost their way and instead of reaching the asura colony where they lived, they reached the sage's hermitage. Hoping fervently that the armed men would not attack them in the ashram, they rushed inside to seek refuge.

'Kavyamata was furious after hearing the children's story. She commanded her oldest shishyas to cordon off the walls of the ashram and ensure that none of the armed men pursuing the children were allowed to enter. To the cowering children who had sought shelter under her roof, she spoke gently, "Don't worry young ones; no harm shall come to you while you are here. You have the word of a muni dvitiya (wife of a sage)."

'While she was trying to make the asura children comfortable inside the ashram, one of her shishyas came in shaken and said, "Maa, there are more than fifty armed men standing at the gate and they are demanding that we hand over the children to them." Kavyamata looked at her trembling pupil and spoke softly to him, even though her tone was admonishing, "And what do you think, child? Should we fear those barbarians and hand over these defenseless children to them so they can kill them like they did their other companions?" The student lowered his eyes, ashamed at having displayed fear in front of the sage's wife. He whispered, "No, maa, give me permission to fight these evil men and make them leave."

'Kavyamata smiled and patted his head lovingly. "No, child, there is time yet for you to display your prowess. In the absence of your guru, I am responsible for your safety and the security of this ashram. Take me to these men who dare to come armed to a place of learning." The student led the sage's wife to the gate where a battalion of armed men waited impatiently. As soon as they saw Kavyamata, they started jeering and hooting. One of them remarked, "Look who's come...an old crone!" The other men laughed as he continued poking fun at Kavyamata. "We can't even do anything with this old hag. If she had been a little younger, we could at least have had some fun with her!" Kavyamata's face grew tight at the insults and she restrained some of her students who made a move towards the man insulting their guru's wife.

'And then, to the extreme surprise of the armed men, Kavyamata herself opened the gate to the ashram. There was something about her face and the way she looked at them that made even these men suddenly take a step back in fear. But it was too late. Kavyamata had unleashed the potent Jangama mantra that allowed her to control the mind of anyone she looked at. The men standing close to her were all rendered immobile almost immediately. By the time the others realized what was happening, a majority of them had been affected by the hypnosis-inducing mantra and they stood as statues, incapable of moving a limb. Only two of the armed men, who had been standing beyond the line of vision of the sage's wife were unaffected and were able to escape. They ran for their lives shouting threats at Kavyamata, even as they left.

'Kavyamata watched with relief as she saw the two men's retreating back. She looked up at the setting sun and hoped her husband would be back before the men returned with others. She had exhausted herself by using the mantra on so many people at the same time, and she was aware she might not be able to hold back too many more men if they returned.

'A few of the older students waited at the gate while Kavyamata went in to meditate. She hoped to recover some of her lost vitality through her powers of concentration. She told her students to call for her if the men returned while she was in meditation.

'As it grew progressively darker, the children keeping watch at the gate shivered with the cold, and with the fear of the men returning with more warriors. Gradually, they heard the sound of approaching horses. They strained their eyes to see who it was. As the horses drew near, they recognized the two men who had run away earlier. They were accompanied by a third man, wearing a shining white armour. His hair was light brown and it fluttered in the wind. As he rode on his large stallion with his sword held high, he appeared to the students the most dashing and dangerous man they had ever seen in their lives. Mesmerized by the sight of the armoured warrior, they watched in awe as he reached the ashram gate. Before any of them could think of running to warn Kavyamata of the men's arrival, the warrior's sword swung in the air and loped off the heads of three of the oldest students stationed at the gate. As the rest of the students watched in horror, the other two men began to systematically hack each of them to death. The annihilation of the shishyas stationed outside was complete and the three warriors had not yet uttered a word.

'Finally, the man in white armour addressed his two companions and his voice was heavy with rage. "Find every man, woman and child in the ashram and make them taste the metal of your sword. I will deal with the witch who dared to attack my men and gave shelter to the asura children."

'The two armed men combed every inch of the ashram and did a professional job of ruthlessly killing all the children they found. Not a single child was spared; and a special fate awaited the asura children. Their hacked heads were placed on top of the walls of the ashram, as a message for anyone else who dared to offer refuge to an asura, or obstructed the way of the warriors.

'Meanwhile, the third warrior, the one in the white armour, had gone in search of Kavyamata. She was not in the main ashram building, and had gone to meditate at a slight distance, near the stream running behind the hermitage. The warrior gazed at her, sitting serenely by the stream, lost in concentration. For a moment, his mind seemed to waver. Then his face set in a grim expression. His lips curled in an enigmatic smile and with one mighty swoop of his sword, he sliced off her head.'

◆

Devayam stared at Bhargava, as he came to the end of the story. The acharya was looking strangely at him. Without warning, he asked, 'Tell me now Devayam—did you see any evil in this story?'

Devayam answered almost instantaneously, 'Great evil, acharya! The men who killed those children and the defenseless gurumata were evil incarnate.'

'Hmm,' Bhargava nodded, 'and if I were to tell you that this was not the first time these men had committed such dastardly deeds? That they had killed other innocent people before this; what would you say should be done to such people?'

This time, Devayam took longer to reply. When he answered, his voice had dropped to a whisper, 'Such men have no business being alive, acharya. They should be hunted down and destroyed!' Bhargava countered, 'But would that not be evil, Devayam? To kill other men?'

Devayam was vehement. 'How can it be evil to kill such men? They deserve to die!'

Bhargava smiled. 'You have now understood what Brahmarishi Amartya Kalyanesu said to you sometime back.' He paused as he saw the beginnings of comprehension dawn on Devayam. 'To destroy great evil, it may sometimes be justified to commit a lesser one.'

Devayam was silent as he digested this. Then a thought struck him. 'This warrior, acharya...the one in the white armour. Who was he?'

Bhargava gritted his teeth as he got up to leave. 'He goes by the name of Indra.'

Devayam gasped. He saw Bhargava preparing to leave for his evening meditation. Amartya Kalyanesu sat quietly, watching the exchange between Shukra Acharya and his aide.

'Shukra Acharya!' Devayam called after Bhargava's retreating figure. 'Who was that woman in the story—the one called Kavyamata?'

'She was my mother,' Bhargava choked as he walked out of the door.

Battle at Bhairava Van

Vasudev stopped to survey the hazardous terrain ahead of them. The rough pathway was strewn with boulders of varying sizes and the trail they were on suddenly branched into a multitude of narrow byways. It was anyone's guess which of these was the right one and led to the assassin's lair. Vasudev knew each of these byways could be a death trap, and he could well be leading his men to their end.

The platoon of men that Airawat had gathered together for the task force had grown to a full brigade of five hundred hardened soldiers under Vasudev's command. It had taken a month to select the men and train them to achieve the unbelievable standard they had reached before Vasudev finally announced them ready to battle the asura assassins. He had started the training as soon as he had reached Madhuvan from Bateshwar. Airawat had been awed at the intense training regime Vasudev set for his men. Yet the Prince maintained an easy camaraderie with all of them and it was evident to Airawat that he had the loyalty of each man present there.

Two days back, one of Ugrasena's trusted spies had brought news that he had sighted a few suspicious-looking men at Hastinapur. The spy had been keeping watch on their activities for several days and he had finally become convinced that they were assassins in hiding. While they worked within the city, they did not dwell there like the other workers and traders. This in itself was odd. To add to that, they looked vastly different from the other traders and carried themselves with the air of people trained to fight. Finally, one day the spy decided to follow the men to find out where they stayed. He trailed them at a distance, but just when he thought they were reaching their destination, his horse stopped and refused to move further. The spy realized the horse had badly hurt its hoof, and it would be pointless to follow the men on foot. He walked ahead for some distance and came to a point where the road branched into several directions. Rather than follow them further and risk being exposed, the spy had returned to Hastinapur and requested an urgent audience with Dhritarashtra, who was acting as regent of the powerful country in the absence of his younger brother, Pandu, who was currently undergoing penance in the forests of Chaitraratha, along with his two wives. Under the sage advice of his vrddhah (grandfather), Bheeshma, Dhritarashtra handed the spy a communique for Vasudev, giving him permission to enter Hastinapur with his task force.

Vasudev and his men had ridden hard and covered the distance of twenty yojanas from Madhuvan in two days. They had now reached the point where the spy had lost the trail of the men he had been following. Vasudev turned around as Airawat rode ahead with the spy to join him. The rest of the men were halted at a distance waiting for instructions from Vasudev.

'Is this the exact location you lost the men, Aniruddha?' Vasudev looked at the spy.

'Yes, My Lord,' Aniruddha answered, amazed that Vasudev knew his name. He had no idea that Vasudev could have rattled off the name of each of his five hundred men with ease.

Vasudev glanced at Airawat. 'What do you suggest? Each of these paths could be a trap leading the men to their deaths.'

Airawat nodded in agreement. Like Vasudev, he too had made a quick assessment of the situation, which included analysing each of the byways. He had a question for the spy: 'How many men did you say you followed Aniruddha?'

Aniruddha considered for a while. 'I think there must have been about thirty in all, sire.'

Airawat nodded, his expression thoughtful. 'What are the chances that there could be other men...men that you may not be aware of, but are companions of the people you followed that day?'

Aniruddha understood where Airawat was going with his questions. He shook his head ruefully. 'I have no idea, sire. I never saw those men interact with anyone else at Hastinapur. But there is always the chance that there could be other groups like theirs functioning in other parts of the city. And...and all these groups may be dwelling in the same place.'

'In which case it could be both, an advantage as well as a terrible drawback,' Vasudev intervened. Both men stared at him.

'If there are several groups holed up together somewhere up there,' Vasudev said, pointing in the direction of the byways, 'then this would be a brilliant opportunity to catch them all at one go.' He paused, before continuing in a quiet voice, 'If, however, their numbers are too large, then not only will they have the advantage of knowing this terrain, they could also possibly outnumber us by a large margin.'

There was a lull in the conversation as each of the men debated the situation in their own mind. Vasudev was the first to break the uncomfortable silence. 'We have one major advantage though. They don't know we are coming for them.' He grinned at the others and they felt their confidence returning.

'This road branches off into five lanes, My Lord,' Airawat said cogitatively. 'We don't know where they lead to and whether they even link up at a common point. If we were to split our men across each of these lanes, we may end up spreading ourselves too thin.'

'What do you suggest?' Vasudev asked his second-in-command.

Airawat nudged his horse to move forward and signalled Vasudev and Aniruddha to follow him. He stopped and dismounted as they came to the point where the path branched off into different directions. The other two followed suit. Airawat beamed with satisfaction as he pointed to two of the bylanes. The grass grew heavy on these routes and there were no indications of any footprints, of man or horse.

'These don't seem to have been used in a long time, My Lord,' Airawat said with a pleased look. 'That leaves the other three bylanes. I suggest we split up into three groups and see if the roads meet up ahead.'

Vasudev nodded. 'I will take one of the paths. You take another one Airawat.' He paused, 'Who do you think should lead the third route?' 'Tantra!' Airawat's answer was swift.

Vasudev nodded in approval. Airawat had chosen wisely. Tantra was a veteran and he was the oldest in the task force. But despite his age, he could move more nimbly and swiftly than any of the other men. More importantly, he had a clear head on his shoulders and was not rattled easily. In the absence of Vasudev and Airawat, the men would be safe under his command.

'I will take a company of a hundred men with me. You and Tantra take a battalion of two hundred each,' Vasudev said, looking at Airawat.

Airawat looked distinctly uncomfortable with Vasudev's decision of splitting the numbers. He didn't want the prince to go into enemy territory with the smallest force. 'I think Tantra and you should go in with a battalion, My Lord. I will take a hundred men with me.'

Vasudev shook his head in mock exasperation. 'When will you learn to take orders, Airawat?' he joked. 'My decision stands. I will go in with a hundred men. Speak to Tantra and get the men ready. I will join you in a moment.' He dismissed the two men and continued to stare contemplatively at the lane he had chosen to take.

◆

Airawat watched as his scout kneeled down and put his ear to the ground. He had not heard anything, but the scout's keen senses had apparently picked up something. He stayed with his ear pressed to the ground, till he was certain he had the right information.

'Sixty men, sire! And by the sound of it, it looks like they are having a meal,' the scout said with conviction as he raised himself from the ground.

Airawat was impressed with the man's abilities. *I wouldn't have been able to figure out how many men there are, leave alone what they are doing*, he thought to himself with a smile.

'How far do you suppose they are from here?' he asked the scout.

'A quarter of a yojana, sire,' the scout said with a certainty born out of years of experience in reconnoitering.

'Hmm,' Airawat mumbled. Then he gave the order to his men. 'Move at a slow trot. Let's hope the scoundrels are too busy eating to have posted a lookout. When we are within shouting distance of their camp, we will make the charge at full gallop.'

The men nodded wordlessly, their faces agog with excitement at finally encountering the enemy they had been training to destroy for the past few months. Their horses gradually fell in formation as they followed their commander. Airawat had got a special shield made that was attached firmly to the elbow of his left arm. Since the bonara had cut off his hand at the wrist, this was the only way he could carry the shield and protect an assault to his body.

As they approached closer to the assassin's camp, they could hear the raucous banter of the asuras. Airawat was amazed that they hadn't posted any sentinel. But he realized they probably didn't expect anyone to venture into these bylanes. An ordinary person would have got lost in the maze of twists and turns they had encountered since they had split up with the other two groups. It was only their scout's skill that had ensured they stayed on track.

Airawat gave the signal for his men to stop. He unsheathed his sword and held it high, pointed in the direction of the asura camp. His men followed his example and took out their weapons. Then, as Airawat gave the signal to charge, they let out a bloodcurdling roar that seemed to shake the earth. The horses caught the frenzy of their riders and charged with the full might of their breed. Sounds of 'Har Har Mahadev!' rent the air as the men followed their cavalry commander into their first encounter with the assassins sent by Pataal Lok.

The men in the asura camp did not stand a chance as the Madhuvan battalion came at them like a battering ram smashing through everything in its way. Airawat loped off the head of an asura who attempted to assault him with a mace. Out of the corner of his eye, he saw another one hurl a spear in his direction. Airawat barely had time to bring up his shield to ward off the attack. If he had been a second late, the spear would have sliced through his neck. Before the gigantic asura had time to launch a second attack, Airawat goaded the horse in his direction, and leaped off the mount to engage the demon on ground. The asura took out a curved blade from his scabbard and in a series of swift thrusts, forced Airawat to fall back. His opponent was faster and more adept than any warrior Airawat had fought till date, and for a brief moment, Airawat felt the initial symptoms of fear as the asura continued to push him back. In the aftermath of losing his hand in the fight against the bonara, Airawat's self-belief in his abilities had been shaken worse than even Mandki knew. And at this juncture, the absence of confidence was costing him heavily. All around him, there were lusty screams of men killing each other and being killed. His sudden irrational fear left him temporarily paralyzed and his antagonist had him pinned against a tree. The asura suddenly brought down his sword with all his might and the force of the blow was such that it cracked Airawat's shield in half, which then clattered to the ground. Airawat was now completely vulnerable, with only his sword to protect him. The asura gave him a malevolent smile and moved in for the fatal blow.

At that moment, there was a chorus of 'Har Har Mahadev!' from the Madhuvan battalion. The familiar scream of the Madhuvan war cry shook Airawat from his self-induced stupor and served to calm his frayed nerves. He recovered in time to parry a deadly thrust from the asura, who stumbled with the force of his own blow. Before he had time to recover his stance, the tip of Airawat's sword had pierced through his thick neck, jutting out through the other side. The asura's eyes rolled over in pain and disbelief, and he tottered to the ground. Airawat watched his body hit the ground in the same instant that he became aware of the deathly silence around him. He turned around and surveyed the camp site. Not a single assassin had survived. Their torn and bloodied bodies lay slumped on the ground. The entire camp had been decimated.

One of the soldiers approached Airawat, his face betraying his anxiety. 'Sire, your...your hand!' he said hesitantly. The stitches on Airawat's damaged arm had opened up where the shield had been wrenched off by the asura's blow. Blood flowed profusely from the open wound. Airawat compelled himself to ignore the pain. He clenched his teeth to prevent himself from screaming in agony as the soldier made a tourniquet under the arm to stem the flow of blood.

'How many of our men are dead?' he asked wearily.

'Ten of ours, sire! We took all of them though,' the soldier replied proudly.

Airawat shut his eyes momentarily. The loss of his men hung heavy on his shoulders.

'Make arrangements for each of these ten men to be taken back to Madhuvan,' he instructed the soldier, his eyes ablaze with a rare fury.

The soldier saluted smartly, touching his right hand to the left of his chest. 'And what do we do with this place, sire?' he asked tentatively, motioning towards the camp site.

'Burn it down....all of it!' Airawat whispered in muted rage as he walked away from the site.

◆

Vasudev tried to shake off the feeling of foreboding. They had been on the move for a while now and his men were getting restless for action. The unnatural silence around them did not do anything to improve matters. The path they had taken had soon opened into the terrifying Bhairava Van (forest), and there was no way of being certain that they were on the right course. The jungle route was hard and rocky and the men and their horses were not used to this terrain. To make the situation worse, the rocky surface made it nearly impossible to track footprints. It was only the incredible skill of their tracker which gave them some comfort that they were not moving in circles.

'This is not normal, My Lord!' Aniruddha said suddenly. Vasudev looked questioningly at the spy.

'Doesn't the complete absence of wildlife strike you as strange?' Aniruddha asked softly.

Vasudev nodded slowly, understanding dawning on his face. It was rare not to observe any sign of an animal this deep into the forest. Even the occasional chirping of the birds had disappeared for some time now. The implications were too obvious to miss. This part of the woods seemed to have been marked by someone; someone whose presence was deadly enough to have scared away even the natural predators of the jungle.

'The asuras are nearby,' Vasudev whispered, more to himself than to anyone else. *And they seem to be present in large numbers to have this kind of impact on the surroundings,* he reflected, his senses on high alert.

He recalled Narada mentioning in their last meeting that there were at least a thousand asura assassins hidden away in each of the major kingdoms of Mrityulok. Judging by the strategic importance of Hastinapur, Vasudev guessed the size of the assassin module stationed in this city would be considerably larger than a thousand. Assuming that the assassins had built separate encampments, and each of the three bylanes he and his men had taken led to one of those camps, Vasudev's men would probably be up against a force three to four times their own size.

Vasudev held up his hand and called a halt. He didn't know how far they were from the asura site. But if they had to have a reasonable chance of surviving and possibly winning the battle, he would need a more strategic battle formation for his men. Non-verbal signals were swiftly exchanged and the hundred men under his command quietly shifted their positions till he had each warrior exactly where he wanted him. The twenty lancers were placed at the head of the formation. They carried spears extending one gavuta in length and were crafted to pierce even through heavy armour. The strongest men wielded the lances, which an ordinary soldier would have found difficult to raise with both hands, leave aside carry them in one arm, for an extended period of time. Behind the lancers came forty of the regular cavalrymen, wielding swords. They were ideal for hand-to-hand combat and each of them was capable of engaging with several opponents at the same time. The tail end of the structure was brought up by the archers. Vasudev decided they would be the ones to unleash the first part of his lethal assault on the asuras. He gave a grim smile, satisfied at last with the way his small force had been arranged.

The company of a hundred men followed the prince, the adrenaline pumping through their veins beginning to make its presence felt in the way they carried themselves. Each of the men had left behind a declaration of how their assets should be distributed in the event that they failed to return from this mission. They had nothing to fear now. They knew if they died fighting the enemy, their families would be taken care of by the king of Madhuvan. But the lure of money is not what drove them this day. While each of these men had fought earlier as mercenaries, this was the first time they were willing to fight and die for their motherland. Glory awaited them, and it banished any fear of death they might have ever had.

To Vasudev's surprise, the forest ended abruptly and opened

into a vast meadow. At the far end of the meadow, a new stretch of forest started. This one was far denser than the one they had just exited.

The tracker stopped suddenly. Something had attracted his attention at the threshold of the adjoining forest. He peered in its direction, trying to ascertain what it was. There was nothing! Then his trained eyes detected an almost imperceptible movement directly ahead of him, about five hundred paces away. His eyes widened in horror as he understood what he had seen. But the realization dawned too late. He opened his mouth to shout a warning to Vasudev but his scream was cut short by an arrow that went straight through his mouth and exited behind his neck. The tracker dropped to his knees, his sword dropping from his hands. Vasudev and his men watched mesmerized as the tracker's head separated in slow motion from the rest of his body and rolled in their direction, coming to a stop just in front of Vasudev's horse. Vasudev stared at the sightless eyes of the tracker, reflecting all the terror of the dead man, just before the arrow had unerringly found its mark.

Ghora prepared to string another arrow even as Vasudev recovered from the shock of seeing his tracker cut down in front of him. Ghora's next arrow raced through the air and the impact of it threw Aniruddha off his horse. He was dead even before he fell to the ground. The arrow had pierced through the armour and gone right through his heart. Vasudev had never seen an arrow capable of piercing through armour. He knew at once that the enemy showering death on his men was no ordinary warrior. He also knew another thing—he was going to have that warrior's head before this battle was over.

'Shield your bodies!' he shouted to his men as a hail of arrows descended on them. He watched with grim satisfaction as his men rasied their massive shields to protect themselves from the deadly enemy projectiles.

'Agneebaan!' he bellowed to the archers, even as the asura's arrows rained on them from all sides.

The formidable archers of the Madhuvan task force dipped their massive arrows in portable cauldrons of fire; and stringing them on their mighty bows, they let loose their Agneebaans in the direction of the enemy forces. The arrows, laced with oil, erupted in fire even as they left the bow. The archers had fired the arrows in an upward arc, aiming their missiles at the trees which shielded the asura assassins. The dry leaves and wood on the trees served as combustion material and there was a conflagration as the fire spread from tree to tree. The archers continued to fire the Agneebaans and as they descended on the enemy, it looked like the gods were raining down their wrath on the assassins.

Vasudev heard screams of unbearable agony as the assassins poured out of the blazing forest into the meadow. A significant number of these men were half-burnt and would die a torturous death. Vasudev disregarded them for the moment. It was a mistake he would soon regret.

Looking in the direction of those assassins who had somehow miraculously escaped being burnt, he roared a command to his lancers. 'Spears at the ready men!' he bellowed. 'Take the largest of the assassins first.' The lancers raised their spears in front of them and galloped towards these men.

Vasudev looked on as the asuras rapidly re-assembled their badly depleted forces under the command of their leader. He estimated that the forest fire had probably cost the asuras more than half their force. But he could still make out at least four hundred of them. Even with close to a hundred in a burnt state, that still left three hundred enemy survivors; three times the number of his own unit.

Vasudev was too far to see the leader's face but he noticed the calm and assured way with which the man carried himself. He watched with incredulity as the assassin's leader instructed his half-dead men to cover their unharmed comrades. He realized what the asura leader intended to do but it was too late. His lancers were too far and riding too fast for him to shout a warning. He watched as the incredibly strong lancers smashed their way through the enemy wall. But the major share of their charge succeeded only in giving a quick death to the asuras who were already half-dead. By the time, the lancers were done with their charge, more than a hundred asuras lay dead on the ground, their bodies broken by the force of the assault. Unfortunately, this was an empty victory for Vasudev as the asura leader had used his already dying men to exhaust the strongest portion of Vasudev's unit—his lancers. And now the lancers were encircled on all sides by the assassins.

Vasudev realized his twenty lancers stood no chance against the three-hundred-odd assassins who had them surrounded. Without waiting for the rest of his men to follow, Vasudev goaded his horse in the direction of the enemy. The leader of the asuras, astride his own horse saw him coming. He calmly picked up his bow and even as Vasudev looked on, he shot five arrows in quick succession. At first, Vasudev thought the asura had badly miscalculated his aim. Each of the five arrows landed harmlessly in the ground, ahead of him. In the very next instant, he realized that he had deliberately fired the arrows to fall short; they now stood firmly in the ground, arranged horizontally and blocking his way. Too swift to stop in time, Vasudev's horse crashed into the barrier formed by the arrows and he was thrown off his mount. He staggered to his feet and in the distance, saw the asura leader smiling serenely at him.

Vasudev gasped. The man who led the asuras could not have been more than nineteen. His face displayed a vulnerability that was at odds with the calculated brutality he had demonstrated. The contradiction was confusing and terrifying at the same time. The manner in which he had toppled him off the horse told Vasudev this was a master archer; a formidable warrior. And it was in that moment that he realized he was staring at the man who had killed his tracker and Aniruddha.

Ghora smiled unruffled as he felt Vasudev's gaze upon

him. He knew he could have easily shot the commander of the Madhuvan force instead of dislodging him from his horse. But he did not want to give him an easy death. Six hundred of his companions had perished in the fire and another one hundred brave men had been cut down by this man's lancers. He would give him a death that the warrior's people would remember for ages, when they spoke about this battle. But first, he had to deal with the lancers who had ruthlessly killed his men.

'Cut off their heads,' he said softly, as his assassins circled the lancers.

Even as Vasudev jumped on the back of his horse, he saw with horror a horde of assassins descending on each of his twenty lancers. The Madhuvan men fought valiantly but in a matter of seconds, the sheer strength of the enemy's numbers took its toll on them. Twenty heads rolled to the ground, in quick succession.

Vasudev's swordsmen were already engaged in fighting a separate battle with the rest of the asuras. His archers, who had exhausted their supply of arrows in the previous assault, had also taken out their swords and were bravely fighting for their lives and for the honour of their motherland. But it was a futile effort against the superior numbers of the asuras, and Vasudev's men were being killed with frightening speed.

Vasudev knew the battle would be over for him and his men within the next few minutes. But he had a vow to fulfil before he died. He wanted the head of the asura leader; now more than ever before. He nudged his horse in the direction of the enemy.

◆

A loud roar of 'Har Har Mahadev!' temporarily halted the uneven battle between Vasudev's rapidly diminishing force and Ghora's horde of assassins. All eyes turned to see where the deafening war cry of Madhuvan had erupted from. Vasudev breathed in relief as the two battalions swarmed out of the forest behind them, with Airawat and Tantra in the lead. *Thank God they made it in time,*

Vasudev thought with grim satisfaction.

The outlook on the battlefield was suddenly transformed as Airawat and Tantra led their men to the core of Ghora's force. The asuras who had almost tasted victory in their mind were now faced with the immediate prospect of fighting a force much larger than theirs. Vasudev's remaining men battled with regained fervour and the tide started shifting in favour of the men from Madhuvan.

Tantra was fearsome to behold as he chose to attack the three largest opponents on the battlefield. He charged, knocking two of them to the ground as his horse rammed into them. Tantra buried the point of his spear into the chest of one of the men, and as the second one struggled to get up, the veteran commander sliced his neck off with his sword. The third asura recovered quickly from the intensity of the attack and thrust his sword at Tantra's torso, who brought up his shield to parry the blow. The sword slipped out of the asura's hand.

'Burn in hell!' Tantra said calmly as he dug his sword into his opponent's neck. The asura brought both hands up to his throat and tried to stem the rapid flow of blood, but he was beyond salvage. He stumbled and dropped to the ground.

Tantra turned his horse towards Airawat. The cavalry commander was valiantly fighting a large number of assassins who had him completely surrounded. Airawat fought bravely though his strength had been seriously depleted, owing to loss of blood from his new wound. Tantra noticed a change in Airawat. The normally quiet man fought with a passion that was awe-inspiring. His eyes burnt with a strange fury, and he ruthlessly hacked at the men attacking him, even as more of them kept coming at him. Tantra let out a whoop and rushed forward to support Airawat.

Airawat seemed oblivious to Tantra as he battled the enemy, with complete concentration. He seemed to be under some kind of a spell where the blood lust had subdued any other feelings he may have had. Finally, the assassins around him were all dead, lying in an ever expanding pool of their own blood. Airawat stopped swinging his sword, and gradually his body seemed to lose some of its tension. He took in deep breaths of air and felt the blood lust begin to leave his system. He became aware of Tantra staring at him anxiously, and he gave the veteran a grim smile. The two men looked around the battlefield. The serene meadow had been transformed into one huge deathbed of warriors from both sides. Bodies lay strewn all across the field. The entire enemy force had been annihilated. The three hundred and fifty Madhuvan warriors who had survived stood watching a private battle about to take place at the other end of the field. Airawat saw Vasudev face to face with an asura, preparing for single combat.

The colour drained from Airawat's face as he noticed the tattoo on the warrior's arms. The tattoo represented his fighting prowess. In the land of asuras, this tattoo was only worn by someone who had been accorded the status of an Asakya Sura; a warrior who was considered almost invincible. Even the terrible Zataka Upanshughataks were no match for a warrior of this stature. Airawat knew no one had ever fought an Asakya Sura and lived to tell the tale. And even though he had seen Vasudev's incredible talent in sword fighting during his visit to Bateshwar, he wondered if the prince would prove equal to this opponent.

◆

Vasudev faced the warrior who had killed Aniruddha and the tracker. He noticed the strange symbol tattooed on the right arm of his enemy. It had at its centre, a circle from which eight Trishuls emanated, pointing in different directions. Vasudev was incredulous. The trishul was the preferred weapon of the Mahadev. The significance of the eight trishuls did not escape Vasudev's attention either. As a Bharatvanshi, he knew the relevance of the number eight. The loop in the number indicated that we always came back to where we started our journey of life; hence, existence was infinite. When rotated at an angle of ninety degrees, the number took on the sign of infinity, again proving the infiniteness of the universe. Vasudev wondered why this warrior carried on his body a symbol that indicated his respect for Lord Shiva, and why an asura would give importance to a number that was considered holy by the Bharatvanshis of Mrityulok.

While he found all of this immensely surprising, it was the eyes of the Asura leader that left him completely astonished. They looked like a much older man's eyes set in the face of a child. They seemed to contain within their depths a lifetime of pain, and despite his rage at what the asura had done to his people, Vasudev felt himself inexplicably drawn to this man, in a way that was difficult for him to fathom.

Ghora looked around them. His eyes took in the carnage. All his men were dead. Companions with whom he had spent the last few months; thought of as family, all of them were gone. He had failed them as their leader. And he had also failed Ugra, the one man he had learnt to love and respect.

'You are their leader?' the harsh voice of Vasudev broke into his thoughts.

'Yes, I am!' Ghora answered, meeting Vasudev's gaze. 'Or should I say, I was...' He left the sentence incomplete.

'They got what they deserved,' Vasudev retorted unforgiving. 'And by Vishnu, you shall soon join them soon!' he whispered softly, his eyes not leaving his opponent even for a moment.

Ghora smiled. It was a sad smile, but he appeared unruffled. 'Then you shouldn't waste time talking, should you?' he said quietly.

Vasudev was astounded at the uncanny calm his enemy displayed in the face of such daunting circumstances. He wished he could know this strange man better, but too much water had flown under the bridge for that to happen now. The man would have to bear the consequences for what he had done.

Vasudev raised his sword. 'Prepare to fight,' he said, his eyes narrowing.

The two fighters circled each other, each looking for an opening in the other's defense. There was none, on either side. Suddenly Vasudev thrust his sword at Ghora's throat. The blow would have impaled him had he not moved adroitly out of the way. Vasudev pulled back his sword and stepped sideways. The dexterity with which Ghora had avoided his attack surprised him. Vasudev took a deep breath to calm himself. He didn't want to waste his energy on ineffectual manoeuvres. He tried another approach. He made a feinting move, making it appear as if he was aiming for Ghora's torso. Ghora appeared to take the bait and raised his sword sideways to parry the assault on his body, leaving his lower body vulnerable to attack. This is what Vasudev had hoped for. He relaxed his grip on the sword and in one fluid motion, lowered the blade aiming instead for the enemy's feet.

Airawat, watching the fight closely, thought that Vasudev had the asura then, but in an unexpected movement, Ghora simply stepped aside. Vasudev's sword missed the foot and pierced the ground. The impact jarred every bone in Vasudev's body and he made a herculean effort to pull the sword back out again. In the same instant, Ghora brought his sword to Vasudev's throat and a collective gasp went up amongst the onlookers.

'You are dead, my friend!' Ghora whispered, as a trickle of blood started from under Vasudev's chin. 'Make it quick then,' Vasudev replied without a trace of fear.

To his surprise and the bewilderment of the entire Madhuvan force, Ghora shook his head. Pointing in the direction of Vasudev's sword he said, 'Pick it up. We have just about warmed up.' There was a trace of amusement in his voice that both confused and irritated Vasudev. He had never fought a warrior who could move so fast and so unpredictably.

Vasudev pulled out his sword where it was wedged deep inside the ground. He acknowledged his adversary with a slight nod and the fight began again. This time it was Ghora who went on the offensive. In a series of lighting moves, he lunged at Vasudev from different sides, and his thrusts appeared to be everywhere at the same time. It took all of Vasudev's skill to parry the unrelenting attack. Most fighters would make the mistake of coming too close to their opponents while attacking, and it would give a superior warrior the opportunity to seek an opening and move in for the kill. But Ghora was ensuring that with every thrust he made, his sword arrived at the fight before his elbow or his face did. This did not allow Vasudev any chance of striking back. Neither did Ghora stumble or falter while attacking, making it impossible for Vasudev to strike. His complete attention was concentrated in keeping Ghora's attacks at bay and in trying to buy time, hoping the young man would tire soon. But Ghora appeared to be as fresh when they had started off. To his surprise, Vasudev found his own breathing grow ragged with the strain of having to defend himself continuously. And then, as suddenly as he had started, Ghora stopped his offensive.

The two warriors paused to stare at each other. Vasudev knew the other man was playing with him, wanting to reduce him to an exhausted wreck before he made an end of him. He tried to feel his sword but his arms were too tired to have any sensation left in them anymore. They hung limp at his sides, drained of energy and strength. Incredulously, the man facing him hadn't even broken into a sweat. He just continued to stare at Vasudev, as if he wanted to give him time to regain his energy.

Vasudev thought of his impending marriage with Devki, and how she would react when she would hear about his death. *It will break her heart*, he thought. The bile rose into his throat and he spat out the disgusting fluid. *I can't die, not like this...not without seeing Devki*, he resolved. The thought seemed to give him superhuman strength and he felt the apathy fade from his body, as his limbs regained their vitality.

Ghora noticed the change come over his opponent. He prepared himself for what he knew was going to be the last round of the lethal fight. Vasudev didn't wait for Ghora to go on the offensive this time. He realized he had made a terrible mistake in allowing his opponent's unnatural skill to get him rooted to the spot. It was the worst thing a swordsman could do. He started moving lightly on the balls of his feet, much as a boxer would. It was a technique he had learnt from his physical training instructor when the latter had taught him the essentials of hand-to-hand fighting. The dancing movement allowed blood to circulate freely through his lower limbs and also served to confuse an opponent about any intended move. He made a few light lunges towards his adversary, making sure he used his body weight rather than his arms to power the thrusts. The change in technique helped Vasudev control his breathing better and he found the tiredness had all but deserted him.

Finally, Vasudev decided to use a technique he had learnt from one of his tribal friends during his younger days. It was an unconventional move and even classic fighters were unaccustomed to it. Vasudev remembered his friend had bested even their instructor with this style as the trainer had been caught unawares due to the unusual technique.

While a fighter of Ghora's calibre would possibly adapt to it in no time, there was bound to be a brief period of uncertainty. Vasudev intended to use that moment of hesitation to his advantage. He began to circle Ghora, slow at first and then rapidly. As the pace increased, he jumped in the air in an unpredictable move and attacked Ghora sideways from top. Ghora was just in time to defend the blow to his head. By the time he had recovered, Vasudev had begun circling him again, even faster, dancing all the while on the balls of his feet. And again, he jumped in the air and attacked. This time the assault was aimed at Ghora's neck instead of the head. Yet again, Ghora deflected the blow, but this time Vasudev's sword almost nicked the skin off the side of his throat. Ghora felt a slight trickle of blood begin to flow, but it was inconsequential. His attention was focused completely on Vasudev who was circling him faster than ever now. This time

Ghora was prepared for the blow, and as soon as Vasudev made the move to leap up, Ghora brought up his sword to deflect the intended blow. Only this time around, Vasudev did not leap up in the air. He lunged to the side, and before Ghora realized that he had become the victim of a feint, Vasudev had dug the sword sideways into his thigh, severing Ghora's femoral artery.

Ghora stared in disbelief at the man he had been fighting for the past one hora. He had fallen for the most common ruse in swordsmanship—a feint. But the style had been so different that he had not been prepared for it. The blood gushing out of his thigh sapped his energy and his legs revolted against the weight of his body. He staggered to his knees, the sword falling to the ground. He looked up to stare at the man who had finally vanquished him. Vasudev stared into his eyes. He saw no fear there; possibly some regret, but he couldn't be certain.

'Why did you not kill me when you had the chance?' he asked abruptly. Ghora smiled. 'Is this necessary?' he asked, coughing blood.

'It is necessary to me,' Vasudev said, knowing the man would die soon if the blood loss was not stemmed immediately.

Ghora shook his head resignedly. 'My men were all dead. There was no point in killing you. It wouldn't have got them back!'

Vasudev's voice shook in frustrated anger. 'Then why, dammit? Why did you have to fight me?'

'Because I knew you wouldn't be at peace till you had killed the man who was responsible for the deaths of your people,' Ghora rasped, his praana leaving him rapidly. 'And because I would have rather died fighting a warrior then be killed by those men,' he said pointing towards the Madhuvan force, moving towards them.

Vasudev shook his head, the sudden pain in his head beginning to cloud his thoughts. *War is so useless; it makes beasts out of men*, he reflected.

'I wish you were fighting on our side, my friend,' he mumbled, the ache in his voice evident.

'I wish so too. But I am not!'

'I am willing to give you a chance to save your life if you agree to share your knowledge of the other assassin units with us,' Vasudev said quietly. Ghora shook his head, 'I am afraid I can't do that,' Vasudev sighed, 'Then you leave me with no choice.'

'I ask you for one favour,' Ghora said softly. 'When I left home, I told someone that I would not return till I had either completed my mission, or had my head cut off trying.'

Vasudev nodded in understanding. Ghora smiled at him acknowledging the favour his enemy was doing him. He bent his head, his last thoughts dedicated to the man back home who had given him the love of a father during what were destined to be the last days of his life. Some part of his mind was steeped in regret at what could have been and was not. But the larger part of his consciousness was thankful that he was leaving this land forever, to begin a new journey elsewhere...

Ghora's soul had already commenced its passage into the after world when Vasudev's sword granted him the one favour he had asked of him.

◆

Vasudev and the surviving members of the task force started their victorious journey back to Madhuvan. Three hundred and fifty men remained of the five hundred they had started out with. But they had destroyed more than a thousand asura assassins holed up in Hastinapur. Vasudev had dispatched a man to Dhritarashtra's court, informing him of the battle at Bhairava Van, and the annihilation of the asuras hiding there. In his letter, he had also made a plea to Dhritarashtra to set up their own task force that could prevent fresh infusion of assassins into their land and could also be used to help neighbouring countries. He had no doubt that the regent of Hastinapur would do what he had requested.

Airawat and Tantra had brought Vasudev up to date on what had happened after they had gone their separate ways. While

Airawat's group had razed down one asura camp, Tantra and his battalion had not encountered any encampment. The two battalions had met up on the way, and had taken the only route they thought might have been taken by Vasudev and his men. Fortunately, they had been right and they had reached just in time.

While Tantra dropped back to ride with his men, Airawat rode besides Vasudev at the head of the combined task force. He had not failed to notice the despondent mood the prince was in since they left the Bhairava Van. Vasudev had not once spoken about his fight with the fearsome warrior; nor had he shown any joy in their victory. While they had lost a hundred and fifty of their men, Airawat had thought Vasudev might show at least some satisfaction at what they had achieved. But there was none. Vasudev rode on; his face cast in stone.

They had left Hastinapur far behind and were now halfway back to Madhuvan when they saw a cloud of dust in the distance. Airawat moved to unsheathe his sword, but relaxed as he saw it was a messenger approaching. The man was attired in the traditional clothes of Bateshwar. Vasudev recognized him immediately.

'What news from Bateshwar, Ojus?' he asked the messenger. Ojus saluted smartly, 'My Lord, Commander-in-Chief Sini Yadav sends his greetings.' The messenger handed a scroll to Vasudev.

Vasudev quickly broke the seal and extracted a letter written in Sini Yadav's typical laconic style. He read the message with mixed feelings and put the letter back in the scroll.

'Thank you, Ojus. Tell Sini that I am grateful for the news, and let him know I am thrilled at what his team and he have achieved. Tell him I will send him a more detailed letter once I reach Madhuvan.'

Ojus nodded his understanding. And then he smiled. 'My Lord, all of us at Bateshwar wanted to wish you and Princess Devki the best for your impending marriage. May the gods bless this union.'

Vasudev allowed himself the first smile that day. 'Thank you

Ojus. Devki and I are grateful for the sentiments of the people of Bateshwar. And both the princess and I are looking forward to coming back after the marriage is solemnized.'

Ojus grinned. Vasudev's marriage to Devki was the most looked forward to event at Bateshwar these days. He gave a smart salute to both Vasudev and Airawat and galloped away.

Airawat was glad to see Vasudev smiling finally. 'All well at Bateshwar, My Lord?'

Vasudev nodded. 'Sini Yadav and his team discovered a hideout of about six hundred assassins, a little outside Bateshwar. They have wiped them out.'

Airawat looked perspicaciously at the prince. 'There seems to be more than that,' he said hesitantly.

'Yes, there is,' Vasudev replied grimly, his mood again becoming sullen and withdrawn. 'Sini also sends news that signs of chaos and lawlessness have started increasing all over the land. Several kingdoms have reported unprecedented incidents of murder, vandalism and in-fighting within their cities.'

'So it has started!' Airawat exclaimed softly.

'Yes, it has. And the more assassin units we hunt down and destroy, the more they are going to get provoked,' Vasudev said grimly.

They rode quietly for a while, before Vasudev exploded. 'I wish Kansa had returned. It would have been so much easier.'

Airawat did not respond. He had always been a vocal admirer of Kansa; which is why he couldn't understand why the mention of the prince made him so uncomfortable at this moment.

Kansa Gives a Gift to Devki

Ugrasena and Surasena waited for the royal pandit (court priest) to announce the exact date for the vivah sanskar (marriage ceremony). The pandit seemed to be taking his own time in calculating an auspicious time for the event. He knew this was perhaps the only time when two of the most influential kings in Mrityulok waited for him to speak. Surasena winked at Ugrasena, exhorting him to maintain his calm at the delay. He hadn't failed to notice that his friend was unnaturally edgy. While the king of Madhuvan seemed happy about the wedding, the rift between Kansa and him had taken away the joie de vivre out of his existence. Surasena understood this but he carefully refrained from initiating any discussion about the prince.

The pandit looked up at last and smiled. 'The moon stands in Magha at the moment,' he said. 'In three days, when the moon passes through Uttaraphalguni, the vivah sanskar will take place.'

Surasena sighed in relief. The guests had already been informed about the tentative day for the wedding, but it was necessary to have the precise date for the actual ceremony. He was glad the final date fixed by the pandit was not too off the mark. The guests wouldn't have to wait after their arrival.

Ugrasena, too, seemed satisfied with the announcement. He nodded to the pandit. 'Thank you, Ritvick. Prepare for the ceremony. The guests will begin to arrive in two days' time.'

As the pandit left, Surasena looked at Ugrasena. He didn't want to talk to him about Kansa but he was still concerned about the immense change in his friend's disposition since his last visit to Madhuvan. 'You seem troubled, old friend. Is something bothering you?' he asked gently.

Ugrasena was silent for a while. Then his voice quavering, he whispered, 'I have lost my son, Sura. I have lost Kansa forever.'

Surasena shook his head, his friend's obvious grief considerably diluting his own exuberance. 'We don't easily lose the people we love Ugrasena. If he truly cares for you—and I think he does—he will return to you.'

Ugrasena looked at his oldest friend, a faint glimmer of hope reflected in his eyes. 'Are you sure that he will come back to me, to Madhuvan?'

Surasena nodded vigorously. 'He will. And when he does, welcome him with open arms. Don't grudge him whatever has happened between the two of you in the past.'

Ugrasena smiled for the first time in days. 'May Vishnu let this be true!' he said with fresh enthusiasm. 'Come then, we have work to do.'

The two old warriors slapped each other's backs, and laughed the way they used to when they were younger and didn't have the weight of kingly responsibilities upon their mortal shoulders.

◆

Madhuvan resembled a celestial kingdom on this particular day. The entire city was covered with lamps of various sizes and shapes. The citizens had turned out in their finest attire, and the bright colours of their clothes vied with the dazzling hues of the lamps. Since the actual wedding would be privately held within the precincts of the palace, the regular citizens would not get an opportunity to witness the ceremony. Not wanting them to feel left out, Ugrasena had provided for their entertainment too. Circus owners from all over the land had been invited to Madhuvan and they had pitched up their tents just outside the city so that the people of Madhuvan could have their share of revelry. Infants and even adolescents shrieked in glee as they witnessed fire-eaters and lion trainers in action. Surasena had declared that the Bateshwar treasury would bear the expense on food and sweets that were to be circulated as gifts to every citizen of Madhuvan. Ugrasena had already sent an endowment of fifty gold coins to every household in the city. The coins carried images of Devki and Vasudev on either side and were intended as souvenirs that the citizens could keep with them as a memoir of the royal wedding.

The festive atmosphere reached gargantuan proportions with the arrival of Kansa on the eve of the wedding day. Crowds screamed their welcome to the prince of Madhuvan and the more exuberant amongst the children actually ran alongside his horse, cheering for him. Caught up in the excitement of the moment, none of them noticed the subtle changes in Kansa.

Kansa went directly to the palace and bowed to the king, seeking his blessings in full view of the entire court. The courtiers cheered the arrival of the prince. Ugrasena made a gallant effort to keep his emotions in check as he blessed his son. He was so elated at Kansa's sudden arrival that he too failed to notice the transformation in the prince. Kansa took his place on the right-hand side of Ugrasena and he nodded tersely at Vasudev as he caught his old friend staring at him from the other side of the large hall.

Vasudev sat next to Surasena, in a place reserved for the most honoured guests. Seated amongst them were the various kings and royalty from the most powerful countries in Mrityulok. Dhritarashtra from Hastinapur was accompanied by the Kuru grandsire, Bheeshma. Drupada was present from the powerful country of Panchala. Sakuni represented the land of Gandhar. The other notable royals present had come from Salva, Kekaya, Chedi, Avanti, Kosala, Kalinga, Madra, Sindhu and Virata, among others.

Vasudev stared at Kansa. He was the only one there who noticed the change in his demeanour. Kansa had not returned his smile. *Maybe he is tired from the journey*, he mused. Nevertheless Vasudev was delighted that Kansa had returned. He knew Devki would be thrilled and it was nice to have his old friend back. *I have got to share with him all that has happened in the last few weeks*, he thought.

Ugrasena welcomed all the people who had arrived for the wedding and he suggested they retire to the royal quarters readied for them. A group of attendants had been appointed for each guest and now approached to escort them to their respective residences within the palace.

The formal welcome being completed, Ugrasena excused himself and left the court, motioning to Kansa to accompany him. The guests started dispersing as the court broke up. Handshakes were exchanged and there was a lot of back-slapping as several old friends mingled with each other. Everyone present wanted to congratulate Vasudev on his imminent wedding and some of the older warriors even made coarse jokes about Vasudev's approaching wedding night. Vasudev took all the jokes aimed at him good-naturedly. He knew the men meant well. After he had met all the guests present, he left Surasena to handle them and quietly left the court. He was eager to meet Kansa.

◆

'But why do you want to leave so soon?' Ugrasena said agitatedly. 'You have just arrived.'

'I am not leaving, My Lord,' Kansa replied softly. 'I just want time to prepare a surprise for Devki and Vasudev.'

Ugrasena stared hard at Kansa. 'Since when did you need to call me "My Lord", son?'

Kansa averted his gaze and looked away. He didn't trust his voice enough to speak right now. It had taken all his self-control just to come to Madhuvan. If Jarasandha hadn't persuaded him about how important it was for him to return, he would have not come back at all. But to stand in front of the man who had called him his father all these years and then disowned him, was galling for Kansa.

'I said, since when did you need to...' Ugrasena's sentence was cut short by a knock on the door. The guard outside announced the arrival of Prince Vasudev.

Ugrasena shook his head in frustration. He had thought everything was going to be fine when he saw Kansa enter the court in the morning. But there was something different about Kansa. He seemed changed; stiff and reserved as if he were suppressing some strong emotion inside him. Vasudev's arrival put an end to the discussion with Kansa.

'Kansa!' Vasudev exclaimed in delight. 'How have you been?' he said, enveloping him in a bear hug.

Kansa's body was rigid and Vasudev felt unfamiliar cold vibes emanating from his friend. He abruptly let go of Kansa and stepped back. 'Are you okay?' he asked quietly.

Kansa forced himself to smile at Vasudev. A tiny voice in his head, growing in intensity, wanted him to crush the head of the man standing in front of him. But he restrained himself. *This is not the right time*, he murmured to himself.

'He wants to leave already, Vasudev. Why don't you try and reason with him?' Ugrasena goaded his future son-in-law.

'Leave? What, already! Aren't you going to attend the wedding?' Vasudev exclaimed.

'I am going to attend the wedding, Vasudev. That is the reason I returned, after all,' Kansa paused thoughtfully. 'I had planned a surprise for Devki. I need some time to prepare it for her...and for you!'

'What surprise, Kansa?' Vasudev asked, pleasantly surprised. 'Devki will be so happy. Your coming here will be the biggest surprise for her though.'

Kansa smiled. This time it was easier to do it. *Maybe I will get used to smiling at these people finally*, he decided.

He looked at Vasudev, his mind preoccupied with painful memories. 'Devki always told me how much she would miss going away from Madhuvan after her marriage. She felt that once she left for Bateshwar, she would lose a sense of belonging here, at Madhuvan.'

Vasudev nodded, not sure what this had to do with the surprise.

'I wanted to make a separate palace for Devki,' Kansa said softly. 'A place which would be all her own. A home right here in Madhuvan where she could come back any time she wanted to, and it would always be the way she would have left it. Two years back, I started getting the palace made for her. It's located a little outside the main city and is next to a beautiful lake.' Kansa looked Vasudev in the eye. 'I had planned this as a wedding gift for Devki.'

Ugrasena took a sharp intake of breath. 'All this while, I thought you were making that palace for yourself; or for Asti and Prapti in case they wanted to have more privacy away from the main palace.'

Kansa shook his head. 'No, that palace was always intended for Devki. It was to be my gift to her.'

Vasudev held Kansa by his shoulders. 'Devki is lucky to have you, my friend,' he hesitated, wondering whether to say more. 'Kansa, Devki told me about her last meeting with you at Magadha. She didn't give me any details but mentioned something to you towards the end that she shouldn't have. All these days, it has been her wish that you could somehow forget and forgive her that.'

Kansa strained to keep his voice steady as he replied. 'I have already forgotten...everything,' he said softly. *But I may not forgive*, he thought as the agony of Devki's betrayal threatened to overpower him yet again.

He knew he had to leave before his malevolent persona took over. The time was not right, yet. He looked at Ugrasena now. 'I haven't been to that palace since I left for Magadha. It's been a couple of months, and I want to make sure the place is clean and ready for Devki and Vasudev.'

Vasudev looked surprised. 'Why do you want to have it cleaned now? The wedding is tonight and we leave for Bateshwar tomorrow morning, at first light. Devki isn't going to be back for some time, at least!'

Kansa smiled. When he spoke his voice was eerily soft. 'That's the other surprise. Devki and you will consummate your first night in her new palace.'

◆

The rituals for the dead and the Godana rites had already been preformed earlier in the day by Vasudev and his father. Surasena had made a bequest of one hundred thousand gold-horned cows to the various brahmans gathered for the Godana ceremony.

Now, the hour set for the wedding had approached and Vasudev arrived at the temple. He was wearing a sparkling white dhoti, his torso bare, and a red cord of wool tied on his wrist.

Surasena signalled to his son that Devki was already waiting at the altar, and the vivah sanskar could commence without any delay. Vasudev walked towards Devki. His jaw dropped as he looked at her. The mischievous princess of Madhuvan had never appeared so desirable and alluring as she did at this moment. Her bright red sari heightened her ivory complexion. *She looks amazing*, thought Vasudev, his pulse racing. Devki noticed Vasudev staring open mouthed at her and smiled inwardly.

Ugrasena, standing next to his daughter performed the first ritual of the ceremony—the kanyadaan—this was a simple procedure where Ugrasena took Devki's hand and placed it gently in Vasudev's. Vasudev solemnly accepted Devki's hand and as dictated by custom, recited the Kamasukta verse in Ugrasena's presence. Ugrasena then asked Vasudev to not fail his daughter in his pursuit of dharma (righteousness), artha (wealth) and kama (love). Vasudev repeated his commitment to all three pursuits, three times. He looked so serious as he followed the procedure that Devki had to wink at him to get him to lighten up. Vasudev grinned back at her. The declaration of his commitment three times to Ugrasena marked the end of the kanyadaan.

The next ritual was the vivaha-homa rite where Vasudev lit a symbolic fire marking the commencement of a new household with Devki. The panigrahana ceremony came next with both Devki and Vasudev holding each other's hands as a symbol of their impending marital union. Vasudev announced his acceptance of responsibility to four deities—Bhaga (signifying wealth), Aryama (signifying heaven), Savita (signifying a new beginning), and Purandhi (signifying wisdom). As per custom, Vasudev faced west, while the smiling Devki sat in front of him with her face to the east. They held hands while the presiding pandit recited a mantra from the Rig Veda.

The pandit looked on satisfied as the ceremony was done to perfection. The final stage of the vivah sanskar was the saptapadi, which would make the marriage legal and binding, as per the prevalent laws. He motioned to the bride and the groom to rise for the concluding phase. Vasudev got up gingerly. He wanted to make sure he didn't mess anything up. Devki was less careful, and she jumped up in her excitement, colliding with Vasudev and almost knocking him down. She giggled even as the old pandit rolled his eyes at her in disapproval.

'Do you want the pandit to get us married or not?' Vasudev grinned at her.

Devki pouted at him, 'Yes, take that old pandit's side against me now.'

Vasudev tried hard to control his amusement. *I wonder how I am going to manage you*, he thought, his love for Devki evident in his expression.

Vasudev and Devki walked towards the sacred agni (holy fire). The saptapadi ritual involved the two of them conducting seven circuits around the agni, which was meant to be a witness to the vows they would make to each other. Ugrasena came forward to tie the edge of Devki's sari to a loose end of Vasudev's dhoti. Vasudev then took Devki's right hand in his own and she led the two of them around the sacred fire for the first six circuits. Vasudev led in the seventh circuit as Devki now walked behind him. At the end of each circuit, Devki and Vasudev, both took their respective vows of marriage.

Devki mentally chanted the following vows:

त्वत्तो मेऽ खिलसौभाग्यं पुण्यैस्त्वं कृतैः ।
देव! संपादितो महयं वधूरादये पदेऽब्रवीत् ।
कुटुंबं पालयिष्यामि हयावृद्धबालकादिकम् ।
यथालब्धेन संतुष्टा व्रते कन्या द्वितीयके ।
मिष्ठान्नव्यंजनादिनि काले संपादये तव ।
आज्ञासंपादिनी नित्यं तृतीये साऽब्रवीद्वरम् ।
शुचिः शृंगारभूषाऽहं वाङ्मनःकायकर्मभिः ।
क्रीडि घ्यामि त्वया सार्धं तुरीये सा वदेद्वरम् ।
दुःखे धीरे सुखे हृष्टा सुखदुःखविभागिनी ।
नाहं परतरं यामि पंचमे साऽब्रवीद्वरम् ।
सुखेन सर्वकर्माणि करिष्यामि गृहे तव ।
सेवा श्वसुरयोश्चामि बन्धूनां सत्कृतिं तथा ।
यत्र त्वं वा अहं तत्र नाहं वञ्चे प्रियं क्वचित् ।
नाहं प्रियेण वञ्चा हि कन्या षष्ठे पदेऽब्रवीत् ।
होमयज्ञादिकार्येषु भवामि च सहाय्यकृत् ।
धर्मार्थकामकार्येषु मनोवृत्तानुसारिणी ।
सर्वेऽत्र साक्षिणस्त्वं मे पतिर्भूतोऽसि सांप्रतम् ।
देहो मयार्पितस्तुभ्यं सप्तमे साऽब्रवीद्वरम् ।

Vasudev grimly took the vows of the groom:

इष एकपदी भव-सामामनुव्रताभव-पुत्रान्विदावहैबहूंस्तेसंतुजरदष्टयः ।
उजैव्दिपदीभव-सामामनु॰ ।
रायस्पोषायत्रिपदी भव॰ । मायोभव्यायचतुष्पदी भव॰ । प्रजाभ्यः पंचपदी भव॰ ।
ऋतुभ्यःषट् पदी भव॰ । सखासप्तपदी भव॰ ।

At the end of the saptapadi, Devki and Vasudev performed the surya darshan, turning to look in the direction of the sun in order to be blessed with creative life. Next, they completed the dhruva darshan, looking in the direction of the polar star and resolved to remain unshaken and steadfast like the polar star.

A roar of approval went up from the assembled guests as Vasudev and Devki completed the vivah sanskar, which bound them for eternity as man and wife.

Ugrasena approached his daughter and his son-in-law. His face expressed his total contentment. He held Devki's hand and in a loud voice made the final proclamation that would enable Devki to pass from his house to the family of Vasudev. 'My daughter, whom I have loved more than my own life, I set you free from the fetters of Varuna, who is the guardian of the mortal world order, by which the gentle Savitar has bound you till now to your father's family. In the lap of Rita, which embodies the natural and moral law, I give you now in love to your husband, Vasudev.'

Kansa stood in a corner, watching the man he had loved as his father giving away the woman he had considered his sister to the man he had thought of as a brother. All three had betrayed him in their own way. But the final betrayal would be of his doing. And he had already set the stage for that. He smiled in satisfaction as he watched his former family laugh in joy. This would be the last day of their happiness.

◆

Devki squealed in delight as they entered the palace Kansa had built for her. 'Oh Kansa, this is so beautiful!' she exclaimed, hugging her brother impulsively. Kansa flinched at her touch, remembering what she had called him the last time they had met at Magadha. But he forced himself to stay calm. He needed to make sure that Jarasandha was already in the palace with his assassins before he made his intent known to his former family.

'It's late, Devki. Why don't you and Vasudev settle in for the night,' he said forcing himself to take out all sense of revulsion he felt for Vasudev from his mind.

Devki looked like she wanted to explore the entire palace before she retired to the room that had been readied for her and Vasudev for their nuptial night. But Vasudev intervened, 'Kansa is right Devki. We need to leave for Bateshwar early morning tomorrow. We need to get some rest before that. Father has already gone ahead today to prepare the reception for the future queen of Bateshwar.'

'What? Queen of Bateshwar...what does that mean?' Devki asked in genuine surprise.

Vasudev grinned. 'Don't you know? Father has been meaning to retire for a long time now. He was waiting for our marriage and for me to be ready to take over his responsibilities. My coronation as the king of Bateshwar is scheduled a day after we reach Bateshwar.'

Devki was thoughtful. 'And what about Rohini? This won't be fair to her, Vasudev.'

Vasudev sighed. 'Rohini has always known that when you come to Bateshwar you will be queen. She will have all the rights and respect due to her as my wife but she has always been aware that I love only you!'

This was one time in her life when Devki found herself at a loss for words.

'Come now. We need to rest. And I am sure Kansa and tatatulya also need time together,' Vasudev said, smiling at Kansa and Ugrasena. Ugrasena looked on happily as Vasudev and Devki left for their chambers.

'Kansa...' Ugrasena turned to look at his son. He was shocked to see the expression on Kansa's face as he looked at the retreating figure of Vasudev and Devki.

'What...what's wrong my son?' Ugrasena stammered, suddenly afraid of the flash of green he had seen in Kansa's eyes.

'Nothing is wrong,' Kansa replied slowly, his voice sounding as though it were coming from inside a deep tunnel. Then suddenly his persona changed and he smiled at Ugrasena. 'I think you should sleep too now. It's late and there's a lot to do tomorrow.'

Ugrasena nodded his head mutely. He was not sure he recognized this man who had come back from Magadha. He seemed...so different. And so terrifying!

'Goodnight then,' Ugrasena muttered, and he walked in the direction of his room.

Kansa stared after him, his face set in stone.

◆

'How many assassins have you brought with you? Kansa asked tersely.

'There are a hundred of them. They are the Zataka Upanshughataks. All of them are hidden inside the palace compound,' Jarasandha replied. He looked closely at Kansa. The Prince was changing by the day. His behaviour was getting more and more unpredictable.

'Have they been given their orders?' Kansa asked, his hands pressing the sides of his head.

Jarasandha nodded. 'They know what they have to do. They are just waiting for the wine to take effect on the king's bodyguards.'

'Hmm!' Kansa mumbled to himself, the throbbing pain inside his head refusing to relent. Jarasandha waited tolerantly for Kansa to say something, but he remained silent. Finally he lost his patience. 'Have you decided what to do with the bodyguards? They are a risk...an unnecessary threat we can't afford.'

Kansa turned suddenly and his eyes were shining with the light of his malevolent persona. 'Don't raise your voice,' he growled at Jarasandha, and his voice came out like the snarl of an animal. 'It gives me a headache,' he said after a pause, more softly this time.

Jarasandha had never been afraid of any man or beast. But Kansa in his malevolent form terrified him. He cursed himself for having got him involved in the plan. His sisters were now married to a raging paranoid schizophrenic. And the unpredictability of Kansa's moods made him feel uncomfortable.

'Kill them!' Kansa said softly, interrupting Jarasandha's thoughts. 'Kill all the bodyguards.'

'What do we do with their bodies?' Jarasandha asked hesitatingly.

'Throw them in the lake behind the palace. The water is infested with alligators. By the time the sun has risen, there will be no sign that the bodyguards ever existed.'

Jarasandha stared at the man he had known for the past several years; the man who would not harm a fly without a cause. That person had changed forever. *Maybe it is for good. Perhaps he will help me become overlord of Mrityulok when the time comes*, he thought; the idea of unlimited power temporarily banished the future of his sisters with this wreck of a man.

'And Jarasandha...' Kansa said quietly. 'There is a man called Airawat with the bodyguards. He is the cavalry commander of Madhuvan, as well as the chief of the bodyguards.'

'What about him?' Jarasandha questioned.

'I don't want him killed. He...he has helped me in the past.' A part of Kansa's mind that was still capable of thinking coherently went back to the day when Airawat had risked his life to save Kansa and Devki.

'But he is too loyal to the king. He can't be trusted to roam free. Make sure he is securely locked up till I decide what to do with him,' Kansa said as an afterthought.

Jarasandha nodded. He would have wanted to kill Airawat along with the rest of the bodyguards, but he didn't want to antagonize Kansa, especially not in his current frame of mind.

'What about Ugrasena?' he asked.

'Ugrasena has disowned me as his son, even though he pretends to show love for me now,' Kansa said slowly. 'But I cannot order his death. He saved me when my mother wanted me killed. For that, I will spare his life.' He paused. 'But he will not leave this palace.'

Jarasandha had one more question before he left, and he had to know the answer. But he hesitated, not knowing how Kansa would react.

'Vasudev and Devki...what do we do with them?'

Jarasandha stared horrified as Kansa's face underwent a series of transformations, the two personalities within him competing to dominate.

'I will kill the man who dares to lay his hands on Devki,' Kansa said in a hoarse voice. The pain in his head was staggering and he knew a massive seizure was on its way. Jarasandha knew it too and he wanted to get out of the room before that happened and Kansa transformed into a raging animal. But Kansa had not given him a complete answer and Jarasandha did not want to leave before that.

'Vasudev...at least we can kill Vasudev. That man tried to have you assassinated!' Jarasandha shouted, trying to provoke Kansa.

Kansa roared in agony, moments away from the impending seizure. 'Vasudev is necessary for Devki to live. I have condemned her to live out her life within this golden cage. The least I can do is let her have Vasudev with her.'

Jarasandha exploded in impotent rage. 'You will allow her to live with that vile man so that they can freely copulate and give birth to the child who will destroy you one day? Has your love for your sister made you completely insane?'

Kansa leaped out of his chair and lunged at Jarasandha's throat. His vice-like grip threatened to snap his neck any moment. His eyes were shining with the bright green light of Aghasamarthan, the potent asura energy, controlled only by the most powerful demon kings in Pataal Lok. When he spoke his voice was that of Kalanemi, and Jarasandha shook with a mixture of relief and fear as he heard the words whispered in his ear. 'Devki's children will not live to grow old!'

Kansa let go of Jarasandha, and as the king of Magadha

staggered back, the voice of Kalanemi coming through Kansa, commanded him, 'Now go and slaughter the bodyguards!'

◆

Devki put her head on Vasudev's heaving chest. Their love-making had been passionate and desperate. It was as if this moment would never come back. They lay exhausted, their bodies, drenched in perspiration, wound around each other.

'I love you,' Vasudev whispered in her ears.

'I know,' she smiled, her head on his chest. 'I have always known, Vasudev.'

'I wonder what our children will look like,' he grinned in the dark, as his hand groped for what he was looking for.

She slapped his hand away, giggling. 'Isn't it rather early to think about children, my love?' she said contentedly.

'Oh no, it isn't,' he laughed. 'What would the people of Bateshwar say if they found their queen hadn't given them a crown prince within the first year of marriage?' he said in mock horror.

Devki slapped him again, 'You chauvinistic man! Why does it have to be a crown prince; why can't it be a princess?'

Vasudev roared in laughter. 'It's so easy to provoke you, darling. Of course it could be a prince or a princess. But we wouldn't know unless we keep trying, would we now?' he said playfully as his hands started roving again.

Devki laughed. 'And I thought someone wanted us to sleep early so we could be fresh in the morning?' she said coquettishly.

'Really?' Vasudev acted surprised. 'That's strange. I don't know anything about that.' He laughed as he expertly pulled the last of the strings holding up Devki's robe.

Devki sighed in pleasure as she felt his hands finally find what they had been searching for. This time their love-making was slower and gentler. The night had begun to give way to dawn when they finally slept, exhausted, in each other's arms.

◆

Vasudev woke up with a start. His senses honed over a lifetime of training told him that something was radically wrong. He turned towards Devki and breathed a sigh of relief. She was still sleeping, the hint of a smile on her face. Then he heard the noise again. It was the same commotion that had roused him from his slumber. He pulled open the curtains and blinked involuntarily as the bright glare of the morning sun pierced his eyes.

'What the...' he stopped himself from cursing out loud.

'What's the matter, darling?' Devki called softly from the bed, stirring from her sleep.

Vasudev turned to look at her. She looked breathtakingly beautiful, and vulnerable. He had to force himself to take his eyes off her and focus on the situation. 'Something's wrong Devki... I can feel it in my bones. The sun is up. We have obviously overslept. But the strange thing is that no one woke us up.'

Devki was staring at him, her expression betraying her confusion and apprehension. Then she heard the same uproar that had woken up Vasudev.

Her eyes widened in trepidation. 'What could it be?' she asked timorously.

'I don't know yet, but I intend to find out,' Vasudev said grimly, donning his clothes hurriedly. He looked around for his armour and sword. They were gone.

'My sword!' he whispered. 'I can't find it.'

Devki had got into her robe as quickly as she could. 'Let's go out and see what the matter is,' she said.

Vasudev nodded. A part of him wanted Devki to stay back in the safety of the room. But he wasn't sure what the problem was and he decided he would feel better if she were with him instead of being alone in the room.

◆

Vasudev and Devki were baffled at the complete absence of activity in the palace. The place had a deserted look about it that was ominous. Vasudev hadn't got the opportunity to survey the palace when they had arrived the previous night. Now, as he moved through the palace, he studied the entire structure with the eyes of a professional warrior.

The main palace building had three levels to it. The top storey housed the master section, which comprised an enormous bedroom and an assortment of other lodgings. This is where they had spent the night. The next floor had fifteen mid-sized rooms, all residential in nature. *Kansa and tatatulya must have occupied two of the rooms on that level*, Vasudev reflected. The lowermost level was the ground floor, which included a large hall for public meetings and separate rooms, which could presumably be used for private discussions with select guests.

Vasudev did not detect any activity within the main palace building. Whatever noise he had heard earlier must have emanated from somewhere else within the sprawling palace compound. Vasudev's attention was drawn to the considerably sized outhouse on the eastern side of the compound, about fifty gavutas away from the main building. The outhouse normally served as lodgings for the domestic staff working in the palace. The windows of the outhouse were open, and Vasudev could see right inside that building. He couldn't perceive any employee there. And then it occurred to him that he hadn't noticed any staff during the night either. It had struck him as odd even then, but Devki's excitement at seeing the palace had made him uncharacteristically ignore the irregularity. Getting increasingly concerned, he moved quickly down the stairs with Devki following, and reached the ground floor. From where they were standing, they had a full view of the pakasala (kitchen). It should have been bustling with activity, with the paurogava (superintendent of the kitchen) shouting orders at the various kitchen staff. Today, the pakasala was conspicuous by the complete absence of any movement.

Suddenly, he felt Devki nudge him softly. He turned to look at her and saw her pointing in the direction of the aikanga kaksha (bodyguard's lodging). He drew in his breath as he observed the open door. It made creaking noises as it swayed back and forth on its hinges. Vasudev's pulse raced with a multitude of thoughts blazing through his mind. 'Tatatulya's bodyguards...' he whispered. 'I can't see them.'

Devki huddled close to Vasudev as he crept cautiously along the compound, moving in the direction of the aikanga kaksha. She could sense his ragged breathing, and the adrenaline pulsating through his system as he moved forward, measuring each step warily. They reached the open door, and Vasudev brought his finger to his lips, indicating to Devki that he wanted her to move back, away from him. Devki reluctantly took a few steps backwards. The menace in the air was palpable and she didn't want Vasudev facing whatever awaited inside the room alone. But she guessed he stood a better chance of tackling whatever it was if she was not in his way. She watched, her heart thudding against her chest, as Vasudev took a deep breath and dived inside the room. And then she heard him scream.

It raised her hackles as she sensed the mix of rage and agony in Vasudev's voice. Without waiting to think, she rushed towards the door, intending to tear down whatever or whoever had dared to inflict pain on the man she loved more than anything else. She collided with Vasudev as he stumbled out of the room, his expression reflecting utter despair and horror.

'Vasudev, what happ...' Devki cried out in concern as Vasudev held her in a tight embrace. She could feel his heart thumping against her body as he held her close, not wanting her to go inside the room.

'Vishnu have mercy on our souls!' he finally whispered, his anguish transparent in his expression.

Devki lifted her head over his shoulders, and she saw what he hadn't wanted her to glimpse. The floor and the walls inside were splattered in shades of red and scarlet. Beds and pillows were soaked in blood and gore. A singular odour pervaded the air; the sickly sweet smell of blood. The entire room had been witness to a ruthless bloodbath. Devki knew she would never forget the scene or the smell for as long as she lived.

◆

Vasudev heard the noise at the same time that Devki did. It was the same commotion that had woken him up in the morning. It seemed to be coming from one of the rooms on the ground level.

Devki shuddered, 'Kansa... Father...' she whispered, her voice trembling. 'I hope they are safe!'

'Let's find out,' Vasudev said grimly; his composure and self-control returning as he realized he would need all his skill to fight whoever had done this dastardly deed. But first he had to make sure that Kansa and Devki's father were alright.

'Stay behind me, darling,' he said quietly to Devki. She saw his expression and realized that he had used the endearment automatically. His mind was elsewhere. The savage expression on his face scared her almost as much as the horror of the scene they had just witnessed. The Vasudev that stood before her was not the gentle man she had known all her life or the tender lover of the previous night. This person was the warrior she had heard people in the court talk about with awe; the ruthless slayer of assassins.

Vasudev ran in a criss-cross direction towards the source of the commotion, all the time holding Devki's hand and shielding her with his body. He reached the room from where the noise was coming. The door was locked and it was too thick to break through. Vasudev ran to the other side, where he thought he spotted a window to the room. It was open but was barred with thick iron grills. Vasudev tried looking through the closely spaced bars. It was dark inside and impossible to see what or who was within.

'Kansa, is that you?' There was no response.

'Tatatulya, are you in there?' he shouted louder. There was a scuffling sound as someone dragged himself from the other side of the room. There was a groan as the person inside made a herculean effort to raise his body and bring his face next to the grilled window.

'Airawat!' Vasudev gasped as he recognized the Madhuvan cavalry commander. 'How did you get in there? Speak up, man!'

Airawat winced with the effort of standing up. 'They broke my legs,' he said in a hoarse voice. 'The bodyguards were drugged... I think I was too...when I woke up, I saw I was bound in chains.' Airawat shut his eyes as a shiver of unbearable pain coursed through his body. 'They gagged me and carried me out of my room, taking me to the aikanga kaksha, where the bodyguards were lying unconscious. I was made to watch as they hacked the bodyguards in their sleep,' Airawat broke down and tears of frustration flowed down his face.

'Who did this?' Vasudev growled.

'A man called Ugra...he led the assassins,' Airawat replied, his voice registering the horror of having seen his former colleagues and friends being mercilessly hacked to death.

'That man is already dead. I promise you this!' Vasudev swore.

Devki had been silent. She couldn't contain herself any longer. 'Where are Kansa and Father, Airawat? Are they safe?'

Airawat looked at Devki in bewilderment. 'Don't you know?'

'Know what?' Devki's lips trembled. She feared the worst.

'The king has been locked up in a room on the second floor....but he is safe,' Airawat said haltingly, the pain in his legs wracking his entire body.

'And Kansa? Where is he?' Vasudev intervened.

Airawat hung his head. 'Kansa is with the king, My Lord.'

'Thank God!' Vasudev sighed in relief. 'Once I get him out of there, we are going to cut down each and every one of these assassins.'

Airawat laughed harshly. 'I don't think you understand, My Lord!' Vasudev stared at Airawat. 'What do you mean?' he demanded.

'Kansa is holding the king hostage.' Airawat said softly. 'He is the one who hired these assassins!'

◆

Vasudev had still not been able to absorb the full import of what Airawat had just told him when his attention was distracted by the sound of several feet running softly over the ground. He turned around to see a hundred assassins standing in a large semi-circle. They were led by a giant of a man, holding an axe in one hand and a sword in the other. Vasudev's eyes narrowed as he recognized the sword the man was holding. It was his.

'Be careful, My Lord!' Airawat mumbled feebly. 'The man with the axe is Ugra...' Airawat was unable to complete his sentence as the unbearable agony finally took its toll and he slumped to the ground, unconscious.

Ugra smiled at Vasudev. The intensity of his loathing was reflected in his expression.

'Vasudev!' he said softly, the menace in the tone unmistakable.

The news of Kansa's betrayal had paralyzed Vasudev. The sight of the man who had mercilessly hacked the king's bodyguards in their sleep served to bring him back to reality and he felt rage surge through his entire being as he glared at Ugra.

'I am told you are the one who killed my son after he had granted you your life,' Ugra said in muted fury.

Vasudev blinked for an instant as he recalled the fearless young warrior he had almost died battling in the Bhairava Van. 'Your son was a brave warrior. He knew he was fighting on the wrong side but he still had the courage to fight...for your beliefs. You are the one who killed him when you sent him to Hastinapur. I just did what I had to do,' Vasudev retorted.

Ugra seemed to waver for a moment as he remembered Ghora's indecision at the time of going to Hastinapur. *Did I really send him to his death?* He thought with anguish. He shook off the thought from his mind and focused on his enemy, the man who had taken away from him the one person he had really cared about in his whole life.

'I will not be as forgiving as my boy was,' Ugra snarled. 'Prepare to die!' he roared as he threw Vasudev's sword to him.

Vasudev caught the sword mid-air. He saw Ugra charging at him with his axe held high, and he pushed Devki to the side, preparing himself to face his daunting adversary.

Ugra brought the axe down with all his might. Vasudev jumped nimbly aside, as the axe made contact with the stone corridor, shattering the floor in a shower of fragments. Vasudev was flabbergasted at the speed of the asura. He moved with astonishing agility for a man of his size and even before Vasudev had got his bearings, Ugra landed another massive blow. This time, Vasudev was not quick enough and the axe dug itself in his sandals, a nails breadth away from his toe. The sandal was useless and would only inhibit further movement. Vasudev slipped out of both his sandals and flexed his toes to get the blood flowing. *This man is not in the same class as his son; but the difference in their ability is more than made up by his size and his inhuman strength*, thought Vasudev.

Ugra was swirling the axe in a manner that made it almost impossible to get inside his circle of defense. Vasudev knew he might only get one chance to strike. He had no intention of losing that opportunity whenever and if it presented itself. He decided to confuse the assassin. He knew the technique he had tried with Ghora may not work with this opponent, given the asura's height and the unpredictability of his weapon. He tried a different tactic. Instead of waiting for him to strike, Vasudev began to twist his body sideways, transferring his sword from one hand to the other as he did so. Just when Ugra thought he had timed Vasudev's moves to predict where he would be next, Vasudev changed the frequency of his body movements. The continuous monitoring of his opponent's movement took Ugra's attention from Vasudev's sword. He did not realize that Vasudev had stopped transferring the sword between his hands, and now held it firmly in his right hand.

When Vasudev was certain the moment was right, he moved his body to the left. He was deliberately slow in order to lull Ugra into a sense of security. As he had thought, Ugra brought down his axe at the spot he calculated Vasudev would be. But Vasudev had shifted his body weight mid-way and the axe slashed through the air, swishing harmlessly on one side of Vasudev. The right flank of the asura lay open and Vasudev thrust his sword in a straight line. Ugra did not see the attack coming. The sword pierced through a barely perceptible opening in his armour near the shoulder, and it cut right across the brachial artery. In one blow, the radial, median and the ulnar nerves were sliced. Ugra felt the axe fall involuntarily from his hand, as complete paralysis of the arm set in. Vasudev stared at the man whose son had once spared his life. He considered for a brief moment, letting the asura live. But the vision of the blood-soaked room came unbidden to his mind, and in a daze of uncontrollable fury, he swung his sword at Ugra.

There was a hush as the Zataka Upanshughataks watched their chief's head separate from his torso and fall to the ground, as though in slow motion. The legendary fighter, whom no law or enemy had been able to subdue, lay vanquished at Vasudev's feet.

There was a bellow of rage from the assassins as they regained their self-possession. They looked at each other, and prepared to charge at the man who had killed their chief. Vasudev knew he would not be able to fight their combined might. He glanced at Devki, silently exhorting her to run away. She shook her head and walked towards him. Vasudev smiled in resignation as he recalled one of the lines from their wedding vows: *We have taken the seven steps together. You have become mine forever. We are word and meaning, united. You are thought and I am sound. You are the song and I am the lyrics. I have become yours. Hereafter, I cannot live without you. Do not live without me.*

◆

Kansa took one last look at Ugrasena. The man who had played the role of his father for the past twenty-nine years sat slumped on the ground. Kansa couldn't believe this was the same man he had admired as a great warrior while growing up. But then, he also couldn't have believed that this very man had once wanted him killed as a child and who had recently disowned him in favour of that back-stabbing Vasudev. *It doesn't matter. I am stronger and more powerful than any of them now*, he thought. *I don't need anyone to love me any longer. Anyone!* He raged as he locked the door on his former father. Ugrasena had given him what he wanted, even without his asking for it.

As he walked out of the room, Kansa's attention was drawn to an uproar from the compound. He peered over the banister and saw the group of assassins moving menacingly in the direction of Vasudev and Devki. Devki had stationed herself on one side of Vasudev who had his arms around her, in a protective gesture.

The part of his mind that still loved Devki asserted itself and Kansa hurled himself over the banister landing on the ground three gavutas below. He stood between the assassins and Devki. The assassins, confused by Kansa's sudden presence, stopped in their tracks. They had seen Ugra bow to the prince of Madhuvan and they were aware that he was the one who had hired their services through Jarasandha. They bowed to him, awaiting further orders, expecting he would instruct them to kill the two mortals like he had asked them to slay the bodyguards. His words shocked the assassins into silence. 'No one will harm these two,' he growled.

Kansa turned around to look at Vasudev and Devki. Vasudev glared at him with a mixture of contempt and fury. 'What have you done with the king?' he demanded.

Kansa smiled. 'The king is safe. He has retired from his kingly duties and desires to relax in this palace for a few years.'

A shiver of fear ran through Devki as she heard Kansa speak.

He looked and sounded exactly as he had when she had left him in Magadha. 'Why are you doing this, Kansa? What's happened to you?'

Vasudev interjected, 'Nothing's happened. This man suddenly wants to be king and he couldn't wait for tatatulya to announce his ascension. This is a sick man and I am galled that I ever called him my friend.' Vasudev paused to get back his breath even as Kansa looked at him with mild amusement. 'You will never succeed in your vile designs Kansa. The people and the army of Madhuvan will never forgive the person who kidnapped their king and was responsible for the merciless killing of his bodyguards. You are a monster amongst men and the people of Madhuvan will treat you as one,' Vasudev spat out in disgust.

'I know I am a monster!' Kansa said quietly. 'My sister and her father have already told me that. But do they know how you actually tried to have me assassinated in Magadha?' Kansa's eyes reflected his pain as he allowed himself to think through the torment he had faced when he got to know that the man behind his assassination attempt was none other than Vasudev.

Vasudev looked at Kansa in disbelief. 'You lie!' he roared. 'You lie to cover your dark deeds. Remember this Kansa. As soon as the army of Madhuvan knows what you have done, they will rebel and you will be paraded around the kingdom of Madhuvan as the murderer you have become.'

'Really?' Kansa snarled, his other persona creeping over him as he listened to Vasudev. 'The king has already signed a letter announcing me as the new sovereign of Madhuvan. The letter bears his seal and it also mentions that he is going on a long journey of self-realization, accompanied by his trusted bodyguard and cavalry commander, Airawat.'

Devki gasped. 'Why would Father do that?'

Vasudev gave a bitter laugh. 'Because this fiend must have threatened him that he would harm you if the king didn't sign the declaration.'

Kansa's eyes flared, the green light of Aghasamarthan fighting to gain control over his senses. 'I didn't have to threaten the king. You see, like you, he doesn't know that I would not talk about harming Devki even in a threat. And like you he believes that I am monster enough to do what you just said,' Kansa paused, his head hanging low. 'He signed the declaration on his own and gave it to me.'

Devki looked pleadingly at her brother. 'Kansa, why have you held all of us here?'

'Madhuvan needs a new king; someone who can do what needs to be done,' he replied vaguely.

Devki couldn't believe Kansa would hold their father prisoner. But she needed to know more. 'And Vasudev and me? Why have you held us here? What have we done?'

Kansa's eyes narrowed. He was having another splitting headache. 'Vasudev tried to assassinate me. He needs to be punished,' he said cradling his head in his hands.

'And Devki? What has she done?' Vasudev glared at him.

The pain in his head was becoming unbearable now. Kansa struggled to stay calm as his thoughts started going into disarray. 'Devki's son will kill me!' he cried out in agony. 'Her boy will betray me just as all of you have done,' he raged, finally losing all control and submitting to the dark force of Aghasamarthan. As the evil energy coursed through his system, he felt the pain in his heart and mind receding. He raised his head and roared; and even the assassins standing there cowered in fear. Devki sobbed as she saw her brother being torn apart by a force she couldn't yet fathom. Without thinking, she advanced towards Kansa, her arms open as they used to be when she was a child, and wanted him to hug her. Kansa looked at her approach, his green eyes boring into her, threatening to devour her.

Vasudev saw Kansa snarl as Devki approached closer. Afraid for her, he shouted at Kansa and charged towards him with his sword held high.

Devki saw Vasudev move to attack Kansa. 'No, Vasudev, don't!' she screamed at him to stop.

Kansa stared at Devki and then at the charging Vasudev. Ignoring Devki, he caught Vasudev's sword with his bare hand and twisted it out of his grip, throwing the mangled blade to the ground. With a howl that sent shivers down her spine, Kansa bodily lifted Vasudev and dashed him to the ground.

Devki watched in horror as Vasudev's body convulsed and quivered for a while and then went completely limp. She still stood as she had with her arms open, too shocked to move. Kansa moved towards her, the force of Aghasamarthan beginning to leave his body and his mortal self gaining dominance over it once again. He held her hands. 'Devki,' he said softly, wanting her to hug him like she used to.

At the sound of his voice, Devki snapped back to the present. She stared at the motionless body of Vasudev, and an involuntary sob escaped her mouth. 'You have killed him, you bastard!' she screamed. And then her voice dropped to a whisper. 'You are right. My son will kill you, you monster.'

◆

Kansa looked at the woman he loved despite all that she had said and done. She was bent over Vasudev trying to revive him. Kansa was too tired to linger there any longer. The headache had returned as the force of Aghasamarthan left his system. He looked at one of the assassins. 'Take the two of them to their room.' As the assassin stared at him in disbelief, he said quietly, 'Make sure no harm comes to either of them.'

Staggering from the pain in his head, and the constant ache in his heart, Kansa left the scene. He didn't notice Devki staring at his retreating back with tears in her eyes; torn between the husband she loved and the brother she couldn't help.

The assassins all stared at one another. The law of the Zataka Upanshughataks demanded that they avenge the murder of one of their clansmen. And the man who had died today was their Chief. But the person forbidding them to follow their law was not a mortal. He had the fire of Aghasamarthan burning in his eyes and to disobey his word would mean instant death. Two of the assassins moved forward to help Devki lift Vasudev, even as the others slowly slunk away.

◆

Sini Yadav was on the way back with his task force when they were met by a messenger from Bateshwar. The man was badly wounded and would not survive, even though Sini had ensured that he was given immediate medical aid. Sini read the urgent message from Surasena with incredulity. Surasena had been ambushed on the way back from Madhuvan and the small battalion escorting him had been decimated by Jarasandha's outsized forces. Jarasandha had then proceeded to attack Bateshwar and taken the army there unawares. It had been an easy task; not only had the army not expected an attack, but the people who could have inspired the army to fight back—Vasudev and Sini Yadav—were both not there. And Surasena himself was in confinement and unable to do anything. Surasena also wrote that Jarasandha had boasted that Madhuvan was now under the command of Kansa who had taken his father Ugrasena captive. And that Vasudev and Devki were also incarcerated by the prince of Madhuvan, who was now the sovereign of the country.

Sini Yadav's jaw clenched in anger as he read the bit about Vasudev being a prisoner. He cursed himself for not having gone to the wedding.

In his letter, Surasena specifically commanded Sini not to come to Bateshwar or go to Madhuvan as he would surely be taken prisoner or worse, be killed on sight. He was instructed to go to Hastinapur at once and meet Dhritarashtra with news of what had happened. Surasena was certain that Dhritarashtra may be able to help. His final instructions were that Sini should stay away till such time that either Hastinapur decided to assist them or till Surasena sent him a new communiqué. At the conclusion of the letter, Surasena had given him the name of the person he could stay with while he was in Hastinapur.

Sini read the name mentioned in the letter—Kripa Acharya.

The Carnage Begins

Nine months had elapsed since Kansa had taken over as king of Madhuvan and Jarasandha had added Bateshwar to Magadha's list of conquests.

There had been a few murmurs when Kansa presented himself two days after Devki's wedding and told the senior members of the royal court that Ugrasena had declared him king and gone on an indefinite pilgrimage. But Ugrasena's letter signed in his own hand and carrying the royal seal had put all rumors to rest. Also, there were enough people who had seen Kansa return from Magadha and being cordially received by Ugrasena on the day of the wedding. Airawat's absence too corroborated what the king had written in his letter. Kansa was crowned as the new king of Madhuvan and the court members enthusiastically pledged loyalty to their new sovereign.

Mandki was the only person convinced that something was terribly wrong. She knew Airawat would not have left without meeting her. They had decided to get married immediately after Vasudev and Devki's wedding was consecrated. His sudden departure didn't make sense and Mandki became increasingly concerned that something was wrong as the weeks went by without any news from Airawat.

And then everyone heard about Jarasandha's conquest of Bateshwar. Mandki was horrified at the news. She wondered what had happened to Vasudev and Devki after Bateshwar fell into Jarasandha's hands. The biggest surprise was that Kansa did nothing about it. *Why hasn't he done anything to help Vasudev?* she thought. *How could Jarasandha dare to attack Bateshwar when he knows that Kansa's sister is married to the prince of Bateshwar. And why doesn't Kansa talk to Jarasandha about this? After all, Jarasandha's sisters are married to him.*

Mandki started keeping a close watch on Kansa. She observed that he had systematically removed all those people from court who had been close to Ugrasena. It was done subtly and always with good reason, but it was too much of a coincidence to ignore. Gradually, the senior-most members of the court were all people that Kansa had personally handpicked. And then there were all the strange-looking people who suddenly began arriving at Madhuvan. They dressed like people of the city but they were clearly outsiders. Some of them did not even look like mortals, with their distorted faces and their misshapen bodies. The crime rate had increased in the kingdom but Kansa appeared to turn a blind eye to it all. It was as if he was either not bothered about what happened to Madhuvan or it was all being done with his consent. Mandki refused to believe that Kansa could participate in something like that. She remembered him risking his life for Devki on the Shiva hill.

But then why doesn't he do anything? she thought in frustration.

She continued to keep a tab on Kansa's activities, including the people he met and the places he went to. With Devki and Airawat not being there, she had all the time in the world, and lately, it had become an obsession with Mandki to find an answer to all the strange events happening around her.

Then one day, she saw Kansa ride away from the palace. Mandki rode at a distance, careful not to let her presence be known. Kansa did not seem to be headed in any particular direction. His path kept meandering and it looked like he was simply out for a ride. Just when she was about to give up and turn back towards the city, she saw Kansa give a furtive look over his shoulder. Satisfied that he was not being followed, he took a sharp turn and rode at a gallop. Mandki followed as fast as she could. The zig-zag route continued for a while. As she took a particularly sharp bend, she realized she had lost him. She rode along the road and came to a beautiful palace built beside a lake. She recognized it as the palace Kansa had built for his sister. Her sharp eyes perceived the fresh hoof marks on the ground and Mandki realized that Kansa had entered the palace compound.

She stayed on her horse, lost in thought. And then making up her mind, she started the horse at a trot entering the palace gates. She had a feeling that the answer to all her questions lay within the walls of the palace.

◆

Kansa sat perched on the tree as he waited for the person following him to enter the palace gates. He had been aware that he was being stalked for many days now. He had seen the same person showing up wherever he went and it was too much of a coincidence to ignore. Kansa did not believe in coincidences. But he had been unable to make out the features of the person because the stalker's face was always covered by a cloak. He had noticed the same stalker trailing him today. To make sure that the rider was actually following him, he had taken several meandering paths. The stalker had stuck with him all through. There was no doubt now in Kansa's mind that he was being followed. He wanted to know who this person was.

As the horse came through the gates, Kansa took a deep breath and jumped from the tree, pouncing on the rider. Both Kansa and the stalker fell to the ground with a jarring thud. In one swift move, Kansa was astride the stalker and he viciously pulled off the cloak covering his pursuer's face.

'Mandki!' he gasped. 'Why have you been following me?' he demanded.

Mandki winced in pain. The fall had badly shaken her and as she looked into Kansa's eyes, she felt inexplicably lost in the strange power she saw blazing there.

'I...I wanted to know what was in the palace,' she stammered.

Kansa looked at her quietly and she felt the cold finger of death rest on her soul as she stared into his cold eyes.

'You have all your life to find out what is within the palace, my dear,' he whispered menacingly.

Mandki looked at him, her face reflecting her confusion.

Kansa laughed harshly. 'Devki has been pining for someone to talk to. Who could be better than her childhood friend to keep her company?'

Mandki stared at him, horrified at the implication of his words.

The fear she had been feeling in his presence transformed into a frenzy of terror as she saw the pisaca and the bonara approach from a distance. She screamed in terror, and then darkness engulfed her as she lost consciousness.

◆

Mandki got up with a start. There was total darkness. She had had a terrible nightmare. She had dreamed that two of the assassins she had seen on the Shiva hill were coming to kill her and Kansa was smiling at her, even as they approached. She shivered at the memory of the pisaca's quivering tentacles and the bonara's razor sharp talons.

She became aware of the bed she was lying on. It didn't feel like her own. She looked around her and as her eyes adjusted to the darkness, she realized with a tremor that she was lying in a strange room. She screamed in terror in the same instant that she realized it hadn't been a nightmare. It had all been real—Kansa's blazing green eyes boring into her, the two assassins coming towards her and then...total darkness.

An urgent knock on her door made her scramble up from the bed. She frantically looked for a place to hide herself. The door opened and someone entered her room, holding a candle. Mandki trembled in fear hoping for a quick death. She didn't want the assassins ravaging and torturing her.

'Mandki!' the face behind the candle whispered softly. Mandki knew the voice. Even as her dazed mind recalled what Kansa had said to her before she fainted, the face behind the candle became visible. Mandki gasped in relief and rushed into the arms of the person holding the candle.

◆

Devki got Mandki up to date with all that had happened since her wedding night. She was not overtly surprised when Mandki told her about Jarasandha's conquest of Bateshwar. She had known that would happen after Kansa had held Vasudev and her hostage. If Bateshwar hadn't been conquered, their army would certainly have created a problem for Kansa when Vasudev failed to return to his country.

Mandki was thrilled to know that Airawat and the king were safe, even though they were in confinement. Airawat had recovered from his wounds but was not allowed outside his room. The king, however, was free to walk around in the palace compound, though he had voluntarily decided not to leave his room after his last interaction with Kansa. Devki would visit Ugrasena in his room, every day. She too had the freedom of moving around within the palace and the outer compound. The assassins were everywhere, out of sight. It was futile to try and escape.

Mandki looked closely at her friend. The stress of being held by her own brother had matured Devki beyond her years. But the hopeless look in her once-mischievous eyes told Mandki that there was something more than that; something so terrible that it had killed all the joy inside Devki. And then it struck her. Devki had spoken about everyone else, including Airawat. But she had carefully refrained from talking about Vasudev, except for one or two occasions when she had to.

'Devki, where's Vasudev?' Mandki asked unable to contain her apprehension.

Devki did not answer. Her eyes were as expressionless as her face. Mandki grew increasingly perturbed as she asked again, 'Where is Vasudev?'

Devki got up abruptly. She held Mandki's hand and silently pulled her behind her as they entered the inner chambers of the vast residential area. They reached the bed where a figure lay huddled under a blanket. Mandki gaped in horror as she saw the motionless body of Vasudev. His eyes gazed expressionlessly at her, his mouth twisted in a constant grimace. His once muscular body had atrophied to becoming almost skeletal.

'He has been completely paralyzed since the day Kansa threw him to the ground,' Devki said softly. 'He hasn't spoken or moved since that day.'

Mandki stared at her friend who had always been transparent with her emotions. But the Devki standing next to her displayed even lesser sensation than the man who had been lying motionless on the bed for the past nine months.

Mandki sobbed unable to restrain her own feelings. 'Devki, how have you lived with...with all this?' she said marvelling at the princess's stoicism.

Devki touched her stomach. 'This...I live for this!' she whispered. And Mandki's attention was drawn for the first time to the signs of life growing rapidly inside Devki's enormously protruding belly.

◆

Brahma listened carefully to Narada. The news from Mrityulok was not encouraging. In the last few months, there had been grave incidents of unrest and violence in various kingdoms of the mortal world. Most of them had occurred in Bharat, which comprised majority of the civilized portion of Mrityulok. Brahma shuddered as Narada narrated stories of murders, theft, vandalism and all other forms of bestiality.

'It has started then,' Brahma muttered to himself.

'Did you say something, My Lord?' Narada asked hesitatingly, not sure what his father had said.

Brahma ignored the question. He knew he couldn't explain his greatest fears to Narada without mentioning Amartya Kalyanesu. The last thing he wanted right now was to talk about that. Like Shiva, Narada too would look down on him if he realized the current crisis in Mrityulok was a consequence of what he had done to Amartya two hundred years ago.

'What news from Pataal Lok?' he asked, changing the subject abruptly.

Narada shook his head. 'Devayam has disappeared. He was my source for most of the news from the netherworld.' He paused. 'I do know that Vrushaparva, the asura king, has given his consent to assemble a large army of every kind of asura. But no one seems to know whether it has been assembled yet or by when it would be done.'

Brahma nodded. 'That is some good news, at least. What is the latest on Kansa and Jarasandha?'

Narada's face darkened at the mention of Jarasandha's name. 'Jarasandha has shown himself to be worse than the worst asura. 'He has conquered several kingdoms including Bateshwar and he seems to be the mastermind behind the asura assassins entering into Mrityulok. His generals and commanders managing the conquered kingdoms on his behalf have given free rein to these assassins who are committing every conceivable evil on the hapless mortals.'

'What about Kansa?' Brahma enquired.

Narada shook his head in frustration. 'Kansa does not seem to be getting any better. By some inexplicable turn of fate, he has gone from being one of the noblest men to becoming a raging madman. Unlike Jarasandha, he is not committing atrocities on his people directly. But neither is he doing anything to stop the carnage in his kingdom. It looks like he is supporting the entry of the assassins into Madhuvan and is also conniving with

Jarasandha in the overall plan.'

'It is his destiny. He has to bear the consequences of his actions,' Brahma said softly.

Narada snapped uncharacteristically. 'Father, his destiny is affecting other people's lives as hundreds of innocents die every week in his kingdom; victims of the assassins he has allowed into Madhuvan. We need to do something,' he ended emphatically.

Brahma got up abruptly. 'I need to meet the Mahadev,' he said, urgency evident in his voice. 'You return to Mrityulok and try to get other countries to form their own task forces against the assassins.'

Narada nodded and was preparing to leave, when Brahma called after him. 'You have done well, my son! Take care of yourself while you are there.'

Narada stared at his father. This was the first time Brahma had praised him for anything in his life.

◆

Mandki hovered around excitedly as Devki's contractions began. The ardhadhara (surgeon) nodded to her assistant and indicated that the uterus had contracted sufficiently and the cervix was dilated enough for the baby to be pushed out. She asked Devki to push gently. Devki looked anxiously at her but the ardhadhara's serene smile made her feel relaxed.

Mandki watched in amazement as the baby came out. 'It's a beautiful boy,' she whispered reverentially as she saw the surgeon's assistant clean up the howling baby and wrap it in a fine muslin cloth.

'Get ready for the next one,' the ardhadhara smiled at Devki.

'The next...next what?' Mandki asked bewildered.

The ardhadhara looked up calmly towards Mandki. 'The next baby; she is having sextuplets.'

'Sex...sex what?' Mandki stammered.

'Sextuplets! Six babies,' the ardhadhara smiled at her. 'Now don't just stand there. There's going to be a lot of cleaning up to do here.'

◆

Shiva nodded thoughtfully as Brahma related to him all that Narada had told him. He sat contemplatively, lost in his thoughts. After a while, he looked up, his mind seemingly made up. Brahma stared at the Mahadev and he realized that Shiva had put up a cosmic shield around them to ensure that no one would be able to eavesdrop into their consciousness through cosmic telepathy.

Shiva quickly conveyed his instructions. Brahma stared uncomprehendingly as he tried to make sense of what Shiva had asked him to do.

Shiva smiled at his former student, 'Just make sure it is done. Narada needs to be back with it as soon as he can.'

Brahma nodded, the urgency in Shiva's voice leaving him in no doubt about the significance of what he had been asked to do.

'Aum-Num-Ha-Shi-Vai,' he said reverentially, as he took Shiva's leave. He would have to tell Narada what the Mahadev wanted before Narada left for Mrityulok.

◆

Kansa was at the Shiva temple hill praying, when he heard about Devki's childbirth. He had been a devotee of the Mahadev for several years, and praying to Shiva had always imbued him with a sense of peace. Of late, he had started visiting the temple regularly and he realized it made him feel better. The headaches had become less frequent and the lapses into his malevolent self had also reduced dramatically.

The last two days he had been in an especially buoyant mood. His wife, Asti had told him yesterday that she was pregnant; Kansa had been thrilled at the news. Asti and he had been trying to have a child for a very long time and they had not been successful. His other wife Prapti had been diagnosed during the early days of their marriage with a condition that made it impossible for her to ever have a child of her own. Kansa had wondered if he would ever become a father. Now that Asti was finally pregnant, Kansa had started imagining how life would be with a child in the house. He was certain it would be a boy. *He will get all the love that I didn't receive*, he resolved.

As he stepped out of the temple, he looked around the hill top. This was the same place he had fought the pisaca and the other assassins who had tried to kill Devki. With a jolt, it hit Kansa that the same assassins he had battled to save his sister were now guarding her on his instructions. *When did I change sides?* he asked himself, as he walked to the point where he had fallen after the bonara had attacked him. The image of Devki standing over him, willing to risk her life to protect him from the pisaca came unbidden to his mind, and he doubled over in agony at the realization that he had been keeping his sister a prisoner all these months.

I need to get her out of there. I will make everything fine between us again, he determined as he began to walk down the hill. And then the messenger came with the news of Devki's childbirth. In his current state of mind, this was the best news he could have received. It was a great opportunity to make amends with Devki. *I will take a gift with me*, he thought. *And then I will get Devki out of there.*

He ran down the hill in his excitement. After what seemed like an eternity, he was beginning to feel like his old self. He made a brief halt at his palace, and debated what he could take as a gift for Devki. He wished Asti and Prapti had been there, but both sisters had left for Magadha in the morning. As per tradition, the mother was supposed to spend the entire duration of her pregnancy at her maternal home. Though Asti and Prapti's parents were no longer alive, Jarasandha had played the role of both, a father and mother to them. The sisters would spend the next few months at Magadha till Asti gave birth.

Kansa excitedly looked around for something that he could take as a gift for Devki's children. He wanted it to be something really different; something appropriate. And then it came to him. What could be a better gift than the traditional chaddar? The chaddar upacara was the age-old ceremony followed by Kansa's ancestors. It involved a male member of the family putting a coverlet over a newborn, which symbolized the fact that the person doing so vowed to shield the baby from all calamities throughout his life.

Kansa smiled in satisfaction. He would himself undertake the chaddar upacara for all of Devki's six children. The symbolic gesture would tell her more than anything else he could do that he still loved her and was vowing to protect her children forever.

He selected a gold-braided coverlet which was wide enough to cover the six babies. It was made of fine silk and would be fitting for the newborn princes.

◆

Mandki glared at Kansa as he came bounding up the stairs. She stood protectively at the doorsill, her arms folded across her chest. She would not allow him to hurt her friend anymore. Kansa observed her aggressive stance and was slightly taken aback at the immense hostility emanating from her.

'What do you want?' Mandki demanded, her voice quivering with a mixture of fear and anger, at the man who had almost totally destroyed her friend's life, and her own.

Kansa looked at her, awed by the loyalty she displayed towards Devki. He could have simply brushed her aside, but he was determined to make things better between Devki and himself. Antagonizing and hurting her best friend would not help do that.

Kansa smiled patiently at her. 'I have come to put this over Devki's children,' he said gently, holding out the gold-braided coverlet for her to see.

Mandki saw the blanket he carried. She was well aware of the significance of the chaddar upacara. Once Kansa performed the act of putting the coverlet over the newborns, he would be bound by the law of his ancestors to protect the children throughout his life. She hesitated, unsure what to do. This man had almost killed Vasudev and imprisoned his sister and father. And her Airawat... he had hurt him so much too. She stared at Kansa, trying to comprehend his motives. *He looks so eager, and so...so sincere*, she thought, her resolve wavering.

'Let me come in Mandki. I have come to make everything alright between Devki and me,' Kansa said quietly.

Mandki looked closely at him. He seemed to be like his earlier self. *His eyes...they no longer blaze with that insane green light*, she noted with relief.

Her resolve faltered further. 'Devki is sleeping,' she said hesitatingly. 'She...uh...she was exhausted after the childbirth and the ardhadhara gave her a strong medicine to make her sleep.'

Kansa grinned. 'Not a day old yet, and they have already started exhausting their mother,' he said lightly.

Mandki looked at Kansa in amazement. He seemed to be the same prince everyone had loved.

'Should I wake Devki?' she asked, undecided.

Kansa shook his head. 'No. Let her sleep. She needs rest. I will come back later to meet her,' he paused. 'Can I at least put the coverlet on the babies?'

Mandki considered the situation. She knew the chaddar upacara would bind Kansa to protect the children in the future. More importantly, it looked like he genuinely wanted to make things better with Devki.

Mandki made up her mind. 'Okay, you can perform the ceremony,' she said slowly. 'But for God's sake don't let the babies wake up. I have spent the last three horas just trying to put them to sleep,' she said in mock horror.

Kansa laughed genially as he followed Mandki to the room where the babies were sleeping.

◆

Kansa gazed upon the babies, sleeping peacefully in their cot. They looked beautiful, and he could see Devki's features mirrored unmistakably in their faces. Kansa sighed as he remembered how Devki had been as a child. *These children will be like her*, he thought nostalgically.

'Can you get me some water, Mandki?' Kansa said, his throat feeling parched all of a sudden.

Mandki nodded slowly, not sure whether she should leave him alone with the babies. But he looked so peaceful as he gazed adoringly at Devki's offspring. She turned to leave, to fetch the water, leaving him standing near the babies' cot. Kansa gently put the coverlet over the sleeping children. Reciting the mantras he knew by heart, he commenced the chaddar upacara that would bind him to these babies forever.

Mandki stood at the door, watching him mutter the mantras. She groaned as she heard one of the babies get up from his sleep. And then the other five also began to move around and making wailing noises. Thinking they had got scared of seeing a strange face looking at them, she took a step forward to calm them. She came to a sudden halt as she heard Kansa pause in his mantras to talk gently to the children. She looked on fascinated as the babies settled down and started making happy gurgling sounds. Kansa laughed with them; and they seemed to like the sound of his deep laughter. Mandki smiled to herself and left to get the water for Kansa.

◆

Kansa playfully tickled the feet of one of the babies, making it gurgle happily. The other children lying in the cot seemed to take offense at being ignored and tried attracting Kansa's attention, by raising their arms in his direction. Kansa smiled and obliged the other children by tickling their feet too, one at a time. But each child craved individual attention and demanded it by trying to babble louder than the others.

Kansa began to experience the beginnings of a headache as the babbling of the children grew louder. He pressed his hands to his temples in an effort to quell the increasingly throbbing pain in his head. But the agonizing ache refused to go away. He looked at the babies and felt suddenly that they had stopped making their gurgling sounds. Ignoring the growing pain in his head, he tried to make funny faces at them to make them burble in mirth. It worked. The babies started to laugh as they saw the comical expressions he was making. They raised their arms to him again, wanting him to pick them up.

As Kansa looked at them through the haze of his pain, it seemed to him that they were no longer laughing with him. They now appeared to be laughing *at* him. Their raised arms seemed to point accusingly at him as they continued to laugh at him. The sound of their laughter threatened to split open his head. Kansa put his hands to his ears in an effort to drown out the sound, but it only seemed to increase in intensity. And then the laughter seemed to erupt from inside his head, and his entire body twisted in pain, the seizure taking hold of him. In a desperate attempt to quieten the babies, he covered their faces with the gold-braided blanket he had placed over them. He pressed down with all his might, and stayed that way till the laughter gradually faded.

As the force of his seizure left him, and the green light of Aghasamarthan faded from his eyes, he gazed in confusion at the babies in the cot. They lay still, their faces shrouded by the blanket he had brought for them. With trembling hands, he lifted the edge of the blanket and stared at the eternally quiet faces of Devki's six children.

A howl escaped his lips as he looked at the expression on their innocent faces.

◆

Mandki was returning with the water when she heard the howl.

It shook her to the core and the goblet of water dropped from her hand, clattering to the ground. She raced towards the babies' room and stared in dismay at the vacant room. Kansa was no longer there. With an ominous feeling she crept slowly towards the baby cot. She forced herself to look at what she was by now certain she would see. But the shock of seeing left her horrified. All six of Devki's babies had been mercilessly strangulated.

◆

Mandki waited for the drug to take effect before she entered Vasudev and Devki's bed chambers. Devki had gone insane when she woke up to find all her children murdered. She had raged at Mandki for allowing Kansa to meet the babies. For the first time in their life, Devki had refused to talk to Mandki as she stormed out of the room, tearing at her hair and calling on the gods to end the life of the brother she had once loved more than anyone else.

Concerned for Devki's sanity, Mandki had called the Ardhadhara who arrived and gave her a potent dose of a medicine that would help Devki sleep. The ardhadhara instructed Mandki to keep Devki on the drug for the next few days, till she was able to absorb the reality of her children's death. Mandki had been following the doctor's instructions for the past two days, and she had just given Devki her dose for the night. She looked at Devki sleeping next to Vasudev; two vibrant people whose lives had been reduced to a vegetative state by the one man they had both loved above everything else.

Mandki approached their bed, trying not to make any sound that could rouse them. In her hand, she held the sterile packet that had been given to her an hour earlier by a man she now knew she could trust completely. She had never met the man before in her life but she had heard of him from Airawat and she knew he had implicit faith in this person. She didn't know how the stranger was able to reach her room without being apprehended by the assassin guards who were stationed all over the palace compound, but he had somehow managed to give all of them the slip. He had then handed her a sterilized packet and told her what he wanted her to do with it. When he saw her waver, he had told her his name and suggested she confirm with Airawat if she could trust him. Mandki had made a quick trip to Airawat's cell. The guards did not stop her as they were used to her regular visits to his place of confinement. When she told Airawat the man's name, he asked her to describe him. After hearing his description, he gave her a smile full of hope. The only thing he said was, 'If you can't trust this man, you can't trust anyone!'

Mandki returned to her room and told the man she would do what he wanted. But first she would have to give Devki her dose of medicine for the night. She had done that some time back and the drug seemed to have taken effect. Devki slept soundly. Vasudev lay next to her, immobile as usual. Mandki approached Vasudev first. She touched his head, and carefully picked out a strand of his hair. Then tracing the strand to where it emanated from his scalp, she gave a sudden tug and it came out in her hand. Vasudev did not make any sound. He lay in the same manner he had since the day Kansa had dashed him to the ground. Mandki opened the sterilized packet the man had given to her. She placed the strand of hair, its root dangling at one end, inside the packet, taking care not to let her fingers touch the inside. She repeated the same procedure with Devki's hair, a little more cautiously. Devki groaned briefly as the strand of hair was pulled out along with its root, but then she settled down. Mandki sighed in relief, as she placed Devki's hair along with Vasudev's in the same packet.

Sealing the packet carefully, she quickly left the room.

◆

Narada gave Mandki a relieved smile as he took the packet from her. He peered inside, holding the packet close to his eyes, as he observed the roots of both strands of hair. The bulbs were intact, he noticed with satisfaction.

He smiled benevolently at Mandki. 'Thank you, my child. The world will thank you someday for what you have done today!'

Leaving behind a confused Mandki, Narada hastened to return to Brahma. He had obtained what the Mahadev had instructed Brahma to get.

He Is on His Way

Bhargava sighed as he heard the Dark Lord tell him about Kansa. 'I know I should be happy that Kansa is lending the final shape to our plans. I wonder why it is then that I feel no joy in this.'

Amartya Kalyanesu gave him a sad smile. 'Perhaps because you are a good man, Bhargava. People like you don't derive any personal joy from destroying a noble man's soul, and the carnage that comes along with the death of that spirit.'

'And you? Are you happy?' Bhargava questioned.

'My happiness or the lack of it is not significant. This is not a personal war against Brahma or Indra or even the devas. Maybe it was when I started off.' Amartya paused, wondering how to explain himself. 'I realized later that what Brahma did to me was because he felt he had the power to do it and get away with it. He did not just destroy a brahmarishi the day he unjustly punished me. He was making a point that anyone with power could do whatever they wanted, to anyone they wanted to. And he is one of the three supreme gods. If a god is allowed to get away with this, can you begin to imagine what other people would do with that kind of power?'

Amartya's question hung in air as Bhargava tried to understand what he had just said. His thoughts were no different from Amartya, even though his motives might have been so. But there was a question that had been bothering him, and he knew if he didn't ask Amartya now, he might never be able to ask him again.

'Why blame Brahma alone? Wasn't Indra equally to blame for what Brahma did to you?'

At the mention of Indra's name, Amartya's body visibly stiffened and Bhargava feared he had gone too far. They hadn't discussed this in the last two hundred years. After Bhargava had taken Amartya away from the hell of Tamastamah Prabha, he had made discreet enquiries through his trusted sources in Swarglok and he had found that Indra had been the one primarily responsible for Amartya's fate. He had shared it with Amartya and the brahmarishi had listened quietly. At the end of it, he had told Bhargava he did not want to discuss Indra's role in the matter, ever again. But it was right after that discussion that Amartya had started making his plan of joining forces from Pataal Lok and Mrityulok to launch a full-scale war on Swarglok. Amartya had never said it in so many words, but Bhargava knew that it wasn't just Brahma who was the target; Amartya intended to teach Indra and his devas a lesson too. And that suited Bhargava because Indra had been the one to ruthlessly kill his mother.

Amartya read Bhargava's thoughts. 'Yes, Indra definitely influenced Brahma's actions. But Brahma alone was responsible for what he did. Both of them will have to answer for their deeds.'

'Then why launch a war on all of Swarglok? Why not just teach Indra and Brahma a lesson?' This was the one aspect of their plan that had always baffled Bhargava, even though he had done everything in his power to help Amartya.

Amartya sighed. Even Bhargava with all his knowledge showed limitations at times. 'Brahma hurt me, Bhargava; and Indra caused you grievous injury. But if that was the only reason we were fighting them, we would be no better than any other person who sought to avenge themselves on their antagonist.'

Bhargava shook his head. 'I still don't understand,' he said.

Amartya decided to elaborate. 'This war is not just about Indra and Brahma, or what they did to you and me. This is about the extent of rot and corruption that has set inside every corner of the celestial world. Swarglok today abounds with every kind of rogue. The devas are drunk with power and under Indra's command, they have lost all sense of purpose. The Mahadev is too busy with his penance to castigate them. And Lord Vishnu has shut himself in Svetadvipa, refusing to meet anyone. The other brahmarishis, angered at the behavior of the devas have left Swarglok and gone far away. Brahma, the God who embodies a storehouse of knowledge within himself, is unable to control his senses and his rage and allows the devas to manipulate him, as Indra did in my case.'

Amartya took a deep breath to calm himself, 'Do you have any idea how many people's lives have been wrecked by these same devas who were supposed to be their protectors? If the decay and vices they have caused are not stopped today, they will do the same thing with Swarglok and Mrityulok what the asuras did with Pataal Lok several thousand years ago. No Bhargava—make no mistake—this war is not about you or me. This war is about all those people who have been betrayed by their gods; those same gods who have not lifted a finger to stop the devas from their vile actions. You and I are going to force the gods to step in and do something about it. That is the only reason this war is being fought. And if it means that noble men like Kansa have to be sacrificed at the altar of this revolution, then it will be so.'

Bhargava looked at the animated face of Amartya Kalyanesu, and he wondered how he had ever thought that this man—this brahmarishi—could ever wage a war against Swarglok merely for his own revenge.

One thing bothered him though. 'What about your promise to the asura council that you will infuse them with the power of Brahman? Won't they misuse the potent force it wields?' he queried.

Amartya laughed. 'It is impossible to infuse a person with the force of Brahman within whom the dark forces of Aghasamarthan already exist. The two forces are contrary in nature. No one who willfully wields Aghasamarthan can ever absorb the pure energy of Brahman.'

Bhargava was puzzled. 'Then why did you tell the council that you would teach them to use Brahman energy?'

'One of the things Brahma taught me well was that you deal with people in the same currency that they understand. The asura council and King Vrushaparva would never have allowed you to train the assassins on their land unless they knew there was something in it for them. And what could have been a more powerful attraction than being able to wield the force of Brahman.'

Bhargava couldn't help admiring Amartya's astuteness. He had understood the psyche of the asura king and his council members to perfection. 'But what about these asura assassins we are training? Aren't we adding to the rot the devas have already accumulated in the world?

Amartya Kalyanesu smiled at the man who had befriended him during the most difficult part of his life. When he spoke his voice was gentle. 'Each of the asura assassins is doing what their destiny wills them to do Bhargava. They have set the wheels of fate in motion but they will all die, like Ghora and Ugra already have. Some of them will die for money and some for the sake of the great men who trained them. But all of them will find salvation at the end of the road.'

'And Jarasandha! What about him? You made a commitment to him that you will make him lord of Mrityulok for all the help he is extending to us in our plan?' Bhargava queried, his face betraying his sadness at the fate that awaited the men who had trained under the mighty Ugra.

'Jarasandha will never be lord of Mrityulok. He will gain victory over a large part of the mortal world. But his end will come through the same man who will give Kansa his salvation.'

Bhargava's face went pale. 'Who is this man who will be able to destroy warriors such as Kansa and Jarasandha?'

Amartya looked at his friend, but his mind was elsewhere,

hovering over a land called Svetadvipa where he knew the slayer of evil would originate.

'I don't know his name yet. The universe is silent on that as of now. But I do know that he is on his way.'

Krishna! Krishna! Krishna!

She gazed at the mountain in front of her. Try as she might, she couldn't stretch her head far back enough to see the top. It seemed that only the base of the mountain was visible to the eye. It rose so high that the greater part of the mountain was enveloped in dense stretches of fog. No one knew how far up it went, and there weren't too many people who had ever reached the top of Kailas, the abode of the God of Gods; of Shiva—the destroyer of evil and the most feared God in all the three worlds.

The beautiful maiden had braved the steep climbs of Kailas only once before in her life. But that time she had Brahma as her companion. His mere presence had been enough to ease her tired limbs as she scaled the mountain. Today, however, she was alone, and though she was a goddess herself, the treacherous terrain of Kailas was testing the limits of even her endurance. And it wasn't just that. Every now and then, she would feel some presence around her. It was as if something was trying to throttle her as she slept or in an unguarded moment. But then, these feelings and sensations would go away almost immediately and she would feel safe and calm. She shook her head frequently in an attempt to clear her mind of these feelings. She put down the sensations to an overactive imagination. But somehow, she wasn't sure if it was just her imagination.

Bhoomi Devi—the keeper of earth and the mortal world— sighed as she told herself to trudge on. She knew that in a few days the dusty and dry terrain would give way to expose the true beauty of Kailas and reveal the mountain to her in its full glory.

On the fourth day of her travel, just as the hour of noon was approaching, Bhoomi Devi came to a point where there were four different paths to choose from. Each path took you to the top of Kailas from a different side of the mountain. Each side was made up of a singular material. The north was made of crystal; the east of ruby; the south face of the mountain was pure gold and the western front was made of lapis lazuli. The whole mountain of Kailas itself was located at the heart of six mountain ranges, symbolizing a lotus.

Bhoomi Devi paused to consider which of the four routes she should take. The lapis lazuli pathway on the western front fascinated her but the last time she had been to the mountain, Brahma had taken her through the south side, and that route had been fast and unhindered. While she was tempted to experiment with a different path today, her pragmatic side favoured taking the old route, especially since she was in a hurry and needed to meet Shiva urgently. *I can't afford to waste time*, she thought to herself. *If the gods don't help me soon, the demons will destroy the mortal world.* Her breath quickened as she considered this, and she hastened her steps in the direction of Shiva's abode on the peak of Mount Kailas.

◆

Shiva was in deep meditation when Bhoomi Devi reached the summit. Even though his eyes were closed, his cosmic vision saw everything. He knew why a senior goddess like Bhoomi Devi had personally travelled all the way from Mrityulok to meet him. He also knew what she wanted from him. *It's a pity I won't be able to help her though*, he thought with a sigh, still in meditation.

Bhoomi Devi waited patiently for Shiva to come out of his meditative state. She knew it could take days or even weeks before this happened, but disturbing Shiva in meditation could invite his wrath. That was the last thing she wanted to do at this moment. She knew that sometimes supreme gods like Shiva could decide to communicate telepathically with other gods or demi-gods. They could do this while still in meditation. *I wish he would communicate with me now,* thought Bhoomi Devi, trying to suppress her anxiety. *They never use telepathy when you want them to,* She couldn't help thinking sardonically.

Her mind had not even completed the thought when she felt a sudden jolt; it was as if something had entered her mind, unbidden, a force quantum times stronger than her own. 'So, we never use telepathy when you want, is that right?' growled Shiva. Bhoomi Devi jumped at the sound of his voice. It was as if Shiva was speaking from inside her head. She looked at his face; He was still meditating and his face was inscrutable. *Oh Lord, he is using cosmic telepathy,* she suddenly realized.

Cosmic telepathy was a rare power wielded by the three supreme gods and the brahmarishis. While basic telepathy allowed communication between two people, through the transmission of information from one person to another without using any sensory channels or physical interaction, cosmic telepathy went much beyond that. Using cosmic telepathy, the supreme gods could read and control the minds of life forms on multiple planets at once. They could transmit and receive information from multiple planets, while also creating illusions and controlling emotions of the same scale.

Bhoomi Devi felt rather than heard Shiva laughing inside her head. It was his typical deep-throated and clear laughter. 'My Lord, this is not fair. You should have warned me you were entering my mind,' she said, a little upset with Shiva. The laughter died down as quickly as it had started, and Shiva spoke to her in a kind tone. 'Forgive me, dear, I get carried away with this cosmic telepathy thing sometimes. Tell me what I can do for you.'

She couldn't help smiling. It was impossible to stay upset with Shiva. Even though Vishnu was generally considered to be the charmer, she personally found Shiva's rustic charm more appealing. She never mentioned this to anyone, though. She knew

Shiva's wife, Parvati, would kill her if she caught her admiring her husband, even from a distance. Suppressing a smile, Bhoomi Devi forced herself to return to the matter at hand.

'Lord, since you are using cosmic telepathy, you would already know why I am here,' Bhoomi Devi said softly.

'I do, goddess, I do.' Shiva sounded thoughtful.

'Then will you help?' Bhoomi Devi's voice was pleading.

'I am not the one who will help you, Bhoomi Devi. Your saviour is elsewhere.' Shiva's cryptic answer confused her even more.

'Who?' Bhoomi Devi started to say as the voice of Shiva in her mind interrupted her.

'You need to go to Svetadvipa. Reach there as soon as you can. Brahma is already waiting for you there.'

'Brahma? But he doesn't like to leave his abode in Brahmlok for any reason whatsoever. How has he gone to Svetadvipa?' Bhoomi Devi was genuinely taken aback.

'The situation demands his presence there,' Shiva said. 'You should know how serious it is. After all, that's why you came to me, didn't you?'

'Y-yes, My Lord, I did. But I came to you for *your* help. Why are you sending me to Svetadvipa and why did you say you can't help in this situation?'

'Patience, goddess. So many questions!' Shiva admonished her gently. 'As the keeper of the earth, you came to me because you felt that the force of evil has become stronger than that of good and it threatens to destroy Mrityulok. But it is not I who will destroy that evil. In this case, it will be done through Vishnu. And he is currently at his celestial abode at Svetadvipa.'

Bhoomi Devi nodded as she began to understand somewhat. What Shiva said was logical. Though Shiva had destroyed forces of evil on numerous occasions, it was a fact that whenever Mrityulok had been threatened by dark forces, Vishnu had come to the rescue and decimated the evil. She remembered an occasion several ages back when the demon Hiranyaksha had abducted her and taken her to the Netherworld. It had been Vishnu who had come to her rescue and saved her then.

She understood now why she had to go to Svetadvipa. But she still wasn't clear why Brahma was also there. Shiva read her thoughts through and continued, 'You are aware that any god, demi-god or mortal can go up to Brahmlok and see Brahma when they face a problem in their world. And all those who can bear to climb the formidable Kailas are welcome to my humble abode, too. But it is different when it comes to seeing Vishnu.'

'Why, My Lord? What's different about meeting Vishnu?'

'Vishnu has confined himself to his island at Svetadvipa for the past several years now. He hasn't been too happy with the way things have been here.'

'That still doesn't explain why Brahma is going to Svetadvipa,' Bhoomi Devi said, puzzled.

'There are two reasons for that. The first is that he is carrying something I had instructed Narada to get from Mrityulok. Vishnu is going to need it if he has to help you.'

'And the second reason?' Bhoomi Devi asked, her curiosity piqued.

Shiva sighed. He had been hoping he wouldn't have to explain that. But Bhoomi Devi was too smart to fool. 'Brahma is there at Svetadvipa to use his force to cleanse that place of all evil. You may not be aware but the dark forces know of your coming to us for help. And they have sent some of their potent energies to try and harm you. You probably didn't see them because they were invisible but they followed you all the way to my abode. If Parvati hadn't been around you, they would have likely tried to attack you on the way here.'

'Parvati? She was there with me on the way uphill?' Bhoomi Devi said in a stunned tone. And then it struck her. She remembered the feeling of being strangulated at times when she was resting or sleeping on the way to Kailas. *That must have been the dark energies at work, trying to throttle me.* And then she recalled how these feelings would suddenly disappear and be replaced with sensations of calmness. *Ah, that would have been Parvati. She would have scared away the dark ones and used her own positive potency to calm me.* Bhoomi Devi mentally thanked Parvati for her help.

'My Lord, if the dark energies followed me to Kailas, won't they also come after me on the way to Svetadvipa?' Bhoomi Devi's voice was shaky as she asked the question.

'They will, goddess,' answered Shiva's voice inside her head.

'Then who will protect me on the way to Svetadvipa? Who will ensure I reach there safely?'

There was a long silence, making her think that the Mahadev had gone into deep meditation and was no longer tuned into her mind. But then she heard him, and his words left her both, secure and terrified at the same time.

'Have no fear. I will come with you to Svetadvipa!' Shiva's words seemed to echo in her head. There could be no bigger comfort than knowing that Shiva himself was escorting her to her destination. The same thing also scared her out of her wits because she knew that Shiva would only come along if the dark forces had unleashed their most potent and deadly energies against her. She wondered what would happen to her when Brahma, Shiva, Vishnu or Parvati were no longer there to protect her.

In that instant, she saw Shiva's eyes open and before she knew it she was being whisked away in a cocoon fuelled by his vital force. She couldn't see Shiva around but she could feel his presence and as the cocoon flew away from Kailas, she saw looming in the distance, the milky waters of Svetadvipa, home to one who some considered the greatest god of all—the all-seeing Vishnu.

◆

Brahma was standing on the shores of Svetadvipa. He wiped the slimy fluids off his body. The dark forces could make themselves invisible at will, but their cloak of invisibility did not deceive him. After all Brahma wielded the force of Brahman, which gave him powers beyond the imagination of any dark force.

He was breathing a little heavily after three continuous horas of battling the dark forces. When Shiva had told him about the possibility of the evil ones following Bhoomi Devi to Svetadvipa, Brahma had initially thought Shiva was being overcautious. After all, Svetadvipa was inhabited by Vishnu himself. And not even the dark forces could be as stupid or brash as to violate his domain. But he had been wrong. They had violated Vishnu's most treasured environ, the place where he resided with his wife and most loyal followers.

However, this was not the only thing that bothered Brahma. He found it strange that it had taken him three horas to overcome the creatures sent from Pataal Lok. Normally, it would be a few moments' work for him to restrain these demons. But today, the vile creatures seemed imbued with an uncanny energy and an eerie power—a power that did not seem to be their own; an energy force that seemed like it was being controlled from somewhere else or by someone else. Brahma recognized the presence of Aghasamarthan, the opposing force of Brahman. He knew Amartya couldn't be the one behind this because the Brahman energy that flowed through Amartya would make it impossible for him to use the contrary power of Aghasamarthan. It had to be someone else in Pataal Lok; but who?

He looked around him. The place was secure now. He hoped Shiva would arrive soon. The packet that Narada had given him would need to be handed to Vishnu quickly if it had to be of any use.

◆

Vishnu waited patiently for Shiva to arrive. The Mahadev had already communicated with him telepathically and Vishnu knew what he wanted him to do. It annoyed him that Brahma was accompanying Shiva. Vishnu had been voluble in his castigation of Brahma after what he had done to Amartya Kalyanesu. He had taken care to avoid Brahma all these years, not being sure how he would react if he saw him.

Vishnu had also understood from Shiva what was happening in Mrityulok, and the reason for Bhoomi Devi's arrival. *All of this is because of Brahma,* he fumed silently, his anger at Brahma's banishment of Amartya rising afresh. He was tempted to punish Brahma for his misdeed. Realizing he was dissipating his vital force by indulging his anger, he forced himself to be calm and concentrated on the universal energy of Brahman flowing through his Sahasrara Chakra.

A deed done in anger cannot be rectified by another act of rage, he reflected as he finally began the process of forgiving Brahma for what he had done two hundred years ago.

◆

Shiva sat facing Vishnu, with Brahma and Bhoomi Devi on either side of him. He smiled as he realized Vishnu had finally forgiven Brahma. *None too soon either,* he smiled inwardly as he realized what would have happened to Brahma if Vishnu had not tempered his anger before they arrived.

'Have you brought what the Mahadev asked you to?' Vishnu's question was directed at Brahma. He hurriedly took out the packet Narada had given him. 'Yes, My Lord. Narada got it for me.'

Vishnu looked closely at the packet. 'How long back were these samples taken?' he asked Brahma, his eyebrows raised.

'Two days ago, My Lord,' Brahma stuttered, concerned that he had unwittingly made some grave error.

'Perefct!' Vishnu smiled, as he got up to leave.

'My Lord,' Bhoomi Devi cried out, worried that the meeting with Vishnu was already over. 'I wanted to share my concerns with you.'

'I am aware of the problem that is bothering you,' Vishnu

smiled gallantly at her. 'I was on my way to get you the solution to that very problem.'

Bhoomi Devi stared in confusion at Vishnu's departing figure.

◆

Vishnu sat in the pratiroop kaksh (cloning room), surrounded by all manner of lab equipment. He looked intently at the samples of hair Narada had brought from Mrityulok. He examined the bulbs. They were in perfect condition. The nuclear DNA could be easily extracted from the root, while the hair strand carried sufficient quantity of the mitochondrial DNA. Put together, he would be able to isolate all the vital properties from both Vasudev and Devki's DNA.

But that won't be enough, he smiled, as he plucked out one strand of his own hair and kept it under the scanner.

He debated which of his genes he should extract from his own DNA sample. The last seven times he had cloned himself, it had been easy. He had simply separated the few characteristics that were required and recombined them to form a partial clone. But this time was different. The situation in the mortal world was so dire that a partial clone would not help. The clone would need to have all his representative genes.

He tapped the table unconsciously as he debated whether he could afford to do that. Having two Vishnus could upset the world order. Then he smiled as he realized the fallacy of his thinking. The clone would have all his representative genes but would also carry within him the mortal genes of Vasudev and Devki. He would, however, be his only mortal poorna avatar (complete clone).

Working at a rapid pace, Vishnu combined the genes from Vasudev and Devki's DNA with the entire range of his own genes. Then he began the process of immunizing it, so that it could last through the journey back to Mrityulok. Within a few minutes, the cloning capsule was ready and immunized. He put the capsule into a bottle and wondered what name he should give to this avatar. *Everyone will be attracted to him*, Vishnu thought. Since he carried the essence of Vishnu, people would find happiness merely by being in his presence. He would be the essence of attractiveness (Krish) and bliss (Na). Vishnu wrote the name 'Krishna' on the bottle.

As he got up to leave, another thought struck him. The last time he had created a partial clone of himself, he had called him Ram. Ram's younger brother had been named Lakshman and had carried the genetic code of Vishnu's closest friend, Sheshnaag. Vishnu recalled Sheshnaag joking that at some time, he hoped one of his clones could have the comfort of being older than Vishnu's clone.

Vishnu laughed to himself as he thought. *Krishna will require a brother who can keep him company on his mission.* Without a moment's hesitation, he went to one of the bottles resting on his lab shelf. He found the one he was looking for. It contained the genetic code of Sheshnaag. He emptied the contents of the bottle and mixed it with the remaining genes of Devki and Vasudev. The process of immunizing the resultant genes was done equally quickly and he put the freshly made cloning capsule into another bottle. He wondered what name to give Sheshnaag's latest clone. It would have to be something that encompassed all of his friend's qualities— someone who was a powerful force in whoever's life he touched, and would value truth, justice and discipline above everything else. The name came to him as all of Sheshnaag's traits breezed across his mind. He etched on the second bottle the one name that represented all these qualities—'Balarama'.

◆

Shiva was standing at the edge of the island called Svetadvipa, when he saw Vishnu approaching, followed by Brahma and Bhoomi Devi. Vishnu had a huge grin on his face and Shiva's own countenance broke into a broad smile as he read Vishnu's mind.

'It is done!' Vishnu said softly, his face growing serious.

He handed the bottle containing Balarama's clone capsule to Bhoomi Devi. 'Take this to Vasudev's first wife, Rohini. She needs to take this capsule orally. It will find its own way into her womb and she will give birth to a warrior who will train other formidable warriors.'

Bhoomi Devi was confused. 'Why not give it to Devki?' she asked.

'Because Kansa will not allow the child to live. These two children have to be reared away from Madhuvan for the initial few years,' Vishnu answered quietly.

Bhoomi Devi nodded her understanding.

The mountains were silent and the water surrounding the island of Svetadvipa halted its constant flow, as Vishnu held the other bottle in his hand. 'Take this one to Vasudev's brother, Nand. His wife Yashoda has not had a child yet.'

The keeper of the earth accepted the bottle though her face still registered her doubts. 'But what about the one who will save Mrityulok from all the carnage that is taking place today?'

Vishnu replied quietly. 'Ask Yashoda to swallow the capsule tonight. The saviour will be born to her at midnight, nine months from tomorrow. He will be the foremost warrior in all the three worlds!'

Bhoomi Devi looked in awe at the bottle she held in her hand. 'What...what will his name be?' she asked, her voice quivering in anticipation.

The name of the warrior was murmured softly by the lord of Svetadvipa, and it was taken up by all the people present, till the hushed whisperings reached a crescendo and one name echoed throughout the land—Krishna! Krishna! Krishna!

Acknowledgements

There is not enough space here to thank all the people I would like to. However, I would still like to acknowledge a few people without whom this book and the Krishna Trilogy would not have been possible.

Komal, my wife: If you had not listened patiently to all my ideas, they would never have been translated into a story that had me in an obsessive writing fit all through the months it took to complete the first volume.

The twin orbs of my eyes, Bhoomi and Arya: If you had not allowed your mother and me to discuss the plot and its twists and turns at the dining table, the story would as yet be unborn.

My parents: You pushed me to move away from non-fiction and write a story that could excite lovers of mythology and take them 5,500 years back in time.

My publisher, Kapish Mehra, who was excited about the idea from the word go and was a pillar of strength through the arduous process of taking this book from my study to the readers.

The entire team at Rupa Publications, who patiently listened to my suggestions and extended themselves beyond what any publishing team can possibly do.

To all those people across the country who helped me, over a period of nine long years, to research one of the most complex characters in our culture—Krishna.

To all those people who have picked up this book to commence a journey I myself started almost a decade ago.

And mostly to that conqueror of souls; the master of masters;

the mortal whom the world turned into the god of gods—Krishna! Thank you for guiding my pen to tell your story in a way it has never been told before.